MEMORY LANE

by Gary Gentile

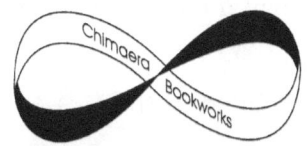

Chimaera Bookworks
P.O. Box 57137
Philadelphia, PA 19111

Additional copies of this book may be purchased from the same address by sending a check or money order in the amount of $20 U.S. for each copy (plus $3 postage per order, not per book, in the U.S. Inquire for shipping cost to foreign countries). Alternatively, copies may be purchased from the author's website, and paid by credit card:

http://www.ggentile.com

The cover photographs were taken by the author. The front cover inset is courtesy of Siemens Medical Solutions USA; colorization by the author.

International Standard Book Numbers (ISBN)
1-883056-28-4
978-1-883056-28-5

Original copyright - 1994

Printed in the U.S.A.

Chapter 1

Grant was still fumbling with his key, trying to twist it in the lock, when the bolt snapped back, the knob twisted hard, and the door swung open with a jerk, yanking the key chain out of his hand. This was very odd because this was his house, and he lived alone.

The porch light flared on and a gruff voice grumbled, "Whaddaya think yer doing?"

Grant was nonplussed. In the utter silence that followed, he heard the keys rattling on their chain like a wind chime in a storm. He opened his mouth and worked his jaw, but his throat was gripped with a strange paralysis that let no sound escape.

Coming from the side, the porch light cast the man's face in a garish shadow. He could have been a gargoyle perched atop a French cathedral. Bushy brows formed shallow arches over dark, fathomless eyes, and a bulbous, red-veined nose protruded beyond a chiseled face whose features Grant did not recognize. The man's blue flannel shirt hung loose outside faded dungarees; the laces of his tan leather work shoes were untied.

An eerie heaviness filled Grant's skull. He had a headache like none he had ever had. It was not the throbbing temple twinge caused by tension or overwork, nor the frontal pressure of sinus congestion, nor the massive occipital agony of a migraine. Instead, it emanated from within. His hair stood out on end as if his scalp were charged with static electricity.

"Well?" That single word rang out like a condemnation. The man held the door with one hand, leaned against the frame with the other. Thick thumbs curled around the pine veneer. The room behind him was as dark as a dungeon.

Grant tried hard to find his voice. After several false starts and a couple of guttural clacks, he stuttered, "I—I—I live here." It came out almost as a question.

The man's face neither hardened nor softened, but his brows pinched in a tight clot and joined together to form a single hairy band that could have been a fat caterpillar in mid stride. His forehead wrinkled.

"That is—I thought I did." Grant's enunciation was practically a slur but speech was becoming easier. "Is this—is this—" He had to strain to remember. "—14 Cedar Place?" The brass numbers were in easy view next to the door, and readable despite the patina.

The man's face could have been carved from wood. The keys had stopped tinkling, and now in the background stillness Grant heard the ticking of a clock. A table lamp switched on in an adjacent room. There was an illusion of movement. A small, white-haired woman appeared behind the man's arm, the one against the doorframe. She wore a mauve paisley robe over matching pajamas. Her feet were clad in furred slippers.

She peered over the crook of the man's elbow. "It is. But you must want Cedar Way. You're on the wrong street."

Grant's consternation persisted. "Cedar Way?" he croaked stupidly.

That was the trouble with housing developments. All the streets looked alike, all the houses were the same, and sometimes even the neighbors were indistinguishable from one another, as if they were backdrops built into the design so the community conformed to the image of middle-class America that the rest of the world perceived. Grant certainly did not know these people, and it slowly dawned on him as he peered past the couple in the doorway that although he recognized the wallpaper—whose pastel floral design he had always thought insipid—the furnishings in view were not his own. He broke into a sweat caused by the growing heat of embarrassment. He felt so foolish.

"Now, Ed, put that thing down or you'll scare the poor man." The woman pulled Ed's hand away from the doorframe. The pistol he gripped in his huge paw looked frighteningly ominous. She smiled at Grant. "He's harmless, really."

Grant heard the click of the safety mechanism. Was it now on or off? "I—I—I'm sorry if I've disturbed you. I really thought . . . "

What did he think?

Ed never took his eyes off Grant, did not utter a sound.

The pale woman pulled Grant's keys from the lock and held them out to him. "It's on the other side of the development. Near the pond."

Mindlessly, he shoved the keys into his jacket pocket. "The pond?"

Ed exploded with a voice that could have been a loud peal of thunder. "You live around here, you know where the pond is."

"The pond?" Grant was totally disoriented. He had to concentrate hard in order to make sense out of the situation. "Oh! Woodland Pond." It was beginning to come back to him. "Down the hill from the Hub."

"The east side of the hill," the woman cooed. She cast a whimsical glance up at Ed. "I know just how you feel. Got lost in the mall the other day. Got completely turned around, went out the wrong door, couldn't find my car, and reported it stolen. I felt so simple-minded when the police took me right to it at the other end of the parking lot. The way they build things these days . . . I don't know."

Grant backed away, looking from Ed to the woman to Ed again. He stumbled off the porch and dropped nine inches to the pavement, lost his balance, and twisted around to catch himself with his other foot. Flailing wildly, he fell forward several steps before he regained his equilibrium. When he turned around he saw Ed's stony face staring blankly from the doorway. The woman smiled and nodded slowly. Then she closed the door.

His antics would have been funny if this had been a scene in a sitcom. He could almost hear the canned laughter from off-stage. Under the present circumstances, though, Grant was totally demoralized. He felt like an intoxicated buffoon instead of a sober scientist, especially with his head buzzing like a beehive.

The porch light stayed on. Grant reached the sidewalk and turned to survey the house from beyond the cone of light, where he hoped that Ed and the woman could not see him. At first glance the structure reminded him of his own: a red brick ranch house with a garage at one end, a chimney at the other.

As he studied the house in detail he observed subtle differences. The white trim around the windows was dull and peeling, whereas his had been bright and freshly painted. The red brick facade was faded and dirty. The front door was weathered. The brass address numbers were green with verdigris. The garage door panels were cracked. The driveway was stained with ugly black oil marks. The shrubbery was much fuller and more extensive, and the willow tree—most of whose long, thin leaves were now brown and sere—was at least twice as tall, towering above the house to a height which was three times that of the black shingled roof.

The porch light went out. In the semidarkness afforded by the starlit, moonless sky, the house again took on a hauntingly familiar appearance, as if the dissimilarities between the image in Grant's mind and the structure before him could be wiped out merely by the flick of a switch. He looked around for something that was distinctly his—some alteration that he might have made—but knew that there was little likelihood of finding such a brand because he spent so little time at home. His principal place of abode was the building that held his office and laboratory. That explained why his marriage had fallen apart.

Nonetheless, Grant's spine tingled with a powerful sense of dé·jà vu. He was sure he had been here before. But then, Woodland Acres was not that big of a development that one could not see all of it during the course of an average constitutional. And since walking was Grant's primary method of exercise—he usually walked to and from the lab while dictating notes to his voice recorder—it followed that he must have strolled along this street often during his wanderings and musings.

But that was a long way from mistaking this house for his own, despite the similarities in the designs of the dwellings in the development. Only five models were offered.

Grant knew that dé·jà vu was a mental aberration which, admittedly, was not fully understood. It could be a neurological phenomenon in which the two hemispheres of the brain lapsed temporarily out of phase, so that one side perceived an event a fraction of a second after the other side; the secondary input was interpreted by the mind as an event that had already occurred. It could also be a psychiatric disorder characterized not as much by false recognition of the past but by the negation of the present. The pharmacological explanation was that it was triggered by a transient chemical imbalance. Or it could be a temporal lobe lesion.

Whatever the reason, these mental ramblings were not going to help Grant find his way home, or explain how he had confused Cedar Place with Cedar Way. How could he have forgotten the name of the street on which he had lived for so many years?

Part of him could not help but chuckle at how he had found his place but lost his way. Oh, the people at the office were going to tease him unmercifully when he told them that he had outdone himself: that he had been so preoccupied that he had gone to the wrong house, on the wrong street, on the wrong side of the development. Not that it was unusual for him to lose his train of thought, but this time he had lost the whole railroad. They did not call him "the absent-minded professor" for nothing. In fact, they had christened him Fred, after the actor MacMurray who played the part in the film.

Many were the times that Grant left his desk to get a reference manual or to check details with a technician—and totally forgot what he was going for when he got to where he was going, because in the mean time his mind had run off in half a dozen different directions. In order to get back on course he usually had to retrace his steps, physically as well as mentally: go back to his desk, return to what he was doing, pick up his previous line of thought, and, when he reached the point which had initiated the original diversion, write down his purpose for going. Like a lost child, he walked around the building with notes in his hand and pieces of paper in his pockets.

Consequently, his co-workers constantly played good-natured tricks on him: moving lab equipment from one room to another, stealing file folders off his desk, placing erroneous memos on his bulletin board, forging notes in his handwriting and sticking them in his pockets. Sometimes it was frustrating for him, but it was far better than the nagging he had received at home.

As Grant ambled along the sidewalk he noticed that quite a few houses were the same model as his. But none emanated the same aura of reminiscence. All exhibited clearly discernible differences: stone paths, garden walls, wooden fences, smaller or larger lawns, or a carport instead of a garage. Each had an individuality that was different from his own.

Cedar Place curved through Woodland Acres like an old river through a forest, a designer concept that offered a semblance of seclusion and outback similitude. Instead of being clear-cut, the land was left natural wherever possible. Trees, creeks, and underbrush dominated a landscape punctuated by inset houses which were connected to each other and to the populated world by narrow black ribbons of macadam. Grant reached an unlighted intersection, then instinctively turned left onto Hardwood Pass and headed up the hill toward the Hub.

He passed streets with a deciduous litany: Chestnut Place, Walnut Place, Locust Place, Birch Place. At the top of the hill was the Great Divide: the major artery that separated the two sides of Woodland Acres like the corpus callosum split the brain down the middle. The four corners of the central intersection were occupied by the clubhouse, the community hall, the pool, and the spa, where he sometimes worked out. Social activity in the development, such as it was, occurred at the Hub, as the four buildings were referred to collectively. A few cars moved in and out of the parking lots, but street traffic was light.

Grant crossed the brightly lit intersection and started down the hill on the other side—the east side of Woodland Acres—past Birch Way, Locust Way, Walnut Way, and Chestnut way, until he reached Cedar Way, where deciduous street names gave way to coniferous. Beyond were Spruce Way, Pine Way, and Cypress Way. There was a definite system here, but one that was perhaps more confounding than a random taxonomic arrangement. Only the pond between Spruce and Pine broke the lumbering harmony.

He turned left onto Cedar Way and followed the curving sidewalk until he reached number 14. A creepy tingling sensation coursed along his spine and crawled into his scalp, exacerbating the ever-present headache. The residence on the lot was a two-story stone manor house.

Grant stared dumbfounded at the strange dwelling while his mind raced through the possible scenarios that could account for his present situation. The inevitable conclusion was that he had been right all along: that he did live at 14 Cedar Place. But then, who were the people there now, and why did the house look different?

For a brief moment he countenanced the thought that this was an elaborate practical joke, and that even now his co-workers were hiding in the bushes trying to conceal their laughter while his furniture was being moved back into his house. But in the back of his mind he knew that the explanation for his confusion could not be so contrived, that something was very seriously amiss. After deep reflection, Grant decided that he must fall back on the reliable system of scientific method: if a laboratory experiment yielded uncertain results, the next logical step was to repeat the experiment under more controlled conditions, in which strict attention was paid to previously unobserved variables.

With this resolve Grant walked a little farther, to 15 Cedar Way on the opposite side of the street, then on to 16 Cedar Way. Neither dwelling was a ranch house. He then walked back toward Hardwood Pass. The last house before the intersection was number 11. He crossed Hardwood Pass and continued on Cedar Way. The first house he came to was number 10, and beyond that was number 9. He kept going until he reached number 1, where the street ended abruptly at a stand of tall oaks. That eliminated the possibility of there being a North Cedar Way and a South Cedar Way.

He climbed the gradual hill to the Hub at the top and continued on down the other side. He went north on Cedar Place and again encountered number 10. He went one house farther to make sure it was number 9. Perplexed but at least with a formula to follow (a comfort to any scientist working blind) he reversed his direction and returned to his own house—he could not think of it otherwise—continued past it to number 15, then to number 16, and gave up at number 17. The whole neighborhood shrieked with familiarity.

Again came the haunting sensation of dé·jà vu. What about the "good match" theory? One school of thought held that the brain did not store events like an indivisible chain, with each link firmly fixed to the links at either end, but that it treated events like discrete particles, or quantized substructures, each of which was coded in sequence, then separated into components which were sequestered in convenient cerebral locations: referred to poetically as "the recesses of the mind." Later, an event was reconstructed by assembling the appropriate isolated components. Errors were introduced during the reassembly process, either by false electrical discharges or by chemical receptor malfunctions, thus altering the way that past events were perceived. The farther one got from the original construction, the more imperfections were introduced. Eventually, through compounding losses and shuffling of components, little more than a blur remained. Thus a new situation could find a match among the billions of stored events in various stages of degeneration. But this was not going to help Grant find his way home, or his place in the world.

Use your intellect, he scolded himself. Attack the problem logically. Could he live at 14 Spruce Place? Or 14 Pine Place? Perhaps he did not live in a coniferous place at all, but in a deciduous way. When he snickered at the thought that he was barking up the wrong tree, he knew that he was scared. Humor was his method of maintaining control in an otherwise uncontrollable situation. He made light of events that affected him emotionally—as he did when Barbara had asked for a divorce.

If Grant had lost his way in the woods, perhaps he could ask his ex-wife for directions back to the path of reason. After their separation, she and their daughter had moved into the adjacent housing development then under construction. With the surge of industrialization entering the area, due largely to the success of Biotech Corporation, the influx of trained and highly paid personnel created a boom in the market for single-unit family dwellings. Real estate values skyrocketed as land was needed for houses, stores, and the inevitable shopping malls. Almost overnight, the fields and forests were converted to modern laboratories for scientists and technicians involved in aerospace research and development. Highland Hills grew from a sleepy Midwest college town to a bustling community of over-educated eccentrics.

Peripheral support industries guaranteed the need for additional, low-cost housing. Thus bloomed the project called Flower Fields—which was where Barbara had moved when she was left with only a teacher's salary for support. She and Dawn lived but a short drive away along the Great Divide, but a half hour's walk on the macadamized bike path which doubled as a sidewalk for those rare instances when an individual chose to go from one community to the other on foot.

He and Barbara maintained an uneasy friendship

based primarily upon providing care and security for Dawn. For all her faults—that is, for those personality traits which conflicted stubbornly with Grant's, and which made their marriage unworkable—she was an intelligent and reasonable woman with a better grasp of day-to-day affairs than Grant could hope—or desire—to have. When they were married, she was the glue which kept Grant from falling off the surface of the world.

He prayed fervently that she could throw a lasso that would pull him down from orbit.

Chapter 2

Flower Fields was gained through a two-lane entranceway which was a floriculturists dream. Trellises covered with climbing vines provided boundaries and separations for a montage of boxed flower beds that contained blossoming plants of every description, including those which were often referred to as weeds: an architectural unification which emphasized nature's wondrous diversity while denying anthropocentric evaluation. Roses were juxtaposed with gray beardtongue, orchids with foxglove, daisies with dandelions.

A large brocade billboard displayed a plot plan of the development. Semicircular byways branched off semicircular byways which themselves branched off semicircular byways, creating an overall pattern reminiscent of a stylistically interpreted bush. Grant had always wondered if Flower Fields was a work of art or the work of a madman. A wooden dispenser offered free maps printed on recycled paper, but Grant knew where he was going. The reclaimed wetlands left a landscape almost mathematically flat.

Another fifteen minutes found Grant on Buttercup Path. Barbara's house was number 228, the fifth one on the left—a small bungalow with a yard just large enough to require a power mower. All the houses were small, and the space between them was little more than an alleyway. The single car garage had enough room for a compact and a bicycle, if the handlebars were turned at an angle. In deference to the firmament whose natural illumination was implicit in the design, the streetlights in Flower Fields were switched on only for emergency purposes, fire drills, and block parties. Each dwelling had a pair of lampposts positioned close to the sidewalk at opposite ends of the property. The lamps were operated and paid for by the owner of the house. Number 228 was dark both inside and out. Barbara was a power saver.

Grant knocked on the front door: softly at first, then, after receiving no response, harder, but not loud enough to alert the neighbors or wake up Dawn. He thumbed the latch and found it locked, as he expected. The door was white painted steel with no glass. He peered through the living room window into Stygian blackness; nothing moved inside. With his hands on the clapboard facade he sidled along the front wall, rounded the corner opposite the garage, and felt his way past the chimney to the back yard. There was no fence between properties; a line of plump azalea bushes separated adjacent yards into symmetrical rectangles. A week ago the azaleas had been resplendent with pink and white blossoms, but already the short flowering season had ended.

He tapped on the pane that was Barbara's bedroom window. "Babs," he called out in a hushed tone. "Babs. It's me. Grant."

After a few seconds he tapped harder, cupped his hands around his mouth, and pressed his palms against the glass. "Babs!"

No answer.

Dawn's bedroom was dark as well, and besides, Barbara would never leave her alone in the house. She was only eleven years old.

The kitchen door was locked. Grant pondered his predicament and what his next step should be. Barbara was never one to stay out late. She liked a routine life without commitments and with her evenings free to prepare for class or mark test papers, with some time leftover to spend with her daughter, watch the news, or read an entertaining novel: nothing too heavy. Grant had no idea what time it was. He looked up at the stars, but the celestial clock was meaningless to him. He knew it was spring by his mental calendar and the chill in the air, certainly not by recognizing the positions of the constellations. In fact, he had very little awareness of the stars at all, or the phases of the moon. The only sign of the Zodiac he knew by sight was the Big Dipper, and he was never quite sure whether the quarter moon was waxing or waning. For one who had spent his entire academic life working for the aerospace industry, he was amazingly ignorant of astronomy; it was a topic beyond his sphere of reference. He never looked up at night. He was too busy making sense of the world around him and thinking about his ongoing projects at the lab.

By logical deduction, he presumed that Barbara was attending a PTA meeting or some similar school function, and had taken Dawn with her because a sitter was unavailable. Barbara did not visit friends or go to movies. And except for those rare weekend jaunts and even rarer vacations they had shared, she always slept in her own bed at night. Barbara was a homebody.

He looked for the spare key in the fake rock at the base of the lilac bush, but it was not there. This was odd, because Barbara rarely moved anything but the furniture. He checked the other bushes and dug frantically in the dirt, all with no success. With no other options available to him, Grant decided to wait. Dawn was sure to bring her home soon, he quipped to himself.

He walked around to the front of the house and tried the front door again. It was still locked. He peered in all the windows. He wandered around the back yard as far as the hedgerow of tall forsythias which provided privacy while doubling as the property line between the houses on Buttercup Path and those on Marigold Path. He paid special attention to avoid stepping on Dawn's scattered toys, and marveled when he encountered none; for once she must have picked up all of them. He would have to give her some positive feedback—no, that was the scientist talking, not the father. He would have to give her some loving praise, buy her a new doll, or take her for a swim. She loved the water.

The chill in the air soon became a bite. Grant walked in circles with his hands in his pockets, but the night was a bit too nippy for him the way he was dressed: thin slacks, cotton shirt, and sport coat—even if it was wool; he buttoned it all the way. After a while he decided that he would either have to go for another long walk, in order to get his blood circulating, or break into the house. His legs were tired, his head hurt miserably, and he needed some aspirin—and perhaps a shot of hard stuff to calm his nerves. A windowpane was easily replaced: one of the few household jobs which Grant could tackle alone.

He took a log from the woodpile to smash in one of the kitchen windows. After all, he thought wryly, it's my house. He had bought it after their divorce, mostly out of guilt, so Dawn would have a place to live. But then, money meant very little to him.

Grant doffed his jacket and placed it against the glass, then stove in the window with the blunt end of the log. The thick wool tweed muffled most of the noise. He donned the jacket, then held his sleeve by the cuff as he reached inside and flipped over the latch, careful of jagged shards that might tear the fabric or lacerate his skin. He lifted. With a slight sucking sound caused by the rubber gasket, the window rose smoothly in its casement.

Now came the difficult part—getting his paunch up high enough to rest it on the ledge. He leaned the log against the wall beneath the window, stepped on it lightly to check its steadiness, then stood on it gradually until it supported all his weight. The log wobbled a little, but as long as he was careful and made no jerky movements, he could maintain a delicate balance.

Grant used his sleeve to brush broken glass off the sill. The shards tinkled when they dropped onto the counter top and into the sink. He was barely high enough to reach in and hook his elbows on the inside of the sill. He pushed himself up on tiptoe, felt the log tilting out from under him, heaved with his feet and pulled with his arms—then hung there momentarily when the log fell away. He squirmed upward with his hips, his legs kicking wildly in the air, and used the muscles in his chest and upper arms to pull himself inward. He strained awkwardly. His strength was just about to fail when he passed the balance point and was able to pause with his pelvis on the sill. He gasped for air but could not rest where he was because he was lying on the faucet and the pressure against his diaphragm prevented him from inhaling. He wriggled like an earthworm until he got the faucet under his belly. It was not a comfortable position, but at least he could breathe.

Within seconds his forearms began to ache from supporting his upper body weight on the narrow lip that was the outer edge of the sink. He took a few deep breaths, then lurched to the side, sweeping dinnerware to the floor with a resounding crash. The window was not wide enough to enable him to get his bent knees through. He had to keep wriggling. He jackknifed his body sideways onto the counter top and almost went over the edge when his jacket snagged. He barely had time to think "saved by a button" when the snag let loose and he careened over the edge. The slight hesitation enabled him to duck his head into a curl. More by accident than by design he hit the floor with his right shoulder and rolled head over heels in a semblance of a somersault. His legs crashed hard on the linoleum with little acrobatic aplomb. He lay there stunned and stinging.

At least, he thought, that damnable headache wasn't so bad any more because my body hurts so much.

Grant climbed to his knees with a groan. He rubbed a few bruises, more concerned over his lack of physical conditioning than the aches and pains from his fall. He did not realize that he was so pitifully out of shape. With a solemn promise to spend more time at the spa, he pulled himself up to a standing position. The sudden rise momentarily drained the blood from his head. He gripped the counter as if it were the edge of the world and he were about to fall off. He squeezed his eyes shut until the vertigo passed. When the stars stopped spinning, he acknowledged that disequilibrium under the circumstances was due to postural hypotension, which was usually brought about by low blood pressure. He promised to check it out as soon as he got hold of a sphygmomanometer.

He oriented himself with relation to the sink, reached out to the wall, located the switch, and turned on the garbage disposal. The raucous grinding noise sent shivers along his spine. He switched off the disposal and tried the switch next to it. The small overhead fluorescent tube flickered undecidedly for a moment, then came on and cast a dim white light on the washing area. He viewed with dismay the mess on the floor: dirty Melmac dishes and silverware and a couple of plastic mugs. This was unusual because Barbara was meticulously neat. She never could get used to Grant losing things or leaving them lie about.

Neither bones nor dinnerware were broken. He placed everything in a heap on the counter and opened the cabinet where the aspirin was kept. Instead of sundries he found cups and saucers and drinking glasses. This was strange because Barbara never moved things about once they had been assigned a permanent location. A place for everything and everything in its place, was her motto. He tried the cabinet to the right as well as the two on the other side of the sink. The one that usually had cereal and crackers was full of plates and bowls. Where he expected to find the plates and bowls he found stacked plastic containers and a tray full of lids. Where the glasses should have been were the pots and pans and a teakettle.

He was still mystified about the changes in venue when he heard the garage door open. A moment later a car door slammed, followed by an engine whine as a car pulled into the garage. The engine shut down. A car door opened and closed, then another car door opened and closed. Grant had a statement prepared when the fire door swung wide. He did not want to scare anyone.

"Sorry about the mess, Babs. I was shivering outside so I let myself in through—"

The woman halted in midstride as if an unseen puppeteer had yanked in her strings. She let out a startled gasp and nearly dropped the bag of groceries she held in her arms.

Grant was nearly as surprised. He had expected his ex-wife to be the first to enter, with Dawn right behind her, not a woman he had never met before. He held his hands out in front of him. "It's okay. I'm Barbara's ex-hus—"

The grocery bag could have been launched by a basketball player. A bag of potato chips and a loaf of bread flew up into the air with the sudden thrust, while the heavier items within the confines of the paper sack soared past Grant's outstretched hands. He side-stepped instinctively, but the bagful of soup cans hit his hip with a glancing blow before crashing into the cabinet behind him. By the time he recovered his wits, the woman was gone.

He dashed into the garage in time to see her race across the yard and down the street. "Wait!" he called after her, knowing it was no use. She was not lingering for explanations. Grant realized that from her perspective he could be anything from a burglar to a rapist. And Barbara was not there to back him up. More groceries in the back seat of the car explained the second door closing he had heard.

Frantically, Grant rushed back into the bungalow, afraid to chase the terrified woman or to be seen in the street by neighbors aroused by her fearful screams.

This is crazy, he thought. How could I go to two wrong houses in the same night? Or ever, for that matter.

There was no time to reflect on it now. He had to get out of there. The back door had a safety lock that could not be opened from inside without a key. He tried to jump onto the lip of the sink, found that his legs did not respond the way he expected, and succeeded only in barking his shin on the metal curvature. He rubbed the bone for a few seconds, then ignored the pain and slowly clambered onto the counter top. His legs seemed unnaturally stiff.

He did not go out the window headfirst. He spun around and stuck out his legs one at a time, squirmed across the sill until he was seated, then rolled over and

let himself slide over the edge. Without the log as a plat-
form, he dropped awkwardly onto the ground, scraping
his chest across the sill. Levered outward by his arms,
he fell flat on his back on the grass and had the wind
knocked out of him. A cat burglar he was not.

The crisis of the moment forced Grant into motion
before his body recovered from the shock. It required
supreme effort and will power to roll over and get up on
his knuckles and knees. Still panting for air, he rose
partially erect and stumbled toward the hedgerow. He
angled away from the Flower Fields entranceway, away
from the path taken by the screaming woman, away
from the direction from which the police were likely to
come.

The rustling of leaves as Grant scuttled across the
adjacent back yards was thunderous in Grant's ears.
The ground seemed to be covered with them, and he
kept plowing through huge piles that had been raked
up against the hedgerow. A dog barked from its kennel
as Grant ran by. He heard the rattle of a dragging chain
and the tingle of metal vaccination tags, then a momentary silence as the dog reached the end of its leash. By
the time it began barking again, Grant was already
past.

The hedgerow terminated at the end of the street.
The lawns of the last two yards merged, then yielded to
a barrier of tall weeds where the residents stopped
mowing. Grant scrabbled to a halt, bent over and rested his hands on his knees, and sucked in air as hard
and as fast as he could. A full minute passed, during
which each labored breath felt like the tenth inhalation
from a balloon. His lungs burned. Another two minutes
went by before he was able to stand erect and focus his
attention on his surroundings. This was disconcerting
because, thought Grant, a man in his early forties
should be in better shape.

Flower Fields was suffused with a preternatural
silence: no children sang, no women screamed, no
sirens howled. In the hush of the moment, Grant could
almost believe that everything he had been through in

the past couple of hours was nothing more than a bad dream. He barely had time to regain some composure when the streetlights winked on row after row. In seconds, one entire quadrant of the development was flooded with the sunlike brilliance of powerful mercury vapor lamps. Grant was suddenly exposed in full view to anyone who happened to be looking his way. He felt horribly out of place, and so alarmed that his natural flare for word plays fell flat and humorless in dire afterthought. In the eyes of the world at large he was no longer just a lost pedestrian in search of somewhere to hang his hat, but a prowler on the loose.

The light worked to his advantage. Now he could see the beginning of a narrow dirt trail that led through the tall brush. Without hesitation he ducked into the natural sanctum provided by the thick vegetation. It swallowed him like a pitcher plant engulfing a fly. He was immediately surrounded by blackness so intense that he should have been discomfited. Under the circumstances, however, he was glad to screen his departure. The chirrups he heard could have been crickets or frogs or nesting birds: natural sounds which had a calming effect on him.

Soon Grant felt his shoes slurping in mud. Not all the marshland had been reclaimed for the development of Flower Fields, and he was afraid that he might soon find himself wading through a swamp. Instead, the path rose to higher and dryer ground and soon opened onto a broad meadow surrounded by a wire fence with rough-hewn wooden posts. Drifting clouds now partially obscured the starlight. The diffuse heavenly glow created a splotchy shadow effect which turned the field into a bleak and desolate otherworld landscape. Black hillocks punctuated the otherwise flat and featureless plain.

When Grant found his way along the fence blocked by heavy brush, he climbed between the wire strands, careful not to get hung up on the barbs.

Footing was poor due to mounds of earth and dumps of vegetation irregularly spaced among shoe-sized divots, causing him to stagger across the field like a drunk on a weekend binge. He saw another fence in the distance and what appeared to be a roadway or country trail curving up a slight grade and leading away from a huge, two-story barn. He headed in that direction not knowing where he was going—not quite sure where he was coming from.

For a respite from the terra infirma, Grant leaped onto one of the large dark mounds. His foot came down on something soft, something that yielded to his weight like loose topsoil covered with thick spongy moss. No sooner did he register this impression than the mound undulated beneath him, pitching him off. He flapped his arms for balance, stubbed his toe on something hard and unyielding, and fell against another mound with an "oof" escaping from his lungs. The second mound heaved upward with a long, drawn-out "moo-oo-oo." Grant was tossed backward onto the ground.

They were Black Angus cows, startled from their sleep by Grant's fumbling intrusion. He lay sprawled on a pile of desiccated dung in the middle of a pasture.

Black shapes arose from the earth like giant specters in a monotone phantasmagoria. Grant scrambled to his feet so as not to get trampled by the stampeding herd, but the cows merely mooed in discontent and sauntered away en masse at a pace that registered annoyance rather than alarm. Hooves kicked up clods of dirt that plopped on the ground like grapeshot against a mud bank. Particles hovered in the air long after the cattle came to rest in a less active part of the field. Coughing and fanning dust from his eyes, Grant headed once again for the opposite fence.

He snagged his coat when he ducked through the barbed wire, tearing one wedge out of the sleeve and another out of the breast. It did not seem to matter. Without knowing why, he turned left on the dirt farm trail and followed the ruts up the hill. After a while he came to a paved road with a hump in the middle and narrow stone shoulders, each of which curved down to a weed-filled drainage ditch. As he looked both ways along the endless road, he was filled with dreadful inde-cision.

He knew that he could not stand still, that he had to keep moving. Not because the nip in the air would soon chill him to the bone, but because the terrible, fearful piercing cold which was numbing his inner core was likely to consume his sanity if he did not soon make sense out of the night's absurd events. But he also knew that he could not meander around the coun-tryside creating disorder, that he must have a direction in which to move, some goal in mind which could pro-vide a solution to his quandary. He needed orientation as defined in terms of psychology: individual awareness of the objective world in its relation to the self.

Grant held his hands out in front of him, flexed his fingers until the nails bit hard into the flesh of his palms. He felt pain; he felt tactile sensation. That was good. It meant that his body was real.

Cogito, ergo sum—I think, therefore I am. In the deep Cartesian well of philosophy, the very fact of self-awareness implied personal existence. But was the mind inseparable from the body? Descartes thought not; he believed in dualism, that the universe consist-ed of two radically different kinds of substance—physi-cal and mental, the body and the mind—and that one could live without the other. Modern scientists and philosophers, whose perception of reality was based upon the study of the structure of the brain, thought otherwise.

By logical deduction, because Grant could breathe and think and be aware of both, he was alive. The ques-tion that bothered him, though, was one that was infi-nitely more profound: Was he sane? Furthermore, how could he tell the difference between sanity and insanity when he could perceive the world only through a mind which was being deceived by contradictory evidence? By knowing one thing and experiencing another? Was truth a matter of perspective, or a quantitative absolute independent of viewpoint? Was truth even a valid con-cept in universal terms, or was it a human simplification for manifestations of reality?

Grant shivered—not from the cold but from the meaninglessness of his rambling speculations. Once again he forced himself to think rationally, in terms of scientific method. In order to pick up the ties of his life he had to return to the point at which he had gotten off the track, a point from which his thought processes could be reconstructed. And the only siding he could park on was the one with which he was the most familiar—his experiments at the lab.

He was a neurologist, a cyberneticist, a practicing scientist who worked for one of the most innovative laboratories in the country—a private consortium which was dedicated to the development of computer intelligence augmentation through biological analogue and the implementation of programmable heuristic logic circuits for robotic vehicles in space: the Biotech Corporation.

Deep in Grant's subconscious mind crawled incomplete notions and half-hidden ideas. Suddenly he knew where he had to go, knew where he must find the answers to all his mystical questions.

Memory Lane.

Everything he needed to know could be found on Memory Lane.

Chapter 3

Grant lay motionless in the drainage ditch until after the headlights passed. A glimpse through parted weeds revealed that it was the same car that had gone by a few minutes previous, in the opposite direction: a shiny metallic gray four-door sedan which might have been a Lincoln or a Cadillac—Grant knew very little about automobiles other than how to drive them. Probably someone who lives on this road, he soliloquized silently. Someone with lots of money. Some sprawling, affluent horse ranches were nestled in this neck of the woods, a few with thoroughbreds well known in the racing circuits; also a couple of stud farms.

When the taillights dropped behind the nearby rise, Grant climbed out of concealment, brushed himself off as best he could, and continued on his way. Shortly he reached the intersection with the main road: a two-lane finely paved highway that connected the suburban housing developments with town. He did not walk along the hard-packed shoulder, but kept to the mown grass at the edge of the tree line. Whenever a vehicle barreled into view, he ducked into the woods and waited for it to pass. Twice, police cars hummed by in no particular hurry. After climbing through a window, sloshing through the swamp, falling in a cow pasture, and hiding in ditches, Grant figured that his appearance more closely resembled that of a tramp or prowler than a late-night perambulator. It behooved him to stay out of sight.

There was little traffic at this hour of the night—whatever hour it was; just enough to be a nuisance. The stars shone bright above scudding cumulus: stellar emanation that made navigation easy when the clouds dispersed, difficult when they gathered together. Signposts were clearly legible, although Grant knew where he was and how to get to the place he was going, and did not need to read street names to find his way—

or his lane. He chuckled to himself. His humor was returning now that he had an objective.

He quickly grew weary of the endless game of hide-and-seek, especially on those occasions when a car no sooner sped past than another appeared behind it or approached from the other direction. Such interludes in the bushes gave him the opportunity to rest, but Grant wanted to be walking rather than crouching and shivering. By the time he reached the cutoff to Memory Lane, the stars close to the horizon were becoming less distinct, and the purple firmament had faded to a dark blue.

Memory Lane was more properly a private driveway than a public thoroughfare. It had been carved out of the pristine forest when the Biotech office-lab complex was built. There was only one postal address on its half-mile length: Biotech Corporation, 101 Memory Lane. The paved surface was supported by an extra-thick concrete foundation in order to withstand the constant flow of heavy-duty delivery trucks, and had withstood the trauma of usage much better than the secondary roads that funneled into it. The sidewalk was broad and flat, and doubled as a bike trail for those so inclined to ride.

Grant expected the building to be darkened, but he thought that at least the nightlights would be lit. There was nearly always someone catching up on paperwork or performing after-hours experiments, especially those that drew a great deal of electrical power; and a watch-men patrolled the building constantly in order to ensure against fire, theft, and, of potentially greater consequence, industrial sabotage. Quite a few competing companies would love to download Biotech's main-frame onto transportable hard drives while injecting a computer virus that would infect the host data. A mosquito program was much to be feared, difficult to slap, and its byte impossible to inoculate against.

Biotech had two entrances from Memory Lane. The first turned into the parking lot, the second—on the far side of the grounds—led to the loading docks at the back of the building. Grant turned into the darkened lot where not a car was parked. This was just as odd as the building lights being extinguished. The ground floor looked like a cavern opening behind ceiling-height glass panels that stretched the full width of the lobby.

Grant pressed his face against a thick pane and cupped his eyes with his hands. Since there was no glare from lights in the parking lot, it made no difference. He could see nothing inside but vague, unmoving shapes and shadows. The building appeared to be deserted. Could this be the result of a maintenance shutdown or a new energy saving policy? In either case, Grant should have heard about it. Perhaps it was one of those announcements which he normally put out of mind. Whatever was going on, it was the first time in Biotech's history that the building had been blacked out and totally devoid of personnel.

Grant rattled the door in disbelief. It was locked, and the glass was too thick to break with anything less than a sledgehammer. Keep moving, he said to himself. Keeping searching. There's a rational explanation for everything.

The Biotech building was twice as deep as it was wide. Both sides were lined with shrubbery which separated the red brick facade from the sidewalk, and which provided some seclusion for people in the first floor offices when the vertical blinds were opened to let in the sun. Now all the blinds were closed, and the windows which Grant could reach through the bushes, were latched. The grounds keeper did not appear to be doing his job, for the shrubs were ragged and untrimmed and had grown far too tall. Furthermore, the grass was uncut and dead leaves littered the ground in dire need of raking.

The side door that Grant normally used to reach his office was locked. Without conscious thought he pulled the key chain from his jacket pocket, selected the proper key, and inserted it in the keyhole. The key slid in smoothly, was a little difficult to turn, but unlocked the bolt with a satisfying click. The door pulled open with a squeal of unoiled hinges. This surprised him, as nothing else this night had gone as anticipated.

By now the eastern sky was tinted with the faintest splash of pink. Grant put his keys back in his pocket, then stepped into the unlit entry. The cement floor was overlaid with black and white linoleum tiles. An aisle led to the inner fire door, while to the right was a set of red painted steel stairs leading up to the second floor. Behind him, the outer door closed by dint of a hydraulic piston, plunging the interior into utter blackness. Grant fumbled for the wall switch, found it, and flipped it up then down then up again. The stairwell lights did not illuminate.

Grant knew the building by heart, so had no trepidation about feeling his way up the stairs in the dark. He let himself into the second floor hallway, then played blind-man's--bluff along the corridor until he arrived at his office. He pushed open the door. The blackness was near absolute because the blinds were closed, and remained so when the fluorescent tubes in the recessed ceiling fixtures failed to come on when he flipped the switch. He crouched down low, held his hands out in front of him, and tread lightly across the room swinging his arms back and forth. In his mind he pictured the filing cabinets against the left wall, his desk against the right, and chairs, wastepaper basket, and boxes of samples and test products in the middle. His course direction was faultless: he banged into nothing. Not even the workstation under the window.

He opened the blinds to let in the faint glow of first light. The room was totally vacant.

There were no filing cabinets, no chairs, no boxes, no desk, and no mess. Even the carpet had been pulled up. Grant felt a pang in his chest that was like the stab of a stiletto, only it hurt much, much more. He swallowed hard despite the lump in his throat. His breathing came in gasps. Think it through, he thought, trying to remain calm. There's got to be a rational explanation. But he could not remain calm. His spine tingled with trepidation that quickly escalated to panic.

He felt lost, so utterly lost in a world in which he no longer seemed to have a part. His house was not his own, his family had been supplanted, now his office was a hollow shell which had been swept clean of all evidence of his tenancy—as though he had been dispossessed of his existence. Or as if the act of turning the key in the front door of his home had unlocked a portal to another dimension—a parallel time stream in which Grant had never been born.

But that doesn't make sense, he reasoned. That is the stuff of science fiction and theoretical physics, not life in the real world. Use your brain, he reminded himself. You're a neuroscientist and computer expert. You work on the brain and analyze its functions every day of the week. Use that experience and knowledge to rationalize real-time events.

He groped for the office door, ran his hands along the fine-grained paneling. There was no name plaque, only screw holes to show that it had been removed. He opened all the other doors in the hallway—every room was as devoid of furniture as the first; none had a name plaque. The conference chamber was a large void without tables or chairs or bookcases. The restroom was as dark as a pocket, and when Grant twisted the faucets there was not the slightest gurgle or hiss. Even the secretarial pool was dry.

The laboratory sections were equally as barren. Gone were the workbenches, storage cabinets, shelving, computer consoles, specimen boxes, glass enclosed experiment cases, and all the diagnostic equipment. The clean room was immaculate as always, but it was missing the operating table, hospital furnishings, surgical instruments, and testing and recording apparatus. Of the ceiling mounted video cameras, only the brackets remained. There were no signs of the prototype board production center or the master chip miniaturization tools or the photographic reduction cameras. Every bit of machinery and all the conveyor belts in the vast assembly room had been removed. And the storage vault had been cleaned out.

Grant backed against the wall in the corner of the tech lab where in some other life, in some other world or dimension or time warp, in some bizarre solipsistic plane of existence, he had once worked at his secondary desk and auxiliary computer station. Memory Lane had been his last bastion of hope, but he had found no comfort here. He was inexplicably lost in the maze of emptiness around and within him, trapped in a dream from which he could not awake.

He no longer had the strength to go on, or even the strength to stand. Slowly his legs folded beneath him. He slid down the wall in pantomime of a cartoon character who had been conked on the head with a bat. He came to rest with his buttocks on the floor and his legs tucked tight against his chest, so that his heels touched his buttocks. He pushed his feet out to a more comfortable position, wrapped his hands around his shins, and lowered his forehead until it rested against his knees.

Grant's life passed before his eyes in meteoric flashes: faces, places, scenes, and situations; a lifetime of academic achievement from kindergarten finger painting through elementary school spelling bees through middle school science projects to magna cum laude; medical school and postgraduate work; internship at Chancellor Hospital, microchip designer at Cyberdyne Systems, chief scientist at Biotech; his mother, father, grandparents, neighborhood playmates, college girlfriends, fellow students, occupational acquaintances, colleagues and associates, presidents and janitors, wife and daughter. His head was a maelstrom of images and associations the sum of which equaled the persona known as Grant Philip Templeton. After all, who was he—who was anyone—but a chronological collage of experiences? One's past was the essence of oneself.

Grant was overcome with hopelessness.

He wrangled with emotional turmoil. What he knew about himself and his past conflicted with current observable data; nor could he fathom any rational explanation for his paradoxical predicament. He was lost in a dialectical wilderness with no sign of rescue in sight.

For the first time in his life, Grant understood the meaning of alienation and loss of identity. He had bypassed that delicate stage of adolescent development that drove many parents mad and some teenagers to suicide. Once a child prodigy, then adult savant, he now felt himself slipping—retrogressing—to the kind of person whose direction in life was motivated less by intellectual pursuits than by insecurity, emotional instability, and the soul-wrenching search for a sense of belonging. Grant had never needed to belong to anything.

Now, with a flash of horrifying insight, he knew what it meant to be alone, knew how a little child must feel when its mother passed away, knew how much of his fellow man a person is a part. And with this flash of insight, Grant also knew despair. He could not help but give in to emotions that were surging within his breast.

Finally, in despondency, he permitted himself to do what he had not permitted himself to do since childhood.

He cried.

Chapter 4

Grant did not awaken fully alert as he usually did in the morning. Instead, he felt groggy and bleary-eyed, as if he had drunk too many vodka gimlets the night before. Not that he went out on all-night benders or drank himself into oblivion when he was in the house alone, but he usually had a nip or two when he arrived home from work, and a couple more before bedtime in order to help him sleep. He had cut down consumption considerably when the trauma of divorce had begun to fade. Now he only imbibed to that extent when he felt particularly maudlin—perhaps two or three times per week. He certainly was not an alcoholic.

He found himself on a concrete floor lying on his side, and curled into a fetal position in order to conserve his body heat. His right side was numb from cold and restricted circulation. When he pushed himself up to a sitting position, a groan escaped from his lips. He ached all over. And he had a headache which neither throbbed nor pounded, but which seemed to rattle through his skull as if had used a running engine block for a pillow.

The grogginess lingered. For a long time he did not recognize where he was nor remember how he got there. Then, when the night's preposterous episode finally came to mind, he wished he had remained in ignorance. The empty lab told him that this was not the dawn of a new day and a return to the routine, but the continuation of madness.

He climbed to his feet by pressing his hands against the wall. He shook his head to clear it of cobwebs, but succeeded only in aggravating the headache. For several minutes he wandered through the abandoned building, reaffirming in the light of day what he had already ascertained: that if he had ever worked here as he thought he had—no, as he *knew* he had—then it was a long time ago.

Grant's mouth felt like a wad of cotton. He could sure use a drink—liquor preferred, but tea or coffee would suffice in a pinch. He felt his way into the windowless lavatory and again tried the faucets; again nothing came out. Even the toilet bowls were dry. He lifted the porcelain tops off the tanks, and in the third one found a puddle of dark water at the bottom. He cupped his hand, scooped out some water, and held it to his nose. There was a faint mineral odor but nothing particularly foul. He splashed the water into his eyes to rub out the dried sleepy matter that clouded his vision, and got a real fright.

A thick mat of hair covered his entire face, as if he had not shaved in months, or years. He ran wet fingers along both cheeks and his throat, scarcely daring to imagine how he had grown such a beard overnight. It seemed impossible—but then, so did everything else that had occurred in the past few hours. Ignoring the matter in his eyes, he took the toilet tank top to the mirror over the sink, squinted and glanced away, and smashed the glass with the heavy porcelain ram. When the glass stopped tinkling, he put down the tank top, carefully felt in the sink for a sizable chunk of mirror, and carried it out into the corridor. Sunlight streaming in from the window at the far end of the hall offered enough illumination for him to see the startling truth. Whiskers at least an inch long concealed all facial skin except for a wrinkled forehead, elongated crow's feet, and bags under hard brown eyes. He hardly recognized himself.

The face Grant beheld in the mirrored shard was like a fairy tale reincarnation of Rip Van Winkle. After the initial shock, when he felt himself slipping once again into despair, he recalled his commitment before lapsing into sleep, and bolstered his resolve to venture boldly into the world into which he had been thrust, to meet coming affairs on their own terms, and to try to decipher the cause and the meaning of his apparent displacement. Either that or admit that he had suddenly become psychotic.

Grant left the Biotech building the same way he entered: through the side door. The long shadows and heavy eyelids reminded him of the early hour. Despite his fatigue, he was too fired up to sleep. He crossed the parking lot, paused at the entrance gate, and looked back at what had once been the headquarters of the most sophisticated biomechanical engineering firm in the world. He stemmed the flood of nostalgia with a sibilant, quixotic, "Damn," laughed at his own witticism, and turned his back on the past.

He was walking along the bike path admiring the vivid autumnal color when another incongruity struck him. Yesterday it had been spring and the flowers were coming into full bloom; today the leaves were dropping from the trees in preparation for winter. Maples with their red and orange, and oaks with their auburns, blended prismatically with the bright yellows of interspersed sassafras. Take it easy, he thought when he felt his pulse quicken. He forced himself to calm down, made a mental notation, and chalked it up as another mystery to be solved.

At the highway he turned right and headed toward town, walking openly along the shoulder as cars and trucks whizzed by at high speed a few feet away. Blasts of air spun his curly hair into wind-blown disarray, which was indistinguishable from his usual coiffure. He thought of sticking out his thumb and hitching a ride into town, but decided against it. There were too many kooks on the road—at least, there were in the world he was used to.

The telephone booth on the side of the highway next to the gas station at the intersection gave Grant a sudden inspiration. He let his fingers do the walking until he found the page on which his name and number should have been printed. Three Templetons were listed, but none was named Grant or Barbara. Anonymity was one thing, nonentity quite another. He shrugged off the tingles that ran along his spine. Have a little backbone, he laughed to himself. The phone company could not tell him that he did not exist; he knew otherwise.

He tapped the touchpad for directory assistance.

The voice that answered was surprisingly soft and feminine, without the nasal tonal quality stereotypically applied to telephone operators. "What city, please?"

Why did they always ask what city you wanted when you were calling from the city in which the operator was located? "Highland Hills, Illinois."

"What number, please?"

"I'd like the number of Grant Templeton."

Grant held his breath during the slight pause. "I'm sorry, sir. There is no one listed by that name."

"Can you tell me if the number is unlisted?"

"I'm sorry, sir, I don't have that information."

You do so have it. You just won't give it out. "Okay. How about Barbara Templeton?"

Another pause.

Grant wiped his sweaty palm on his pants, shifted the receiver to his right ear, then wiped off his other palm.

"I'm sorry, sir. There is no one listed by that name."

"She's at 228 Buttercup Path."

"I'm sorry, sir. We have no Templeton listed at that address."

Think fast. "Uh, do you have a, uh, a Bob Lerner? Robert Lerner?"

She was quick this time. "I'm sorry, sir. There is no Robert Lerner listed."

"Okay, how about—" Whom should he ask for next? "—how about Francine Baker?"

He found it odd that after requesting his co-worker's number he should next ask for that of his secretary, instead of the numbers of other members of the Board of Directors or officers in the company.

With exasperation, "No, sir. There is no Francine Baker."

Now he was getting desperate. He forced himself to control his emotions. "Okay. Okay. Uh, can you place a call for me? A local call?" He remembered that Francine's number, like Lerner's, was unlisted. Fortunately, he knew Francine's home phone number by heart.

"This is directory assistance, sir. Dial zero if you need to make an operator assisted call."

"Uh, okay. Okay. Thank you, uh—" What did you call a directory assistance person if not an operator? "Thanks." He hung up the phone, waited a few seconds, picked it up, and tapped out Francine's number.

The dial tone went silent. After an appreciable interval, a recording came on and announced, "Your call cannot be completed as dialed. You must deposit seventy-five cents for the first three minutes."

Local calls had gone up drastically in price. Grant rummaged through his front pants pockets for change and, finding none, hung up, waited half an eternity, and tapped zero.

"Operator. How may I help you?" This woman's voice began as pleasantly as the previous one's.

"I'd like to make a call, please, and, uh, reverse the charges." Surely Francine would advance him a few quarters.

"What is the number, please?"

"Seven-one-three, one-four-six-eight."

"What area code is that, sir?"

"Eight-one-five."

"Sir, that is a local call. We cannot reverse charges on local calls."

"What? Why not?"

"We can only reverse charges on long distance calls." As if that were an answer. "I can connect you if you will deposit seventy-five cents, please."

Grant switched the phone back to his left ear, cocked his head, and jammed the receiver against his shoulder while he rummaged through his pockets again. "Uh, I don't seem to have any quarters."

"Nickels and dimes will work, sir, as long as they equal seventy-five cents. No pennies, please."

Grant's jacket pocket yielded his key chain and voice recorder; he had not a single coin in his possession. He scanned the floor and the tiny shelf, and checked the coin return hopper. Seeing no money, he frantically tripped the coin release lever, but nothing dropped into the hopper. "Uh, I don't seem to have any change at all, operator. Uh, are you sure I can't reverse the charges?"

"Not for a local call, sir."

"Then can I charge it to my home phone?"

"Not for a local call." The absence of the "sir" was evident.

"Okay, I understand. It's just that that I need to call someone in town and I don't have any change." He thought quickly, reverse the burden of responsibility by asking her for help. "How can I do that?"

"Sir, I am not authorized to place unpaid calls, but if it is an emergency you can call nine-one-one or I can connect you directly."

He had thought about going to the police, about throwing himself on their mercy, explaining his situation, and letting them call around to verify who he was, where he lived, where he worked, where he belonged. Perhaps they could account for his strange dissociation. On the other hand, perhaps they would lock him up as a nut case or have him committed to an institution where he would be helpless to help himself.

The ache in his head had diminished to a vibratory purr: enough to be annoying without being debilitating. Grant formed his words slowly. "No, this is not an emergency. That is, not that kind of emergency. I just need to talk to—" Francine Baker? Okay, so they had started seeing each other socially since his divorce, and since her husband had passed away. That was hardly a reason for needing to talk with her. Who else could he call? "All right. I'll make a long distance call and reverse the charges."

"What number, please?"

"Area code five-oh-three, four-two-two, nine-eight-seven-zero."

"And who shall I say is calling?"

"Grant." That was all she needed to know, but for some reason he added, "Grant Templeton."

"One moment, please."

He heard the connection being made and the telephone ringing. Too late he realized that Oregon was on Pacific time, and that it was two hours earlier there and probably still dark. Would she be up at this hour? In the middle of the sixth ring came a momentary silence and a clatter of banging plastic, followed by a sleepy voice which croaked, "Hello?" It was a man's voice.

"I have a collect call to anyone from Grant Templeton. Will you pay for the call?"

"From who?"

"Mr. Grant Templeton."

"I don't know no Grant Templing." Click!

"I'm sorry, sir. The party you called will not accept the charges." Why do they always do that? Grant raged inwardly. Don't they know I can hear every word that's being said? "Please try your call later."

"No! I want to try it again, right now. Charge the call to my home phone."

A period of silence was followed by a tone of resignation. "What is your number, please?"

"Seven-one-three, three-three-eight-eight."

"What area code, please?"

"Eight-one-five," he practically screamed.

"Sir," the operator started, this time with a hint of disdain rather than with formality, "That number is no longer in service in this area code."

This proved to Grant that his home phone did not have an unlisted number. "Okay, okay. How about my calling card? Can I use my calling card?"

"Yes, sir. You may. What is your calling card number, please?"

He rattled it off the top of his head, "Eight four-six, two-two-one, nine-three-nine-eight, seven-seven-four-four."

After another appreciable pause, the operator announced with increased inflection, "That is not a valid calling card number, sir."

"What?" How could he have forgotten his calling card number? He stuck his hands into his inside jacket pockets, then his rear pants pockets, then he checked all of his other pockets. Again he found his key ring and voice recorder, but no wallet. He had no identification, no driver's license, no automobile registration card, no cash, no credit cards, no business cards, and no way of verifying the number of his calling card. "Maybe you didn't hear me correctly." He repeated the number.

"I'm sorry, sir. That is not a valid number."

Exasperation dissolved into dismay. He started to lose control again. He took several deep breaths, conscious of the silence which it was his turn to fill. Then he spoke deliberately in a well modulated voice, "Thank you, operator. I'll try again later."

He hung up the phone for about five seconds, took the receiver off the hook, tapped zero, and held his breath while he waited. A different operator answered. They repeated the procedure with the same amount of frustration for both of them and with the same result. He finally asked to speak with the supervisor.

"May I help you?"

"Yes, you can. At least, I hope you can. I know the operator was just doing her job, so she isn't to blame. But I've had an accident and I need to call, uh, someone, to come and pick me up. I have no wallet and no money. But for god's sake, I only want to make a local call. I promise to repay the phone company if you're really that concerned about a few lousy quarters. You can either trust me or bill me. My name is Grant Templeton. But I need to make a call."

"Of course, sir. I'll be glad to put the call through for you."

Grant breathed a soft sigh of relief. "Thank you. I— I really appreciate your help." He inhaled deep once again. He enunciated slowly so as not to make any mistakes, "The number is seven-one-three, one-four-six-eight."

The supervisor tapped out Francine's number. After the tenth ring, she said, "I'm sorry, sir, but there's no answer at that number. Is there another number you would like to try?"

"No," he said resignedly. "No. But I'd like to try again later."

"Yes, sir. Dial oh and ask for Noreen. I'll be glad to help you."

"Thanks."

Grant hung up. For a long time he leaned against the side of the booth, contemplating his next move. Around him, life went on as usual. Cars zipped along the thoroughfare carrying ordinary people to work. Every once in a while, a vehicle slowed and pulled into the lot of the gas station and convenience store. Some people pumped gasoline, some picked up a newspaper, some purchased coffee in Styrofoam cups and perhaps a doughnut or sandwich. They were all strangers to him: with their own destinations, their own desires, their own thoughts, their own troubles.

Or was Grant the stranger? Was *he* real, or were they? The world appeared normal beyond the glass walls of the phone booth: the kind of normality to which Grant desperately wanted to belong, but of which he appeared to be no longer a part. Against that greater reality—a reality which he could observe like a relativistic physicist observing subatomic particles or speed-of-light waveforms, but with which he could not readily interact—he felt totally defenseless, alone, and alienated. But not down and out for the count.

There had to be a rationale for his seemingly impossible circumstance. But because his resources were limited, because time was against him, it was impractical for him to conduct the kinds of tests which a scientist should conduct without blowing up the laboratory and himself into the bargain. It was time to make the world come to him.

He tapped nine-one-one. Already he was ahead of the game because the call cost no money.

Chapter 5

The policeman had a peach fuzz face that could not have required shaving more than once a week. His blue uniform was spick and span, his black shoes were polished like ebony mirrors, and his hat was perched high on the back of his head with the shiny brim pulled down so far in front that it practically covered his bright blue eyes, which were nearly a match for his uniform. He was tall, lithe, broad-chested, and, with firm lips set above a square-set jaw, imposing. Which, as an authority figure, he was supposed to be.

Grant left the security of the phone booth and approached the young cop. "Hello, officer. I'm Grant Templeton. I'm the one who called."

"Patrolman Riley, Mr. Templeton." The policeman's voice was deep and resonant, his carriage sternly official. Long arms hung casually by his side as he walked, with his hands never far from the belt that held the two-way radio, the billy club, and the holstered .38-caliber revolver. He appeared not to notice Grant's unruly mode of dress. "What seems to be the trouble?"

Grant did his best to sound relaxed as he went into his rehearsed speech. "I've had an accident of some kind. Maybe bumped my head. I'm not hurt, but I'm confused and—not sure where I am or what I'm doing here. I didn't know whether they'd send a patrol car or an ambulance or—or what. This isn't really a police matter— I mean, a matter of law enforcement. But I didn't know who else to call."

"The police do a lot more than enforce the law, Mr. Templeton. Helping people in distress is high on our list of priorities."

"Well, I'm in distress." Grant grinned, then paused uncomfortably. "I was hoping you could take me to the station, perhaps make a few phone calls to friends and relatives—someone to come and get me. I've got no wallet or ID. I can't tell you how naked that makes me feel."

Riley leaned close to Grant. "You're eyes are blood-shot, Mr. Templeton. Have you been drinking?"

"Not that I can recall." He knew it was the wrong answer as soon as he said it. "I mean, no."

Riley's expression was noncommittal. "Would you mind taking a Breathalyzer test?"

Grant shrugged. "No, I guess not." He felt embarrassed, however, standing in the open and puffing into the mouthpiece, a sorry sight to passers-by who gawked suspiciously at the bum in tattered clothing on the side of the road. His jacket stank of cow manure and his shoes were wet with swamp water. After conducting the simple test, Riley packed the Breathalyzer kit away but offered no enlightenment of the results. Grant finally asked, "What does it show?"

"You're clean." Riley's face warmed a degree or two. "But I noticed a couple of bruises on the side of your head. One on each side. Mind if I take a look?"

"No. Go ahead."

The patrolman pushed his fingers through Grant's hair, and palpated the area above each ear. "Does that hurt?"

"It's not painful, but I can feel a—a sensitivity."

"The skin's not broken but it's discolored—kind of purplish, with a black dot in the middle."

"How big?"

Riley pursed his lips. "About the size of a dime, maybe smaller. We might want to get it checked out by a doctor."

Grant started to tell the patrolman that *he* was a doctor, but refrained. The saying that came to mind, "Physician, heal thyself," seemed ludicrous under the circumstances. *How can I heal myself when I don't even know myself.* "I'd rather go to the station first."

"Okay, Mr. Templeton." Riley opened the back door of the police car. "I'll be glad to take you."

Grant allowed himself to be ushered onto the rear seat. Not until the patrolman closed the door did he notice that there were no handles on the inside. The wire mesh that separated the cab into two compartments reminded him of a cage.

Riley slid in behind the steering wheel and grabbed the microphone dangling by a coiled cord from the dashboard. "Car eight reporting. I'm bringing in the John Doe, ETA about fifteen minutes. An ambulance is not required. Repeat, not required. Out." A grumbly masculine voice acknowledged receipt of the call.

The engine idled quietly. Riley put the automatic transmission in gear, wheeled the car in a short arc, and eased onto the thoroughfare. The car accelerated smoothly and rapidly with a muffled, high-pitched whine. There was power under the hood.

"Do you always lock people in the back like this, even if they haven't done anything?"

Riley glanced at Grant in the rearview mirror. His lips parted ever so slightly. "Nothing personal, Mr. Templeton. It's SOP. According to regulations, we're not allowed to have passengers up front—only other officers." He paused for several seconds, then explained, "Someone who's hurt, like yourself, might pass out and fall against the driver and cause an accident."

"Yes, I guess I didn't think of that." Nevertheless, Grant did not care for being penned in like a common criminal. If helping people in distress was truly a police priority, then the police should treat those people in a manner that was less humiliating. The authoritarian viewpoint tended to lump criminals and their victims in the same context, so that the victim often became more victimized by the system of follow-up procedure than by the initiating criminal action.

Grant tried a different mode of perception: thinking of Riley as a chauffeur instead of as a patrolman "taking in his man." Feelings were subjective adjuncts to a perceived notion of reality; that is, the kind of reality that was perceptible to the human brain due to its physiological construction. By extrapolation, the limitations of the mind were predicated upon the sensory restrictions of the brain which housed it. "You can't think your way out of your own brain," was an aphorism often touted among neuroscientists, any more than you can fly a car, because the engine and chassis were not designed for flight. Emotions, on the other hand, could be partially controlled or directed by a strong will and a desire to maintain objectivity despite perceived threats to one's mental well being. At least, that was the theory. In his heart, Grant doubted his ability to "think" or "feel" his way out of his present predicament. And he knew too well from recent experience that as subjective as scientists claimed feelings to be—and he used to make the same claim himself before the trauma of divorce made him wiser—no one was immune to the anguish of psychological stress, even if that stress was purely imaginary. Pain that was "all in your head" was no less painful than a blow to the skull, because man is an emotional animal who cannot escape his own evolution.

"Do you live around here, Mr. Templeton?"

Grant brought his eyes back into focus. "Uh, yes. I do. I work for Biotech." Too late he realized that from what he discovered last night, Biotech no longer existed. Not in this world. Perhaps he should have said "used to work." He stared out the window as they passed a strip mall that he had never noticed before, and used it to change the subject. "I can't believe how this town has grown. They keep building like there's no tomorrow."

Riley shed another layer of officialdom with a smile. "The big companies are still moving in and bringing people with them. Good class of people, not riffraff, although we get some troublemakers with the support service workers and their families—teenagers, mostly, but not the college types. And most of them are just rabble-rousers, not hardened offenders of the law. The kind of kids who aren't going anywhere, just spending time on Earth."

Grant thought that was an astute observation for a person so close to his own adolescence. Patrolman Riley was either older than he looked or wise beyond his years.

"I've always felt safe here," Grant allowed. The sun

was still fairly low on the horizon. Rays penetrating the rear window caressed his back with welcome warmth. He rubbed his icy hands. "It doesn't seem very crowded today. Where is everyone?"

"Saturday mornings start out slow. Come Monday rush hour the boulevard will be a parking lot."

Now Grant knew what day it was. By entering the appropriate prompts, what else could he learn about the world into which he had been thrust without giving away his ignorance? He had to be careful with what he said and how he said it, and to speak in generalities.

They passed a sprawling supermarket that was already open for business. It was new to Grant, but he did not mention that fact as he did not want to seem too unfamiliar with the layout of the town. His plan—as he conceived it after his frustrating conversations with the telephone operators—was to use the official resources that were available to the police in order to determine what had happened to him—not to let the authorities turn him over to an asylum under psychiatric lock and key.

"Our company has always promoted flex time for all salaried and hourly-wage personnel, whether management or staff. The system is mutually beneficial because the people are guaranteed forty hours pay per week, and the company is guaranteed forty hours work. In addition, both sides earn perquisites. The people have the flexibility to deal with personal matters during normal working hours—taking the kids to school or picking them up, doctor's appointments, getting the car fixed, and so forth—while the company obtains increased productivity and an incredible sense of loyalty. Throw in stock options for everyone from the janitor on up, and we wind up with a company that is treated like an extended family member. The building is like a second home, with people stopping in all the time to make sure their work is caught up. Our doors are never closed."

Except for this morning, he thought wryly.

The patrolman nodded gently and puckered his

lips, obviously impressed. "It sounds very progressive. Now if we could just get all these high-tech companies to stagger their hours, we wouldn't have so much congestion at commuter time."

"That's the second time you've mentioned traffic," Grant said, trying to be friendly and conversational.

Riley laughed. "Believe it or not, traffic control is the police department's biggest headache. I don't know anyone who would rather be directing traffic at an intersection with a broken signal than dealing with prowlers, car thieves, and domestic squabbles."

Mention of prowlers made Grant jolt in his seat. If he had been connected to a polygraph he would have bent the needles. He forced a grin. "Aren't cars less dangerous than crime?"

"Don't take this the wrong way, Mr. Templeton, but most of the time this job is pretty dull. Not that it doesn't have its satisfactions, such as helping people out, like yourself, but it's not as exciting as television makes you think. The cop shows are glamorized all out of proportion, and the newscasters only cover stories that have violence or corruption or personal injury, or that appeal to the viewers' prurient interests. Highland Hills doesn't even have a narcotics division or a homicide department. We call in the State Police for big time crimes. Sometimes I'm so bored that I wish something major would happen to break the monotony." Riley glanced at Grant through the mirror. "Like I said, don't take that the wrong way."

Grant gave the patrolman a grateful grin. "I understand." He was overjoyed to know that he was still in Highland Hills, even if this was not the same Highland Hills that he once knew. Again came that feeling of dé·jà vu, as Grant noticed places that were familiar, but were juxtaposed with those that were not—subtle differences which reminded him that a change had occurred either to him or to the town.

The brick post office stood where it always had, but an annex had been added and the parking lot enlarged. There was the diner where he and Dawn sometimes breakfasted on Sunday mornings, but next to it was a tire shop that he did not recall. The local bookstore was now a pharmacy, and the bookstore had relocated a block away. In this Highland Hills, the downtown service station where Grant took his car for repairs was a furniture store. The library looked the same. People walked the streets oblivious to changes which were obvious to Grant. Outwardly, it appeared to be a typical day.

"What kind of work do you do, Mr. Templeton?"

Grant snapped back to reality—to the reality in which he found himself trapped. His mind went blank for a moment. Was Riley just being friendly, or was this a prelude to interrogation? In either case it did not matter, since this was what Grant had asked for when he had called for assistance. He had to cooperate with the authorities if he expected them to help him find himself in this alternate world.

"There's no single precise term for my occupation. I've been called a bioengineer, a biophysicist, a roboticist, a chip designer, and a few other things I'd rather not mention. If I had to categorize myself within a specific discipline, I'd go back to my primary training and say that I'm a neuroscientist, although most of my workmates would replace 'neuro' with 'mad'." Despite his anxiety, a little of Grant's self-assured, easy-going personality slipped into his dialogue. "What I actually do is a another matter altogether, sometimes incomprehensible even to my employers, who want to see tangible results so they can prepare progress reports for their investors." He let out a humph. "How can I tell them what I'm doing when I never know myself?"

Riley suppressed a smirk. "You sound like a research scientist."

Now Grant grinned madly. "With that attitude you should run for the board of directors. I'd like reporting to someone with an open mind for a change. Don't get me wrong. I love my job because it's challenging, inventive, and intellectually stimulating; and, in my opinion, worthwhile. If the nitwits at the higher echelons would let me conduct experiments in my own way, I could achieve the kind of success for the company that they desire so much to achieve. What they don't understand or refuse to accept is that pure research does not always produce immediate and predictable results. That's not the way discovery works. If you knew in advance what you were going to find at the end of a trail—whether it be a wilderness trail or a biochemical trail—then it wouldn't be a discovery. By the same token, it's easy to discover what is already known—it's the unknown that takes time and perseverance to . . . "

Grant drifted off when he realized where the succession of ideas was leading. Perhaps if he heeded his own advice and remained receptive to his new sense of awareness, without carrying over the prejudice of past cognition, he might learn more about where his present course was taking him.

"Sorry, I usually only get riled like that when I'm forced to deal with corporate hardheads who know nothing about science and scientific method but who insist on telling me how to run my lab. I didn't mean anything personal."

"No offense taken, Mr. Templeton." Riley halted at a red light where cross traffic was heavy. The sleepy town was coming to life. "But I still don't understand. What is it you research?"

"Forget it. I just fired you from the board of directors for being too inquisitive." Then, seeing that Riley was taking the matter more seriously than Grant intended, he rushed on, "Only teasing. I know that you can't get answers if you don't ask questions." He commenced to squeeze his chin while he formulated his thoughts, but jerked back his hand when he felt the unruly beard: a reminder that his presence here was not a straight-line continuation of his previous existence.

"I started out as a computer whiz kid and built my own hard drive, wrote my own programs, created my own games, that kind of stuff. My specialty was breaking access codes with a math coprocessor that I designed just for the purpose. Never did any mischief, you understand; I just did it for kicks. But what decided me on medical school was my father's death, when I was a teenager. He was only forty-five when he developed early Alzheimer's disease. It was a traumatic experience for all of us—Mom, Dad, and me—as his mind slowly degenerated. He was a brilliant man, a good man, but the disorder took all that away from him and turned him into a hopeless vegetable. It is the nature of the disease that the victim is unable to comprehend what is happening to him. As Dad's intellect declined and he progressively lost his motor skills, he became angry, depressed, frustrated, and increasingly difficult to live with. His whole personality changed. He was no longer the person I once knew and loved."

Grant paused for a moment, finding it strange that he could talk about his father's cognitive impairment and eventual death with such detachment, without any sense of emotional involvement, as if his father had been a character in a movie which he had seen long ago. Nor did Grant's response have anything to do with Riley's original question. Confused, but unable to stop, he went on with his story.

"So I decided on a career in medicine. I was going to become a brain surgeon and save people from diseases of the brain. Only, during my internship I discovered that what I really wanted was to save my father—who by that time was long dead. I had no desire for neurosurgery. That was just a dream to help me overcome my pain and bitterness. I didn't want to cut into people. And I especially didn't want to be a neurologist: the poor guy who spends most of his time diagnosing patients with fatal diseases and prescribing placebos for the terminally ill. I wanted to work where there was life, where I could be creative."

He still did not understand why he was saying any of this. It was not like him to try to impress people with his background and accomplishments. Nonetheless, he went on, as if driven.

"So I reverted to my original love. I went to graduate

school and majored in computer technology, then got a job designing high-density microchips. By applying some innovative techniques, I was able to increase both storage capacity and processing speed. But I eventually came to grasp that there was a limit to what silicon-based chips could do. A static matrix is bounded by the parameters of chemistry and physics. Then came Biotech and the search for Artificial Intelligence."

Riley sucked in his breath. "You mean, like computers that can think for themselves?"

"No, no, no. Nothing like that. Nothing as simple or as complex, as AI is understood by most people who know only what the media feeds them. I'm not talking about network systems that can take over the world, but microprocessing units that can be programmed to append their primary databases with newly encountered information, the same as people do—what we call heuristic computers. The basic idea is that if you input enough data and integrate enough looping circuits, you can simulate the function of the human brain, not so the computer becomes sentient or has a sense of self-awareness, but so it can correct its own mistakes. The problem is that when you install the amount of memory needed to support a peripheral data acquisition program so the processing unit allows near instantaneous feedback, you've got a computer so big that it can't be housed in the ordinary robot. And before you jump to conclusions, by 'robot' I mean any automated mechanical device designed to operate independently of a remotely controlled system, human or otherwise, hardwired or broadcast. A machine that can act on its own, like a hot dog sorter in a meat processing plant, or a drill press in a sheet metal factory, or an automated soft drink dispenser.

"You see, when a computer makes what to us is a simple mathematical calculation, say, multiplying twelve by thirteen, it has to scan its entire memory bank in order to retrieve the appropriate combination of numbers. In the strictest definition of the word, it doesn't 'compute' at all: it compares data and eliminates wrong answers. The illusion of speed is a function of electronic circuitry, not efficiency of the system. The human brain, on the other hand, operates at a comparatively slow speed, by sending impulses along a neuronal pathway consisting of axons whose membranes consist of a semi-fluid lipid which is permeable to some hydrated ions and not to others—"

"Excuse me, Mr. Templeton, but you're losing me," Riley interrupted. "What I know about computers and the brain you could fit on the head of a pin. I mean, I can touch-type on a keyboard and input data, and retrieve police files by entering the proper codes. But when it comes to how computers operate, I'm completely lost."

"Okay. Okay. Just the short version. Indulge me, please." It was suddenly important to Grant that the patrolman accept his credibility. "In simple terms, the human brain makes up for its lack of speed by utilizing shortcuts, by automatically dismissing huge quantities of stored information. You don't 'know' the product of twelve by thirteen any more than a computer does, but you have a pretty good idea, just off the top of your head, that it can't be more than a couple hundred. After thinking about it for a moment, you'll come up with the correct answer without having to go through a lifetime of acquired knowledge. In other words, the human brain does intuitively what the computer does logically according to programmed instructions. Now, if you wait five minutes and ask the computer the same question, it has to go through its entire storehouse of data all over again, and run the same routine that it ran the first time. You, on the other hand, remember the answer right away. You've learned. And that is the quintessential difference between the human brain and an electronic processing unit."

Riley slowed the car and turned into a driveway, nodding slowly, comprehendingly. "I think I see what you're getting at."

"So my research is directed toward finding a way to simulate human intelligence within the architecture of currently available hardware, by designing feedback receptors that enable a computer to learn from experience and remember what it has learned, and to increase the complexity of computer circuitry without increasing its overall dimensions. And the best model we have, the closest convenient analogue, is the human brain. That is what I study."

By this time Grant was practically breathless. His heart beat faster than usual, and beads of perspiration rolled slowly down from his armpits. But at last he comprehended what was driving him to speak. He was trying to establish an identity in this world and to justify his existence. Not to Riley. To himself.

The patrolman parked the car next to others which were similarly marked with police insignia and rooftop strobe-light racks. He switched off the ignition. When he turned around to look at Grant without the use of a mirror, his face revealed a mixture of wavering authority and hesitant solicitude. Tentatively, he asked, "So how's the research coming?"

When Grant thought about it, his mind went blank. "I haven't the faintest idea."

Chapter 6

Riley poured the black brew from the autodrip pitcher into the thick mug which he held in his hand by the handle, then held out the mug to Grant. "There's no telling how long it's been sitting, Mr. Templeton, but you're welcome to it."

Grant wrapped his hands around the smooth white porcelain and soaked in the warmth through his palms as if it were living energy. "The first cup doesn't have to taste good, it just has to work." He did not address the policeman by name because "Riley" sounded impertinent and "Patrolman Riley" too formal. At Biotech, everyone went by first names. "So, do you get many nut cases like me?"

Patrolman Riley twitched his cheeks as if it would be out of character to smile in the station. "You'd be surprised." He poured another cup of coffee for himself. "We've got fake sugar and chemical creamer." He added some of each to his cup, and stirred.

"Black is fine." Grant inhaled the viscous steam and licked his lips after every sip. "If it were any stronger it would walk away." He glanced at the wall clock perched above the row of filing cabinets. "I thought you got off duty at eight." Already it was ten minutes past the hour.

The patrolman nodded imperceptibly. "That's right, Mr. Templeton. But 'off duty' only means off the street. It usually takes an hour or so to file the night's reports." He sat behind the cluttered oak desk, then indicated the notepad in front of Grant. "Is that the list of names and numbers?"

Grant had forgotten names before, and places and companies and titles, but never had his entire life been on the tip of his tongue. "It's the best I can do for now." He rotated the notepad so it faced the patrolman, and ticked off the lines with a pencil. "This is my secretary, and her phone number and address. There was no answer when I called her this morning. I work with Bob Lerner but never had occasion to call his house before, so I don't know his home phone number. This is my mother, in Oregon. This is—"

"Are all the other numbers local?"

"Yes, my mother is the only one who is out of town." Except for me, he thought wryly. "This is my ex-wife. And these other people are work associates, any one of whom will know me."

"And you said you were employed by Biotech." It was more of a statement than a question.

Grant felt an icy stab of fear in his chest. He had omitted mention of his nocturnal activities, and now regretted that he had told Riley about working at a place that was abandoned and obviously out of business. If Riley investigated the premises, he would know right away that Grant's tale of accident and disorientation had more than a few holes in it.

He gestured with his hands. "Unless I've been fired."

Riley gave a curt nod. "And this place—this Biotech—you said they manufacture memory chips and microprocessors for NASA."

Nodding, "And we've recently gotten into the production end of the business. Most of our components come from subcontractors that specialize in mechanics, hydraulics, power cell construction, and so on, but we've begun assembling the units at our facility so we can perform whole-body diagnostics tests and motor skill functions prior to delivery. The idea is to eventually become a full service robotics company, from nuts to bolts, so to speak."

Riley nodded noncommittally. "And you don't know where you live."

The patrolman said it politely, without accusation. Nevertheless, confessing to such ignorance or mindlessness made Grant feel like a fool. Although, not as foolish as he would feel if he tried to explain how in reality he did not live here at all, but in a parallel spacetime continuum. He made another faint-hearted gesture with his hands.

"What about neighbors?"

Grant tilted his head and shrugged. "Can't say that I ever got to know them very well. I wasn't home that much." He stifled the thoughts that brought back images of his broken family life. "One's name was Ted; he lived across the street. On the left was an elderly couple: Brewer, or Brouwer, or something like that. On the right was a grove of trees, and the next house was half a block away so I never had much contact with the people who lived there other than to smile as I walked by."

Riley made notations at the bottom of the sheet. "This should be enough to start with. I can place a few calls—" He glanced at Grant. "The police can obtain phone numbers that are unavailable to the public, and we can interrupt busy lines for emergencies and official duties. There should be someone on this list we can track down."

Grant noticed the time again. "I hope I'm not putting you out. I know you should be filing your reports so you can go home . . . "

"That's what we're here for, Mr. Templeton." Riley managed a weak grin. "Police work is never a nine-to-five job—those are just the hours we get paid for. We're on duty round the clock and then some." He paused. "Besides, it was a slow night. Other than checking out a prowler story and a botched break-and-entry, and some middle-aged pranksters opening doors at the girl's dormitory, I spent most of the night cruising the neighborhoods or sitting in the parking lot at the doughnut shop, drinking coffee and reading the paper. Other than the bizarre assassination of an army general named Brinkley—he was shot twice in the head, once on either side—the doughnut was more interesting."

Grant could not help but feel gratitude and relief. "I—I certainly appreciate your efforts. You can't know what it's like to suddenly wake up and discover that nothing makes sense any more. It's so—so lonely."

"I'm sure it must be disturbing, Mr. Templeton.

That's why I'm doing what I can to help. I've already notified the State Police and filed a missing persons warrant—I did that as soon as we checked in. They'll run it through the FBI's computer files."

A cold chill gripped Grant by the backbone. "Will they have me on record?"

"Only if you've been reported missing." Then, after a moment, "Or committed a crime, of course."

Grand nodded dumbly.

"The next step is to check with the police departments of neighboring districts, to see if any traffic accidents occurred last night in which you may have been involved. We'll also look for abandoned vehicles, lost property—in case someone turns in your wallet—potential witnesses, hospital admissions—for other victims—unusual reports from local citizens, and we will be especially vigilant for calls from concerned friends and relatives who might be wondering where you are. Did you have any appointments today?"

Again with the hand gesture, "Not that I can think of."

Riley acknowledged with a single nod. "The official wheels are in motion, Mr. Templeton. We'll check first with the Department of Transportation—do you have a driver's license or own a car?"

Grant nodded.

"Then we can get your address from Springfield. We've got quite a system, with feelers going out in a multitude of directions, so I have no doubt that before long we'll be able to establish your identity and clear up—"

"I already know who I am!" Grant heard himself shout as he leaped to his feet, sloshing his coffee in the process. His words pealed uncommonly loud in relation to the patrolman's soft tone of voice. Grant stared in horror at Riley's impassive face, realizing at once that his outburst was uncalled for. He was seeing threats where none existed. "I'm sorry. I didn't mean to . . . "

Riley looked up at Grant and cocked his head slightly, like a robin on the lookout for a worm. "I was not implying that you are an imposter. It's part of police procedure in any investigation—accident, domestic, or criminal—to establish the identity of all parties involved and write a report of the incident. It's a legal formality that serves many functions, such as aiding in the processing of insurance claims, for example."

"Yes. Yes, I see your point." Grant eased himself back down into the wooden chair. "I'm sorry. I'm overwrought and—I was jumping to conclusions."

Riley acknowledged with his characteristic nod. "Are you sure you wouldn't rather have a medical examination?"

Grant read "medical examination" as "psychiatric evaluation." Something in the back of his mind told him at all costs to stay away from hospitals and doctors and so-called therapists, lest he find himself placed under restraint. He had seen it happen to his father. And he had made rounds long enough to know that once a patient was admitted to a hospital, he gave up his personal identity and became instead a number on a chart, an interesting case history, an object of study, a rare disease to cure or an injury to heal: a prisoner of the ward no longer responsible for his own well-being. He ate what was given to him, drank when he was told, swallowed pills at the nurse's whim, and bared his arms or buttocks for injections intended to sedate him or to make him more tractable. And if he did not survive the medical institutionalization, the only afterlife available to him was a brief stint in the morgue undergoing the dehumanizing ritual called autopsy.

Despite Riley's avowed personal concern, Grant was beginning to feel trapped by the complicated process of bureaucracy which he initiated when no other alternatives seemed available to him. Now he was afraid that he might have opened a Pandora's box, that he might be smothered by a system whose organization relied upon rigid rules and regulations and modes of operation which did not allow for situations without precedent, nor which permitted individual enterprise contrary to written standards of procedure. Riley was just as enmeshed in the inflexible bureaucratic machinery as Grant, perhaps more so due to his training and indoctrination. An event that was too out of the ordinary was bound to be swept under the carpet of officialdom, and forgotten.

He fought down his paranoia and tried to appear calm. "Not right now."

Riley accepted Grant's decision with equanimity. "How about a photograph?"

"A mug shot, you mean?"

"No. A Polaroid that we can circulate with a physical description to affiliated agencies."

"I suppose you want my fingerprints, too?"

"It might help, but it's not necessary at this time."

Grant knew that he was making a difficult situation desperate. He finished his coffee and put the mug on the desk. "I didn't sleep last night. I was cold. I was miserable. I was lost and—and—and I'm not usually like this."

"There's no need to apologize, Mr. Templeton. Accident victims are usually disoriented—whatever the cause. One time I rolled my squad car chasing a hit-and-run driver, and when I got out of the wreckage I was so dazed I hardly knew my own name. The effects of shock can take a long time to wear off. But if you expect anyone to help, then you've got to get yourself under control."

Grant fidgeted nervously. "Thanks. I guess—I don't like being here. In a police station. It's . . . "

"I know. It's a place where criminals are brought for jailing and law-abiding citizens are treated like convicts. That's the way police are perceived by society these days. A guy puts on a uniform and people call him a pig—until they break down on the highway or have their expensive car stolen, until they get mugged or assaulted or burglarized, until they want someone to break up a domestic squabble and take a knife or a loaded gun away from an enraged family member. Then we become tolerable—like a loud smelly watchdog let out of the basement whenever his owners go out for the evening and want their precious property guarded. Even my high school chums view me like that, as if I betrayed them by working on the side of law and order. We don't get credit for doing a good job, but we get crucified by the media for every mistake we make no matter how minor.

"About the only satisfaction we get comes from solving a case or resolving a situation. But no matter how hard we work or how many hours we put in, no matter how much effort we invest in sleuthing and surveillance and tracking down the frauds and swindlers and desperadoes, the sad fact remains that we seldom bring criminals to justice. As fast as we can lock 'em up, the courts let 'em go. They're usually back out on the streets before we complete the paperwork, making it all seem so pointless. No wonder so many damn fine officers are disillusioned by the legal system and leave the force before retirement, their allegiance betrayed. It's not an easy job, Mr. Templeton. And you aren't making it any easier."

Riley's delivery was smooth and soft and without hostile inflection, but his manner was decidedly firm. Grant was struck aback, caught off guard between the stern patrolman's unsolicited polemics and what Grant perceived as youthful impertinence, despite his recognition that authority was not a matter of age, but of rank.

"It would help facilitate matters if you would be more cooperative. You're not under suspicion of anything so there's no need for reticence."

"Well, uh, I'm sorry if I seem, uh—"

The door opened and the captain of the Highland Hills police force stuck his head into the room. "Riley, can I see you for a minute?" To Grant, "You can stay where you are, Mr., ah, Templeton."

Riley stood up and strode out of the room. "Help yourself to more coffee, Mr. Templeton." He closed the door behind him.

Grant poured a second cup which was stronger than the first, which tasted just as bitter, and which he drank just as greedily. He tried to make himself at ease, but no matter how he sat he could not find a position of comfort. The problem was not the chair, whose rough wooden contour was probably intended to keep people from relaxing. The problem was Grant's emotional turmoil. He finished the coffee, thought about having a third cup, then decided against it and placed the mug on the desk. A quarter of an hour passed before the door creaked open.

Riley entered with a lackluster grin on his cheeks. "Looks like you're in luck, Mr. Templeton. Seems as if you had a date last night, and the gal you stood up came looking for you."

Grant jumped to his feet nearly knocking over the chair, and for some unknown reason blurted, "Francine?"

The woman who followed Riley into the room had long, ebony tresses which bounced off narrow shoulders like willow leaves in a spring zephyr. Her beautiful tanned features were just as airy. An overabundance of makeup accentuated light brown eyes which sparkled with a clear inner light. The heavily rouged cheekbones were set high, and bulged prominently. Her long green dress was pulled in at the waist with a patent leather belt, accentuating large breasts, but otherwise hid her form in loose folds of material. The straps of her shoes wrapped around shapely ankles, while the spiked heels forced her calves into a delicate yet muscular arch.

Her smile was like the sun at noon. "Hello, Dr. Templeton. I'm Sarah Mason."

Grant did not know her from Adam. Or Eve.

Chapter 7

Sarah Mason extended her hand in greeting. Grant responded automatically by holding out his own, but with more than a little trepidation due to his inability to recall either her name or her face. Her grasp was as firm and assured as her manner, with warmth and strength to match. Long nails rasped against Grant's inner wrist, sending tingles along his arm and raising goose bumps all the way to the shoulder. He might not recognize her enchanting lineaments, but he knew without a doubt that she was the kind of woman no man in his right mind would willingly leave in the lurch.

His face must have registered his discomposure, for she pulled back her hand abruptly, and blurted, "Of course you don't know me, Dr. Templeton. We've never met." She rifled through the black leather purse which hung by a strap from her shoulder. "I know I've got one in here somewhere—ah, here it is." She passed over a glossy business card bearing an embossed logo of blue, sharp-pointed waves running across the top border. Underneath was the company logo and address, and in the lower right corner was her name and telephone number. "I'm from Benthic Products, Incorporated."

Grant was none the wiser. "I'm afraid, uh, that I don't—"

"Of course, Dr. Templeton. I understand you're a little disturbed this morning and have other things on your mind." She cast a glance at Riley. "It's just that when you didn't show up for our appointment last night at the Neanderthal Club, I figured something more important must have come up. I might be new in this business, but I'm sophisticated enough to know that on the priority list of a busy scientist, a meeting with a sales rep is pretty close to the bottom. Still, just in case you had a breakdown on the way, I called your office last night and left a message for you, to remind you that I was in town. I called again this morning but got no answer. Then I got this queer kind of feeling, like when my mother skidded on the ice and smashed her car into a pole, and ended up in the hospital? Kind of a creepy feeling, you know, like tingles up your spine? Well, I started calling around and finally found out where she was, and she was okay but she wasn't able to call me because I was waiting for her at the park where there were no telephones. So I thought, maybe Dr. Templeton got held up or something and can't get through to me because he doesn't know what hotel I'm staying at. So I looked in the phone book and saw there was only one hospital in town, and when I called they said you weren't there. Well, really, they said that no new patients had been admitted who gave your name or fitted your description. I didn't get really worried until this morning, though, when I called Biotech and found out they were closed. I mean, the phone just rang and rang and rang and nobody ever answered, which is odd for a big company like Biotech not to have someone on duty or at least to have an answering service, because it's required that defense contractors be available twenty-four hours around the clock. So just on the off chance that you might have had an accident and nobody knew about it, I called the police and asked them if anyone fitting your name or description had been reported and they said you just came in with amnesia and they were looking for friends and relatives to come and get you. Well, I don't know if I qualify as a friend or relative, but I know who you are and all about you, so I thought maybe I could help, since we were supposed to meet last night anyway, I mean."

Grant was exhausted by the time she wound down, and addled by her rapid nonstop delivery, but he was also exhilarated by the fact that someone here knew him—or knew of him, and that he really had—or used to have—an office at a company known as Biotech. No sooner did he succumb to the seductive bliss of relief, however, than an eerie and troubling thought crossed his mind. Suppose this world already had a Grant Templeton, and now there were two of them, and the Grant Templeton she was supposed to meet was the one who belonged here? That made himself an interloper. On the other hand, if that were the case, what were the chances that the other Grant Templeton had not shown up for his appointment with Sarah Mason? And where was he? Was Grant going to bump into him? Or had they traded places, and the other Grant Templeton now occupied his—this Grant's—world. It all sounded so crazy. Or perhaps he was crazy and the world was somehow sane.

Grant held up his hands like a road worker holding up traffic at a highway construction site. "Miss, uh, Ms. Mason—"

"Call me Sarah," she cooed with a grin as wide as the Rio Grande. "I hate formalities as much as you do."

"Well, uh, okay. Good. And call me Grant. Everyone else does."

If there was a Grant Templeton who lived in this world, he could not be very different from himself. And if Grant was going to imitate him and insinuate himself into his life, or take his place (or way), he was going to have to think fast and pick up cues from people who were acquainted with him.

Without lowering his hands, he continued, "But can we go a bit slower? I'm a little hazy on recent events, so if you could fill me in on the details . . . "

Sarah waved nonchalantly with one hand. "Oh, sure, Grant. I know you've been busy lately and have lots of fingers in the pie. It's just that I'm really nervous because this could be a big sale for me and mean a big bonus in the envelope. Even though my boss said you had already seen the pre-production model of our deep-sea retriever, he thought you'd be more impressed by a hands-on demonstration—" She laughed skittishly. "Sorry, it's an in-joke. You'll understand later. Anyway, he thought you'd be impressed with our topside model so he arranged this meeting so I could convince you to sell us your latest generation microprocessing chips even though we're competitors in a sense, although we've already got the Disney contract and Biotech withdrew their bid, but in the future we might compete for other jobs if we decide to expand our business into other topside markets. Not that we have any inclinations of entering the aerospace industry. Anyway, I don't mean to give it away up front but I'm supposed to high-pressure you—" She laughed again. "That's another in-joke. Our standard one. High pressure. Because we built underwater robotic retrieval systems." She seemed intent on explaining it to Grant in order to wring a chuckle from him. "Anyway, I'm supposed to show you our demo—which I brought with me, by the way; it's in my hotel room—and a videotape of our prototype dummy for the Disney contract, so you'll know what we can provide if you get behind on your other contracts, and at the same time see if you'll work with us to improve the articulation and feedback response by licensing us to implant the Memchip 201. Well, that's it in a nutshell. So, would you care to see the demo and the movie clip?"

It was an awful lot for Grant to absorb all at once, even if it was in a nutshell. A coconut shell. "Well, I'm not . . . "

Sarah turned to the patrolman. "He's free to go, isn't he, Mr. Riley?"

"We're not holding him. He's here voluntarily." To Grant, "Mr. Templeton—or should I say Dr. Templeton—although we've begun an investigation based upon the information you've provided us, and proper procedure obliges us to file a report on the case, you're not under police custody, and technically you can leave any time you want. We've already discussed this with— Ms. Mason and Captain Hendry—and as long as you go with her of your own free will, we have no authority to stop you. It's the same as leaving under your own recognizance. She has agreed to take you to the hospital for an exam—"

"No. I don't want to go to the hospital. I feel fine physically. And I'm sure this—mental dislocation—will heal itself in time."

"Well, how about if I take you home?"

"No!" Grant cried, more loudly than he should. He needed more information from this garrulous sales representative before facing once again the fact that his home was no longer his own. "I mean, not right away. I'd—I'd like to see this demonstration first. After all," he hastily ad-libbed, facing Sarah Mason, "If you've come all the way from California for a private consultation, one that was pre-arranged between your company and mine, the least I can do is to live up to my end of the bargain and give you the time to demonstrate your product. Any other course of action would be—unprofessional."

"Then it's settled," Sarah beamed. "I have a rental car and I'd be more than happy to be your chauffeur about town. Is that okay, Mr. Riley?"

The patrolman stood like an automaton, expressionless. "Like I said, there's no law that can keep him here against his wishes."

Sarah faced the door, twisted her body, held out her hand behind and to the side, and took Grant by the arm. "Come on. Let's go before the nice policeman changes his mind and decides to arrest us both." To the patrolman, with a smile, "You're too kind, Mr. Riley." High heels clacking, she proceeded to drag Grant out of the room and into the hall.

"Thanks for your help," Grant had time to say, before he was whisked into the corridor and out of the patrolman's sight. He nodded at the police captain on the fly as they passed by his office.

"Everything's under control, Captain Hendry," Sarah cooed.

The corridor opened into a wide, high-ceiling room crammed with half a dozen unoccupied desks which were all cluttered with books and stacks of loose papers with no semblance of organization. Fluorescent fixtures flush-mounted in the drop ceiling shed an even white glow throughout the room despite bright sunbeams which stabbed through the glass on the building's east side. A lone tub of a sergeant sat at the radio dispatch station with a sandwich in one hand, a pencil in the other, and a headset covering his ears.

Sarah wiggled her fingers coquettishly. "Too-da-loo."

Outside, she steered Grant across the parking lot toward a powder blue two-door sedan. "This is my car. Well, it belongs to the rental agency, really, but I call it mine. Isn't it just the cutest little thing you ever did see?"

Grant had no mind for cars. They were machines that got him where he wanted to go, and as long as they functioned as they were supposed to, they held no more meaning to him than a good toaster or a microwave oven. "Looks great."

"It's open. I didn't bother locking it. I mean, after all, we are in a police station." Sarah pulled open the driver's side door and slid behind the wheel with precision and grace. She might have been an actress in a television commercial. Her black hair flowed from side to side like a bouquet of flowers in a gentle breeze.

Grant's muscles were stiff and sore after his unprecedented nocturnal excursions. He shambled awkwardly, each movement attended by an ache or twinge which he did his best to conceal. The seat and backrest were luxuriously soft, the blue pile upholstery plush. The cushions conformed so nicely to his body that he could have fallen asleep instantly without a thought or a care to his peculiar situation. A sharp pain stabbed his shoulder as he reached out for the door, and the joint locked up for a moment. Grant massaged the shoulder, grimacing. He had taken one tumble too many for a man his age.

Sarah showed a look of concern. "Are you okay?"

"I'll live." He slammed the door shut, then gave in to the pleasures of the flesh and let himself melt into the seat. "I could use some heat, though."

"No problem." Sarah twisted the key in the ignition and held it down too long, causing the starter to grind. "Oops. Sorry."

Motors whirred as the passive restraints lowered

the safety harness into position. "Must be something new," Grant said, feeling a bit like a country bumpkin. An airbag annunciator light glowed dimly.

"Welcome to the twenty-first century." Sarah grinned expansively. "The rental agencies always have the latest models off the shelf. Competition, you know. This thing's got more electronics than a space shuttle, with digital gauges for just about everything, including gas mileage and consumption. I tell you what, the cars they got today will do everything but your laundry."

Although the interior was filled with warmth due to the sun streaming in through the windshield, Grant still felt a chill, almost as if he were coming down with something. Probably he was just worn out. Sarah threw the fan switch on high, blasting cool air from an unheated engine across Grant's feet. She put the car in gear, backed out of the parking spot, and pulled up to the street.

"So, you're place or mine?" Before Grant could respond, Sarah went on, "Only kidding." She squeezed his arm and scrunched up her heavily rouged cheeks with a conspiratorial grimace. "All the stuff's at my hotel so we've got to go there anyway."

She turned too sharply into the street and went off the edge of the apron. One rear tire bounced over the curb. The car came down hard with the metal under-carriage scraping raucously on cement, and the tires squealed because she stomped the accelerator pedal. "Gotta get used to this thing."

With a shiver, Grant looked around for police.

"I hope you don't think I'm being too forward. I guess I'm a little nervous, you know, meeting you for the first time, and all. You a renowned scientist and me a parasitic sales rep. I can't tell you how honored I am to have this opportunity to be with you, one on one, you know, to give you a private showing of my wares—I mean, my company's wares. Oh, you know what I mean. I've read all about you, you know, in the maga-zines and newspapers, so I guess I'm a little, you know, in awe. Honestly, Grant, I admire what you've accomplished in the field of robotics and microchip design, and I say that because I feel it, not because I want to make this deal go through. Besides, the boss said that everything was already set, and that this was just a courtesy call, a formality, so you could write up a report and make recommendations to the higher-ups. Now, I don't profess to understand big business, so I don't understand why it's necessary for me to even be here. I mean, it seems like this could be done over the telephone, you know? But the boss said, 'Go see Grant Templeton and give him the usual sales pitch,' so that's what I'm doing. Like I said, it's good money, and all the expenses are on the house and paid for by the company. My company, that is. Not yours."

Grant was content to let Sarah drone on with her drivel in order to pick up information which might prove useful later on. As long as she was willing to talk, he was willing to listen—if only he could stay awake. He specifically wanted to know about the Memchip 201 she mentioned, because he had no recollection of such a device in Biotech's sales catalogue, nor did he remember being involved in research and development of such an item.

Grant nudged her along. "Have any contractual negotiations been initiated as far as the Memchip 201 is concerned?"

"Contract work is not my department, but as far as I know you're still withholding distribution pending patent approval. Biotech, that is, not you personally, 'cause the boss said you were all for worldwide marketing since you're a scientist before you're a business person, and how you thought a discovery like this should be for all mankind and not held by any one company or nation. And since the patent has been applied for in your name, you being a major stockholder in the company and all that, you should have the final say-so. I have to hand it to you, Grant, the Memchip 201 is a major breakthrough, although all that science stuff is way above my head. I mean, 'memory in ionic flux instead of silicon stasis' may be in my head, according to your theory, but it doesn't mean anything to a person whose got my kind of head on her shoulders."

"Sometimes I wonder if I understand it myself," Grant said, giving a curt laugh at the irony of his statement. His return to humor implied restored self-confidence. Now for a hot shower, a warm bed, and the love of a good woman, and the world might begin to look good again. He glanced sideways at the sexy bundle of beauty beside him. If she were not such an airhead he would probably find her attractive. It's a wonder she's not blonde, he jested inwardly.

"Well, don't expect me to explain it to you. I've got enough trouble understanding Nietzsche much less computer lingo. That's why I'm a sales rep, 'cause I'm a good talker. I can grasp the basic workings of Benthic Products' products enough to sell the product. Beyond that I'm computer illiterate. Now, they gave me a crash course in robotics so I'd know one when I saw one, like the roves of our own product line—"

"The what? The roves?"

"Sorry, Grant. That's the industry abbreviation for 'remotely operated vehicle.' ROV, pronounced 'rove.' Plural 'roves." They're unmanned submersible platforms that are lowered to the bottom of the sea to take pictures and bring back samples. Biologists, geologists, oceanographers, and salvage outfits use them all the time. They come with cameras and lights and manipulator arms, which is where you come in. Not with the cameras and lights, but the manipulator arms, that are actually robotic extremities like human hands. That's what led us to expanding into the topside robotic market because we build manipulator arms with fingers so coordinated they can pick up a gold doubloon without stirring the sand, or a glass test tube without crushing it. Feedback control, with high-grade memory chips, enables precision hydraulic response almost as good as the human body."

"I see," Grant said, even though he did not. Underwater robotic systems were not too different from aerospace robotic systems: each discipline required machines which were designed to operate in hostile environments at opposite extremes of the pressure gradient, but which performed essentially the same tasks. "But tell me, Sarah—" Her name had a nice ring to it. "How does this fit in with Biotech and the, uh, Memchip 201?"

"Two ways. One because of the Disney contract, the other because of advanced untethered robotic technologies. You see, all our roves are connected to the surface support craft with umbilical cords: waterproof cables that carry communications from the operator in the boat to the rove on the bottom. The videocameras are the operator's eyes, the manipulators his hands, the thruster motors his wings. He flies the rove like a remote controlled airplane. The umbilical also connects the rove to the topside CPU, which is kind of like saying that the rove's brain is on the boat and its body is on the bottom. With the current state of the art, roves need a mainframe computer because of the required memory and processing speed requirements. What we're getting into now is untethered platforms so we don't have to worry about thousands of feet of cable being deployed from the boat and getting hung up on shipwrecks or geological outcrops. But we can't put a mainframe computer in an underwater housing because it's too big—and too expensive to lose if the housing floods at depth. So, what we need in order to go untethered is greater onboard memory capacity so the rove can operate its systems without topside feedback. Ergo, the Memchip 201."

The air churned out by the fan finally turned warm and caressed Grant's legs with heat. As he listened to Sarah's lengthy explanation, he wondered if she were smarter than she made out to be; if part of her strategy was to let her male clients feel superior. She spoke with great animation, flinging one hand in the air like an orchestra leader directing the finale of William Tell's Overture, and arching black languorous eyebrows in tune with the silent composition. Fluttering eyelashes thick with mascara gave expression to her words, and matched her articulation for emphasis.

"Secondly, the developing technology has applications in other fields of robotics. That's how we got the contract for Disney Planet in Houston. You see—"

"They're building another one?" Grant said in astonishment. It seemed as if Highland Hills was not the only community that was growing without his notice.

"Where've you been, living in a cellar? I mean, after all, you did turn down the contract to produce the simulacra."

Grant chastised himself for talking instead of listening. There were bound to be differences between this world and the one he was used to. He shrugged. "I don't have anything to do with sales. And I may not live in a cellar, but sometimes the lab can be just as dark and dank."

Sarah tilted her head in thought. "Yeah, I guess you're right. And you do have a reputation for being a recluse." She passed a line of cars which were backed up in the left lane awaiting a pickup truck whose left turn was stymied by oncoming traffic. "Well, anyway, because of our experience building underwater equipment—you did know that 'benthic' means 'deep sea,' didn't you—we got the job of supplying the roves for Disney Planet's aquarium. One thing led to another, and the next thing you know we got the job to build the simulacra—the automated dummies that are part of the story board."

"Robots, you mean, in human form."

"Well, kinda, but limited in capacity by their programming. Oops, I almost passed it. Here's the Tuck Me Inn."

Sarah spun the wheel and turned the car into a tree-lined driveway, throwing Grant against her shoulder and his face into her hair. The fragrance of perfume accentuated her sensuality, causing arousal despite his exhaustion. Boys will be boys, he thought. And so will men.

Said Grant, "I wish somebody would."

Chapter 8

The Tuck Me Inn was a motel rather than a hotel, as Sarah had called it, but one which catered to expensive tastes and which provided all the amenities furnished by its high-rise brethren. The lounges, fountains, and well-kept grounds were decorated with enough kitsch to fill a two-story barn. If the inn's patrons considered money an object of affection, here it was no object.

Grant felt no guilt about taking advantage of his host's generosity and unlimited expense account. "I could sure use a drink."

"No problem, Grant. Make yourself at home." There was no sarcasm in Sarah's voice; she truly meant it. "I'll call room service. How about some breakfast?"

The coffee had done much to fill the empty void in his stomach. "Maybe later." He plopped down on the queen-size waterbed and bobbed for a moment with the waves. It had been a rough night, and he had long since exceeded the limit of his reserves, both physically and emotionally. He rubbed his coarse beard with distaste.

Sarah loosened her belt and shoe straps, kicked off her high-heels, and pranced around the room in her stockings. She picked up the phone on the nightstand. "What would you like?"

Grant tried hard to keep his eyes fastened on hers while his imagination wandered elsewhere. He fancied the firm, female anatomy that pulsed with life under the jade green dress, and it made him tremble with desire. He had been divorced for too long, and without female companionship and the tender touch of love. Francine's was a platonic relationship only, although it might become something more if they worked at it. "A bottle of vodka and some fresh limes."

If Sarah considered it too early for cocktails, she kept the thought to herself. She ordered hot tea and a couple of biscuits, and a bucket of ice for the vodka.

"The stuff'll be here in five minutes." She hoisted a reinforced metal trunk onto the suitcase stand and unlocked the hasp with a key from her purse. "Can't be too careful with company secrets, you know." She flung open the lid to reveal an interior packed with foam which was cut into blocks. "Here's the movie clip." She tossed the digital videodisk onto the bed. "There's a player under the television, but I want you to see our prototype 'arm' first."

She pulled out some foam packing blocks and exposed a highly polished metallic tube which was folded in two by means of a ball joint in the middle of its length. It could have been two sections of smooth drainpipe connected by a fat hinge. She lifted the tube from its bedding, hefted it in the air, and handed it to Grant. "The chassis is titanium so it's a lot lighter than it looks."

Grant did not really feel up to a complete demonstration, but neither could he afford to brush Sarah off with a cursory examination of her wares.

After all, that was why she brought him here, that was the purpose of last night's appointment, and it was critically important that he learn what he was about in this world. Despite his fatigue, he forced himself to concentrate as she went into her spiel, and to show some interest in the product.

"Now these are just protective sleeves to keep dust and foam out of the inner workings during transport. Hold tight on this end." Grant gripped the thick shaft on one side of the joint while she pulled the cylindrical tube off the other shaft. Underneath lay a complicated mass of multicolored wires and hydraulic tubing, connector blocks and wiring harnesses, piston pumps and solenoids. "On the underwater models the sleeves are thicker and double-hulled, with crosshatched bulkheads throughout, pressurized interstitial spaces packed with polyabsorbant material, and watertight gaskets at either end. For topside use we've removed the pressure-proof housing and replaced it with a synthetic tegument that can be stretched over the frame to give the look and the feel of skin."

Sarah never skipped a beat as she pulled a control box from the trunk, plugged the power lead into a wall socket, and snapped the downlink cable array onto the pin connector of the prototype arm's output module. "If you don't mind me blowing my own company's horn, Benthic Products is way ahead of the other companies who bid on the Disney job—even those in the aerospace field, like Biotech—because for years we've been manufacturing roves that have to survive the most stringent conditions encountered at depth. In outer space, an insulation deficit on a microconductor might not cause a problem because of the background vacuum; you won't have a short circuit or current flow to ground unless the potential is large enough to spark across the gap. But at the bottom of the ocean or a deep inland lake, a single drop of water extruded through the casing under pressure can compromise the integrity of the entire system. We're used to building tough machines to operate in an unforgiving environment.

"For us, a human simulacrum is a step down from what we're used to manufacturing. We took the specifications from our benthic models and scaled them down, to create a mechanical device in human form that is stronger, more stable, and more responsive than anything anyone else can build, including, we believe, Biotech. That's why we won the Disney contract."

She took a mechanical hand from the trunk and snapped it onto the wrist of the arm that Grant was holding in awe. Then she manipulated a miniature joystick on the control box and actuated the fingers. Micromotors whirred ever so slightly as she caused the hand to make a fist, extend the fingers one at a time, and pull certain fingers back in various combinations in order to make familiar expressive gestures such as the "V" for victory, a hex sign, the Boy Scout salute, and a single digit salutation of disrespect. Then the hand rotated round and round on a ball joint socket.

"That's a valuable maneuver for oil rig companies when they have to capped wellheads or screw-down bolts on pipeline brackets. I've got the specs on sheer strength, torque, and applied force, if you need them. But for the Disney simulacra, where we're only mimicking motion, the requirements fall far below our ordinary standards."

Grant sat up straight, impressed by the demonstration. "This—this is amazing. We don't have anything even close to this."

"Well, now, Grant, there's no need to knock your own product. Biotech has quite a reputation in the aerospace industry. I've seen the shuttlecraft mockups and they're very impressive. It's just that your company and mine work in different mediums. Or is it media? I always forget. Anyway, when you come right down to it, we've both refined robotics and articulated joint technology for different applications. Now, if we could just work together on—"

There came a knock on the door.

"That must be room service." Sarah took the arm from Grant, folded it at the elbow joint, stuffed it back in the trunk, piled the control box and wires on top of it, and closed the lid. "You can look at it more later on." She opened the door only wide enough to take the silver tray and the bucket of ice, said "Thank you," and took the refreshments to the counter top which was provided for the purpose. "Vodka gimlet, right?"

"Not just yet." Grant stood up awkwardly. Despite the stimulation provided by the novelty of the Benthic Products manipulator arm, he felt enervated by the strain of disorientation. With the arm out of sight, his attention span matched his level of fatigue. "What I could use the most right now is a shower. Would you mind?"

Sarah already had a biscuit stuffed in her mouth. She cupped one hand under her chin in order to catch loose crumbs. "Hey, go right ahead. There's plenty of towels and washcloths. You want the vodka on ice?"

"No. I stir ice into the drink after it's mixed."

"Whatever." Sarah poured hot tea from the pitcher into a delicate china cup, added two spoonfuls of sugar, and gulped it down noisily. "I'm a beer drinker, myself."

Yes, it fits the mold. If only she weren't so damned attractive. Grant groaned as he slipped off his jacket and headed toward the bathroom. "If I'm not out in half an hour, send in a rescue party."

"I may be your sole means of delivery, Grant." She cast a look which could be interpreted as one of wistful longing—Grant was predisposed at the moment to harbor such fantasies—but which more likely was an attempt at humor. "Hey, seriously, how's about I get your clothes cleaned while you're washing up? They've got a dry cleaner on the premises and they guarantee service in under an hour. You can put on a towel in the meantime."

Grant paused at the bathroom door. "You know, this is the strangest sales meeting I've ever had. Yet you seem to take it all in stride."

She shrugged. "You do what you gotta do."

Grant could not help but be put at ease by her manner. His initial intimidation by her overt voluptuousness was gradually giving way to an appreciation of her professional ingenuousness. After years of dealing with pompous blowhards pushing the hard sell for products which were obviously substandard, he found her frankness refreshing as well as befitting the product. If her lack of sophistication was an act to keep him off his guard, it was working to perfection.

He smiled whimsically. "But here I am, a strange man who misses an appointment he can't remember making, and the next morning you find him in a police station and take him back to your room and let him have free rein of the facilities. You're too good to be true."

"You're not so strange. Or are you?" Sarah sashayed toward him until she stood close enough for him to smell her sweet breath above the scent of her powerful perfume. "My boss says that any meeting that ends up in the hotel room can't be a total loss. Now don't get any wrong ideas about what that means. It's just his way of saying that there's more than one way to keep relations between companies. He believes in the personal touch—people meeting as ordinary folks instead of as stuffed shirts trying to cheat each other. He also says that you sell yourself as much as the product. And don't misinterpret that meaning either. You've got a reputation in the business as an honest kind of a guy, and until I see otherwise I'll accept it. So why shouldn't I extend a courtesy to you that I would've made to anyone else I found in trouble? You think I should abandon you to police bureaucracy just because we're supposed to abide by strict hierarchical rules—you the big mahoff and me the lowly sales person? Now that doesn't make any sense, does it?"

"Well, when you put it like that . . . "

"Now you just get in there and take your shower. When I hear the water running I'll slip in and take your clothes. Go ahead. Go." She placed her hand in the small of his back and pushed him through the doorway. "Don't make such a big deal out of nothing."

Grant closed the door behind him. The bathroom was large and luxurious, with enough decorative ceramic to tile a basilica and with a tub big enough for an army, or at least a couple of platoons. He was usually a shower man, but once he saw the accommodations he changed his mind and decided on a long soak in bath oil. He opened the hot water faucet and poured in the lotion provided by the management, then stripped off his grimy clothes and piled them on the marble countertop. When he bent over to unlace his shoes he discovered how sore he was from the night's activities. He had aches in muscles that he never knew he had. And while he knew that he would recover, he did not have much hope for his clothing and footwear. The soles and uppers were caked with mud, the socks were still sodden, the jacket and trousers had tears, the white shirt was stained brown, and the underclothes stank. He felt as if he should trash the whole outfit and buy a new ensemble. Except that at the moment he had no money or established line of credit.

His nakedness disappointed him. He had put on

weight, lost muscle tone, and appeared to be losing the battle of the midriff bulge. With a woman who had a body like Sarah's standing only a few feet away—albeit on the other side of an opaque door—he felt woefully inadequate, and any delusions he had entertained about consummating a relationship with the sexy but flaky sales rep were terminated upon due consideration of the condition of his wares. Benevolence went only so far.

He stirred cold water into the bath until, wincing with pain, he could ease his foot into the oily solution. He lowered himself by degrees until the ripples lapped at his chin.

There came an insistent knock at the door. "Coming in," Sarah singsonged. Grant hastily pulled the semi-transparent shower curtain into place. Before he could give her the okay, the door swung open and Sarah marched in. She scooped up his clothes. "Now you stay in there as long as you like, you hear?"

"I'll be fine."

"If I'm not back when you get out, feel free to call room service for anything you need. Okay?"

"I'll do that, Sarah. Thanks."

The door closed and she was gone. Grant steeped in the hot water like a used teabag, and felt just as weak. Periodically, he added more hot water until his skin glowed cherry red, like an overcooked lobster in the pot. And still he soaked in the warmth and the comfort. When his pores felt satiated with the stinging heat, he opened the drain and stood up to rinse off the bath oil under the shower. He washed his hair and lathered his skin, then rinsed off for another five minutes. Okay, maybe ten. When he finally turned off the fine spray it was mostly due to a sense of guilt at using up the motel's entire supply of hot water.

He toweled off slowly because his muscles refused to work at speed; nor could he dry his skin completely because of the density of the steam in the room. He flipped the switches for the exhaust fan and the infrared lights, and wiped the condensation off the mirror with a towel.

Grant did not like the look of the beard; it had to come off. The motel did not furnish shaving supplies, but Sarah had left her cosmetic kit next to the sink, and, in addition to dozens of jars, tubes, and bottles of every color and description, it contained a can of shaving cream and plastic disposable razors. Grant indulged himself. He lathered his face liberally before applying the blade. The whiskers sloughed off easily with sure, deft strokes, and in five minutes his face was shorn of the ugly black bristles. He felt like a new man, but upon close inspection his skin showed wrinkles that were not all caused by worry.

With a large bath towel wrapped around his somewhat portly middle, Grant peered into the bedroom, saw that it was empty, and walked to the bed and sat down. He stared at the trunk whose lid was closed but not locked. He was up in a flash. He brought the manipulator arm back to the bed and studied it again, this time paying particular attention to the motionless hydraulic systems. Little wonder that Benthic Products had beat out Biotech on the Disney job. The mechanics and architecture of the manipulator arm were much more sophisticated than anything Biotech's robotic division had in stock, making Biotech's space probe arms seem cheap and cumbersome by comparison.

Grant's job at Biotech was to design microchips and central processing units which operated the various devices and mechanical components which the engineers constructed largely for aerospace applications. He also spent as much time as possible conducting research in three dimensional crystal lattice mnemonics, which he believed might become the next generation in mechanical memory systems. Nonetheless, he kept up-to-date on advances in the robotics field since it was critically important to have a whole-body understanding of the products which Biotech sold, and which subsidized his research.

After several minutes spent inspecting the mechanical arm, he remembered the movie clip. He laid the arm aside. The DVD player was a brand he had never heard of—another Japanese clone like so many that glutted the market these days—but the operation was fairly basic. He slipped the disk into the drawer compartment, switched on the television, depressed the play button, and waited for an image to appear on the screen.

At first he thought he must have actuated the cable channel selector by mistake, for Humphrey Bogart came into view in a casual, stereotypic pose. He wore a white suit and talked from behind a plain table in a scene that could have been an outtake from *Casablanca* or *The Maltese Falcon*. There was no mistaking the distinctive voice and the solemn, punched-out delivery.

"Of all the gin joints in all the towns in all the world, why should you buy your simulacrum from Benthic Products? Now, you might say, what's a robot like me doing in a place that makes remote underwater camera platforms and sample recovery sleds. Well, I'll tell you. Benthic Products is coming up in the world. That's right, up from the bottom of the sea to the planetary surface where the technological advances that made its name synonymous with success in underwater operations will be more visible to the world at large. We're entering the field of human form robotics, and we're doing it with lifelike simulacra. Oh, I can do more than sit here like a dummy and read a script. A lot more."

Bogie pushed back the wooden chair and stood up behind the desk. There was something odd about the way he did it, as if he were suffering from a slipped disc or lower back inflammation, for instead of leaning slightly forward as a normal person would, he rose straight up with his trunk perfectly vertical. He sidestepped around the edge of the desk on legs that seemed too heavy to lift. But the real shock came when he stood in full view of the camera and Grant saw that he was not wearing any pants.

There were no genital parts to expose. The lower chassis consisted of a titanium frame—according to Bogie's soliloquy—whose various extremities were linked to each other by universal ball joints and which were operated by servomechanisms. One leg was covered with a skinlike tegument which was padded to give appropriate muscle bulges, and insulated to deaden the sound of moving mechanical and electrical parts such as hydraulic pistons and solenoids; it even had hair. The other leg appeared like the manipulator arm on the bed: packed with tubing, sensors, servomotors, and color-coded wires and pin-type connector blocks. The simulacrum walked with a stiff-legged gait.

"I maintain my equilibrium in this unbalanced world of ours by means of a gyroscope that fills most of my thoracic and abdominal cavity. For you nonscientific types, a gyroscope is a spinning mass—now let me see if I can get this right— 'the spin axis of which turns between two low-friction supports, and which maintains its angular orientation with respect to pre-set inertial coordinates when not subjected to overpowering external torque.' In simpler terms, I've got a child's top built into my chest, and it'll keep me upright if you don't slap me too hard on the back or pull the rug out from under my feet. A horizontal stainless steel disk is kept rotating at high speed by a powerful electric motor whose copper windings give me most of my weight. Dieting doesn't help.

"The skull casing houses a rechargeable energy cell that can keep me going for eight hours at a sitting, but only for two or three hours if I'm walking and talking. My brain is where you would expect to find it in the average human male: in the pelvic girdle. Like most men, I think with my groin.

"Well, there's only one tale left to tell, and it's quite a tale. In fact, it *is* a tail." The Bogie simulacrum turned around slowly to reveal a black cable running out of his rump. "In most settings I'm able to hide it, or disguise it so it blends in with the backdrop. And as long as I face the camera—" He took a frontal pose. "—you can't see it at all. On the other hand, so to speak, it does keep me from running away or chasing after the ladies." When he laughed, the cheeks and lips formed facial expressions which were amazingly realistic. "Well, now that you know who I am—or should I say, 'what' I am—let me strut my stuff, put on a little act, and show you what I can do." He looked off-stage. "Play it again, Sam."

The Bogie simulacrum performed a complex series of steps and gestures which were executed slowly but with incredible precision. There was a slight loss of rhythm when music was added to his movements, as if his synchronizing circuits were somewhat out of phase; and the feet did not get very high off the floor. Nevertheless, it was the best simulation of robotic dancing which Grant could remember seeing. The finale was a song and dance routine from *The Wizard of Oz*—the Tin Woodsman's number, "If I Only Had A Heart"—complete with sound effects and funnel hoots. The voice synthesizer even changed its vocalization while singing the lyrics in order to sound like Jack Haley.

Someone at Benthic Products had a sick sense of humor.

Bogie returned to his seat behind the desk and resumed his original voice.

"Well, it's time for me to recharge my batteries and, since I like to dine alone, I'll be signing off. Keep in mind that what you've just seen is only the beginning of what Benthic Products has planned for the future. We are staying on top of emerging technologies in all aspects of robotics, and we expect to stay on top. Here's looking at you, kid."

Grant suddenly had the urge for a drink. He switched off the disk player, then padded over to the hospitality counter. Room service had thoughtfully provided glasses and utensils. He sliced a lime in half, squeezed the juice into the bottom of a long-stemmed goblet, opened the liquor bottle and poured out a shot of vodka, then stirred in some ice. The resulting concoction should have stimulated his taste buds. Instead, the gimlet tasted harsh and acrid, and had a bite that made him grimace. He swallowed quickly and took another sip; it was not quite as bad, but neither did it go down as smoothly as it should have. He chugged the rest and mixed another one.

Back in front of the disk player he felt a warm glow that went too fast to his head. The alcohol was making him woozy. He switched on the disk player, tapped the play button, and lay back on the bed next to the mechanical arm, glancing from it to the television screen as Bogie went through his act again. His toes got cold, so he pulled the covers over his feet and legs. He sipped his drink pensively. The simulacrum was not just interesting, it was fascinating. And it was far in advance of anything that Biotech could produce, now or in the next five years. If Sarah wanted to bargain, to trade information for something she thought that Grant had, he was going to have to play along with her. It would not pay to alienate a competitor who might conceivably put Biotech out of business.

Deep down inside, that concept hurt. Grant had been on top of the industrial heap for so long that it pained him to admit that someone better was coming along, that he and his company might be superseded by a latecomer to the field. He was going to have to tread cautiously and follow her lead.

If he had made any mistakes in the last world, he did not want to duplicate them in this one.

Chapter 9

"Hey, Lover Boy!"

Patrolman Frank Riley looked up from the computer screen at Captain George Hendry, whose large form filled the doorway like a defensive fullback. Riley answered with his eyes while his fingers continued to punch away on the keyboard.

"That luscious hunk of female that finds something attractive about you—though what it is, is beyond me—is on the phone, and the redhead is glowing hot." He shook his hand as if he had scorched it on an electric burner. "Something about a luncheon engagement?"

Riley's fingers halted in the middle of a word, his expression momentarily blank. Then, caught off his official guard, his tanned face dissolved through a sequence of transitory contortions which reflected perfectly his thought processes and which were as legible as the printed page. The final facade was one of consternation tempered with dread, like a little boy who knew he had done something bad and was about to get spanked.

"I forgot all about it." Riley glanced at his watch and let out a groan. "George, tell her—"

"No, you tell her. I'm through making excuses for you. You wanna get wrapped up in your work, that's fine by me. Makes me look good and the office run like clockwork. But you gotta handle your own social calendar."

"But—"

"But nothing. I'm your boss, not your old man." Captain Hendry hooked his thumbs on the belt that girdled his considerable waist. "But I will give you a little fatherly advice. Sweet talk the girl like there's no tomorrow, or take back that gun you gave her for target practice. Leastways, remove the bullets. She don't know how to aim the thing much less load it."

The self-assured patrolman who was all business

on the street was now unsure of himself. His mind raced frantically to think up excuses that were not overused.

"I've already told her you were working on a case. But that's as far as I go."

A relieved grin washed over Riley's taut features. "Thanks, George."

"Now pick up the phone before she thinks I'm lying to her and you're out with another girl." Hendry pointed to the telephone with his finger. "Line two." He stuck out his chin, and left.

The flashing red annunciator on the base unit reminded Riley of a nuclear reactor warning light. He took a deep breath, picked up the receiver, and pressed the connection button. "Hello, Sandy? I'm glad you called. I'm sorry about lunch but I got tied up—"

What followed was a one-sided diatribe which Riley accepted with equanimity. He inserted "buts" every now and then, and tried to apologize for his forgetfulness, but he was never able to complete a sentence or make an effective response before Sandy drowned him out with angry accusations about how little attention he paid to her on the rare occasions when their off-duty schedules coincided. Nurses worked shifts also. After several minutes of back peddling and offers to make amends, he submissively took his medicine. Mentally, he made a dangerous comparison between Sandy's impatience and lack of understanding, and Sarah's mature poise with respect to Grant's nonappearance. Notions like that could lead only to trouble. It was safer and more reasonable to accept Sandy for who she was: a warm and affectionate woman who needed—no, demanded—love, commitment, and punctuality. And not necessarily in that order.

When he finally replaced the receiver, he did so with thumb and forefinger; the plastic was too hot to handle. "Whew," he said aloud. He would rather face a gang of bank robbers or a crowd of drunken sailors in a bar-room brawl than Sandy's Irish wrath. After sitting a moment to regain his composure, he ripped the spreadsheet out of the printer and dashed into Captain Hendry's office.

"George, I've found some peculiarities in this story that Grant Templeton told us. Things that don't make immediate sense. Can I bounce a few of them off you?"

Captain Hendry peered over the top of his half-frame reading glasses. "Frank, you aren't an MP any more and this isn't the army. Things are done different in civilian life. We're not here to defend the city like it was an ICBM missile base, we don't check up on people just because they act funny, and we don't conduct investigations unless they're called for. We've got enough work to do without creating more, and not enough men on the force or hours in the day to do it all. The rule of thumb is: don't make a case where there isn't one, and don't carry a case beyond its end."

"I was an SP in the Navy: Shore Patrol, not Military Police. And I was stationed at a nuclear submarine base."

Hendry shrugged it off. "Same difference."

"There are still parts of Templeton's story that don't add up."

"That doesn't make him a lawbreaker. The guy was lost and confused and he turned himself in voluntarily—not the MO of your everyday criminal. And the eyeful that came in for him knew all about him: where he lived and worked, what he did for a living, even had his business card. You know how these genius types are: can fly a rocket to the moon and back but can't remember to put socks on in the morning. Why do you want to give the guy more trouble than he's already got?"

"Let's call it a hunch."

Hendry took off his glasses and placed them on the desk, then pinched his eyes with the thumb and forefinger of his right hand. "And I've got a hunch that you're not gonna let this go away. Okay, show me what you got."

Riley was all business. He neither smiled nor glowered. "So far I've got mostly negative information. Neither his co-worker nor his secretary answer their phones. The number he gave me for his mother belongs to someone else, and directory assistance has no such listing for her. His ex-wife does not live in this city, or if she does, she's using her maiden name, and I don't know what that is. No one is answering the phones at Biotech, just like Sarah Mason said. And I can't find listings for any of his other work associates."

Hendry cocked bushy eyebrows. "None of them?"

"Not a one. On the other hand, the Bureau of Motor Vehicles confirmed the address for Templeton that Sarah Mason gave us: One Panther Cove."

"Yes, I remember she said that, although I couldn't quite place it, what with new streets popping up on the city register every day."

"It's in Feline Estates."

The eyebrows arched even higher. "That swanky new high-priced development on the west end of town?"

Riley gave a single tilt of the head. "They're million dollar houses situated on closed loops, with vehicular access funneled down a long drive barred by a heavy-duty, remote-controlled gate."

"Town's getting too big too fast," Captain Hendry sighed. "And I've been behind a desk for so long that I'm losing touch with it. Times past I used to know every back alley, every hangout, every lover's lane, every pool hall, bar, and bowling alley. Now I only recognize them as control grids on a demographic chart." He thrust an errant thumb over his shoulder at the large-scale map on the wall behind him.

"We had some problems with minor theft when the houses were being built," Riley explained. "Mostly lumber and kegs of nails, which were attributed to college pranks, like how far someone could run with a sheet of plywood on his head or a fifty pound keg of sixteen-penny nails under his arm."

"At least that much hasn't changed." The chair creaked noisily as Hendry leaned forward and placed his elbows on the desk. "Okay, so the guy's got dough. What else you got?"

"Keller at the State Police is networking with surrounding districts. So far he's come up with no missing persons, no unusual accidents, no unexplained reports, and no activities within the past forty-eight hours that appear to have any bearing on Templeton."

"So what's the beef? Seems like you should let the guy alone. He's in good hands. Real good hands, from what I could see through these." Hendry indicated the reading glasses. "Better hands than you'll ever be in." He added hastily, "Not meaning any disrespect for your significant other, of course."

Riley did not take Captain Hendry's comments personally. "Because I got a lot of negative information on Sarah Mason, too."

"What? Seems like she's the only straight thread in the quilt."

"I know she showed us identification, but so far she doesn't check out. The number on her business card is Benthic Products, but there's no answer there—not unusual considering it's the weekend. I can't follow it up till Monday. But there's no Sarah Mason living anywhere in the greater Los Angeles area, where Benthic Products is based, nor does she have a California driver's license or have a car registered in the state. That makes her an unknown quantity."

Captain Hendry groaned and leaned back in his chair, which creaked just as loud as it had before. He thrust his hands behind his head. "Now you're clutching for straws. She said she was new to the company, so maybe she doesn't have a private phone yet. Or maybe she's living in a sublet apartment and the phone's in another name. Or maybe Benthic Products has offices in other cities and she just takes messages at the number on her card. You've got to look at all the angles, Frank."

"Okay, but try this side. We let a sick man walk off with a woman who's a stranger to him, whose identity cannot now be verified, and whose appearance in retrospect seems oddly coincidental, almost fortuitous. Throw in the fact that Templeton has a top secret security clearance and—"

"Now where'd you get that information?"

"FBI files. I tapped into the central data bank to see if he was reported missing or had a criminal record. Negative on both counts. But the FBI conducted a thorough investigation of Templeton when Biotech landed a large defense contract five years ago. He came through clean. What I don't like is the fact that he appears to be having a nervous breakdown, he's got a head full of military secrets, and we sent him off with a woman whose identity cannot be verified. For the moment."

Captain Hendry appeared thoughtful. He stared up at the ceiling with his hands still behind his head, and remained silent for nearly half a minute. "It's not *mostly* negative info, it's *all* negative. And each piece of information, taken separately, is harmless by itself. But when you put all the pieces together you could make an interpretation that smacks of conspiracy." He leaned forward and put his elbows back on the desk. "But it's more likely to be an innocent combination of events. Something we gotta be careful of in this business. We're so used to dealing with criminals and wrongdoers that we begin to look at everyone with a jaundiced eye. I know I've made an ass out of myself too many times."

"I don't disagree with you, George. And I'm not suggesting that we haul Templeton and the woman back in here for more questioning. I'm only saying that there's enough suspicion to keep the case open at least until we get some more information."

Captain Hendry squinted. "You got things working?"

"Because of Templeton's security clearance, I thought the FBI should know his current status, so I submitted an incident report. They can check with the Department of Defense, and if they have any concerns about Templeton or any sensitive information he might divulge given his present state of mind, they'll get back to us."

"That was smart."

"I faxed them a set of fingerprints—just as a matter of procedure." Hendry bolted back in his chair, causing another squeak. "I thought he refused to be printed?"

Riley let escape a conspiratorial smile. "When I offered him coffee I gave it to him in a clean mug. I dusted the mug after he left, and got three perfect prints and a couple others that were smudged."

"I didn't know you knew how to use the fingerprint kit," Hendry said, startled. "You holding out on me?"

"The graveyard shift is mighty slow. I use the slack time to read up on investigative technique. And I've been experimenting with taking latent prints off all kinds of things. Smooth surfaces work the best—"

"You're not telling me anything I don't already know. I just didn't know *you* knew." Captain Hendry grinned. "If I don't watch out, you'll become an expert in everything and the next thing you know you'll be taking over my job."

Riley's tan face brightened to a mild shade of red. "That wasn't what I intended—"

"Never mind. Just tell me what else you've gone and done."

The patrolman glanced down at the spreadsheet more to divert his eyes from the captain's hard stare than to remind himself of the morning's course of action. "I wrote out a physical description of Sarah Mason and everything we know about her, which isn't too much, and sent it to the FBI on the datalink. Naturally, if she's not on the up-and-up she'll be using an alias and forged identification. There wasn't much more I could do on that score."

"That's fine. Give the feds something to do besides watching Saturday afternoon football." Hendry leaned back again in the creaking chair. "Frank, you done good. Even if nothing comes of it we'll make some brownie points for making proper notification. The FBI is always on our tail for not bringing them in on cases they think they should have jurisdiction over. And when you think about it, Templeton's cockamamie story about waking up and not knowing where he was smacks of somebody with a guilty conscience trying to lay an alibi, although he seemed like a nice enough guy to me, like a victim of circumstance."

"I still think we should have insisted on taking him to the hospital. He had those burn marks on his scalp."

Hendry's jowls wattled with vigorous negative shakes. "I told you, Frank, the law won't let us be everybody's keeper. Highland Hills—or any city for that matter—isn't a military stockade with gunnery control over the inmates. You gotta get that MP attitude out of your head. SP. Whatever. We're civilians just like everybody else. Worse, we're second-class citizens. The badge doesn't hold the respect it used to. You push somebody just an eentsy-teentsy little bit too hard and the next thing you know the Civil Liberties Union is screaming police brutality. We gotta step lightly when we're dealing with the public—especially innocent bystanders like Templeton, because we got nothing on him besides our own paranoid suspicions. If there's a fly in the ointment here it's that dolled up dame. Too smooth a character for my tastes."

"She does come off a bit strong," Riley allowed. "What threw me was that she knew so much about Templeton and Biotech, all of it accurate as far as I've been able to ascertain so far."

"Highland Hills used to be a quiet little community before Biotech moved into town—must be ten or twelve years ago. Now, I've been too busy keeping the peace to keep up on socio-economics, if that's the right word for it, but Biotech's what put this community on the map and brought in all the other industries. But this Templeton's always been a low-keyed kind of guy. Genius, like I said, but you rarely hear anything about him. A lab rat, they call him. No wonder he's finally gone off the deep end."

"Do we have a file on him?"

Hendry shook his head. "Don't think he's ever gotten so much as a parking ticket. Low keyed, like I said. You have to understand, Frank, that what I know about this town is lopsided even though I grew up here. I can tell you everything there is to know about Slippery Dick Hannah and the Bobby twins and that sleaze joint out on Tanner Street 'cause we do a lot of business with those folks. But the corporation people are law-abiding citizens that don't grab my attention unless they get into domestic squabbles or fights with the neighbors."

Riley shifted his weight in the silence that followed. "So, what do you think about all this?" He waved the spreadsheet for emphasis.

"I think you're wasting your time." Captain Hendry leaned forward, put on his reading glasses, and reached out with one hamlike arm. "But at the very least we ought to let Templeton's friends and relatives know what's going on. Gimme me that paper and let me do some checking. You go home and get some rest."

Chapter 10

The room was pitch black when Grant woke up—groggily, as if he had been drugged. Which in a sense he had.

The bitter taste of alcohol lay thick on his tongue: the final ingredient in the recipe for a trip to dreamland. Take a long night of terror alleviated by only a brief nap on a concrete floor, mix in physical exhaustion and mental disorientation, chill for twelve hours, and there was little cause to wonder why the vodka had gone straight to his head.

He pushed himself up to a sitting position, arched his back and stretched his arms and legs, and took stock of his condition. Although his head ached dully and his muscles were somewhat sore, the shower and sleep had refreshed him. He remembered where he was and what had recently occurred, not without detachment. He accepted the situation and would face what might come. His only major concern was the way his feelings alternated from one moment to the next between unbounded exhilaration and stark depression: like a high-speed manic-depressive. Mood swings were not part of his personality. He felt certain that Sarah could help relieve his anxiety.

He threw aside the covers and swung his legs out over the side of the bed. The sensation was similar to sitting on an inflatable surf mat in a heated swimming pool. The towel had slipped off his waist while he slept and was now wrapped around one leg. He stood up, hitched the towel in place, and, hands held out in front of him, tread lightly on the deep pile carpet toward a faint vertical strip of light, feeling his way across the spacious suite like a soldier traversing an enemy minefield. When he thrust aside the curtains, the room did not get perceptibly brighter. It was nighttime, and he had slept the day away.

He groped toward the opposite wall, ran his hands

along the blue felt wallpaper until he located the light switch, and switched on the shaded ornamental lamp which perched on the glass table. In front of the lamp was a covered silver tray with a sheet of paper pierced by the knob on the lid. Grant read the note inscribed in black ink with flowering scroll-like script complete with loops and whirls as if each letter had been penned by an expert calligrapher.

"grant if you wake up before I get back, here's the lunch you missed. call room service if you need anything else. sarah." There was also a postscript. "your clothes are in the bathroom."

Forget the clothes; he was famished. He removed the lid and scooped up one of the triple-decker sandwich quarters, took a large bite out of it, and, drooling lettuce parts and tomato drippings, carried the tray back to the bed where he squatted and leaned over the tray while he finished the first quarter.

The second one went down nearly as fast. After he caught his breath, he sampled the chilled chef's salad and potato salad, which were lying in a bed of partially melted ice. In short order he completed the entire meal down to the last breadcrumb and scrap of celery stalk, without taking the time to notice what kind of meat and cheese lay between the slices of bread. He felt as if he could consume a second helping of everything. Which was unusual in that a platter of food that size normally satisfied his hunger. That's what happens when you don't eat for a day, he thought.

He made another vodka gimlet. It tasted as bad as the others, so he pushed it aside and decided to drink water instead. While he was filling the glass from the bathroom tap he saw his jacket, pants, and shirt, spotless and neatly pressed, draped over a plastic hanger which hung from a brass hook on the inside of the door. The shoes on the floor shone with a high-gloss polish. His underwear was folded and neatly piled on the counter, with his keys and voice recorder on top. He downed one glass of water, refilled the glass, then took it and his recorder into the bedroom.

I wonder what messages I left myself. His mind was a blank as he idly fingered the control buttons. Which was precisely why he recorded his thoughts—he was too prone to forget the ideas he developed during his ambles to and from work, no matter how important they were. The mark of true genius, he was wont to quote, was not in how much a person remembered but in how quickly he forgot. The thwarted logic of the statement implied that once a creative concept was formulated and understood in the genius mind, it was then put aside so the mind was free to conceptualize other thoughts. Well, there's only one way to find out.

He pressed in the rewind button. The tape whirred at high speed for about ten seconds, then came to an abrupt halt when it reached the beginning. He pressed the play button. For several seconds there was grating static, as on a poorly tuned radio, followed by a silence that lasted until the unmistakable Dopplering whoosh of a passing vehicle faded in the distance. Then he heard his voice.

"Grant, tomorrow is trash day, so don't forget to put the trash out tonight. It's really piling up because you forgot to do it last week." This was not exactly the revelation that Grant was hoping to hear, but it was typical of him to address himself in that manner and to remind himself about chores and other household trivia which he subconsciously chose to disremember. "And the week before."

After a pause, "Charlotte would like you to bring back the Fenton file so she can put it on disk. You know how these secretaries are. She was quite insistent." Charlotte? Grant did not know anyone by that name, least of all a secretary at Biotech. And what was the Fenton file?

A barely audible click signified that the recording mode had been switched off and then later switched back on. The interval between entries could have been anywhere from seconds to days; he never keyed time references. "Okay, bright boy, where did you put the memchip matrix sequencing data? Connie wants to know." Who is Connie? And what did he—did I—mean by memchip matrix sequencing data?

Sarah had mentioned the Memchip 201 as if it should have meant something to him. He had no recollection of it at all.

Click. "Grant, you know you've been putting this off but you simply have to go through Dawn's trunk in the attic and find her transcript. She needs it." Which was befuddling, because elementary school graduates did not have transcripts; they had report cards.

Click. "Bob tried to break into the memchip design program. He tripped every alarm in the system, and almost burned out the access trunk line. Better change axes. He's getting too close." Bob? Not Bob Lerner. Must be another Bob. And why is the program protected? I never use access codes because I'm too prone to forget them due to my abominable preoccupation. And fellow workers need immediate access.

Click. "Send a handwritten sympathy card to Martha Vanderbilt. Say something like 'I can't tell you how much sorrow I feel over Randy's unfortunate accident. It was a once-in-a-lifetime—no, scratch that. Bad choice of words. 'It was an occurrence so rare that it couldn't happen again in a million years'—no, that's too informal. 'It was an occurrence so rare that we—all of us at Biotech—are stunned, and find it hard to accept—no—difficult to accept that it actually happened. A proper investigation into the circumstances is being conducted so it can never happen again, but, of course, that won't bring back your beloved husband. You have my fullest sympathy, and the sympathy of all of us here at Biotech. We will miss Randy terribly—no— we will miss Randy, uh—' think of something appropriate. Damn it, Randy, what was going through your mind—besides fifty thousand volts of electricity—when you disconnected the power leads without checking the potentiometer?"

True gallows humor, Grant reflected ruefully, which helped to alleviate the pain and sense of loss of someone he had worked with closely in the lab. He could hardly believe it—Randy Vanderbilt gone. In fact, he was not sure he *should* believe it. He had no recollection of such a dreadful event. Yet that was his voice on the recorder. How could he forget the death of a lab technician he saw every day?

Click. "Too many deaths. Too much for coincidence." What did it mean?

Click. "Hide the backup disk at Kenny Grahame's. Just in case." Grant did not know any Kenny Grahame.

Click. "Don't let him trick you. Bob can't be one of them." Bob who?

Click. "Or else he would have known about the BP connection." The oil company?

Click. "Initiate the memchip modem virus. This time it wasn't Bob who attempted the unauthorized access. It was someone from outside the company. Whoever it was tried to use the red herring entry code. Don't get paranoid now, but there may be factions involved that would stop at nothing short of war. Maybe not even then." What the hell is going on?

Click. "Oh, god, I think Bob's been replaced. That would explain a lot." He could hear the mounting alarm in his recorded voice. The implication of danger went far beyond job loss or corporate competition.

Click. "Shunt the sterilizer circuits before it's too late, scramble the discrimination foci, and boot the old program with the first lane tracking overlay. Maybe they can't tell the difference." None of it made sense.

Click. Static followed by heavy breathing. "The password is Saratoga. And don't forget your keys. The new set."

The tape droned on mutely for several minutes, then reached the end of the spool and stopped. Grant flipped over the cassette and played the other side. While listening to the soft and monotonous machine hiss, he pondered the import of his recorded words. The icy chill that spread over his body was not all due to the cold water he was drinking or his state of undress. Something terrible was happening to the Grant Templeton in this parallel world—something that *that* Grant appeared to have escaped, while he—*this* Grant—was left to face the consequences of actions which he had had no part in contriving.

So be it. Grant was resolved to play his part and see where it would lead. This was not to say that he did not still harbor feelings of doubt about his role, only that he had subjugated those feelings with scientific ratiocination. Even though the mechanisms of space-time discontinuity were far afield from his basic lines of research, the scientist within found intriguing the concept of parallel universes, of alternate realities, of the rich variety of possible outcomes to initiating events. What constituted destiny in one realm of existence was but fantasy in another.

Again he found himself vacillating. Were these speculations an honest assessment of his natural curiosity, or another manifestation of manic digression? It was difficult to know, when the experimenter was also the subject of the experiment. Grant now found himself in a curious predicament: after years of putting thousands of mice through the mazes, in order to study their brain wave patterns as they implemented learned responses for a reward of food, he was the mouse in the maze. His scalp crawled with the thought.

He wriggled his fingers through his hair, feeling for the wounds which Patrolman Riley had seen and examined. About an inch above the top of each ear was a small scab, not sensitive to the touch other than to elicit a mild tingling sensation in the surrounding skin. He rose from the bed with his fingers still rubbing the wounds, and walked into the bathroom. By twisting his head and looking askance in the mirror, he could see the marks through parted hair. They looked like bee stings.

Rapidly he massaged his head: his prescribed method of combing the unruly mop of curly hair. There were strands of gray that he had never noticed before, to go along with the worry wrinkles. He was aging prematurely. He shrugged it off and pulled on his clothes. The pants and jacket had not only been cleaned, they had been stitched as well, and a very good job at that.

The door in the bedroom opened and shut. "Hi, Honey. I'm home."

Grant hastily finished buttoning his shirt. "Sarah?"

"Only teasing, love. Are you decent?" She swept across the room as radiant as always. "I see you've eaten all your food."

He donned the jacket but left it unbuttoned, stuck the key chain in the left pocket, and stepped through the bathroom doorway with a jaunt that was only partially put on. "I was famished." The scent of her perfume was pleasant if a bit overpowering.

"Oh, my." She halted in midstride, and raised eyelashes that were overweighted with mascara. "You look different without the beard."

His hand sprang to his face. Grant squeezed his smooth cheeks as if he were testing a peach for ripeness. "Couldn't stand it any longer. It was too scratchy."

Sarah tilted her doll-like head in sublime imitation of an animated character from Babes in Toyland. "I like it." Her cheerfulness seemed to fill the room. She had changed her green dress for a black pantsuit, but wore the same patent leather belt and high-heel shoes.

Grant laughed. "Get used to it because I'm going to keep it this way."

"Oh, my. You nicked yourself." Sarah ran cool fingers along Grant's neck, giving him tingles which he tried hard to hide. She inspected his face close up. "You'll live. It's not deep at all."

"You'd better get a new razor, though; I think I ruined yours."

She waved her hand at him. "No bother. They're throwaways anyhow." After a short pause, "So, did you get your nap out?"

He took a deep breath and puffed his cheeks as he exhaled. "Yes, and it felt great." He thought, Too bad you couldn't have been here to snuggle with. "Although I didn't mean to sleep all day. Uh, it is still the same day, isn't it?"

She laughed easily. "The last time I checked. But don't feel bad. You must have needed the rest. 'The wise person listens to his body when it talks because it usually knows what it needs.' That's what my mother used to say."

Grant knew exactly what his body needed right now, but it was not offered on the menu. "She sounds like a wise person herself."

Sarah nodded. "So, what did you think of the movie clip?" Her hand flew to her open mouth. "Oh, I'm sorry. I didn't mean to sound so pushy, getting right down to business like this."

"No, that's okay. That's why you're here. I understand." He picked up the voice recorder from the bed and shoved it in the right pocket of his jacket, then stooped in front of the disk player and hit the eject button. When the disk drawer popped open, he plucked out the disk, then stood up and hefted it for a moment. "You know, I'll never be able to watch *Casablanca* the same way again."

"Oh, that." She waved one hand in the air while with the other she took the disk which Grant was proffering. "One of the re-enactments at Disney Planet is a scene from the movie. And they're going to do *The Wizard of Oz*, too. Isn't that just one of your favorites?" She tossed the disk in the trunk with the mechanical arm and snapped down the lid. "Although the Scarecrow's song is more appropriate, when Dorothy meets him at the crossroads—'If I only had a Brain'—because that's the whole purpose of this rendezvous. The funny part about it is that without the Biotech memchip, we can't store enough data to get the required feedback time for a dance that fast or that complicated, especially the way Ray Bolger does it. I mean, with the hydraulic verniers driven by a remote mainframe through a cable, you lose the fluidity of the movements. The lack of verimisal, veridismal—"

"Verisimilitude."

"That's the word. When you don't have that the simulacrum looks jumpy and jittery, like an early silent film from the old days. If we increase the speed without improving the response time, we get Keystone Cops stuff, like fast action with frames missing. The simulacra also fall down a lot. Can't get their feet back on the ground in time—no pun intended." She laughed uproariously, but when Grant's stare remained blank, she explained, " 'In time,' like 'fast enough' and 'in time with the music'?"

A slow grin grew on his face. "Oh, I get it." Then he laughed. It was his kind of humor, like the jokes in *Boy's Life.*

"Anyhow, the theme of the disk is the same as the movie. If we had a brain—the Memchip 201—then we wouldn't need the cable feed for the mainframe linkup, and the simulacrum could stand on its own." Again she laughed at her own joke, and Grant joined her with a chuckle. "I hope you don't think I'm being too familiar with you. I mean, I don't like to be always throwing a sales pitch, but, as you said, that's what I'm here for. And see, just because you agreed to buy some of our robotic manipulators for conversion to outer space applications doesn't mean that you'll license us to implant the memchip on our underwater models or Disney Planet simulacra. But that's what we're hoping."

Grant found her persistence in no way grating. To a woman who in his opinion could disarm an incoming missile with charm alone, he was soft clay begging to be molded into any shape she wanted. That was probably why she had been sent to meet with him, instead of a more experienced salesperson with a haughtily professional air. But until he had a better grasp of the corporate position on the subject, it behooved him to play the part of diplomacy.

"I certainly hope that we can work out an agreement that will prove beneficial to all parties concerned."

She shrugged. "We'll give it our best shot." After a pause, "So, how's about some fresh air? Feel well enough to travel?"

"I guess. Where shall we go?"

"We've already been to my place. How about yours?"

Chapter 11

Grant did not know how long he could carry on the deception before he gave away the fact that he was a novice in this world. As he was discovering, there were major differences between alternate realities, and sooner or later he was bound to get tripped up over details. This plane was more advanced technologically than his own—the Humphrey Bogart simulacrum proved that—which placed him at a disadvantage despite his educational background. In retrospect, he shuddered at the outburst he had made at what he had perceived to be a suggestion of imposture on Patrolman Riley's part. Now he was afraid that he was about to be exposed for the fraud that he was.

His refusal to go home at first was nothing more than a delaying tactic—to give him an orientation period in which to adjust to current conditions and to learn what Sarah knew about him and Biotech. The excuse he had used—to view Sarah's wares in her room—had been slender at best, yet Sarah had taken it in stride and had even responded enthusiastically to the suggestion. Nor had she balked at his taking a bath in her suite and sleeping in her bed. She must want this sale pretty bad.

"I did my homework, Grant. I looked it up on a map to see where your house was."

He thought, But where did you get the address? It's not in the phone book.

Sarah grinned proudly. "I even drove out here today while you were asleep to check it out. Of course I couldn't get past the gate, but the grounds looked really sumptuous from what I could see from the road. What I like about it the most is the isolation. Nobody to bother you, no neighbors to complain when you want to crank up the music, no kids playing in the street and making a lot of noise. But, boy, do you have grass to cut and leaves to rake."

Grant sat quietly in the rental car and stared intently out the window. He recognized the road as the one he had crept along—was it only this morning—after his flight from the pasture; the one on which he had seen the expensive sedan; the one next to which he had lain in a ditch. "I have someone come around every other week to take care of the lawn." That was the truth. He hoped it was the correct response.

"But it has a kind of simplicity, you know. I mean, the house is elegant and all that, but not garish, not ostentious—no, that's not right. Not ostenterous—"

"Ostentatious."

"That's the word. Not ostentatious. I read an article about you in *Personalities* magazine, and they said you were one of those people who wasn't flashy with his money. They said you weren't like most nouveau riche—people who earned their money instead of inheriting it because you didn't let it go to your head. How you didn't care what money could buy, but how it could be used to advance the causes you promoted. I like that in a person. I hope I have enough money someday to be like that."

On one side of the road stood a wooden fence which kept the livestock from escaping; on the other side spread an endless soybean field lying fallow. Sweetgums and rosebuds dappled the landscape with satisfying irregularity, as if they had been planted—or left standing—with architectural intent. The clear, cloudless sky sparkled with stars untwinkling: there were no heat inversions. Patches of fog hugged the ground.

"I don't believe I've seen that article. Is there any chance I can get a copy?"

"No problem. It's still on the newsstands, but I've got the mag back at the hotel. I was hoping to get you to sign it. Do you mind?"

For some reason, the thought of signing autographs gave Grant a shudder. "Well, I guess not."

The road curved to the left around the fenced in pasture, then broadened suddenly to a finely paved surface. To a tall post on the right was nailed a simple teak shingle with jagged edges. The words "Feline Estates" were routed into the wood and painted white.

"Neat trick, that, leaving the county road natural to trick outsiders into believing there's nothing back here but farms."

Grant observed without comment. The pasture ended at a stand of sassafras trees whose leaves had already turned bright yellow. Maples sprinkled throughout the woods added a blend of red and orange. A rabbit dashed across the headlight beams and disappeared into the dense forest on the right. Half a mile down the road, further travel was barred by a metal mesh gate with a stout wooden fence extending to the trees on either side. Mercury vapor lamps standing on thin aluminum poles provided illumination for residents as well as for the video camera. Post office boxes and a shed for packages and oversized envelopes were protected from the elements by a flat wooden canopy.

Sarah halted the car next to an electronic control box. She held out a dainty hand. "Let me have your keys."

Grant took a deep breath. The time had come when he had to admit that he had no recollection of Feline Estates, no idea of where his—the other Grant's—house was located, and certainly no way to gain entrance. "Sarah—"

She reached into his jacket pocket and pulled out the chain, then fanned through the keys on top of the dashboard where they glinted in the light of the mercury vapor lamps. "I saw the key on here when I took them out of your pocket this morning. Here it is! The little one." It looked like the key to a locket.

She rolled down the window, stuck the tiny key in the slot, and twisted. A contactor clacked like a rifle retort. The right lane gate swung outward on well-oiled hinges and a single plastic wheel. "Sorry, love. I don't mean to be in a rush but these lights are bothering me." She retrieved the key and handed the chain to Grant. "Night vision, you know?" As soon as the car passed the photoelectric cell on the inside of the compound, the contactor clacked and the gate swung shut.

Dumfounded, Grant studied the keys in his hand. Was this the same set of keys he had possessed last night when he had tried to force his way into the house on Cedar Place? He thought, It doesn't make sense. Where did I get a key to a lock I've never seen before? The car was plunged into darkness once the lighted gateway was left behind. Recovering quickly from the shock, he shoved the keys back into his pocket. Don't fall apart now. Just take it as it comes.

The forest was unbroken for the next quarter mile. The road curved slightly to the right and then to the left. With the trees crowding close to the shoulder on either side, the gateway light faded into obscurity. On the right, they passed a driveway which was marked by a wooden post with a jagged shingle sign similar to the one that marked the main entrance. Routed into the wood was "Catamount Cove." After another hundred yards they passed a driveway on the left; it was designated Cougar Cove. Then came Panther Cove on the right.

Sarah snickered. "Very clever. They're all local names for the American mountain lion. What comes next? African tigers?"

Grant was noncommittal. "You wouldn't expect to find a dingo in Feline Estates, would you?"

She turned the car into Panther Cove, laughing. "No, but I see you've got nothing against canine trees." The driveway was long and sinuous, and lined on both sides with dogwoods which were no longer in bloom.

Grant choked off a laconic chuckle when he saw the huge weeping willow which occupied the front yard and the incredibly tall oaks which surrounded the house like Olympian guards. "Hey, how did you see the house from the gate, if you couldn't get through this afternoon?"

The driveway turned into a teardrop-shaped closed loop which encompassed the monstrous willow with a low stone parapet, then split part way around so the right tine of the fork headed straight alongside the house to the attached garage at the rear, while the left tine broadened to provide parking for guests in front of the two-story twin columns which bestrode the landing and the wide brick steps. The columns were fluted but not otherwise ornate. The double doors were hung with massive brass knockers which were shaped like valentine hearts. The shuttered windows were dark.

Sarah eased the car into place at the base of the steps. "From pictures. You know?" She held her hands in front of her face, with the thumb and forefinger of the left hand describing a right angle while she flicked the index finger of her right hand close to her eye. "Cameras? The article had an inset photo shot from the other side of the wall." She indicated the parapet. "Taken during the interview, I guess."

Grant nodded, hardly aware of the movement. "I guess you did do your homework."

She grinned like the Cheshire cat. "Know your man, make your sale. That's what I always say. Shall we go in?" Without waiting for a reply, she opened the door and climbed out, her large purse swinging by means of a narrow leather strap which she flung over her head to the opposite shoulder.

Grant continued to sit, pondering his next move. He had an uneasy feeling that her knowledge of his life went far beyond and long before last month's magazine article.

Sarah left him little alternative as she walked around the front of the car and invited him by placing one foot on the bottom step and winking one brown hypnotic eye. She held out her hand with an alluring demeanor. "Come on. I told the nice policemen I would take care of you and make sure you got home safe. You wouldn't want me to go back on my promise, now, would you?"

Reluctantly Grant acknowledged to himself that the woman had the power to make strong men weep, and a presence which defied the aura of a highbred queen. He wished only for a leash, that he might be totally at her command. He stepped into the brisk night air.

"You are a shy one, aren't you? I guess that's why you haven't gotten remarried after all these years of your divorce."

Grant stuck his hands into his pockets in order to avoid the magic touch of her skin. He fumbled with his keys and recorder. "Sometimes the shy ones are the best ones."

Her hand flew to her mouth to hide a churlish smile. "Oh, Grant, you're beginning to show some promise." She caught herself quickly. "Now, come on, let's be adults about this. We're professionals, remember?"

"Very little, but that's beside the point." He was feeling much too jaunty. Another manic swing? "Let's just hope I have the key to the problem."

"You are a joker." She slid her arm around the crook of his elbow and walked with him up the steps to the massive double doors. "You might not be the easiest sale I ever made, but you're the most unpredictable."

You haven't made me yet, but if I play my cards right, I hope you get your chance. "And you thought you had the corner on that market." The confidence of his words belied a weak inner tremor. If one key worked, why not another? His hands were shaking minutely as he pulled out the key chain and fumbled for the right key. Close contact with Sarah increased his nervousness. He selected what appeared to be a common house key, slid it into the lock, and turned.

The latch slid back without protest. Grant breathed a tremendous sigh of relief.

Sarah depressed the thumb latch and pushed open the door with the key still in the lock. The interior was dark, but she soon found the light switches on the adjacent wall and flipped all of them on. The two-story entry was flooded with incandescence which shone off the gilt banister and glossy white posts like the sun reflecting sharply off pools of molten gold and quicksilver. The room was simply appointed, the only articles of furniture being a maroon upholstered loveseat under the semi-spiral staircase and a plain glass end table adjacent to it, on which reposed an empty white porcelain vase.

"Pardon me for saying so, but it could use some flowers."

"Huhn?" Grant was still marveling that the key had actually worked, and had not yet taken in his surroundings.

"The vase?" Sarah pointed a slender finger. "That's what they're for, you know?"

Grant deliberated. "But flowers have to be watered."

Sarah scowled playfully. "If the whole house is like this I'd have to say it could use a woman's touch. But then, you've only been here a couple of months, right?"

He guessed. "Something like that."

"Well, how about a tour? Downstairs first."

The house was as much a revelation to Grant as it was to Sarah, except that he did not "ooh" and "ah" as she did over the spaciousness and the more luxurious manner in which the rest of the house was furnished. Hardwood flooring extended throughout. By the simple expedient of preceding her, he flipped on lights and was able to announce the names of the rooms as they entered. The dining room suite was constructed of polished cherry and included a capacious china cabinet which was devoid of dinnerware.

"Must dine in the kitchen," Sarah commented dryly.

The living room was amply filled with matching modern sofas and chairs which looked so much alike that they gave the appearance of display pieces on a show room floor. Only the price tags were missing. The half-bath was the size of most normal full baths. The huge den was carpeted wall-to-wall in low-pile red fiber and dotted with a variety of casual lounge chairs. Tiered shelving on one side of the fireplace held a full assortment of audio and video equipment; the shelves on the other side of the fireplace were filled with books.

"Looks cozy."

When Grant opened the next door and switched on the lights, he found himself standing in a three-car garage which was empty except for a shiny, cobalt-blue Porsche sitting in the middle bay. "The garage."

"Nice car," Sarah cooed.

Grant grimaced. "I like the color." He did not know enough about Porsches—or any car, for that matter—to recognize the model or to describe its features. He switched off the lights and closed the door quickly. "Over here's the kitchen." Luckily, he could see the counters and cabinets in the light from the hall.

"You could cook for an army in this place."

"And undoubtedly kill them in the process." Grant's greatest culinary skill was buttered bread; for a hot meal he made toast. "I eat out a lot."

Sarah was expressionless. "I like that." After a momentary pause, "I mean, it saves time washing dishes." She grinned. "So, what's upstairs?"

At the top of the staircase was a short hall that led to the bedrooms. The first two were spares complete with beds, linen, and bureaus; the third was the master which had a king-sized bed with a cream satin spread to match the curtains and wallpaper, mahogany dresser and chest of drawers, matching mahogany end tables under Tiffany swag lamps, and a secretary desk and chair.

Playing the gracious host, Grant made believe he knew the layout. He opened one door and made a sweeping gesture. "The bath."

Sarah peered in without entering. "Makes the one at the hotel seem like a shower stall."

When he opened the adjacent door, the overhead fluorescent fixture flickered on automatically, illuminating in stark white a walk-in closet that held more clothes than he had owned in his entire life. "And the department store." If this was the way the Grant Templeton of this world suffered to live, Grant was going to find it easy to get used to.

"Oh, Grant, I didn't realize you had such good taste." Sarah viewed the rows of suits, pants, shirts, jackets, and ties with high regard. "Would you mind—I mean—I know your jacket has been mended, but—"

She plucked a brown tweed cardigan off the rack and held it up against his chest. "This one goes with your pants." Her hand flew to her mouth. "Oh, I'm sorry. Am I being too forward? I keep forgetting I'm only a sales rep and not your girlfriend."

Grant viewed her discomfort with amusement. "Don't feel bad. Since I got divorced—when I no longer had a wife to pick out my clothes for me—the gals at the office are always getting on my case about my outfits not matching. I'm used to it." He snorted, then removed his jacket and tossed it on the bed. "I'm happier in a lab smock, but I don't seem to have any in stock."

She took the cardigan off the molded plastic hanger, replaced the hanger, and handed the jacket to Grant. She shook her head wistfully. "You're so easygoing. Nothing seems to bother you."

"It comes from years of practice." He donned the jacket and shook the sleeves down to his wrists.

Sarah pulled out the shoulders, tugged down on the front, and stood back admiringly. "It looks great on you."

The jacket fit perfectly. Grant should not have been surprised, but he was. What was more surprising was the way he was beginning to feel at home in this unfamiliar world, to believe in the parallel universe theory, perhaps even to like it. Here he was a financial success.

"Maybe you'll let me pick out a different shirt? And another pair of pants?" Sarah rushed on when he scowled. "Okay, I know. I'm pushing it. But that's what women do."

Grant was completely disarmed. He thought, This woman is really getting under my skin. He laughed uproariously. If I can only get her out of her clothes. "Sarah, I've never met anyone quite like you."

"I know." She took his hand in both of hers and squeezed. "I'm a weirdo." Then she brightened. "So show me the study."

That burst his bubble, for he was almost to the point of pulling her close and kissing her. Damn!

She pulled him out of the bedroom and along past

the guest bathroom to the room at the end of the hall, almost as if she knew the way. It was the only room in the house they had not yet seen. "So this is where you spend your nights alone."

The study was the size of an average bedroom. Because it was on the corner it had two windows: one facing the great weeping willow, the other looking over the side drive. In the middle of the room sat a large oak office desk and at right angles to it stood a computer workstation complete with dual keyboards, color monitors, and printers. Filing cabinets and glass display cases full of books lined the two walls which were without windows. Illumination was provided by low-wattage lamps and high-intensity flood lights which slid in tracks secured to the ceiling, and which were switched on independently.

"Not quite homey, not quite worky," was Sarah's simple assessment. "But definitely practical."

It was all new to Grant. "I like it." He walked into the room like a fly through syrup and gazed in awe at his newfound opulence. The desk was new and just the kind he had always wanted, with plenty of drawers for miscellaneous storage and within easy reach of his files and books, all merely a heel-push away on the leather-backed, swivel-tilt chair on casters. The computer set-up was more sophisticated than the one he employed at the lab, and familiarization would no doubt require some time with a good training manual.

His first shock came when he spotted the gold and crystal paperweight/pen-holder which Barbara had presented to him for his fortieth birthday, and the fourteen-carat gold ballpoint pen which his daughter had bought to fit. He was overcome with a wave of nostalgia. That same week his daughter had turned ten, and he had presented her with a conundrum he had been saving for the occasion:

"You're real good at math, Dawn, so see if you can figure this one out. Right now I'm forty years old and you're only ten, which means I'm four times older than you are. But in five years, when I'm forty-five and you're fifteen, I'll only be three times older than you. Then, in another, say, fifteen years, I'll be sixty and you'll be thirty, making me only twice as old as you. How many years have to go by before you catch up to me?"

Dawn deliberated for a long, long time, screwing up her face into a repertoire of contortions which were intended to help her think. Finally, she said, "I don't know, Daddy. How long?" He laughed. "When you figure it out, tell me and we'll both know." Whining, "Come on, Daddy. How long?" He shook his head. "You tell me." She punched him playfully, he fell over clutching his arm in mock pain, then she jumped on him and they rolled around on the floor as she cried out for an answer. The last time he saw her, she still had not figured it out.

The flashback had taken only a split second, and Sarah seemed oblivious to his temporarily frozen posture. He shuddered, took a deep breath, and walked around the room. Among the bric-a-brac on the shelves and walls he recognized additional personal items from his past: his father's gold pocket watch, dinosaur figurines from a grade-school fieldtrip, high school scholastic letters, college textbooks, diplomas, and gifts from friends and relatives: all his cherished items. And his license to practice medicine was adorned with his signature—his own unmistakable chicken scratch. Yes, he belonged in this world.

Furthermore, the studio portrait on the desk was undeniably Grant Templeton. A younger Grant to be sure, full of vigor and without the beard or the lines on his face which he had seen that morning in the mirror, but it was definitely his picture, and he remembered when it was taken. Confusingly, next to it perched a color photograph of a young woman who could have been his ex-wife Barbara—but not quite, as if she were her younger sister. In this world, had Grant married Barbara's sister June after their divorce? To be sure, June took sympathy with Grant when he and Barbara had broken up—but had they fallen in love?

"Looks like you've got company."

Grant had been so wrapped up in memorabilia that he was hardly aware of Sarah's presence. He looked up dully. "Wha-what?"

She pointed out the front window. "Cars. More than one."

It looked like three sets of headlights coming down the driveway. One by one they peeled off to the left and circled the weeping willow, finally coming to a halt in a line that blocked in the rental car by the steps. The lead vehicle was a Chevrolet van, the other two were Lincoln Continentals. Doors flew open and a horde of men wearing expensive business suits stepped into the light from the porch. Three of them approached the front door, the others hung back behind the cars.

Grant did not recognize any of them.

"I think we'd better go see what they want." The pleasantry had gone out of Sarah's voice, and her lips were grimly set.

Grant nodded perfunctorily. He did not look forward to confronting new acquaintances this early in the game. But he had no choice.

Chapter 12

Grant and Sarah had hardly reached the top landing when the front doors burst open and crashed against the white painted walls. Standing in the middle of the double doorway with his hands stretched out high and to his sides was the biggest hunk of manhood which Grant had ever seen. He stood well over six and a half feet tall, and had a chest with the girth of a fifty-five gallon drum. His face was expressionless as two other men, miniatures by comparison, ducked under his arms on either side and strode belligerently into the entry.

Grant halted halfway down the stairs, stunned at the unexpected intrusion, but Sarah, who was prancing downward like a gazelle, high-heels thudding on the rubber treads, did not stop until she reached the newel post a step above the highly buffed floor. Her purse swung at her side like a dying pendulum. She gasped, and covered her mouth with one delicate hand.

The two men in front looked up at Grant with piercing eyes. The one in the gray pinstripe suit spoke in a deep guttural voice which was not in the least bit friendly. "We've been looking for you, Templeton. Where've you been hiding?"

Grant did not know what to say to these strangers. He leaned against the gilt topped railing with his mouth agape.

"And who's the broad?" squeaked the one in blue serge suit. "Another one of your bimbos?"

"Excuse me!" Sarah marched forward with the demeanor of a wet cat, wearing an uncharacteristic ferocious snarl. She stood defiantly in front of the blue serge and glowered at him with fury eyes. "I don't like being called a bimbo, especially by a couple of over-dressed baboons."

"Oh, a bimbo with spunk. Well, we'll fix that." The blue serge reached out and grabbed her by the throat with both hands. If he thought he was going to throttle her like a newborn kitten, he quickly discovered to his dismay that he had dared to tangle with an angry full-grown tiger.

In one fluid motion Sarah clapped her palms together and thrust her arms upward like a rocket launched from its pad, rising between her assailant's arms and breaking his grip with ease. She curled her fingers at the apex of her reach, then chopped downward with all her might and broke both clavicles with a single loud crunch, making a sharp sound like that of a dry twig snapping. Immediately she drove her left knee into his groin. The force of the kick knocked him backward at the same time he doubled up in pain. She finished him off with an open-handed slap to the left side of the head, which ruptured his eardrum and slammed him sideways behind his companion.

The gray pinstripe opened his mouth in disbelieving shock. His eyes went as round as saucers. Then he reached inside his jacket and yanked a revolver out of its shoulder holster.

Sarah took one step toward him, planted her left foot on the floor, twisted, and kicked upward with her right. The outside of her heel caught his wrist just as it was pulling past his lapel. His fist flew up like a steam-driven lever, and the barrel of the gun smashed hard against his chin, breaking his jaw at the same time that the gun discharged and sent a wild shot into the ornate plaster ceiling dome. As Sarah brought back her upraised leg, she tucked and executed a perfect pirouette, spinning counterclockwise halfway around, then slammed the back of her left elbow against the man's left temple. He dropped to the floor like a sack of wet cement.

The entire action took place in less than half a dozen seconds.

Sarah spun sharply on her toes and stopped in midstride like a still-framed whirlwind, facing the only opponent left standing. She crouched into a two-fisted self-defense posture, one foot leading the other, and with one arm extended and the other tucked tight against her rib cage. The giant never moved, he just continued to block the doorway with his tremendous bulk and his outstretched, gorilla-like arms: cold defiance weighing in at more than double Sarah's measure. The David-and-Goliath standoff lasted for no longer than a second. Then the giant took a short step forward, stiff-legged, like a weight lifter whose bunched thigh muscles were so massive that they hindered coordination.

The giant had taken only two steps toward Sarah when she plunged her hand into her purse. Instantly, a long red flame burst through the tooled black leather, accompanied by an explosion which reverberated off the walls of the entry like a broadside from an attacking frigate. The bullet slammed into the giant's broad chest a little high and to the left, checking his forward momentum and spinning him backward with the force of the impact imparted by the high-speed projectile.

Sarah pulled the forty-four Magnum out of her purse, crouched on one knee, aimed, and fired past the stunned giant at the men who were unlimbering guns as they dashed up the red brick steps. One man howled in pain and fell to the ground rolling. The others could not fire at Sarah because the giant was gyrating in their line of sight while trying to maintain his balance, oblivious to the possibility of crossfire.

As hot lead poured out of the entry, men ducked behind cars and scrambled for cover in the bushes or behind the low parapet encircling the front yard. It took but a moment after Sarah emptied her gun for her to pull another clip from a compartment in her purse and to slam it into the bottom of the Magnum's plastic-gripped handle. She cocked and fired, letting the rabble know that she was still armed and dangerous, then scrabbled sideways for cover. The giant was performing a macabre dance that would have been amusing under different circumstances. Sarah placed the barrel of her gun against his lower abdomen and casually pulled the trigger in passing. He staggered across the entry and crashed against the mahogany door he had only recently burst apart.

Shooting in order to gain fire superiority, Sarah reached the protection of the wall just as a hail of incoming bullets spanged off the exterior brick facade and whooshed through the doorway into the base of the stairs. The flowerless vase was shattered and the loveseat was shot full of holes. She flipped down the switches and plunged the entry into semidarkness, then fired around the corner and sprayed bullets through the windows of her own car, winging a man who was crouched on the other side and who must have thought that bullets could not penetrate glass and cheap paneling.

She reloaded again as the giant, whose sightless gaze was fixated into space, slid down to the floor like a sagging cartoon character. "Grant! Get the hell off the stairs!"

Grant was mesmerized by the spectacle unfolding before him, as if he had suddenly been thrust against the screen of a three-dimensional movie which did not require trick glasses to observe. But bullets thudding against plaster directly beneath him, and Sarah's stentorian cry of warning, galvanized him to action, and fear lent wings to his feet. He skipped down the steps taking two at a time and dived headlong into the living room, thinking as he did in his gallows humorous way that it might well prove to be his dying room.

"Kill the lights!"

He did not need to be told twice. He reached over his head and pulled down the switches, but felt no safer under the cloak of darkness.

Sarah slammed one of the front doors shut, and pulled out Grant's key ring in the process. Automatic weapons fire quickly reduced the center panel to kindling. "Stay put, Grant. I'll get to you." Separated as they were by the opened double door, against which the dead giant had finally come to rest, there was no way she could cross the intervening space without being scythed by lead like a stalk of wheat. As if to impress the point upon her, the hinges were shot to pieces and the door fell inward, bouncing hard enough to knock the brass heart from its place and send it rolling and clanking across the polished floor. She fired a stay-put shot at a momentarily exposed head, reloaded from her handbag armory, then carefully aimed at the rear quarter panel of the Continental, whose trunk extended beyond the body of her rental car. She knew that her shots had been effective in their purpose by the temporary lull in the shooting, and by the frantic shouts of impending disaster.

She waited for the gasoline to pool beneath the spurting holes, then winged a couple of shots into the metal and across the macadam. One of them ignited a spark which instantly turned the driveway into a sea of flames. Bodies scuttled off like fear-crazed rats, enabling Sarah to pick off one who got in her sights just before the gas tank exploded.

The rear of the Continental was blasted a good ten feet in the air, and for a moment the car hung with its trunk held high like a Stuka in a nose dive. Then the chassis slammed down against the driveway as the tires were either melted by the heat or blown out by the blast. The Continental became a raging inferno which transmitted its condition to the rental car.

After firing a parting shot, Sarah ducked into the dining room, doused the lights, and charged through the short connecting hall into the kitchen, where already someone was breaking in the glass of the back door. She fired two shots through the right upper pane at point blank range. The explosion of the forty-four Magnum and the slight tinkle of shattering glass were practically simultaneous. The thud of a body hitting the porch deck was delayed by a second. She switched off the lights, too.

Sarah entered the darkened living room from the rear and dragged a nearly insensible Grant to his feet. "Are you okay?" When he responded with only a glassy stare, she shook him by the shoulders. "Are you hurt?"

"N-n-n-n-no. I'm fine." And after a pause, "I think."

"Come out of it, Grant. They've got the place surrounded and we have to get out of here."

In the diffused light provided by the blazing vehicles, the three bodies in the entry presented a nightmare pageant where only minutes before had been a picture of residential tranquility. The giant, slow in life and even slower to die, had finally fallen over onto his side, bloodless as if he had merely gone to sleep on the job. Contrasting sharply with this image of serenity were the blue serge, whose head was encircled by a pool of blood still seeping from his ear, and the gray pinstripe, whose blood-frothed mouth gaped above sightless eyes.

"Come on." Sarah grabbed his arm and dragged him across the living room toward the rear of the house.

The back door burst in and an Uzi was stuck into the kitchen. It sprayed enough lead to poison a small lake. Sarah ducked behind the wall, fired off a shot, then reloaded.

"Who are these people?" Grant whined. "What do they want?"

"I was hoping you could tell me."

He shook his head with a mixture of dejection and disbelief. "I don't know. I don't know what's going on."

Sarah fired a round into the kitchen just to let them know that she was not out of ammunition and had plenty of fight left in her. "They must want you pretty bad to suffer these kinds of losses." She kicked her high-heel hard against the floor, knocking off the spike so that it clung to her shoe by a false rubber sole. She grabbed the dangling spike and yanked off the false sole over the toe, leaving a liner which was an athletic shoe. Then she did the same with the other shoe. She deposited the false heels in her purse. "And it's not over yet."

She picked up a stuffed easy chair, ran with it a few paces, and hurled it through the side window. Glass and wood flew out across the lawn. She poked out her head to see if the coast was clear. "Let's go." She made sure Grant was behind her before she jumped up onto the window ledge and leaped out onto the grass. "Come on! Hurry!"

Shuffling noises in the adjacent rooms did more to urge him along than Sarah's hushed importunities. As he rested the sleeves of his jacket against the splintered sides of the casement, it occurred to him that this was the second time in less than twenty-four hours that he had escaped trouble through a broken window. He hoped that it was not becoming a pattern.

Sarah pulled the chair away from the landing zone, and held out her arms to catch him when he landed. After helping to break his fall, she again took hold of his arm and dragged him toward the back yard as if he were a naughty child. Their pursuers appeared to have gone into the house at the same time that she and Grant had vacated the premises. For the moment, at least, no one was in sight outside, and the kitchen door beckoned darkly.

Sarah still had the silver key ring in hand. She deftly slid the proper key into the walk-in door of the garage, entered with Grant in tow, and eased the door closed behind them. "Get in the car," she whispered, as she stalked across the concrete pad and locked the latch on the door to the house.

Grant was disarranged enough to be sluggish to respond. He reacted like an automaton, taking Sarah's orders only because he did not know what else to do that might save his life from the wanton destruction being meted out by the strangers invading his new-found home. He groped around the front of the car and fumbled for the recessed handle in the dark. He could not find it at first, and when he did, he found that it was locked. Sarah unlocked the driver's door with the key. The dome light winked on when she climbed inside. She hit the electric door-lock button and let Grant in. She stuck another key in the ignition but did not crank over the engine.

"Fasten your seatbelt," she said through tight-set teeth, following her own advice. She pressed the button on one of the two control boxes which were clipped to the visor above her black curly tresses. When nothing happened, she pressed the button on the other plastic box. An electronic signal activated the automatic door opener at the same time she started the engine. The Porsche roared to life immediately. She gunned the engine while the garage door was sliding up on its rails, dropped the clutch suddenly, and, with a high-pitched whine and a squeal of protesting rubber, shot out of the bay like a race car from the starting gate.

Grant ducked instinctively when he thought they were going to hit the bottom lip of the door, but the low roof cleared it by millimeters. As soon as the front tires hit the apron Sarah spun the steering wheel and threw the car into a controlled skid. The Porsche turned in a tight arc around the concrete pad with all four tires sideslipping. Grant braced himself by stiff-arming the dashboard and the driver's seat.

Sarah had not yet turned on the headlights. The Porsche rounded the corner of the house like a darkened blue streak, and charged along the side driveway with gathering speed. Just before reaching the circular drive at the front of the house, the Continental which had not gone up in flames backed across the turn-off and blocked the exit. Sarah slammed on the brakes. Before the car had come to a stop she threw the gearshift lever into reverse and floored the accelerator pedal. The strain on the transmission was awful as the chassis continued to move forward at the same time the wheels were spinning in reverse. A dense black cloud surrounded the Porsche, and the air was thick with the odor of burning rubber and overheated oil and transmission fluid.

The car changed direction so slowly that a gunman was able to overtake it and run alongside while pointing his pistol threateningly at the window next to Grant's head. He checked his fire, however, and shouted instead for them to halt.

Sarah chose to disobey the directive. She jerked the steering wheel and threw the front of the car to the right. The fender caught the man at the knees and knocked his legs out from under him. His upper body fell across the hood, the gun discharged harmlessly, then, as the car swung back the other way, he slid off the finely waxed finish and struck the ground with such force that the sickening thud of his head hitting the macadam was audible above the whine of the engine and the scream of the tires.

The Porsche oscillated wildly as Sarah overcompensated with the steering wheel. Grant was slammed from side to side and hit his head on the roof as if he were strapped inside the cockpit of a jet plane which was plummeting to earth from the stratosphere. Sarah lost control of the car. She jammed on the brakes before they crashed into the house or against the stone retaining wall which kept vehicles from driving off the pavement and chewing up the lawn. The Porsche executed a one-eighty and wound up on the concrete pad and facing the back yard. The car was still rocking as Sarah slammed the gearshift lever into the forward position and dropped the clutch. A slug hit the rear fender down low, then the car was gouging grass and dirt and leaving a rooster tail of green lawn which had been churned to mulch.

"Where are you going?" Grant screamed.

"Away," was Sarah's succinct reply. She turned on the headlights.

Several shots rang out behind them but none hit the car. The burp of an Uzi was accompanied by a series of muzzle flashes behind them. Then the high beams of the Continental flooded the driveway and the luxury car raced after the Porsche in hot pursuit.

The Porsche's tires sliced a dual path through the nicely trimmed lawn, leaving dirty brown ruts which the most inexperienced tracker could not fail to follow. The car zipped between a pair of stately oaks, then curved around a stand of maples nearly shorn of leaves, which had accumulated on the ground and trapped moisture, creating a slick surface. The tires lost traction and the car fishtailed fiercely. Sarah reduced speed in order to regain control, but almost immediately she was spurred on by a fusillade of lead whose retorts were deadened by the forest like champagne corks popping at a New Year's festival.

"Time to pay a call on the neighbors." Sarah was a demon behind the wheel. She sideswiped a few bushes but by and large the trees were widely spaced and permitted easy passage. At a speed that would have made a strong man weak with fear, she carved an unerring trail to the back yard of the adjacent house. "Looks like a swimming pool."

With the Continental hot on their tail and firing guns at them out of the open windows, they could not afford to stop for a chat or to sip a mint julep. The Porsche surrendered to Sarah's will by sliding sideways around the high wooden fence which prevented them from actually seeing the pool it encompassed. The tires caught traction on the tennis court and, responding as only a Porsche can respond, the car turned in a short curve that brought it perilously close to the greenhouse wall and onto the concrete pad behind the two-story English Tudor. Dirt and dust flew everywhere and the tires squealed as they grabbed the pavement and torqued the car up the driveway.

The lumbering Continental did not possess the same measure of control as the low-slung sports car. It clipped the corner off the wooden fence and mowed down two of the posts, skidded through the tennis net and snapped off the top wire, splintering the windshield in the process, then entered the sidewall of the rectangular greenhouse and exited through the door with a crash of glass and flying flower pots and half a ton of topsoil, all accompanied by a cacophony that pierced the air like the baying hounds of Hell.

Sarah turned sharply at the end of Catamount Cove and headed for the entrance gate. The Continental, having taken a more direct route through the neighbor's back yard, had not lost much ground and was fairly close behind. Sarah worked the gearshift lever with speed and precision, and her feet coordinated perfectly with the clutch and accelerator pedal.

"Uh, oh."

Grant merely gulped.

The van which they had left at the house was now parked outside the entrance gate. Three men wearing crisp business suits and brandishing automatic weapons were splayed out in a row on the estate side of the fence. All three aimed their guns directly at the windshield as the Porsche slowed and Sarah deliberated . . .

. . . for about half a second. She did several things in such close sequence that everything seemed to happen at once. She hit the actuating button on the control box clipped to the visor, she powered down the driver's side window, she threw the transmission into a lower gear, and she stuck her forty-four Magnum out the window and fired at the men blocking their way. She did not hit anyone, but two of the men dived for cover in a shrub while the third leaped the fence and ran for the van.

The gate began to swing open ever so slowly. Sarah saved ammunition by taking spaced-out potshots which kept down enemy heads. The Porsche continued to accelerate and drift off course—she was steering with her knees—but she soon brought it back on line. When they reached the entranceway the gate was only partway open. Sarah jammed on the brake then immediately hit the gas, the interruption being just long enough for the space to widen and let the car through the opening. The right side of the car grated against the moving metal post with a crunch and a screech. Sarah pulled the steering wheel and managed to miss the row of mailboxes but not the center post of the canopy.

The wooden post snapped in two and smashed the left headlight. The canopy collapsed onto the top of the mailboxes, where it came to rest on a slant. The car spun off the road and threatened to roll over as it skidded across the stone shoulder then bounded through a patch of briars, but the low center of gravity saved it from toppling. It did two three-sixties before coming to a halt at the edge of the forest.

Sarah twisted in her seat in order to get her bearings, took in the situation at a glance, and hit the button on the control box. The gate motor was undamaged; it reversed direction and dragged the gate closed on a wobbly wheel. Grant was in shock at the speed of events, and had a grand view through the windshield of subsequent actions.

When the Continental reached the entrance there was not enough room to pass. The driver tried to avoid the closing post by veering to the left. The post hit the right fender at the same time the left fender smashed through the corner of the mailbox structure, which was supported by a steel girder sunk into a buried cement block. The girder ripped through the left axle as if it were made of paper. The rear quarter of the Continental crashed through the mailboxes, which then disintegrated into their component parts. The top-heavy luxury car flipped over and over and over, careening through the briars and spitting metal parts like wood chips shooting out of a tree limb grinder. When the Continental came to rest practically on the hood of the Porsche, there was very little left of it that looked like a car.

The Porsche's engine purred smoothly, as if car chases and crashes were common occurrences. It helped that Sarah had kept the clutch depressed throughout the protracted rotation. Without waiting for Grant to regain his wits, she threw the transmission into first gear and drove the car back onto the road, blind on the left side but with the right headlight describing an arc through the trees.

Already the van was on the move and accelerating rapidly. The two gunmen who had dived for the bushes ignored the possible fate of their companions in the battered Continental, and jumped through the open side door of the van as it pulled past the collapsed canopy. No sooner were they aboard than flashes of light erupted from the passenger side window.

Bullets ricocheted off the cold macadam and darted past the Porsche like a horde of angry bees routing a despoiler of the hive. Sarah slammed through the gears and kept her foot hard on the gas pedal; the car leaped forward with pent-up power and torque.

At first the van closed the distance, but as the Porsche hit high gear with its engine screaming, it quickly pulled away.

"Watch out for that hairpin curve!" Grant's knuckles were white as he pressed his hands hard against the foam-padded dashboard.

"I can't slow down or they'll pick us to pieces."

"But you'll never make the turn at this speed."

"You don't know Porsches like I do." Sarah's voice was firm but she spoke without strain. "You ever drive this thing over fifty?"

Grant made no reply. The blood drained from his face until he was the color of an unripe honeydew melon. He kept his eyes straight ahead.

One bullet plunked into the back of the car, and several more skipped past at the level of the road. The Porsche was going ninety miles per hour and still accelerating, and the van was doing its best to keep up. Another bullet bounced off the macadam and thudded against the undercarriage.

Sarah was defiant. "They'll get us for sure."

She swerved into the opposing traffic lane and, just before the Porsche reached the outside of the curve, she took her foot off the accelerator, dropped to a lower gear, and let the transmission torque do its job. Although she did not touch the break, the car bucked so hard that they were both thrown forward against the seat restraints. She turned the steering wheel ever so slightly. The Porsche responded like the fine-tuned machine that it was, and hugged the road like it was part of the pavement, maintaining an almost even keel.

The car cut across the inner arc of the curve going at least seventy. Which was about five miles per hour too fast for that particular angle of bend. The left tires went off the smooth paved surface and chattered along the rough cut stone of the shoulder, and the car still might have been saved had it not been for the uneven slag that left gaps in the poured tar, causing the tires to bounce and the car to jog further down the slight embankment. As Sarah tightened the wheel, the car began to slew sideways and go out of control. The only way she could save it was by straightening the wheel. She did, and the Porsche veered across the sandy soy field plowing furrows where none had been before.

The top-heavy van could not even begin to negotiate the curve, and from the way it shot off the road it appeared that the driver either did not anticipate the turn or did not remember until too late that it was there. It continued going straight until its speed was reduced to a maneuverable rate, then it turned in a wide arc that eventually brought it around onto the Porsche's starlit path.

Sarah angled the car across the field to where it intercepted the farm trail that ran perpendicular to the road. Again she miscalculated the Porsche's speed and turning radius. The car went up the sloped shoulder with so much forward momentum that it flew completely over the ruts and went straight off the other side, taking down a metal fence post that blew out the remaining sealed beam, and tearing through several tiers of barbed wire.

The van was right on their tail. Without the tight suspension of a Porsche, it romped across the soybean field like an unbroken colt, making gunplay useless, and followed them in the air across the road.

The Porsche hit a bale of hay which exploded upon contact, spewing fodder across the windshield and engulfing the car momentarily. No sooner did the visibility clear than the car rammed the corner of another bale, knocking it aside and breaking it open in the process. More dark shapes appeared ahead, dimly seen in the starlight without the advantage of headlamps.

"I know this place!" Grant screamed, at the top of his lungs. "Those are cows! Those are sleeping cows!"

Sarah spun the wheel sharply and narrowly averted disaster. The Porsche sped past the edge of the herd, taking the hair off more than one hide. The wind of passage brought the cattle to their feet, startled. There was no opportunity for the van to turn; it smashed into a rising cow broadside, performed a complete forward roll, and landed on its roof amid meat and moo. The Porsche bowled through another barbed wire fence and streaked toward a huge silhouette that loomed suddenly in front of the car. Sarah stood on the brake. The tires screeched in protest as the front end smashed through the side of a wooden barn. When the car rocked to a halt it was more than halfway inside.

Silence.

Mooing.

Loose boards falling.

Sarah inhaled, exhaled, then inhaled again. "Whew." She looked at Grant. It was so dark inside the barn that she could not even see the whites of his eyes. "Honey, are you okay?"

Grant sat like a stone. After a long time, he swallowed. His jaw worked and a scratchy sound emerged, but it was unintelligible.

"Same here." The engine purred like a kitten, so Sarah moved the gearshift lever into neutral and released the clutch, then engaged the hand brake. "Don't go away. I'll be right back."

Grant was incapable of movement.

The door would not open so Sarah was forced to climb out through the window. By feel she found the inner latch on the barn door and flung it wide open, shedding a little light onto the scratched and battered Porsche. The car was wrapped in barbed wire tighter than a Christmas package. "Whew."

With the forty-four Magnum once again in her hand, Sarah trotted back to the pasture to see if there were any survivors from the crash. Only cows. The van was crushed down like a closed accordion, making it impossible for her to get inside and recover any weapons for which the occupants had no further use. She was going to have to get by with her trusty Magnum and her dwindling supply of ammunition.

Grant was still in a daze when she returned to the

Porsche. She tried to get him to help her extricate the vehicle from its snare, but he could barely comprehend that she was addressing him. It was up to her to pull off the wire strands and kick out the loose planks that wedged the car against the splintered sides of the wall. In some places the barbed wire had been pulled so taut that it had gouged deep grooves in the metal paneling. She had to rend and yank it loose bit by bit, and not until she had cleared the mess of every last vestige of sharp metal did she open the car door, climb in, wipe the blood off her hands, and back out of the barn.

"I think my place is safer."

Chapter 13

Patrolman Riley eased his Toyota past the Biotech building in the dark. The parking lot was empty, the lights were out, and no telltale signs of smoke escaped from either chimney. The complex appeared to be damped down for the weekend, as was usual for businesses whose hours of operation were regulated by time-clock procedures. But Grant had said that Biotech worked on flextime, and had been quite proud of the fact. That made it odd that the building should be unoccupied by at least a night watchman. He decided to investigate.

He parked by the curb, then walked around the corner to the side of the building that faced the parking lot, where the front entrance was located. Twenty feet from the glass and aluminum facing of the lobby, an infrared proximity sensor tripped an electrical contactor which switched on the external floodlights. This was usually enough to scare off the most insistent burglar, especially when two video cameras were recording his every movement.

Riley approached the entrance with flashlight in hand. He tried the handle and found the door locked. Peering through the glass panels, with the flashlight held off to one side in order to reduce the glare, he shone the steady beam into every corner of the lobby. He banged on the glass for a good five minutes before a door opened in the back and the interior fluorescent lights flickered into full brilliance.

The woman was not wearing a guard's uniform, but instead wore a white lab smock over a beige blouse and skirt. Her feet were shod in sneakers. She took a large key ring from smock pocket, stuck one of the keys into the heavy-duty lock, twisted, and pulled the door about twelve inches from the frame. She stuck her head into the crack. Her round face and round eyes reminded Riley of a poorly made rag doll with hair of straw.

She did not invite him in. "Can I help you, officer?"

Riley did not smile, but he allowed his features to lighten. "I'm looking for Dr. Grant Templeton."

Eyebrows arched instantly. It was a full five seconds before she responded. "Dr. Templeton is unavailable at the moment."

"If you will tell him that Patrolman Frank Riley is here, I'm sure he'll make himself available." Then he added, "I can wait if he's in the middle of something."

Another hesitation. "Well, he, uh, he usually doesn't come in on weekends, you know."

"I understand." He contemplated for a moment. "Are you saying that he's not here?"

A pause. "I haven't seen him."

She was definitely evading his questions with indirect answers. "Where can I reach him at this hour?"

A long hesitation. "Well, I really don't know."

More direct, police interrogation style: "When was the last time you saw him, Ms.—?"

She did not offer to give her name. "I really don't know anything about his present whereabouts."

Riley pocketed the flashlight and pulled out a pen and a leather-bound notepad. He flipped to an empty page. "What is your name, ma'am?"

The woman eyed him warily. "Look, officer, there's really nothing wrong here. What is it you want?"

"I want to see Dr. Grant Templeton."

"I've already told you he isn't here. Now what more do you want? I can't help you, really."

Riley became very precise with his enunciation. "You did not say that Dr. Templeton was not here. You said that he was unavailable at the moment and that you had not seen him."

"Well, then, he's not here. Okay? Now, if you don't mind, I'm very busy."

The woman backed away and started to close the door. Riley stopped her in her tracks by squinting his eyes and sharpening the focus of his stare—a simple, nonaggressive, yet usually effective performance which often achieved results far in excess of the amount of effort put into it. The voice of authority spoke by means of silent communication. She backed down under his facial assault, but continued to block the doorway protectively.

Riley put pen to pad. "What is your name, please?"

She rolled her eyes and let out double cheeks full of air. "Dr. Nora Constantinescu."

"In what capacity do you work here, Doctor?"

Pouting, "I'm a cybernetician, if that means anything to you."

Ways for dealing with recalcitrant witnesses were a routine part of police training. Riley did not take the woman's hostility personally. Maintaining control of his emotions, he kept his voice smooth and even, almost machinelike, and was careful not to make inflections which could cause offense or which could be misinterpreted as accusatory.

"When was the last time you saw Dr. Templeton?"

"Really, now, what's the purpose of all this?"

He repeated the question without insistence.

"I don't know. A couple of days ago, I guess."

"That would be Thursday?"

"I guess so. Perhaps it was Friday."

Riley made a notation on his pad. "At what time of the day did you last see him?"

"I don't know," she whined. "Late afternoon, I guess. Maybe early evening."

"Where did you see him?"

"Here, in his office. In the lab."

Riley scribbled down her answers. "Have you spoken with him since? On the telephone, perhaps?"

"No."

"Has anyone you know spoken with him since?"

"Since when? Thursday?"

"Yes, ma'am."

She sighed. "I really don't know. I'm not in the habit of keeping tabs on people."

"I understand. Is anyone else on the premises at this time? Anyone who might have seen or spoken with Dr. Templeton more recently?"

Dr. Constantinescu hesitated. "There are a few people downstairs, but we really can't be disturbed at this time. Look, what's the point of all this. Why are the police interested?"

"Do you work with Dr. Templeton?"

"Of course. I said that."

She had not said anything of the kind, although it could very easily be inferred. "How long have you worked with Dr. Templeton?"

"A couple of years. Maybe three or four." An uncertain spread.

"Has anyone mentioned any concerns about him?"

She humphed. "He's a big boy. He can take care of himself."

Riley had intended to let someone at Biotech know about Grant's "accident." He had not been able to contact any of the people on Grant's list, repeated calls to his home went unanswered, as did calls to Biotech, so making the rounds before going on duty seemed like the only thing left to do. But Dr. Nora Constantinescu, who admitted to working with Grant Templeton and to having known him for several years, showed no regard for his well-being. She had not even asked if he were hurt, which was the first thought that came to mind when the police inquired about citizens who were non-suspicious characters. Instead, in a crass and callous manner, this woman acted as if she were under interrogation, as if she were being asked to inform on someone to whom police involvement suggested trouble with the law.

"Thank you for your cooperation." He closed his notepad and shoved it into his pocket, along with the pen. He tilted his head once. "Sorry to have troubled you, ma'am."

He executed an about face and walked away. He heard the door slam behind him, and the key twist in the lock, but he did not turn around to see what the woman did afterward. Back in the car, he sat for a few minutes and made a mental list of oddities. There were people in the building but no cars in the lot. The people were at work, but without showing lights. Downstairs probably meant basement facilities. Nora Constantinescu knew Grant Templeton, but gave no indication that she thought he was missing or was in any kind of trouble. Her lack of direct replies to his queries implied that she was hiding something; or she could have been just another eccentric scientist who viewed his intrusion as an unpardonable interruption of ongoing experiments. Riley did not jump to any conclusions.

The floodlight switch timed out and the Biotech building was again plunged into darkness. Riley started the car, made a U-turn, and headed toward Feline Estates. He still had a couple of hours to himself before he had to report for duty, and he was eager to get to the station early in order to read any reports on Templeton that may have come in during the afternoon, but he also wanted to know if Sarah Mason had taken Templeton home as she had promised.

Deep in thought, he was speeding along the country road to the Estates when a black silhouette appeared suddenly in the beam of his lights, as if a vehicle without headlamps had stopped in the middle of the road. He jammed on the brakes and jerked the steering wheel. The car skidded straight, but a split second before a collision occurred, Riley took his foot off the pedal. The car veered sharply to the right and barely avoided the crash. He spun the steering wheel back immediately but did not prevent the car from careening off the road. The tires spewed dirt and rocks when they hit the unpaved shoulder. Riley stomped on the gas. For a moment the acceleration drove the car farther off the road, but just before it slid into the ditch, the tires gained traction and pulled the car up onto the pavement at a sharp angle. He hit the brakes again. The car skidded sideways out of control, then halted broadside to the road. The heat that ran along his spine threatened to incinerate him, and his arms and legs were shaking.

He cursed himself for hotrodding like some crazy

college kid, for not being more attentive. He would hate to have to explain to the captain how he had wrecked his car in a ditch, even if the county did not own the car.

The object he had nearly hit was now on the move. Fear instantly changed to anger. Riley was going to give hell to whoever had left his car in the road without leaving on the hazard lights. And he was going to give him a ticket, too; maybe even take him in to the station. He backed up a couple of feet until he felt the rear end crunch onto the shoulder, then turned the steering wheel and drove forward until the car was facing the way it had come.

He felt pretty silly when he saw the Black Angus strolling along the middle of the road.

He stopped a couple feet from the swishing tail and stepped out into the nighttime air. He heard mooing on both sides, and when he pointed his flashlight into the fields he saw scattered black dots ambling along in the same direction. Headlights topped the rise behind him. Riley stood by the open door until the pickup truck came to a halt along side, then he walked around to the driver's door.

The rancher rolled down his window and stuck out his head, careful not to knock off the big brown Stetson. "Howdy, officer. You watchin' out fer traffic while we round up the herd?"

Riley did not recognize the man. "No. I just happened to be driving by and almost hit that cow down the road." He pointed with his thumb.

The rancher peered ahead. "That there's a steer, not a cow. But it'd bust up yer car just the same. 'Specially a little compack like that." He redirected his gaze at Riley. "I got flares in the back, and the sergeant, he said to stick 'em down by the highway. Less'n you already planted some."

"Has this already been reported?"

"Reported!" The rancher spat on the macadam to accentuate his dander. "Hell, dern near ever' cop in the county is over there at the 'States. Few loose cattle's the least o' yer worries. Got a whole slew o' accidents an' none of 'em to blame on teenage rowdies. A van went through ma fence an' made meatloaf outa two prime studs, now the rest o' ma beef is on the hoof. Passengers was killed. Another vee-hickle tore a hole through ma barn an' got clean away. Then up at the gate to the 'States a brand new Lincoln drove through the fence an' overturned. All dead. An', at one o' them fancy new mansions, from what I hear tell, another car blew up and killed a coupla folks. Gas tank er something."

Riley was too shocked to respond. The rancher's succinct account sounded like an interstate pile up, or a year's worth of accidents for a quiet community like Highland Hills.

"Anyhow, ya better git up there an' lend a hand officiatin'. I got cattle to round up. Ma boys'll be here pronto with ropes and hobbles. An' I'll take care o' the flares at the highway. Don' wanna be supplyin' steak ta all the fokes in the neighborhood." He drove off slowly, flashing his lights at the steer on the road and bumping his rump until he walked off into the field.

Riley jumped into his car. It took three back-ups to make a U-turn, then he charged like a lion toward Feline Estates. "What am I doing?" he said aloud, when he realized how fast he was going. He slowed down to thirty miles per hour, switched on his high beams, and kept an ever-watchful eye on the roadway ahead.

A wrecker was working on the overturned Continental outside the gateway to the Estates, and three squad cars, a fire truck, and two ambulances were parked on the pavement nearby, all with strobes and emergency lights flashing. At least a dozen people were milling on the grass: police, fire fighters, and emergency medical technicians. Riley decelerated and crept along slowly, looking also at the damage to the canopy and the fence.

A uniformed officer strode out from the crowd and waved him off with a flashlight. "Hold it right there, mister. Hold it right there. We got enough trouble without reporters and rubberneckers coming around."

Riley stopped and got out of the car. "Sarge?" He had never seen the portly Sergeant Benson do anything other than monitor the dispatch station. "What are you doing here?"

Recognition flashed in the sergeant's eyes. "Oh, it's you, Frank."

"What's going on?"

"I told you to put a radio in that thing. George's been calling you for the past half hour. There's hell to pay at the Templeton place. Crashed cars and bodies everywhere like it was a demolition derby. Every available man's on the job, and they pulled in volunteers to run the station house. You go right on through. See the opening in the fence over there?" He pointed to where the posts had been knocked down and the planks were gone. "That's where the fire truck went through when they couldn't get through the canopy wreckage. 'Bout half a mile down, second drive on the right. Place is lit up like a Christmas tree. You can't miss it."

A couple of minutes later, Riley turned down the driveway marked Panther Cove. There was such a long line of vehicles that he was forced to park at the fork of the circle. He jogged the rest of the way, stunned by the extent of the carnage. Fire fighters were chasing down small gasoline blazes with hand-held extinguishers. Two cars were burned out cinders but were still spurning clouds of thick, black smoke into the air. The grass was singed, the shrubbery was practically consumed. The front of the house was still spouting fire wherever there was wood: the door, the trim, the shutters, and especially the towering columns, which were now blackened and smoldering. The red brick was scorched with soot.

Two horribly burned bodies lay ignored on the driveway, their limbs contorted into gravity-defying positions. Neither one had a face nor any skin remaining; they were dried husks which were charred beyond recognition. The smell was nauseating: a noxious blend of burnt rubber, plastic, and flesh. Frank felt as if he were part of a scene in a war documentary. It was all he could do to keep from vomiting.

There was surprisingly little activity considering the tragedy of events. Other than a few fire fighters pulling hoses from the trucks and directing streams of water at existing spot fires, most of the people were standing in small groups, talking and gesticulating. By this time it was mostly a clean-up operation.

" . . . don't care how much money they got, there's an ordnance against having a locked gate that official vehicles can't get through. I'm going straight to the mayor with this, and the inspector who issued the building permit is gonna hang from the tallest . . . "

Riley recognized the fire marshal as he walked past the group of fire fighters in their back-brim hats, long black cloaks, and rubber boots. The police appeared to be conducting their dialogue in the lighted entry, and as soon as Riley ascended the water-soaked steps he spotted Captain George Hendry holding a heated discussion inside. Riley stayed on the fringe of the clot of policemen and -women, and exchanged nods with his companions as he examined the three bodies which lay sprawled grotesquely on the floor. He was relieved to find that Grant Templeton was not among the recognizable dead.

Captain Hendry noticed Riley's presence, but nearly five minutes passed before he finished giving orders and assigning tasks, and he could break away for a private consultation. Then he dragged Riley into the living room where the smashed window offered some fresh air to alleviate the stench of death. "I guess I don't need to tell you we got a major a problem here."

Riley got right down to business. "Is either one of those two bodies out front Dr. Templeton's?"

"No. Both too tall and too thin. And neither is the one around the side of the house or the one on the back deck. They still got faces."

"My god, how many bodies are there?"

"A baker's dozen counting the ones in the car by the gate and the van in the pasture. Templeton was here all right. We found his jacket in the bedroom. Got a voice recorder in the pocket with a lot of nonsense on it. Frank, I don't mind telling you—I'm scared. We all are. We're way out of our league here. This is no smalltime heist or simple break-and-entry. These people are military professionals. Uzis, bombs, high-power assault rifles, and enough ammo to take on a small garrison."

Riley shivered with a chill at the captain's pronouncement. "If the dead ones are professionals, does that mean there's an army in town that wiped them out?"

"That's what's got me worried. Hell, the dead ain't gonna hurt nobody no more." The strain which Captain Hendry was under was evidenced by his language deficits. "But the outfit that did this . . . I'm concerned for the men. And the women. We ain't trained to deal with the kind of folks that would blow you away at the blink of an eye. Hell, I can't even remember the last time I pulled my gun out of my holster except to clean it."

"Have you called for backup?"

"Hell, yes. I got everybody and his grandmother strapping on iron. Keller's taking a squad of troopers off highway patrol to cover home base so's the State forensic team can make sense out of this mess. The counties are pulling a couple of men off each of the districts to handle local enforcement so our people can be mobile. Lending us some squad cars, too. And I called the governor in on this one. He's thinking about mobilizing the National Guard. Asked me if I wouldn't mind cooperating with them. Hell, I told him, I'm looking for people to cooperate with. That's me: Mr. Cooperation."

Hendry's fear was infectious. Riley felt raw emotion emanating from his boss like heat from an oven. "Have you alerted the feds?"

"First thing. Even before the governor. That's what I wanted to talk to you about."

'In the next room an officer was drawing chalk lines around the three bodies. The photographer had arrived, and he was taking pictures with a flash camera from every possible angle. A woman in uniform was counting the bullet holes in the wall beneath the stairs and digging out samples of lead. Another woman was dusting the switch plates for fingerprints.

Hendry's voice dropped to a raspy whisper. "It looks like you were right to let the feds know about Templeton. He's got something going that's so hush-hush even the FBI don't know what it is, only that the Defense Department issued an all-points bulletin for his apprehension as soon as they heard the story. Not that he's done anything wrong, you understand—at least, nothing the feds are admitting to—but they want him brought in for his own protection. Told me to find him at all costs and guard him with my life. Now where have you ever heard that before except in the movies?"

Riley's comment was interrupted by Richard Anderson, a tall patrolman in his mid twenties. "Hi, Frank. Got you out of bed, too, I see." Turning to the captain, "George, you were right about the car. Even though the paint was blistered off and the plate was buckled, I could feel the bumps good enough to make out the numbers. It belongs to the Aviary Rental Company here in town. They're closed now, so we can't find out who they rented it to till Monday morning."

"You're wrong there, Richy. You call one of their airport offices and find out who the local manager is, then go rustle him out of the sack. You tell him this is a criminal investigation."

"Yeah, you're right. They'll be open twenty-four hours. Okay, I'm on it." He made a pistol out of his hand, cocked it at the captain, and left.

Hendry confided to Riley, "There's no doubt in my mind it's the Mason woman's car, but I want to have proof for the feds when they get here."

"Is the FBI dispatching a field agent?"

"No, they're dispatching an office. A jumbo jet filled with agents and electronics. Be here first thing in the morning. I'm telling you, Frank, whatever we got ourselves into is real big time. National Security, and all that."

"Did they say so?"

"Hell, no. Wouldn't admit nothing to me. I got no 'need to know.' But put two and two together. Templeton's got a top security clearance. He's the head of a big—maybe the biggest—robotics company in the country. Biotech has defense contracts with the government in addition to the work they do for NASA. And the feds want Templeton so bad they're chartering the Air Force to come get him. To say nothing of the fact that his house has been declared a war zone by unknown elements and we got a morgue full of bodies with no identification. Now that don't add up to no penny ante stock scandal or cost overrun swindle. You fight that kinda stuff with congressional rhetoric, not machine guns."

Riley nodded. "What's the media situation?"

"Too soon to tell. They started calling in as soon as they picked up the radio broadcasts. Bob's gonna keep them from getting past the gate—"

"Yes, he stopped me at first because I was in my own car."

"Good. We're not letting them know anything about Templeton or the action here. We've already sworn the neighbors to secrecy and threatened to put them in jail if they squeak a word. Next door called us in when they heard gunshots and an explosion and someone drove a car through their greenhouse. Called the fire department, too, when they saw flames through the trees."

"How do their names tally with the one's Templeton gave us?"

"Not even close. Nor any of the others or the physical layout." The captain shrugged his shoulders. "Anyhow, the cover story is some drag racers crashed the gates and lost control of their vehicles."

"In a Continental?"

"And the one in the pasture was a van. I know it's thin, but it's all we got for now. And we'll be lucky if the firemen don't blab it all over town anyhow, although Casey already read them the riot act if they do. Trouble is, the fire marshal has no authority over volunteers. Can't fire unpaid workers. But we'll go through the motions and hope for the best. Trouble is, once the reporters start counting bodies and ambulances, they're gonna put six and seven together and come up with more than a couple of overturned vehicles. But that's what the feds told me to do, so I'm doing it."

Riley nodded in a businesslike manner. "Now get this. I went out to the Dew Drop Inn, where the Mason woman said she was staying, and found that her room had been broken into and burglarized—that is, the place was trashed like a burglary had taken place. No one has seen her since yesterday. And you want to hear something else that's strange?"

Hendry blinked weary eyes. "Not really, but I have a feeling you're gonna tell me anyhow."

Riley filled him in on the scene which transpired at Biotech.

Hendry grunted. "Either she's a cold one, or she doesn't have any reason to suspect that Templeton's got problems."

The patrolman nodded. "I also picked up some biographical information on Templeton."

"You get any sleep today?"

"A couple of hours. I went to the library right from the station and scanned microfilm till I couldn't keep my eyes open. Then I went back just before they closed at nine and ran off some photocopies of a recent interview. I've got a set for you."

"Figured as much."

Riley pulled a folded packet of material from his back pocket and handed it to the captain. "I haven't read all of it yet, but you were right about him being low-keyed. He likes to avoid reporters and publicity, and more than one complained about how hard he is to pin down for an interview—even on the phone. He's accomplished quite a bit in the field of robotics. Not the mechanical end as much as designing systems for compacting data on microchips. But his big breakthrough is what they call a 'fluxion device,' which they also describe as a 'living memory chip.' They claim you can transfer the entire history and intelligence of a human being onto a 'moving matrix' that's smaller than the average brain."

"Sounds kooky. What's it mean?"

Riley shrugged. "I've only just managed to work out the access codes on the police computer. This stuff is way beyond me." The two men stared at each other thoughtfully. A coincidental lack of activity in the other room lent a preternatural silence to the air that made the hair on the back of Riley's neck stand on end. "But I have a feeling that we're going to find out. And soon."

Captain Hendry pursed his lips and let out a long breath of air. "Looks like it's gonna be a long night for everybody."

Riley nodded. "So what do you want me to do?"

"Get back to the station and work the computer."

Chapter 14

If he lived to be a hundred, Grant would never forget the time he was nearly killed in an interstate highway crash on the way to Chicago. He was the keynote speaker for a three-day conference on Artificial Intelligence, and Barbara opted to accompany him so she could visit her parents in the Windy City. It was a blustery day in March, with the temperature hovering around the freezing point and with precipitation falling from low-lying, dark gray clouds in a blinding blend of rain and snow. As they passed an exit sign which advertised the next available gas stations and restaurants, Barbara said she was hungry and would like to stop for lunch. Grant obligingly pulled into the right lane behind a long line of traffic and took his foot off the accelerator pedal.

Several hundred feet ahead, a green van caught a blast of air which was funneled through a break in the roadside forest. With the phenomenal speed at which highway events proceed, all three lanes became a snarling madhouse of braking, swerving, dodging vehicles. Patches of ice and pools of water aggravated the pandemonium, sending cars and trucks into skids and spinning them like colliding tops. More by luck than by skill, Grant wove a circuitous path through the caroming cars, avoided a jackknifing tractor-trailer, drove halfway off the shoulder and back across all three lanes of gyrating traffic, then screeched to a halt only inches away from a concrete bridge abutment. His heart was in this throat and beating wildly.

In the stillness that followed, Grant marveled at the ability of the human brain and nervous system to respond so swiftly and instinctively to potentially life-threatening stimuli. Then, after that moment of quiet revelation, he jumped out of his car and rushed toward the pile-up in order to render assistance. Miraculously, no one was killed or seriously injured. He treated a few people who had bumps and scratches, and one person complaining of a sprained wrist; no one required hospitalization. Several vehicles had to be towed away, but the damage that was done was not permanent and, to Grant's way of thinking, inconsequential. The losses could be put to right by the simple expenditure of money.

Not until he turned into the restaurant parking lot did he discover that his wife was completely immobilized and still trembling with fear. For Grant, once a situation of stress was over, his response to that stress ceased. Such was the case as Sarah Mason wheeled the battered Porsche past the motel's weathered and vine-covered sign.

Grant had not uttered a word since they had backed out of the barn. After the initial shock had worn off, his mind raced with possible explanations for the abrupt turn of events and the escalation of unknown dangers. "This isn't the Tuck Me Inn."

Sarah glanced at him gravely. "My face is known there. We can't go back."

Grant accepted her statement at face value. "Who are you? And what was that all about?"

She drove slowly to the far end of the Come On Inn, where the row of dilapidated single-story units yielded to a cluster of unkempt cabins which wallowed in a sea of paper litter and unraked leaves. "I could ask the same of you."

The Grant Templeton of this world must have known who those men were and what they wanted. *He* had no idea. "It seems as if we both have our secrets."

"You could say that." Sarah steered around the spreading lower limbs of a live oak which intruded upon the cracked pavement, and headed toward the darkened end of the lot where no artificial light reached. The stars shone down with cold, untwinkling brilliance. She eased the car over a low curb and onto the ragged lawn between two cabins, turned behind the cabin on the right, stopped, and switched off the ignition. She stared at him icily. "Would you care to elucidate?"

The sounds of the engine block cooling and contracting in the nighttime stillness sounded to Grant like gunshots. "Would *you*?"

Sarah reached into her purse. Grant stiffened, expecting to find himself looking down the barrel of a forty-four Magnum. She pulled out a worn key attached by a twisted strand of wire to a small wooden block. "Let's discuss it inside."

"Do you have a room here?"

She nodded. "Under an alias." She left the car unlocked with the key in the ignition, and led the way to the front of the cabin. "We should be safe for a while, until they start looking for us."

Grant wondered who "they" were; or, more precisely, which "they" she was referring to. He did not ask for clarification. After seeing the way she handled herself against seemingly invincible odds, he did not want to antagonize her. It was better to play word games until he knew the ground rules and the lay of this new land. "That won't be long."

Sarah placed her hand on his chest and pressed hard. "Stay here, but keep talking." She peered around the front corner, tiptoed quickly past the curtained window, and slid the key noiselessly into the lock. She looked back at him with light brown eyes whose whites sparkled brightly despite the enveloping shadows. She pointed to her lips with a delicately manicured finger, then made a waving motion with her hand. It was no shushing gesture.

Grant interpreted her pantomime and spoke in a purposely loud voice. "You play them close to your chest, don't you?"

With smooth coordination she shoved open the door, flipped on the lights, and panned the interior with the gun that had only recently spilled blood. She moved wraithlike through the cabin, making not a sound. Lights appearing around the edges of the shades informed Grant of her progress. A moment later she reappeared at the doorway and motioned for him to enter. "You can't be too careful in this world."

It sounded like a comment that he should have made instead of Sarah. "After what happened tonight, I agree."

She closed the door behind him, and locked it. "And that, I fear, is not the end of it."

Yet she did not speak with fear. And after Grant had seen her in action, he did not suppose that she could experience fear the way that he thought of it. Sarah was a woman transformed: no longer the simple sales rep whose bubble-headed affectation was comforting if barely tolerable, but the glamorous executioner whose looks alone could kill. He regarded her with a mixture of misgiving and admiration.

Grant cringed at her apparent lack of mercy and remorse, and he felt powerless in her presence. "Remind me never to call you a bimbo."

"That word is not part of your vocabulary." She tossed her purse on the threadbare blanket that covered the single bed. "I know, because I've read up on you. And not just the tripe they publish in the rag sheets, but your official dossier."

Grant took in the sparse surroundings. The headboard was chipped after years of hard use, the bureau's cheap veneer was peeling, and the cane seat on the solitary wooden chair was missing more reeds than it retained. "Why the interest?"

"Because of who you are." Sarah rummaged through a suitcase which sat atop the bureau. She pulled out a small cosmetic case and several bottles of fluid and cleansing cream. "And what you mean to the future of robotics."

Grant thought fast. He had to know what was going on without giving away his ignorance. "So you could gain access to the Memchip 201?"

She faced him. No longer did she smile coyly. "Partly that."

"And what else?"

"To make sure the secret of the process didn't die with you."

He winced at the frigidity of her tone. "How imper-sonal."

"You should talk!" Her eyes flashed like burnished steel blades. "After the trouble you've caused, and the lives that have been lost. . . . " She choked up so sud-denly that spittle flew from her mouth and her face became an unreadable caricature. The blades of steel flowed wetly. "Do you think I took pleasure in what I had to do back there? Do you think that killing is part of the profession that we take in stride? Do you think I have no humanitarian feelings?"

"Well, I—"

"You don't have the faintest notion about what it means to kill a fellow human being, even in self defense. I did what I had to do because I had no choice. They gave me no alternative. But for god's sake, don't believe for an instant that I enjoyed it. And you can bet your last microchip that I'll have to live with those memories for the rest of my life." She sniffled. "For that I have you to thank."

"I didn't mean . . . " Grant trailed off because Sarah was right—or at least partly so. He had not an inkling about the intrigues in which this world's Grant Temple-ton was involved, about the machinations he had fos-tered, about the adversities he had caused and the hor-rible chain of events he had set in motion before trad-ing places, intentionally or otherwise. Even though he was not responsible for the terrible state of affairs, he could not expect Sarah—or anyone, for that matter—to believe an unsubstantiated tale of interdimensional betrayal. Nor did he want to believe it himself, for to presume that another Grant Templeton had copped out of his troubles implied that every Grant Templeton pos-sessed concealed character flaws which were serious in nature. There had to be an explanation that was more to his liking.

Grant's initial reaction was to divorce himself of all responsibility for murderous happenstances, the way a tourist scoffs at traffic violations which occur in foreign countries. One can laugh at local constables and toss the tickets in the trash. No one will ever be extradited for nonpayment of the fine.

Similarly, this was not Grant's world, nor had he established the rules of engagement. He was a victim of circumstance, thrust onto the field of battle without his consent. The difference between analogy and reality was that he could not leave this land whenever he chose to do so. The mysterious forces that deposited him here were unknown to him. He could not simply click his heels three times, recite, "There's no place like home," and wake up in his own bed at 14 Cedar Place. Nor could he expect a Scarecrow to show him the way, with or without an expanded memory chip.

Grant was into this venture over his head and was digging himself in deeper. "I—I'm sorry, Sarah. I didn't mean it like that. It's just that . . . " He swallowed hard and glanced at her purse on the bed. "With all the death and mayhem, I'm wondering if I'm next on the hit list."

"You mean, if you're next on *my* hit list?"

His mouth was as dry as desert cotton. "Well, I—I don't know who you are any more. Or what you want with me. You're a hell of a lot more than what you've made yourself out to be. Unless corporate competition has gotten more cutthroat—" He blanched at his unfortunate choice of words. "I'm sorry, I didn't mean it that way."

For a moment she remained expressionless. Then, the corners of her mouth slowly turned up into a hint of a smile. "No, I like it. In fact, it's pretty funny when you think about it." She grabbed a handful of beautifully coiffed curls on the top of her head, pulled back hard, yanked off the black-haired wig, and tossed it into the suitcase as if it were nothing more than an old sock. She had silky blonde hair which was plastered against her head and which was pulled back from her face into a three-inch ponytail. "My name is Margaret Witherspoon, and my job is to protect you."

Grant was stunned at her latest transformation. After glaring like an idiot while dust accumulated on his tongue, all he could think to say was, "I liked Sarah better."

She laughed. "So do I and so do all my friends. It's my middle name. If you ever want to see me in a fury, call me Maggie."

Grant grinned and made mock gestures of defense. "I wouldn't think of it." His emotions soared with relief. After the evening's traumatic occurrences, he liked the idea of protection. He wilted into the too-soft mattress like day-old lettuce. "I could sure use a drink."

"You're supposed to have given up alcohol."

"Well, this is a special occasion."

Sarah rummaged again through the suitcase and came up with a liquor bottle that was barely four inches tall. She tossed it to Grant. "Will you settle for gin? It's an airline sample that I thought I might find a use for—other than imbibing."

"At the moment I'd be happy with Sterno." He unscrewed the cap and swilled a mouthful. It burned with a white heat and tasted like rubbing alcohol, and he spat it into a convenient ashtray. "What awful stuff. Maybe I should give it up." He looked up at Sarah. "But, as we used to say in the operating room, I'd rather have a bottle in front of me than a frontal lobotomy."

Sarah stepped into the tiny bathroom and spread her cosmetic accoutrements on the narrow shelf below the mirror. She unbuttoned the loose-fitting blouse, peeled it off and draped it over the towel rack, and stared for a moment at her reflection. Her breasts bulged full and firm beneath the black tanktop.

"I see that Magnum isn't the only forty-four you carry."

She filled the sink with hot water and poured in the contents of one of the bottles, then proceeded to soak her hands. "All your bios bequeath you with an offbeat sense of humor. I guess now I don't have to take that for 'granted'."

"Ho, ho, ho." He put a tiny drop of gin on his tongue. It did not taste any better. "How long have you been saving that line?"

"Long enough." Sarah leaned against the doorjamb and pulled off her fingernails one by one. She slipped the red-painted fakes through the narrow neck of the empty bottle. "And go easy on that gin. I don't want you passing out again like you did this morning."

"You're right." He screwed on the cap and left the bottle on the bed next to Sarah's purse. "It leaves a horrible aftertaste, anyway."

She stared once again at the face in the mirror. "You just can't handle your liquor the way you used to."

Sarah stuck her fingers into her mouth and removed the rubber inserts from above the upper molars; her high cheekbones flattened. Then she pulled the caps off her upper incisors and revealed a gap between them which distorted her dentition's graceful uniformity and made her teeth slightly uneven; the effect was not unappealing. She applied a generous portion of cold cream to her face, which she then rubbed hard with a washcloth, removing gobs of eye shadow, mascara, eyeliner, foundation, and lipstick. Even the suntan came off, revealing an off white complexion with more than a few blemishes. Finally, she plucked out the tinted contact lenses and looked at Grant with clear blue eyes through the open bathroom door.

His mouth was agape. "Is the Porsche going to change into a pumpkin next?"

"No, but we have to dump it anyway. It's too conspicuous, and without headlights we're bound to get stopped by the local flatfoots."

"Aren't the police supposed to be on our side?"

"Not when you're responsible for the deaths of a dozen people, even if they were the bad guys." Sarah pulled the tanktop over her head and laid it across the edge of the sink. Her brassiere was black, also. "I don't think you appreciate the severity of the situation. Those men weren't paying you a social call, you know."

"I know that. But why did they want to kill me?"

"Kill you? Honey, baby, the one thing they did *not* want to do was to cause you bodily harm, even as a last resort. Alive you're worth an incredible fortune, dead you're worth about the same as two hundred pounds of fertilizer."

"But, they were shooting at us."

"No, they were shooting at *me*." Sarah wrinkled thin yellow brows from which the black rinse had been washed. She was no bottle blonde. "You might have gotten hit by a stray shot or a ricochet up there on the stairs, but the body they were trying to fill with lead was mine. Don't you think that guy could have put a bullet into your head through the car window if he had wanted to? And why do you suppose they were trying to shoot out our tires during the getaway, instead of drilling us through the glass?"

"Well, I didn't think . . . "

"Of course you didn't think. You were never trained to notice those things. You're a doctor, a scientist, an inventor, and an expert in a dozen other disciplines whose names I can't even pronounce. This is totally out of your league."

"But why? What have I done to create such a stir?" It seemed like a sensible question no matter what his past.

"You invented the Memchip 201."

Now he was treading water of uncertain depth. "And people will kill for its secret?"

"Not just people, but corporations, syndicates, political factions, and foreign nations." She stood in the doorway and looked down at Grant who was huddled on the bed like an innocent child. She placed her hands on curvaceous hips, posed for a moment in the light, then removed the pads from under the tights and drastically reduced the circumference of her pelvic girdle. "Given that you're an absented-minded professor, you can't be blind to the potential uses for a memory bank of virtually infinite capacity stored in a matrix the size of a walnut, and with the processing speed available through superconductivity. Even with the requisite refrigeration equipment, you can still store enough data in an area no bigger than a baby's shoe box to run all the programs of a small country's defense system."

That much was obvious to Grant. By piecing together tidbits of information which he had picked up from Sarah and the movie clip during the day—had it been only a few hours ago—he was able to formulate a picture of what the Memchip 201 could do, if not how it did it. "Isn't that like putting all your eggs in one basket? It's not a good idea to have so much important data stored on a single chip."

"Use your imagination. With that magnitude of data compression you can switch to fully programmed backups that are scattered over a large geographical area. Besides, I was exaggerating, and that was just an example of what might come to mind to a dictator of a competing third-world nation. Biotech's primary interest is the same as that of Benthic Products: to construct totally independent, remotely operated vehicles that can operate in outer space or under water without constant regulation. Amusement simulacra are a curious sideline of little consequence."

He was beginning to see the light. If only he could frame the thoughts which were formulating in his mind so they did not appear like questions, he might learn a great deal more from his protector. "Yes, with enough programming capacity you can manufacture robotic systems which are self-regulating, self-guiding—which can be programmed to respond to situations unanticipated by the programmer but according to logical but nonsequential prerogatives; which can accumulate new data gained through individual experience; which can, in effect, learn from their mistakes and create novel approaches toward the solution of a problem." My god! He was answering his own question. "If the processing speed is fast enough, you can conceivably create a mobile computer capable of editing its own programs and writing new ones during the interval between observation and response, between action and reaction."

Grant was ecstatic at the implication. Any computer which could produce its own directives was an "Artificial Intelligence!"

Sarah put a damper on his romantic invention. "I wouldn't go as far as to proclaim that self-conscious machine entities are cerebrating about mankind's fate. They're still a few generations in the future. But you can program robotic platforms that don't need to be hardwired to a mainframe computer in order to perform simple but unexpected tasks."

"And life-size simulacra, too." Despite the intoxication of ideas, Grant tried to bring himself back to perceptible reality. "Which explains your involvement, and the Disney contract that Benthic Products has signed."

"No, you're way off base." Sarah reached behind her and unsnapped her bra as casually as if she were removing her hat. Her breasts were reduced in caliber to a pair of free-standing apricots, soft and supple. She tossed the foam-padded falsies into the suitcase. "Sarah Mason is dead, and so is the Benthic Products connection. That was just a cover story designed to get me into the loop without arousing suspicion. Not that all I said in disguise wasn't true, it just has no bearing on the immediate situation."

Grant was confused, and afraid of giving himself away. "You mean, the Humphrey Bogart simulacrum really exists?"

"Of course it does. And Benthic Products would really like to get its hands on the Memchip 201 so its simulacra can operate without a cable connection. Underwater platforms, as well. Those negotiations were proceeding smoothly until a week ago."

Sarah hesitated, and Grant felt as if he were expected to respond. He was distracted by her topless attire. "And what happened then?" He added quickly, "From your perspective."

Her breasts jiggled when she shrugged. "I wasn't brought in until afterwards. Naturally, I had to have complete knowledge of the situation in order to act as Benthic Products' representative, in case my association was questioned by other factions. Like those people tonight, if they had given us the opportunity to talk.

Since Benthic Products conducts clandestine underwater search and recovery operations for the U.S. Navy, we have rather strong ties with the board of directors—"

"We?"

"The Department of Defense. Certain board members provided us with the necessary background information, added me to the payroll and gave me a phone number, and arranged the meeting at the Neanderthal Club. Stop me if any of this sounds familiar or redundant. Anyway, word was leaked from our agent at Biotech that trouble was brewing and that all precautions must be taken in order to prevent the results of secret experiments at Biotech—which were then nearing a successful conclusion and which posed incalculable value to our national defense—from falling into enemy hands. Obviously, we couldn't discuss such sensitive intelligence over an open phone line, so we established a protocol which would confirm the identity of the spokesperson—"

"Saratoga!" Grant blurted.

Sarah eyed him suspiciously. "A password that you could have been given by our agent at Biotech, if you were intended to take his place, or something that you overheard on a voice recorder."

Grant realized ruefully that she had caught him in a trap, one which had been baited with carefully chosen words and whose semantic tongs had been misdirected by bare breasts. "Well, can't that be verified by your agent?"

Blonde eyebrows arched sharply. "I was afraid you might say that."

Grant cringed at the thought that the agent must already be dead, and that he had finally let his ignorance be known. But the truth was worse than that. Much worse.

"You see, our contact at Biotech is Grant Templeton."

Chapter 15

Patrolman Frank Riley was growing continually more ill at ease as each bit of information flashed on the computer screen, or was printed on paper through the Teletype machine. Practically every request for bureau intelligence files or police investigatory reports had been acknowledged immediately with full disclosure, and those records to which the FBI saw fit to deny access—due to customary security measures—resulted in a personal phone call from the sector chief, who explained amicably that the agents who had been dispatched to the scene would provide pertinent details upon their arrival. So far the sector chief had called four times.

"Hey, Lover Boy."

Riley looked up with a strange feeling of déjà vu. When he saw Captain Hendry grimacing from the doorway, he automatically glanced at his watch and tried to remember when he had promised to check in with Sandy. He did not usually call her at night unless she was working the late shift.

"Did you forget your three o'clock date?"

Riley's mind went blank. If he let Sandy down again she would never forgive him. Well, she *would* forgive him, but forgiveness would be costly.

"I told you half an hour ago that Blakey wanted us at the morgue right away."

Ryan Blake was the county medical examiner who roamed the countryside and performed his official duties wherever they were needed. Highland Hills was too small a town to have a separate police morgue, so the town rented space on an as-needed basis under special contract with the Swampwater Regional Medical Center. When necessary, Blake borrowed a couple of interns to act as assistants. Laboratory tests were conducted on site using hospital facilities, and charged to the county.

"He just called again and I can't stall him any more. I've never seen him so fired up before. If you haven't got the goods on Templeton yet it'll just have to wait. You started this mess and you know more about it than anybody, so I want you in on every angle, including the gruesome parts like looking at dead bodies being dissected on the slab."

Riley gathered a stack of printouts, unseparated fanfold, and loose sheets of typing paper, and pushed his chair away from the computer console. "I've got as much as I'm likely to get until the federal investigators arrive. Wait until you hear about his prints—"

"Then come on and you can tell me about it in the car." Hendry charged along the corridor with such uncharacteristic urgency and motivation that Riley practically had to run in order to keep up with him. "You know we really stole a march on this case."

"How is that?" Riley matched Hendry's stride as they passed through the open office area.

"Because you clanged the bell before the horse got away. Or at least before it got too far from the corral and the cowpokes got their spurs on. Just had a call from the Defense Department. Nobody's getting any sleep in Washington tonight. Your tip on Templeton yesterday set off an alarm in their system. Seems like something big is going down in the department—a spy passing intelligence out of the country. And who do you think is mixed up—"

"George! Hey, George!" Patrolman Richard Anderson slammed down the phone and fought his way through an aisle full of desk chairs and wastepaper baskets. He caught the pair just as they were going out the door. "Hi, Frank. George, I got the goods from the Aviary Rental Company. I was just going to bring it to you." He handed a computer printout to Captain Hendry. "Here's a list of the cars they've rented in the past three days. VINs, tag numbers, lessees, the whole bit."

Hendry glanced at the list and passed it on to Riley. "And?"

"It's that one—circled in red. Rented to a gal named Barbara Archbold."

"Damn! Now what the hell is that supposed to mean?"

"Wait a minute, boss. The manager was real helpful. Didn't mind at all being roused out of bed in the middle of the night. Even seemed to like the idea of being involved with the police." In aside to Riley, "I gather that renting cars isn't a real exciting job."

Hendry humphed. "I wish Tom Haskell showed as much interest."

"Judge Haskell?" Riley's eyes widened as he tucked the rental agency printout into the sheaf of papers in his arms.

Hendry nodded. "I called him for a search warrant."

"At this hour of the morning?" Anderson scrunched up his face in disbelief. "Why? The Templeton house is a crime scene. We don't need a warrant."

"Not for his house, for his lab. Frank went nosing around out there and had the door slammed in his face for his efforts. In my opinion, the people out at Biotech know a hell of a lot more than they're owning up to. Got a work party going on out there and they still don't answer the phone."

"Well, I don't think you should—" Anderson thought for a moment, then changed his mind. "If you raid the place I'd like to be in on it."

When Captain Hendry shook his head his jowls jiggled in consort. "Won't be till after ten when the judge gets on the bench. By that time the feds'll be here and I lose my chance at a coup because they'll be taking over the operation." He tilted his head forward and peered over his reading glasses. "The judge was quite perturbed. Now, we're in a rush, me and Frank. You got anything on the car we should know about?"

Anderson blinked his eyes as if to get back on track. "The car. Yes, well, like I said, the guy was real helpful. I asked him to describe the lady and he had no trouble there. Said she looked like a school marm with horn-rimmed glasses and long brown hair tied tight in a bun, and an ankle length dress with pastel flower prints like his grandmother used to wear. Fair skin, five-foot-six or -seven, one hundred forty pounds. Placed her in her late forties, early fifties."

"That doesn't sound like the Mason woman. Nothing like her. Too old, too short, too fat, too plain. She have ID to back up her looks?"

"Illinois driver's license. And before you ask, I haven't been able to get on the computer link because Frank's had it tied up all night. My guess is she was wearing a disguise."

"Isn't that jumping to conclusions?" Riley said.

Anderson shrugged and pinched his nose with thumb and forefinger. "When things smell fishy, the smell is probably coming from a fish." To Hendry, "If the Defense Department has a saboteur in the ranks and a rogue on the loose—"

"Where the hell did you hear that?" Hendry boomed.

Anderson made a fist with thumb and pinky extended, and put it to his ear. "On the telephone. I punched the wrong button and cut in on your line. Then I just kept listening."

Captain Hendry grumbled. "Yeah, well, don't let it go any further. That's privileged information."

Anderson pulled his thumb and forefinger across his mouth. "My lips are sealed."

"But you're right on one account. There's a lot going on that doesn't make sense, like we're peeling leaves off a cabbage to get to the core, and each leaf has different wrinkles. Richy, you get on the link and track this gal down, and let me know what you come up with."

"I'm on it, boss." He made a mock salute and executed an about face. Outside, Captain Hendry shoved his reading glasses in his shirt pocket and led the way to his car. "I'll drive."

Riley nodded and tagged along. "What were you saying about the Defense Department?"

"First I want to know what you found out about the prints. If you did a good enough job to make a match."

"N O F."

Captain Hendry stopped with his fingers on the door handle, and did a double take. "Not on file?" His thumb depressed the latch but he did not open the door. "The man's got a top secret security clearance. He's got to have his prints on file. Complete physical description, too."

Over the roof of the car, "No one knows that better than the FBI. The best guess is that their records have been tampered with—both computer and hard copy—although they're not admitting anything at the moment. They're somewhat embarrassed."

"I guess they are." Hendry opened the door and climbed inside. He waited until Riley was seated next to him before going on. "How about a physical description?"

"They faxed us a couple of recent photos. This was during the day, before the ruckus at his house. Since then they've put a clamp on the Templeton file. The sector chief was apologetic, but his hands are tied. Templeton is no longer a local police matter." Riley snapped the safety belt across his lap. "Anyway, our man looks like the face in the photos, and the physical description fits to a tee: six-foot-one, two hundred and ten pounds, black hair, brown eyes, light complexion, fifty-two years old. I'd put him closer to fifty-five, but then he'd had a rough night before we saw him."

"A beard makes a man look older." Hendry put the squad car in motion and headed toward the hospital along near-deserted streets. "What else you got?"

Riley took a deep breath. "I've got some statistics on him that coincide fairly well with what he told us—he just didn't go into as much detail. He's divorced, he's got a daughter in college—probably the picture we saw on his desk—he's the CEO of Biotech Corporation. Did you read that magazine article I gave you?"

"*Personalities*? Well, I breezed through it."

"Then you know all about his work on robotics and memory chips?"

"What I could make sense of."

"Okay, then get this. They claim he's developed a

new kind of computer chip that has the capacity to record and store in perfect detail every experience that a human being has had in his entire life: everything he's ever done, every fact he's ever learned, every nuance of his existence. And because of a recent break-through in low temperature physics, which virtually eliminates electrical resistance, this chip can operate at a processing speed that allows immediate access to every bit of data: instant recall."

"You're getting beyond me, Frank."

Riley laughed. "Don't feel bad. It's beyond me, too. I'm just telling you what I read. Anyway, the article focused on the military applications of such a device. If you couple the essence of a human being with the reac-tion time of a computer, you can build offensive weapons systems that can outsmart any defense net-work in the world: 'missiles guided by human judg-ment' was the way they put it in the article."

"Okay, Frank, forget about all this scientific mumbo-jumbo. How does it tie in to Templeton? That phone call from the Defense Department claims he's in this spy business up to his eyebrows, and in cahoots with a rogue agent suspected of negotiating the sale of military secrets to third-world countries. Yet he turns himself in to the police, yaks out some nonsense story about waking up in the middle of the road and not knowing where he was, doesn't have a hint of liquor in his blood, then walks out the door with a gal he says he doesn't know and who claims to be a sales rep working with him on an important deal. When she was giving us the lowdown, her words were so honey coated that my fingers are still sticky." He humphed. "Won't be the first time I was bamboozled by feminine sweet talk.

"The Defense Department wouldn't give any more details, only that we were to get Templeton away from the girl and hold them both in protective custody. Went so far as to call Keller and have the state troopers put roadblocks on every cow path leading out of town. Then they phoned the governor to call out the National Guard. They'll be here by sunup, at which time Highland Hills comes under martial law. That means that after dawn you and me are nothing more than messenger boys for the feds."

"You were right, George. Whatever is going on is way over our heads. But Templeton seemed so innocent, as if he truly wanted help. And 'Purloined Letter' or not, a police station is the last place a couple of spies are going to meet for a secret rendezvous so they can trade national secrets. And you want to know what else . . . ?" Riley shuffled through the papers in his lap.

"Maybe the guy's been brainwashed and don't know what he's doing."

"George, listen to this. You remember Templeton gave us the names of people to contact? Well, when I couldn't find any of them in the local phone directory, I checked with Springfield for current driver's licenses and automobile registrations. Couldn't find a one—"

"That's impossible. Somebody's gotta drive—"

"—won't bore you with the way I tracked them down, but what I ended up with in all five cases was a death certificate."

"Huhn?"

"That's right. They're all dead. And all within the past two years."

"And Templeton didn't know this? Or was he sending us on a wild goose chase?"

"I don't want to venture an opinion just yet. But there's a curious connection between the fatalities. One guy drove his car off the road and into a rock wall; one guy got caught in an assembly line conveyor belt and was crushed; one guy was mangled by a steel press—he bled to death; one guy was electrocuted; and one was a woman who drowned in a river."

Captain Hendry squinted askance. "I don't get it. What's the connection?"

"All the deaths were accidental and none occurred in Highland Hills, which was where they all lived and worked."

"Hmmmmnn. It's thin, Frank. It's thin. And the fact that they all worked for Biotech makes it suspicious only because we don't think too kindly of them at the moment. Still . . . "

"There's more."

Hendry raised his eyebrows.

"The one who was electrocuted was Randy Vanderbilt."

"Vanderbilt? Wasn't his name on the tape we found in Templeton's jacket pocket?"

"The same."

"But, why'd he send us out to look for a guy he already knew was dead?"

"I'm just giving you the facts. Vanderbilt, by the way, just moved to DC a couple of months ago. Now, here's something I think we should act on. Francine Baker, Templeton's secretary, and his co-worker Robert Lerner both have addresses in town. Neither are yet answering their phones, and considering the circumstances I think we ought to check their houses and maybe ask the neighbors when they were last seen."

Captain Hendry grabbed the microphone. "Give me their addresses and I'll get someone out there right away."

"Baker is on the north side of town at 2721 Ferdinand Street. Lerner lives on Ocelot Cove."

The captain's eyes widened. "Feline Estates?"

Riley nodded.

"Damn. That don't make a damn bit of—" He called the temporary dispatcher and issued orders as he turned into the hospital parking lot. "Okay, is that it?"

Riley puckered his cheeks. "Now for the clincher." He ruffled through the papers and extracted one with red pencil markings. "I was finally able to track down his mother in Oregon."

"Hallelujah. Something positive for a change. So what did the old gal have to say about the weird behavior of her crackbrained prodigal son?"

"I didn't actually talk to her." Riley tilted the sheet of paper so it caught the light from the mercury vapor lamps atop the tall aluminum poles. "She's currently located at Sleepy Hollow Estates, lane twelve, row four, plot number 423. I spoke with the caretaker of the grounds, and, according to him, Mrs. Agnes Templeton is interred next to her husband. She died eight years ago."

Captain Hendry switched off the ignition and sat in total silence, one hand on the steering wheel, the other seemingly frozen to the key. He stared sightlessly through the windshield. His Adam's apple bobbed as he swallowed long and deep. A full minute passed before he turned and faced the patrolman. "He don't know his own mother is dead?"

Riley responded with a single nod.

"The man don't know what's happened in his own life?"

"He did say he was confused."

"Confused, hell. He's completely loony." Captain Hendry banged his fists on the steering wheel. "We had him in our hands. And it would have been a real feather in our cap if we could have turned him over to the feds. But if he's that crazy, hell, maybe he blew those guys away for trespassing and ran the others off his property. Maybe he's a closet killer. You know, the manic-depressive type that goes off his rocker every once in a while."

"No. To get a top secret security clearance with the Defense Department he would have to undergo psychological testing, polygraph, background investigations, the works. Submarine personnel go through the same procedure. Believe me, if anyone is the least bit unbalanced, the shrinks can spot it right away."

"So, maybe his work unbalanced him, or he's having personal problems, or he's going through a midlife crisis."

"And perhaps he's been out of touch with his family for a while."

"Come on, Frank. That don't wash."

"Neither does anything else we have on him. Like I said, I'm not venturing opinions, just delivering facts."

Captain Hendry rubbed his eyes hard with one hamlike fist. "Yeah, well, let's go see what kind of facts

Blakey's got for us. And hope to hell it gives us some answers instead of more preposterous questions."

They no sooner entered the Swampwater Regional Medical Center than they were accosted by a fiery young redhead in nurse's uniform. She blocked their way to the admission's desk by standing in front of the swinging doors with her hands on her hips. "I expected a call, but I didn't think you'd go out of your way to stop in. Especially with the boss on your tail."

Riley managed a quixotic smile. "Hi, Sandy."

She was a petite woman—not much over five feet tall—with flashing green eyes and a freckled face, and a wild mop of long crinkly hair. She stepped right past him and gave Captain Hendry a resounding smack on the cheek. "Hello, Daddy." Then she gave Riley a quick but quiet peck. "Hi, Frank. Miss me?"

Riley flushed, and hesitated an instant too long.

"The answer is 'yes.' And I'd be mad as a wet hen if I didn't know what was going on." To Captain Hendry, pouting, "Daddy, why didn't you tell me how serious this case was? When you called and told Mom you wouldn't be home for supper, you didn't say the town had been invaded by an army of thugs."

"I didn't want your mother to worry, Kitten. Besides, it's police business, and you know I can't talk about that outside the office. It's confidential. And anyhow, how do you know what we're investigating?"

"Dr. Blake told me all about it—at least, as much as he knows. I volunteered as soon as he asked for assistants, and, being an R.N. and, you know, related to the captain, he took me on, even though I'm only three months out of school. It made me want to puke, seeing those men who were burned and shot and crushed. But I figure it's part of being a well-rounded nurse." Her glistening eyes belied her braggadocio. "Oh, what poor Dawn must be going through."

"Dawn Templeton?" Riley exploded. "Do you know Dawn Templeton?"

"Well, sure. I went to school with her." She grinned weakly. "I went to school with everyone in Highland

Hills." She leaned close to Frank. "It's not that big of a town, you know. Not like Denver."

"Do you know where she lives?"

"Well, with her father, I suppose. She was a grade below me so I didn't talk to her that much. I know that her parents got divorced when she was eight or ten, and that she was fond of them both. But I never went to her house, or anything. And her mother moved to Chicago right after Dawn graduated from high school."

"What about Dawn? What did she do after graduation?"

"Well, I used to see her on campus. She was premed. But I haven't seen her since I got my degree. She's still there, I suppose."

Captain Hendry scowled. "None of those spare bedrooms at the Templeton house had a teenybopper living in them. What do you think, Frank?"

"I'm not sure. Templeton said he had a little girl who lived with her mother, but the way he talked about her made me think she was young—pre-teen. He didn't actually say it, you understand, but—"

"But we already know that he's either a very confused man or not the person he claims to be, even if he is a dead ringer for—"

"Daddy, I hate to interrupt your brainstorming session, but Dr. Blake sent me up here to escort you to the morgue as soon as you arrived, not to chat about Dr. Templeton's family matters. He's got something—to show you that is—quite astonishing. In fact, I'm still not sure whether I believe it or not. But—"

"What is it?"

"Well, it's—it's confidential. You know how it is. Medicine's a lot like police work." She led the way to the stairwell and pushed through the double doors and down the stairs. "Some things you just can't talk about outside the operating room. Anyhow, you wouldn't take my word for it if I told you. *I* wouldn't. So let Dr. Blake demonstrate it for you in his own way."

They found the medical examiner working hard on a sandwich and a cup of coffee, and surrounded by medical forms and loose sheets of paper which were strewn fanlike on the desk before him. He laid aside his snack as the trio entered the room, and held out his hand to Captain Hendry. "George, thanks for coming by." He turned to the patrolman. "And you must be Frank Riley. Heard a lot about you." His handshake was warm and weak, almost effeminate. To Hendry, "Well, I don't have to tell you we've got more corpses in here than we've had in a month of Sundays. You have any idea yet who's responsible for them all?"

"Not a clue, and not much time to gather any. By morning this town will be crawling with federal agents and National Guard units. The governor has declared martial law. Then the responsibility for this ruckus will be out of my hands. But until I'm officially relieved, I'm still the chief peacekeeper."

"Don't envy you." Ryan Blake was a tall man with thinning white hair and a touch of middle-aged spread noticeable only because of his overall leanness. He scratched his receding hairline with one gnarled finger. " 'Specially after what I've got to show you. Follow me."

He swept past one hastily set-up operating room and casually waved his right hand in the direction of the closed doors. "The crispy critters are in here. Unrecognizable, both of them, and I'm leaving them for last. Sandy—"

"Howie's already taken the teeth imprints, Dr. Blake, and counted the fillings, too."

Gulping hard, Riley peered through the wire-framed glass and saw two blackened corpses which reminded him of painted plaster castings like the ones removed from solidified lava at Pompeii. Their limbs were contorted grotesquely. Despite the chemical smell of disinfectants, the reek of burned flesh was overpowering and made him gag.

"Good. Good." To Hendry, "One of 'em's got some bullet holes in him. Won't know till we do the autopsy whether he died of lead poisoning, carbon monoxide, smoke inhalation, or incineration. Don't matter either way, I suppose. Now in this room we've got the victims

from the van." He pointed left. "This one's got the—
What was it? A Lincoln Continental?"

"That's right." Hendry glanced into the room on the
right as they cruised by.

"And here we've got the mystery men." Blake strode
into the last room on the left, his long white smock
flowing behind him so that his hospital greens were
revealed. "Now bear with me on this and listen to what
I tell you. I want to be damned sure you know what
you're up against."

The three corpses which lay supine on gurneys
were the dead men found in the entry of Templeton's
house. They wore white sheets that covered all except
their faces, which were in the process of being pho-
tographed by an intern with a Polaroid camera.

"That'll do for now, Howie."

The intern nodded, pulled up the sheets, and left
the room.

Captain Hendry used his fingers to assist his mental count. "Hey, aren't we missing a couple?"

"Ran out of space. We've got them parked on the
freight elevator till we can make room for them down
here." He drew back the sheet from the head of one of
the victims to reveal the countenance of death underneath. Coagulated blood lay in pools on the plastic tarp
which protected the bedding from contamination. "I'll
make a detailed report later on, but for now I'll belay
the medical jargon and conjugation so you'll know
exactly what I'm talking about."

Riley swallowed hard so as not to vomit. Moments
like this reminded him how much about police work he
had yet to learn and experience. Sandy placed a warm
hand on his arm, and looked up at him with consoling
eyes. He kept swallowing.

Blake pulled on a pair of rubber surgical gloves.
"Death was instantaneous, caused by a well-placed
blow to the temple that ruptured the vessels that supply blood to the anterior portion of the brain." He tilted
the victim's head and exposed a massive purple dot
that bulged around the left temple like half a tennis

ball. "If he was looking the wrong way, he never knew what hit him." He used his finger to draw a circle around the impact area. "Never broke the skin, and there's no indentation from a blunt instrument. The jaw is broken, too, but that's incidental and could have happened in the fall. No other damage, not even super-ficial." He threw the sheet back over the face.

"Now over here . . . " Blake walked quickly to the second corpse, and pulled the sheet down to the knees. The naked body sagged in death like a deflated air mattress. "The man was wearing a gun—a 38-caliber Smith and Wesson in a shoulder holster—but never had time to draw. Can't give you the exact order of the insults, but you'll notice that he was kicked in the balls, had both collarbones broken, and was cupped on the ear." Dried blood still clung to the outer ear and the neck. "The crushed testicles and broken bones caused considerable pain, perhaps incapacitating the victim before delivery of the final blow, which was expertly placed and which caused hemorrhage of the brain. Took a while to die, but he was mercifully unconscious during the death throes."

Blake replaced the sheet with surprising reverence considering his apparent attitude of contempt for the dead. "And here we have Gargantua, the biggest mystery of them all." The figure on the third gurney could have been a whiskey barrel under covers. Blake pulled the sheet down to the belly, exposing the mediastinal incision which bifurcated below the sternum and traced the lower ribcage. Safety pins held the flaps of skin together. "Whereas the other two were dispatched in hand-to-hand combat, this one was terminated with extreme prejudice: a forty-four Magnum. I've got one of the slugs."

Riley nearly lost his lunch when the medical examiner removed his gloves and casually stuck a bare finger into a bloodless hole which was located slightly off center of the middle of the chest.

"Drilled exactly where the heart should be in a normal human being."

"Are you saying he ain't normal?" Captain Hendry asked.

Ryan Blake grinned like the Cheshire cat. "See for yourself."

He pulled the sheet down to the knees. Riley was surprised at the hairless pubic area. Hating himself for a ghoul, he leaned forward and examined the giant's crotch. "He—he's been castrated." He was totally embarrassed by his girlfriend's presence.

"Completely emasculated, you mean." Captain Hendry blushed when he caught his daughter glancing alternately between him and Riley and the figure on the gurney. "His, uh, his penis is gone, too."

Sandy leaned against the other side of the gurney. "You'd better look a little closer, Daddy. Frank. There's no sign of any external genitalia."

The policemen exchanged looks of horror as Blake and Sandy spread the giant's legs and allowed them a posterior view. No shadows were cast by the numerous overhead fluorescent fixtures, making it impossible not to notice that the groin was as bereft of anatomical definition as that of a plastic doll.

"No anal opening, either." Blake undid the safety pins that held together the skin covering the chest and abdomen, then pulled back the thin outer tegument and exposed the metal casing. "I've drained the oil from the major components so you don't have to worry about leakage. Got grease all over everything. I took one bullet out of the gyroscope housing and sent it to forensics for matching. The other bullet is buried in the CPU between the hip junctures. I didn't remove it because some of the motherboards are unbroken, and I thought it might be important to preserve them intact. Except for some hydraulic lines that were severed when the gyroscope wheel flew apart, none of the other machinery is damaged."

Captain Hendry was speechless.

"It's a robot." Riley could barely breathe.

"And a sophisticated one, at that, because it can be operated remotely. Although not, I suspect, without on-site monitoring. Mechanical bodies are way out of my field, but in my medical opinion the carriage architecture is not supported by a sufficiently large enough memory unit. I've done enough prosthetic work to know."

Captain Hendry finally found his voice. "So that's what we're up against. An army of robots that can think for themselves."

"No, George. Not at all. You have missed the point entirely." Ryan Blake beamed with delight. "Unless I miss my guess, free thinking computer systems are a long way in the future. Especially those small enough to walk about. What we have here is something—or someone—far more dangerous."

"How so?"

"Because whoever killed these men and shut down this machine knew exactly what he—or they—were doing. These are not random punches and gunshots, but perfectly directed lethal blows: executed with extreme prejudice and no quarter given. Whoever did this is not only deadly, but very well informed. Not only did he go straight for the noggin, but—" Blake pointed at the robot's central processing unit. "—he knew precisely where the thinker was located."

Chapter 16

"Sarah, I—I know this is going to sound fantastic, especially in view of what's been happening, but you've got to believe—what I'm about to tell you."

"Ah, the moment of truth at last and the end of the subterfuge." Margaret Sarah Witherspoon pulled the black tanktop over her head and tucked the bottom into the elastic band around the waist of her tights. Without the padded hips and breasts she had an almost boyish figure, slender and straight-lined, but with a body which was firm and solid. And without the makeup she looked ten years younger—appearing now to be in her mid to late twenties. "So, tell me who you really are."

"Well, I'm—I'm Grant Templeton, of course. From Biotech. But what I don't know, or can't explain, is exactly how I came to be mixed up in whatever is going on."

"That says a lot," she said, with evident sarcasm.

The situation was too serious for Grant to respond to humor. "I don't mean to patronize you, but—" He made up his mind to stick with the facts as he knew them, and not to conjecture about parallel universes and dissimilar dimensions. "Everything seemed to be going along normally until I tried to go home the other night and discovered that some other family was occupying my house. . . . "

He explained in halting sentences his Friday night travails which began at about the time she had said they were supposed to meet at the Neanderthal Club. Sarah took no notes of his disclosure, and neither interrupted him with questions nor prompted him for details. Nor did she display any expression that could be interpreted as astonishment or disbelief. She simply listened.

Grant maintained his poise completely through to the end of his story, and wound up with their introduction at the police station. "So there you have it, for whatever it's worth. Truly, I'm about as confused about what it all means as you must be. These welts on my head are the only indication of injury, and as a doctor giving an unbiased opinion, I'm forced to admit that they do not have the appearance of nor do they feel like wounds of sufficient impact to cause concussion and subsequent PTA—that is, post-traumatic amnesia. They seem more like burns."

Sarah pondered for a moment before commenting. "What about the headache?"

Grant shook his head. "Almost gone. Although I think I had a bit of a hangover this afternoon. I don't know why the alcohol rushed to my head that way. You'd think with my long history of overindulgence I could drink a couple of cocktails without passing out like the dead."

"You would think." Sarah leaned against the doorjamb and crossed one foot over the other. "So you suddenly 'woke up' with no recollection of recent events and an imperfect memory of the past."

Grant upturned his hands in a gesture of innocence.

"What about the stuff on that voice recorder? What did it mean to you?"

"Did you listen to the recording?"

"Of course I listened to it. It's my job to investigate every angle. I also had a local locksmith make a duplicate set of keys while they were in my possession, then cased the Estate on foot."

A light bulb flashed above Grant's bedraggled head. "Is that why you were so confident that my keys would open the gate and unlock the front door of the house?"

Sarah squinted meaningfully. "Weren't you?"

He slowly shook his head. If he expected her to help him out of his predicament, he had to be forthright with her. "I must also admit that I have no recollection of that house."

"Now that's interesting."

"But I recognized some of the things in the study.

My diplomas and honors, a few gifts from Babs and Dawn. But most of the stuff in there was new to me."

"How about the Porsche?"

He shrugged.

"And you didn't recognize any of those men?"

"I've never seen them before."

Sarah paused in thought. "And the stuff on the tape? Were any of the names familiar?"

"Randy Vanderbilt. A smart young technician just out of college. But I didn't know he had gotten married. I've been so busy lately . . . "

"How about Kenny Grahame?"

"No."

"Connie?"

"No."

"The Fenton file?"

"No."

"And who is your secretary?"

"Franci—" He stopped abruptly, bewildered. "Sarah, I can't afford to lie to you. I know that on the tape I said Charlotte, but as far as I know Francine Baker is still my secretary. I've never heard of any Charlotte working at Biotech."

Sarah seemed undisturbed by his admission. "You do seem to be unusually misinformed about the operations of your own company."

Grant twitched one cheek and raised his eyebrows in a show of peccadillo. "I'm sorry."

"We'll worry about that later. Right now we've got something more important to do."

"Oh?" Grant was surprised that she had accepted his yarn without making recriminations. "What's that?"

"Find the files on the Memchip 201 or the working model itself. Preferably both."

"Why? You said the Benthic Products simulacrum was only a cover story, and that some secret experiments at Biotech were the real reason the Department of Defense was involved."

"Because the military applications of the Memchip 201 are what the experiments are all about. This is a microchip war, and the country with the biggest chip has all the chips in the game of world domination. Those people at the house tonight were enemy agents who planned to kidnap you because they don't know how to program the prototype memchip. It's not you they want, it's what you know. Or what you're supposed to know. Once they get what they want, not only are you no longer indispensable to them, your existence becomes a liability. So let me lay it out for you plain and simple. If the enemy obtains the memchip data, they have to kill you in order to safeguard its secret. If we get it first, then we have something to bargain with for your life. Now, how badly do you want to live?"

Life did not seem like much of an asset until it was nearly lost, or until someone tried to take it away. Then life became the most precious commodity a person possessed. Grant conceded that his instinct for survival overrode all other considerations. For death implied the close to a person's hopes and dreams and desires; death signified the end of awareness and thought; death terminated forever all meaning and purpose. Death was an everlasting state of nothingness: void, vacuum, and oblivion. Death, the mystery of mysteries, the greatest of the great unknowns, was that intangible quantity whose innermost secret was revealed to the questing mind only upon the trice of final embrace, when that mind was no longer able to perceive the moment. Grant's scientific curiosity was not piqued by the ultimate cipher. He was as much afraid of dying as the next man.

Nor did he want just any life; he wanted an identity. He was not content to be an interloper: the revivification of a predecessor, or the leftover memory from someone else's existence. He wanted a life of his own: one which was imbued with a sense of social belonging, one which was full of love and close friendship, one which contained a measure of stability, one in which his individual personality was assured. Put in those terms, he would make any sacrifice to stay alive, and to use that life to mold the world to his liking. Survival was built into his makeup.

"Very much so."

"Then cooperate by telling me what I need to know."

He took a very deep breath. "Sarah, I've got another confession to make. Ever since we met I've been stringing you along, letting you believe I knew more than I did, hoping that you would surrender information I was lacking. But the truth of the matter is that I don't know anything about the Memchip 201, despite the fact that I'm supposed to have invented it. I'd never even heard of it until you ran through your spiel."

Sarah sighed, but remained expressionless. "Well, don't feel bad. I've been playing the same game with you. Dropping hints and asking leading questions to see how you'd respond. Your convenient lapse of memory made me suspicious. And I'm still suspicious. I keep wondering if you've changed your mind about working with us, if you've got some hidden agenda of your own, and you're using us to double-cross your rivals."

"What rivals?" Grant pleaded. "What is going on that I should get involved in international espionage? I'm a scientist, not an undercover agent selling military secrets to foreign countries."

"Someone is."

Grant's raised his brows.

"Someone at Biotech."

"I told you that I went to Biotech last night. The building was abandoned. There's nobody there: no furniture, no files, no workstations, no lab equipment. Nothing."

"But did you go into the basement?"

"No, I didn't go into the basement. There's nothing down there but maintenance facilities: motors, compressors, water heaters, electrical cabinets, and such."

Sarah's eyes narrowed almost imperceptibly. After a pause, "Okay, forget that for now. It doesn't alter the fact that someone at Biotech is selling out the company by merchandising sensitive information to the highest bidder, perhaps to more than one bidder. And at least one prospective customer is in town to guarantee delivery of the product. Granted—sorry, no pun intended—granted that recent circumstances imply that you are the most likely suspect, let's work under the assumption that you set out with good intent on Friday night to meet me at the Neanderthal Club and were somehow waylaid by an accident which has conveniently affected your mind in such a way that you have selectively forgotten events pertinent to the current situation, and appear to have been implanted with false memories of places which—"

"There is such a thing as 'discriminating memory loss' which is not uncommon among patients with lesions in the mediadorsal area of the thalamus or damage to the hippocampus—"

"Stop playing doctor and spare me the neurology lesson. Now is the time for action, not words." She stuffed her blouse and cosmetics into the suitcase, locked it shut, and opened the cabin door. "Let's go."

"Whe-where are we going?"

"To see the only other person who might have access to your computer files. Your close friend and longtime co-worker, Robert Lerner."

They dumped the Porsche on a dirt road just outside of town. Sarah carried the suitcase another half mile through the woods before stashing it under a rotted log and covering it with deadfall. Five minutes of bushwhacking brought them to a deer trail, which they followed for a quarter of an hour until it opened onto a starlit glade.

Sarah tucked the handbag, with the scorched hole in one end, close to her side. "Look familiar?"

Grant studied the surrounding trees and the low-cut lawn ahead. "Not particularly."

"It's the far end of Feline Estates, opposite the gate. I cased the joint this afternoon while you were sleeping off last night's escapades and this morning's vodka."

"You mean, Bob lives here, too?"

"When Biotech hit the big time you both made substantial monetary gains, and invested wisely."

"I hope I get to spend some of it some day."

Sarah punched Grant playfully on the shoulder. "That's the spirit. And the Grant Templeton I want to see, with a touch of humor beneath the facade of solemn scientist."

"I don't feel very funny right now."

"Never mind. Just remember what I told you in the car. If he's the Bob on your voice recorder, if he's mixed up in this scam, then he's likely to have protection on the premises: either gunmen guarding the house, or a surveillance system which can call them in at a moment's notice. I studied the layout through a monocular this afternoon, but it was difficult to tell for sure what kind of protection he has. All the better if he's not home. Then I can root through his files for incriminating evidence. It would be nice to know exactly who the enemy is." She looked him straight in the eyes. "Do you feel comfortable with this?"

"Hell, no. I'm scared to death. Breaking into houses—even my friend's house—isn't something I do on a routine basis. But I seem to be making it a habit lately."

"Are you sure you don't want to back out?"

"I've come this far."

"I know how much you hate confrontation."

"True, but now I don't seem to have much of a choice."

"But we may learn things inside that you don't want to know."

"If Bob can be a Lerner, so can I." He smiled faintly. "I call it 'coping with humor.' He pointed with his chin. "Come on, let's get on with it."

A brisk, ten-minute walk along the tree line brought them to a garden shed behind an Olympic-sized pool fenced in with crosshatched wire strands attached to five-foot-tall steel poles. The sprawling, single-story ranch house was constructed of blond Tennessee stone; deep-set mortar joints zigzagged at random both horizontally and vertically. A profusion of French doors and picture windows gave the house an open-air look.

The back of the house was dark.

"Looks like nobody's home."

"Get down and follow me." Sarah crouched low and crept across the lawn with the stealth of a cat. She stopped when she reached a thin aluminum pole which was pierced with holes the diameter of a ten-penny nail. She studied the pole for a moment, then checked its alignment with identical poles placed to either side at twenty-foot intervals. "The perimeter guard is designed to let rabbits through without tripping the alarm. Can you squeeze in your gut enough to crawl below the bottom hole?" Without waiting for an answer, she rolled over onto her back and slithered forward like a capsized snake.

Grant got down onto his belly and started to crawl.

"Not like that! On your back. So you can gauge your girth."

"This is ridiculous." Grant did as he was told, then carefully wiggled through the grass. He felt like a wallowing hippo. He got his head and shoulders past the pole, then paused and looked down at his protruding belly. "I've got to lose some weight."

Sarah put her hands on his shoulders. "Lie still and suck it in."

"Couldn't we just knock on the front door?"

"Quiet." She grabbed him by the armpits and pulled him along the ground until his feet cleared the pole. She had incredible strength for a bantamweight who was head and shoulders shorter than Grant. "Now get on your knees."

Grant rolled his eyes. "Yes, your highness."

Sarah placed one hand over his mouth and squeezed his cheeks with the other. "Cut it out. This is serious business."

There it was again—the jump from fear to euphoria. The rational mind attempting to make sense out of an irrational world. And each time he swung from one mood to the other, the pendulum rose a bit higher. "Sorry." He followed Sarah to the back of the house, then sat on his haunches as she shone a miniature flashlight with an extended lens cone at the brass lock and around the entire edge of the jamb. Then she fiddled with something at the bottom of the back door and snapped off the light.

She whispered, "I deactivated the electronic sensor." She stuck a key into the lock, turned, gently pushed open the door, and stepped into the blackness inside. Then she pulled Grant in after her and eased the door shut.

Grant wanted to ask her how she happened to have a key, but figured that now was not the time to speak. He followed her into a long hallway whose walls were decorated with glass frames; it was too dark to see whether they contained paintings or photographic enlargements. From somewhere up ahead came a rustling sound, like the faintest push of one sheet of paper across another. They halted in front of an open doorway. Starlight entering the spacious room through the double-width picture window fell on blunt-edged shapes that looked like oddments of furniture arranged haphazardly.

A shape stirred in the shadows. Light glinted off something metallic, like a ring or watchband. Then came the sound of a chair scraping across a plastic rug protector, and a tall figure stood silhouetted against the outside gloom.

"Is someone there?" came a strangely familiar voice.

Icy tingles of fear charged along Grant's spine like ants on a candy cane. He sucked in a breath involuntarily. Sarah, standing next to him, appeared unmoved.

An arm reached out to a shaded lamp. Came a click and a muted incandescent glow. "I knew if I sat here long enough you would pay me a little visit. You are so predictable."

It was not Bob Lerner, not unless he had grown a beard. The man sidled sideways, took a step forward, and halted with one hip leaning against the edge of a polished oak desk.

Grant squinted, straining to see the features that were illuminated by the partially obscured light. His lips separated.

"Don't you know me? Or is your memory so poor that you have forgotten my face?"

Somewhere in the back of his mind, Grant struggled to piece together the black curly hair, the roughly trimmed beard, the hard brown eyes, the wrinkled forehead, the elongated crow's feet. He knew that face. He had seen it recently. Very recently. "It—can't—be."

"But it is," said the man whose name Grant knew but refused to acknowledge. "You know it is."

Grant shook his head slowly in disbelief. His jaw went slack.

"It is all quite baffling to you, I am sure. But there is a simple explanation." The man squeezed his chin between thumb and fingers. "I see you have shaved yours off."

No words could form on Grant's paralyzed tongue.

"And who are you, madam? A friend?"

Sarah clutched her handbag close and took a single step closer to the man. "Dr. Templeton, I presume?"

He bowed slightly. "At your service."

"Sarah Mason. From Saratoga."

"How appropriate. Sarah from Saratoga. And did your father cut stone?"

"Only on weekends."

Templeton extended his hand. "Thank you, Ms. Mason, for bringing it back to me. We were quite concerned, you know, when it wandered off on its own. We were afraid that it might be stolen or come to harm. It represents a considerable investment, as you can well imagine."

"Why didn't you show up last night at the Neanderthal Club? And why were you sitting here in the dark, instead of waiting at Panther Cove?"

Templeton tilted his head. "With the difficulties that have arisen, it was necessary for me to hide—to avoid unnecessary risk. You must know that certain opponents have been causing trouble this evening. Apparently, rival gangs have arrived in town to cash in on Fenton's duplicitous offers. Since Lerner is—no longer with us—and since I was supposed to bring you here anyway, it seemed like the obvious sanctuary. I knew that you would find me eventually, although quite frankly I rather expected you to call ahead instead of appearing personally under, shall we say, surreptitious circumstances. I turned off the light as soon as I detected motion."

"You took quite a chance by letting us get this close, not knowing who or what we were."

Templeton now brought his left hand around the desk. Gripped tightly in his fist was a .45-caliber revolver, which he hefted as if it were a paperweight. "One cannot be too cautious." He pointed the gun casually at Grant. "How did you manage to track it down on your own, when our not inconsiderable resources failed to find any trace of it?"

"The Department of Defense has connections. Our agents started gathering intelligence as soon as the alert went out that trouble was on the way. You could have helped by keeping in touch."

Templeton looked at her askance. "You are no doubt aware that one of your agents has gone rogue, and is at this very moment working in collusion with our warlike foes. Again I say, one cannot be too cautious." He paused, and fixed her with a steady but nonaggressive stare. "It might even have been you."

"And what makes you think I'm innocent?"

Templeton smiled. "I doubt that you are innocent. You are merely less guilty than your competitors. After all, the Department of Defense has purely selfish motives for wishing to protect my invention and me from harm. It is merely the strong-arm component of one government among many which is competing for status in the world. The U.S. desires to maintain the status quo, other countries would like to change it."

Sarah held her gaze on Templeton and the wavering gun in his hand. "At the cost of sounding protectively patriotic, I prefer to characterize the mainspring of American philosophy as a desire to preserve domestic democracy and to promote the spread of human rights."

"My dear Sarah, you are a sadly deluded purist. To be sure, to define authoritarian rule in such virtuous terms has utopian appeal, but there is no such thing as a benevolent government because altruism has no long-term survival benefit. Governments exist not to serve the people, but to perpetuate themselves. They use people the way flowers use bees for pollination. That bees profit from being manipulated is a delusion of viewpoint."

"That's a bitterly cynical perception of civilized behavior. I see government as a codification of law and order for the mutual good of all."

"That point of view is not only idealistic, it is hopelessly naive. That government which governs most, survives best."

"Government is not a conscious entity which makes decisions based upon whim. Government is a collective unity controlled by the people who created it."

Templeton spoke in a modulated tone without stress or resonance, as if he were completely detached from the subject of debate. "However you like to see it." He shrugged his shoulders. "Despite your autocratic hubris, our meeting has nothing to do with politics. We are here to trade money for power. If you have the money, I can give you the power."

"And what about the internal problems at Biotech? The dissidents who have aligned themselves against you."

"Those conflicts have been resolved. The people who disagreed with corporate policy have been persuaded to cooperate despite their previous stance on the ethics of the situation. They simply forgot that Biotech is not a public laboratory in which to conduct pure scientific research, but a private company which has an obligation to its investors to pay dividends and show a return on capital. It is a business."

"Does that mean that you're accepting bids from other potential customers?"

"It means that *our* business is none of *your* business. If, as you proclaim, your only interest is to equalize the balance of power so that no one country is disadvantaged by the technological progress of another, then Biotech's alternative negotiations cannot upset that balance." Templeton squinted one dark brown eye. "That is your purpose, is it not, Sarah from Saratoga?"

"What about the demonstration?"

Templeton pierced his brows. "Ever the skeptic."

"Not at all. It's business." Her voice was as devoid of pitch as his.

"I suppose. The irony is that you had the key to the memchip all along. It is in that brain." Templeton pointed the gun at Grant's head. "If only you had known."

"He's not right inside, though. Something's wrong with his memory. He doesn't know what this is all about, and he doesn't recognize people and places he should. If that's your idea of design perfection, I want a price reduction."

"Any truly innovative technology is bound to have flaws in the prototype stage. Once we go into full production, assembly line memchips will operate at full perfection, and so will our space robots and groundside simulacra."

Headlights swung across the picture window behind Templeton. The dark silhouette of a vehicle turned off the main thoroughfare and trundled along the driveway toward the front of the house. It stopped by the front door and disgorged two men brandishing guns.

"No!" Grant charged across the room with the speed and the fury of a cornered lion. He grabbed his lookalike's gun arm and swung it up. A shot rang out, a bullet tore through the plaster ceiling, then the twin figures wrestled for possession of the firearm, spinning around the desk like partners in a fraternal Danse Macabre. Another shot rang out. The lamp was knocked over in the tussle; for a moment it hung over the edge of the desk by the wire, then it crashed to the floor. The bulb shattered, plunging the room into blackness. The revolver went off again. Man and machine whirled with dizzying speed, a blur of dark silhouettes.

Sarah could not let the real Grant Templeton be killed by his creation. She yanked the forty-four Magnum out of her handbag, aimed quickly, and fired.

Both bodies fell to the floor in a tangle of limbs and electrical cords. Neither one moved.

Chapter 17

"This is the weirdest damn case I've ever had in thirty years of police work." Captain George Hendry shifted uneasily in his seat. "We got robots, assassins, and robot assassins."

Patrolman Frank Riley sat behind the wheel of the squad car. He nudged the brake pedal as he approached a flashing traffic light. "And don't forget the assassinated robot."

"I'll never forget that. Goddamn Blakey, leading us on that way like a college prankster. I nearly swallowed my plate when he stuck his bare finger in that bullet hole. And then spreading the guy's legs—er, the thing's legs—and flashing us a crotch shot. I mean, he coulda warned us." Hendry washed his hands over his face. The lateness of the hour was reflected in the red veins in his eyes. "And in front of my own daughter, too, who was loving every minute of it." He wagged a finger at Riley. "You see what you're in for?"

"I never believed you before."

"Believe me. I wouldn't lie to you. She loves to tease and embarrass. Not in a mean way, just so she can control the situation. And she's worse now than when she was a kid."

"But, how do you put up with it year after year?" Riley turned down a side street and pulled up alongside another squad car.

Hendry slowly shook his head. "I don't know. But you better find out quick if you're still planning to marry her."

"I didn't think I had a choice—"

A uniformed officer approached from a house across the street, and leaned down so she could peer into the driver's window. "Hello, George. Frank. You want a report on Francine Baker?"

"Didn't come out here for the ride, Cindy," Captain Hendry said, wearily but not sourly.

"Well, I've woken up half a dozen neighbors and asked them what they knew. The last time anyone can remember positively seeing her is Thursday night, when she came home from work. One woman saw her car leave Friday morning, at her usual time, but couldn't swear that it was Francine in it because she only saw her from the back when she went out to get her paper."

"Has anyone noticed anything unusual lately, in her behavior? Or has she said anything that might make people think she was in trouble or up to something?"

Cindy shook her head. "No. In fact, she had lunch with one of the neighbors last Sunday and she seemed to be excited over the possibility of getting transferred— to a higher position. She's supposed to get a substantial raise in salary."

"What about relatives?" Riley interjected.

"None in town. Her children married and moved away, and her husband—her second husband—passed away a couple years ago. Lung cancer. Apparently he was a heavy smoker." An uncomfortable silence lasted several seconds. "Do you want me to keep asking around?"

Hendry thought for a moment. "No, let the poor folks get their sleep. No sense in getting everybody mad. You go back to the station and post a report, then see if anyone needs a relief on patrol."

"I'd rather wake people up and get them mad than be out on the street. Everybody's so edgy tonight there's likely to be a couple toes shot off—or worse—from the quick-draw cowboys. Keller's men pulled over a newspaper delivery truck for running a yellow light, and when the driver went to take his wallet from his jacket, he had so many guns staring him in the face he almost passed out. Everybody's jumpy."

"Yeah, well, stay that way. You'll live longer."

The police station was a beehive of activity. Not only was the off-duty staff handling phone lines and radio calls, under Sergeant Benson's able direction, but

Keller's state troopers had moved in to lend assistance, and some volunteer fire fighters had been sworn in as deputies. Hendry spread the word about the robot at the morgue. There was such disbelief that he had to repeat the story several times. The subsequent free-for-all debate got loud and boisterous, with everyone voicing advice and opinions, but there were no conclusions forthcoming. The station house was in an uproar. Finally, Hendry and Riley fought their way through the mob and grabbed some coffee in the back room, where Patrolman Anderson chased them down.

"Boss, I got the run-down on the Archbold woman, and it's fishier than I thought."

"How so?"

"She's alive and well and living in Chicago. She's there this very minute." He paused dramatically to let the ramifications sink in before offering more information. He pulled a pad from his back pocket and flipped it open like a switchblade. "Department of Motor Vehicles verified her license, and the description seems to match. Then I called the old lady at home and got her out of bed—"

"Lot of that going on tonight," Hendry intruded.

"—and asked her if she had rented a car in Highland Hills. And what do you think she said?"

Hendry was in no joking mood. "Quit playing around, Richy."

"She said, 'Does this have anything to do with the kidnapping?' " Both Riley and Hendry shouted "What?" simultaneously.

Richardson smiled smugly. "Boss, we opened a whole can of worms with this one. From what she told me, Thursday night two men tried to hustle her off at gunpoint while she was entering her apartment. She thought she was going to be raped, bit the hand that was clamped over her mouth, and let out a scream that was heard by a couple of undercover detectives who happened to be in the area on an unrelated case. They saw what was going down and broke it up. One kidnapper died of gunshot wounds, the other is in the tank but refuses to talk. Well, he curses in German, but that's about all he says. Now for the kicker. . . . "

After an unbearable pause, Hendry screamed. "Go on!"

"Archbold is her maiden name. She used to be married to none other than Grant Templeton."

Riley wanted to shout "What?" again, realized it would sound redundant, and swallowed instead. The possible implications were endless.

Captain Hendry, despite the expression of amazement on his face, followed proper police procedure. "Had she received any threats? Anonymous phone calls? Was she on the outs with Templeton? Had they had arguments or anything?"

"No threats. No phone calls. No prior troubles of any kind. On good terms with Templeton; divorce was amicable, and her choice, and she still has a great deal of respect for the man. They talk on the phone all the time. And their daughter was living with him till recently."

"Dawn Templeton?" Riley finally found his voice. "Does Barbara Archbold know where the daughter can be found?"

"No." Anderson let a huge grin spread across his face. "But I do."

Hendry was having none of Anderson's histrionics. "Richy, if you don't quit playing games with me I'm gonna rip out your tongue and paste it—"

"She's in the back room." Anderson jerked a thumb over his shoulder. He enjoyed the silence for a moment—but only for a moment. "The college registrar was not happy about being woke up in the middle of the night, but I figured that, with what was going down, we'd better get the girl in here under protective custody. I couldn't get hold of you to get the proper authority—"

Hendry grabbed Anderson's cheeks between two massive hands and shook the patrolman's head like a hound worrying a quail. "Richy, if we were alone I'd kiss you. That's the best damn thing you coulda done. I love you." To Riley, "You see how my policy of encouraging individual initiative pays off in dividends?"

Anderson backed away from the captain's firm embrace. He had completely lost his ever-present smile and nearly all of his innocent ebullience. "George, I like you, too. But let's not get carried away."

Riley broke up a scene which was becoming an embarrassment. "Richy, did you ask Barbara Archbold if her license was in her possession?"

"I did, and it is. That's why I went out and grabbed the girl right away. There's somebody in town that looks like her mother—that's disguised like her mother—and that's using a forged driver's license. And the Mason woman was driving the car that was rented to the Archbold lookalike. Now ain't that fishy?"

"This case makes less sense the deeper we get into it," said Hendry. "I'm more confused than ever."

"That makes the both of us. What else I did was I radioed Cindy to check out the Well Come Inn, where the Archbold lookalike told the rental agency she was staying. She checked in all right, but the room is empty and the bed's never been slept in."

Riley digested this latest intelligence. "How about Dawn? What did she say?"

"She's scared, I can tell you that. She heard the radio report about the ruckus at Feline Estate, but says her father told her to stay away from the house and the lab no matter what. Said he was worried about a major crisis in the company that was coming to a head this weekend and didn't want her around in case there was trouble." Anderson shrugged. "I didn't pump her. I figured you and George would want to be in on any further interrogation."

"You got that right—" Captain Hendry was interrupted by Sergeant Bob Benson, who stuck his head in the door.

"George, I got Blakey on line three. He says it's important."

"Thanks, Bob." The sergeant closed the door behind him. "Richy, you go keep that girl company. Don't let her out of your sight."

"I'm on it." Anderson made a circle with his thumb and forefinger, and left the room.

Hendry scooped up the phone and punched in the red annunciator light. "What you got, Blakey?" He listened for several minutes, uttering an occasional "yeah" and "okay" and "unh hunh." He hung up and took a long draught of coffee before speaking. "Looks like all tonight's victims were European. Least ways, that's where their clothes were made. Blakey also went ahead and extracted the other bullet from the dead robot, like I asked him to, and removed the electronic brain for analysis. The memory boards have patent numbers that can be traced, but I don't think even the President can get those jokers into their office at—" He glanced at his watch. "—three a.m. on a Sunday morning."

"Want me to put a call through to the FBI?"

"Nah. They'll be here in a few hours so we'll just save it for them. But he did find a curious kind of a logo stamped on one of the components. He said it looked like the biological symbol for female—a circle with a cross under it—except that it has a lightning bolt instead of a cross. Does that mean anything to you?"

"Biotech." Riley offered a single nod. "They have the same logo on their building sign. But it doesn't necessarily mean anything. Templeton said they sell parts to other vendors."

Hendry humphed and shrugged it off. "Let's talk to Templeton's daughter and see what she has to say."

In the hallway they bumped into Sergeant Benson with another dispatch. "Just came in from the forensic team working on that van in Powell's pasture. It wasn't a television repair truck like we thought it was. All them TV screens were high-tech surveillance monitors linked to some kind of mobile sensor device. The damn thing was a spy wagon. If what Blakey says is true, it could be the control vehicle for that thing on the slab."

"Bob, pass the word that there may be other non-human predators on the prowl, and to be careful. Machines have no moral compunction against killing people. I want urine samples from everybody on the streets who looks, thinks, or acts suspicious."

"Urine samples? What'll that prove?"

"It'll prove they got urine and the plumbing to deliver it with."

They left the sergeant scratching his head in perplexity.

Dawn Templeton was tall and slender, with long flowing black hair which was as straight and as thin as straw and which swept the lower portion of her back like a broom. She shook the bangs from her dark brown eyes when the two policemen entered the interrogation room.

Hendry made the introductions, and wasted no time in getting right into the meat of the matter. "Now, Ms. Templeton, you already know that your father is in trouble. We don't know what it is, other than some bad guys are after him, but we're doing everything we can to find him and bring him in where we can protect him. I won't mince words with you. His life is in danger. He may already be dead. But if he's still alive, you may be able to help us find him." He hardly gave her time to absorb the seriousness of the situation. "Now, when was the last time you saw your father?"

Dawn bit her lower lip like a scolded child. "Well, I— I guess I—I haven't actually seen him for a week or so. I—I went out to the house to look for some things. Papers I need so I can transfer to MIT next fall. Daddy said they were in a trunk in the attic, and he promised to look for them when he had the time." She shrugged and tilted her head to the side. "Of course, I know how busy he is—always is—but I didn't need them right away, so I let it go. I thought it would give him something to, uh, something to do for me. You see, he always wants to do things for me because we were apart so much when I was growing up. Then, when Mother moved back to Chicago after I graduated from high school, I moved in with him and—we got to know each other a lot better. But I felt funny when Charlotte—"

"Ms. Templeton, please. I don't want to pry into your personal affairs or relationships with your father.

When was the last time you saw him?"

Again Dawn bit her lower lip. "Well, not since he went to Washington—something about government contract work. But he called as soon as he got back—that was on Monday, you know, just to let me know that he was home and that everything was all right. He's always been good about calling. He called again Thursday morning, but he sounded different."

"Different how?"

"Well, I'm not sure. I could say he sounded preoccupied, but anyone who knows Daddy knows that he's always preoccupied. He can stare you in the eyes and hold an intelligent conversation, but you know that deep down inside he's not all there; that a part of his mind is somewhere else, on some other plane, thinking totally different thoughts. There's so much going on in his mind that you just get used to the fact that you never have his full attention. That's why Mother left him. She couldn't accept his duality—the dual nature of his thinking. But that's what makes him so brilliant, because he can handle concepts on so many levels of perception. And he has a unique ability to shift the concentration of those levels at the blink of an eye.

"Anyway, on Thursday he sounded—well, maybe distracted is a better word for it. He was talking in conundrums, almost as if—well—as if he thought someone might be listening. It was like he was talking in a code that he hoped I could decipher."

"Did you understand? Did you know what he was trying to say?"

"I remember the words, but I'm not sure what he meant by them. He said something like big things were in the wind and that, if anything unusual occurred, to remember Mr. Toad."

"Mr. Toad?" Hendry rolled his eyes at Riley and Anderson. " 'Toad' as in 'frog'?"

Nervously biting her lip, "Yes."

"And does that mean anything to you?"

"I have the feeling it should."

Captain Hendry rubbed his hand over his forehead

and gouged his fingers in his eyes. He was standing hunched over the seated girl, and now his back ached something fierce. He stood erect, dug his fingers into his lower spine, and paced around the room like a caged lion. "Mr. Toad." He said it as if the pronouncement might add significance to the name. "Mr. Toad." Where had he heard that before?

"Daddy told me he thought it was about time I went to Chicago to visit Mother, and that to beat the weekend traffic I should leave right away. And he said to make sure I stopped by the house next week to pick up my transcripts."

"And did you? Go to Chicago, I mean?"

"No. He's never told me to visit Mother before. And he certainly would not mention that she lived in Chicago. I know where she lives. I think what he was really trying to say was that I should make myself scarce—to not let anyone know where I was until he contacted me after the weekend. Well, I didn't want to stay with any of my friends because, well, because they talk too much. So I went to Mr. Kraddock, the registrar, who knows Daddy real well because he hires a lot of summer help from the college for on-the-job training. I told him that Daddy wanted me out of the dorm for the weekend—that it was a security matter—and could he find a place for me to stay."

"Didn't he think that was strange?"

"No," she said ingenuously. "Anyone who works with Daddy knows that he does everything with a reason, even if it's not apparent. Mr. Kraddock purposely did not ask me any questions about it. He just made arrangements to have me put up in one of the college guest rooms. I didn't go to class on Friday—I just stayed in the room and studied. All day yesterday, too. Then Mr. Kraddock came in and told me that a couple of my girlfriends said that my mother was on campus looking for me. Then I really knew something was wrong. My mother hasn't been back to Highland Hills since she moved back to Chicago. And she never does anything or goes anywhere on the spur of the moment;

she always calls ahead to verify arrangements. I told Mr. Kraddock that whoever was asking for me wasn't my mother. Then he came back a few hours ago and told me about the news he heard on the radio. Then I was really worried. For Daddy's sake. But I didn't call him. His instructions were explicit. So I just sat there until Mr. Anderson came to bring me in. And he told me about Mother's attempted kidnapping."

Riley got down on one knee and stared up at Dawn's tear-strewn face. "Ms. Templeton, do you know what kind of work your father was doing that would involve the Department of Defense, and that might encourage enemy agents to want to go to such extremes to, uh, exert pressure on him?"

What other reason could there be for trying to kidnap his ex-wife, perhaps his secretary, possibly his co-worker. Something big indeed was in the wind.

Dawn wiped tears from her cheeks with the flats of her hands. Her skin was alabaster white. "Well, most of his work is highly classified—at least, the contract jobs for NASA and the DOD. He wouldn't talk about it even to me. He's always been, well, he took his work seriously and was careful not to let me see, like, his computer screen when he was working at home. He always blanked the screen when I walked into the room so I didn't, uh, accidentally pick up a word or catch-phrase that I might remember subconsciously and repeat in public. He was always careful that way. And I understood. He wasn't hiding anything from me personally. It was his job, and his, uh, his oath, I guess, to keep that kind of information confidential.

"But it's no secret that for the past several years he's been perfecting what he calls the Memchip 201. That's not classified military intelligence, it's corporate information pending patent approval. It's been written up in the scientific journals, and they even did an article on him in *Personalities*, to his great disapproval I'm sure. The Memchip 201 will revolutionize the computer industry the way transistors did when they replaced vacuum tubes. It's a quantum leap in memory technology."

"Will it have applications in the field of robotics?"

Dawn spoke with great composure now that she was on firmer ground. "Oh, definitely. Much of Daddy's contract work for NASA concerns remote robotics, such as minilabs in space or on the Moon that can be operated from Earth. But for interplanetary deployment of scistats—that is, scientific stations—the time lag is a nuisance. That's where an intelligent computer can make a difference in mission success: by being programmed heuristically to deal with unanticipated events—"

"Excuse me, ma'am," said Captain Hendry. " 'Heuristically'?"

"I'm sorry, Captain. A heuristic computer is one that is programmed to learn from its experiences and to adapt thereafter to changing environmental conditions." As an afterthought, "In computerese that doesn't mean a variation in weather patterns, but all external physical conditions that affect the operation of a system, in this case a deep-space probe which might—or will undoubtedly—encounter situations for which the computer is not programmed. Theoretically, a computer with a large enough memory capacity and a fast enough response time can pass the Turing criteria."

Dawn Templeton held up her hands before anyone could interrupt. "The Turing criteria is named after its inventor, Alan Turing: the master cryptanalyst who was chiefly responsible for breaking the German codes during World War Two. Simply stated, if a computer's responses are indistinguishable from those of a human, the computer can be said to be conscious."

"You mean—alive?" asked Anderson.

"No, not alive like you think of life as a function of biological processes, any more than a calculator is alive except in an electronic sense. It just means that for all practical purposes you can't tell the two apart: what we call Artificial Intelligence, ostensibly one without volition or concept of self, but one which can adapt to conditions by overwriting its initial programs. Of course, the philosophical implications—"

"Toad Hall!" Captain Hendry shouted. He faced Dawn Templeton with arms akimbo, bent at the waist, and put on the glimmer of a smile. "Does Toad Hall mean anything to you?"

Dawn looked nonplussed. "Well, I don't think I've ever been to a place with that name—"

"Not some place you ever went. But when Sandy was a little girl, I used to read to her from a book—"

"*The Wind in the Willows!*" Dawn practically screamed.

"And Mr. Toad used to drive around in his car tearing up the neighborhood," Captain Hendry continued. "With the Mole and the Water Rat—"

"And the Otter and dear old Badger. Oh, yes. Daddy used to read it to me all the time." Dawn's eyes dazzled with fond remembrances.

Riley and Anderson exchanged looks of worry and bemusement. "Then it must be part of the code your father—"

Sergeant Benson burst into the interrogation room. "George, there's hell to pay at the Lerner place. One man down and lots o' gun play. You better get out there pronto."

Captain Hendry stood stock still, bent half forward with his head cocked to the side. He glared at the burly sergeant in a frozen tableau for at least a second and a half before straightening and leaping for the door. "Let's go, men."

They were halfway down the corridor before Dawn Templeton jumped to her feet and shouted. "I'm coming, too." All four men halted abruptly, and turned. She looked like a forlorn child, lower lip quivering. "I have to. It concerns my father." After a moment, "And Bob Lerner is like an uncle to me."

Riley nodded. "She might be able to help—"

"Okay, you can come along, but you're not to go anywhere without a police escort. Is that clear? And you take orders."

She stifled her tears, and nodded. Outside, Riley

opened the car door for her and climbed into the back seat beside her. Anderson took the wheel, Hendry rode shotgun.

With sirens blasting and strobe lights flashing, the squad car raced for Feline Estates with half a dozen patrol cars in tow. The canopy wreckage had been cleared from the entrance and the gates had been removed. They passed Panther Cove, went on to the next driveway, which was marked Ocelot Cove, and turned left. The entourage halted behind a small flotilla of vehicles—city and state—which were parked helter-skelter on the lawn. Uniformed officers swarmed over the grounds like ants in a honey frenzy. One policeman lay on his back with his arms clutched across his chest, while two policewomen crouched by his side.

"Phil, you okay?" The concern was evident in Captain Hendry's voice.

Between shallow inhalations Patrolman Philip Handleman managed a weak and twitchy grin. "Hurts like hell, George, but I guess I'm gonna make it. The vest stopped the slug, but the force of that damn bullet spun me twice around and knocked the wind outa me. Maybe broke a couple of ribs. Getting lots of attention, though."

Hendry breathed a sigh of relief.

Patrolwoman Cindy Ballard rose and gave a report to the captain. "The Lerner house was empty earlier, George. I checked it myself. Phil was guarding the Templeton house when he saw a car turn into the driveway, and, knowing that I had been here to check it out, he came over to investigate. He got here just about the time the gunfire started."

"When I saw the car was a Continental," Handleman said between gritted teeth, "I knew it was the bad guys." He sucked hard between sentences. "I called for backup right away. Had no intention of tangling with them, not after the mess I saw over there." He flung an arm in the direction of Templeton's house. "One of 'em must have heard the radio crackle, 'cause he turned fast and plugged me. That's all I remember."

"You did a good job, Phil. Now take it easy and rest up a bit." Captain Hendry dragged Cindy Ballard to the side. "What else we got?"

"Looks like another blood bath. Four bodies: one by the car, another behind the garage, one on the swimming pool fence, and one inside. George, you better take a look inside . . . " She led the four of them into the study where a body lay huddled on the floor in that unnatural attitude of arms and legs that instantly spelled death.

Blood was everywhere, smeared across the jacket and shirt front as if a major artery had been severed. The face was flaxen, lifeless; the eyes were open and unseeing.

Dawn Templeton screamed, then fell to her knees by the body's side and grasped one lifeless hand. She cried hysterically, and repeated over and over, "Daddy. Oh, Daddy. Oh, Daddy. . . . "

Chapter 18

Sarah fired through the picture window at the figures which were fanning out across the front of the house. One hit the ground silently and lay still, the others disappeared from the field of view. One assailant fired a shot: not through the glass, but behind him.

Sarah grabbed Grant by the shoulder and yanked him away from the simulacrum which was jerking spasmodically. Grant extricated himself from the broken lamp and the tangle of extension cords. He was bleeding profusely from a wound in the arm which appeared more bloody than dangerous. She shoved him against the inner wall, then crouched and crawled on her knees to the simulacrum, which was trembling in mechanical seizure. She kicked the fallen revolver out of its reach.

"Don't kill me," it cried. "Please don't kill me."

Sarah aimed the gun where it would do the most good. "Answer some questions and I'll think about it."

"Please let me live. Please let me live. I don't want to die."

"Where is Bob Lerner?"

"Please don't shoot me. Please don't shoot me." It kept wailing plaintively, it's monotonous dialogue overlapping Sarah's questions as if its microphone were damaged and it could not pick up her voice. Its eyes glimmered unblinkingly in the semidarkness, like twin annunciator lights on a control board. "Don't make me die."

"Where is Bob Lerner?"

Faint sounds were audible from the far reaches of the house: sounds that could have been doors swinging and windows sliding.

The Templeton simulacrum placed its hands together in front of its bloodstained chest. It was trying to pray, but the bullet in its chest cavity must have split some hydraulic lines or severed some electrical connections in addition to destroying the gyroscope, for the left arm twitched and the torso convulsed arhythmically. All the limbs were out of synchronism, forcing the simulacrum to make uncoordinated gestures like a humanoid creature in a cheap but gruesome monster movie. "I want to live. I want to keep on living. Please don't take my life away—"

Sarah blew a hole in its central processing unit. Instantly the crying and twitching ceased. Its frozen attitude took on the aspect of a life-size statue whose eyes glared emotionlessly like white painted stone. Sarah ignored it, scampered to the study door on her knees, and fired warning shots both ways down the hall. Then she turned her attention to Grant, who leaned against the wall holding his wounded arm with his hand. Tears streamed down both cheeks, not from pain, but from fear.

"Snap out of it, Grant. We've got to get out of here and the house is surrounded."

Grant worked his jaw, but no words came out. He was in shock, more from emotional response than from his injury. When Sarah pushed the jacket back to expose his left shoulder, he let out a stifled groan of pain. A mass of blood clotted his upper shirtsleeve. Sarah inserted her fingers into the hole which was punctured in the material by the bullet, ripped open a gash to expose his arm, and peered closely at the wound with her miniature flashlight.

"It looks worse than it is, and it's bleeding more than it should."

Grant groaned in pain.

"Probably hurts, too." Sarah snatched the hankie from Grant's jacket pocket and quickly bound it around the furrow that was gouged through the meat. "If you're lucky, you'll live long enough for it to get infected from the gunpowder."

Grant blinked the tears out of his eyes. "How—how—how did you know which one of us—"

"Later. Let's get out of the present situation first. Just remember this: they want you alive at all costs, or everything they've worked for goes down the tubes."

"They! Who the hell are 'they'?"

"The NRL. Nazi Revitalization League."

"But what—"

"Later." She clamped a hand over his mouth. "They won't shoot at you. You got that? They need you alive. So stick close to me and I've got a chance of living through this, too. Now let's go while we only have to tangle with the shock troops. Reinforcements might not be too far behind."

Grant swallowed hard. The dull ache in his arm was more than compensated for by the wild rapture in his heart. He was exhilarated by the fact that he was alive—not just breathing and thinking and talking, but that he was truly alive: a complex biological organism whose origins began in a sea of organic soup many billions of years in the past, amino acids sparked by lightning into self-replicating cells which evolved over millennia to colonial structures to worms to fish to air breathing animals—instead of an inanimate machine made of wires and tubing and hard metallic parts.

He composed himself for whatever might occur. Even if he died in the next few minutes, he would go to his grave happy by knowing that he was fully human. "You're the leader. So lead."

Sarah grinned. "That's the spirit."

Grant grabbed her arm as she leaned into the hallway. "Uh, we could try calling the police, you know."

"Not a good idea at the moment." She stood up in the hallway and ran with her shoulder close to one wall until she reached the back door of the house. Grant was right behind her. She listened intently for a moment, meanwhile reloading her gun. She turned to Grant. "I want you to run for all you're worth for the woods. They won't shoot you. It will give me a chance to spot them."

Grant shuddered at the prospect of facing guns in the open. His faith in Sarah was on the verge of faltering. After all, who was this woman he had met less than a day before? She was a master of physical disguise.

Could she also be disguising her motives? On the other hand, she had put herself in jeopardy and had not abandoned him when last they had been surrounded by a numerically superior force. On that count alone he owed her one. And in the arena in which they were now sparring, he was a sacrificial lamb for the first hungry lion that happened along. "Whatever you say."

Sarah eased open the door, peered through the crack, then yanked the door back, placed her hand in the small of Grant's back, and shoved. Grant hobbled rather than ran—his legs were not used to the amount of exercise they had been getting recently and his muscles were sore, and holding his right hand over the wound in his left arm forced his body into an unnatural twist. He ignored the loud guttural shout and the gunshot. A bullet whizzed over his head uncomfortably close. Sarah, you'd better be right.

An instant later another shot rang out, this time from the direction of the swimming pool. Again, a bullet sped past Grant's unprotected head and left a hollow slap of air in its wake. Then a line of bullets clipped the lawn in front of him, seemingly in an effort to convince him to stop in his tracks. Grant ignored the hopefully hollow threat, and kept running.

He had nearly reached the safety of the tree line when a figure leaped up in front of him, arms outstretched. Grant felt like a rabbit which had been chased into a trap by a couple of shrewd hounds. He skidded to a halt, slipped on the grass, and fell back onto the ground. Shots rang out from the house, and when he twisted his body to look back he saw one gunman tumble head over heels as he was shot on the fly. The other gunman was hit full in the chest as he stood up in front of the swimming pool; the force of the bullet picked him up and tossed him back against the fence. His body went limp, but his suit coat snagged on the triangular wire bail atop the upper horizontal support; the man hung there like a grisly limp rag doll.

When Grant looked up at the antagonist towering above him, he found himself looking into the barrel of a pistol. He kicked out and caught the man in the shin. The gunman lost his balance, swung partway to the side, then was slammed all the way around by a forty-four slug which glanced off his rib cage. He hit the ground hard, and lay there moaning.

"Honey, are you okay?" Sarah knelt above him and slid a hand under his good shoulder.

Grant was more alert after this shootout than the last one. "Yes, I'm fine." He let out a squeal of pain as Sarah helped him to his feet. "I must be getting used to the gun play." He winced. "But I don't want to make a habit out of it."

"That's the stuff—"

The gunman on the ground rolled over and reached out for his fallen pistol. Sarah leaped like a cat and pounced on his hand, digging her heel into the fingers with all her weight and momentum. The bones snapped like uncooked strands of spaghetti. She spun on her heel without stepping off his hand, forcing from his lips a scream of agony. She looked down at him with feral eyes and pointed the Magnum at his head.

"Would you like to say a few last words before going to join your Fuhrer?"

"Don't shoot him!" Grant was breathing hard in the chill night air, puffing streams of white condensation like a locomotive chugging up a steeply angled track. "It would be murder. Cold-blooded murder."

Sarah's eyes narrowed until they were tiny beads of light that shone with the intensity of solar flares. "Death is what he deserves."

"Perhaps, but not like that." Grant glared in horror at the man on the ground, and, despite his fear and trembling and the pain from his wounded arm, found it impossible to pass the death sentence on an enemy already vanquished.

He knew he should hate this man and all he represented, yet he could not watch him die when he so desperately wanted to live—when Grant knew so poignantly what it was like to want to live. All conscious entities, no matter their background or inner makeup, once granted consciousness had a right to survive.

"He'd be dead already if you hadn't kicked him out of my line of fire."

Shrieking in pain, the man grabbed Sarah's slender ankle and tried to pull her foot off his broken hand. She banged his knuckles with the barrel of her gun, breaking more bones in the process.

"But he's not dead. And you can't kill him like this."

"You don't know enough about me, or about what's happening, to say that. And now is not the time for rationalizing the situation." Once again she pointed the gun at the man's head. "You must have noticed that he didn't try to negotiate. And, as corny as it might sound, the fate he had in mind for you was one that was worse than death. Believe me."

Once again, overcome by emotion, tears welled up in Grant's eyes.

"Now I've got to ask him some questions, and I can do it better without any distractions. Go hide in the trees. I'll join you in a moment."

Grant knew what she was going to do—or thought he knew—but was powerless to prevent her. A warrior he was not, so he was at the mercy of anyone who brandished weapons at him or who threatened him with physical harm. It was the bane of being a civilized person in violent and uncivilized surroundings. He cast a parting glower over his injured shoulder, and did as he was told. He stumbled a couple of hundred feet into the forest where he found a sawed-off stump, and sat down for a few moments of quiet contemplation. This world into which he had been thrust was so vastly different from the one which he had left that he thought he might never be able to adapt to it.

Off in the distance he heard the blare of approaching sirens. A single shot rang out from the direction of the house. Suddenly Sarah was standing before him, her approach concealed by stealth.

"He wouldn't talk."

Grant choked down a dozen accusations, confused and benumbed by his savior's brutal conduct and by his own inner turmoil. He could not look her in the eyes despite—or perhaps—because of full acknowledgment that her actions were not unrationalistic, but were in fact appropriate under the circumstances. Hostile intent required—no, demanded—stern measures, taken not in reprisal but in affirmative action.

"Because he was born instead of built doesn't mean that he was human." She placed a soft but strong hand on his shoulder. "It's a cruel world, Grant. If you don't believe me, watch the evening news."

He wiped tears off his cheeks. "But seeing it on television is different from being involved in it."

Gently she lifted him from the stump. "Sulk later, when there's time."

Finally he looked at her. "Will there ever be time?"

"Yes," she said without hesitation.

For the next thirty minutes they traipsed through the woods, crossed creeks and golf courses, passed along deserted neighborhood streets, cut through lawns and driveways, and wound up in another motel called the Please Duck Inn. Sarah re-enacted her check-in procedure, found the room unoccupied, and let Grant into the cramped but tidy motel suite.

"How many rooms did you rent in town?"

Sarah laughed. "Enough so I could keep on the move and leave some false leads in my wake." She locked the door and placed her handbag on the bureau.

Grant put his right knee on the bed and collapsed, hitting the mattress with his right shoulder and rolling over onto his back gently enough not to slam his wounded arm. He stared up at the ceiling. Scenes from the previous day and a half flashed through his mind like a motion picture montage. It was all so unreal—so unimaginable.

"Care for a drink?" Sarah appeared fresh and vibrant, as if no extreme physical demands had been placed against her body, as if no emotional stress had been encountered. She downed one glass and held the other out to Grant. "It's only water."

He winced as he rolled over and rose up on one

elbow, and took the glass in his hand. The water was cool on his lips. He felt no thirst, but drained the glass as if he had been parched. "So how did you know it was me instead of the other one?" Then, as an afterthought, "Or were you shooting at the other one?"

Sarah took back the empty glass. "I always get my man. Don't forget that."

Grant lay back flat. "There are a lot of things I'll never forget." The ceiling was painted flat white; every bump and divot cast a shadow which drew attention to the imperfections in the plaster. "Things I wish I could forget."

"Forget about forgetting. How about trying to remember."

Instead, he tried one of her tactics. "You thought all along I was an imposter, didn't you?"

Sarah brought two more glasses of water from the bathroom, placed them on the nightstand. "It was a strong possibility. Look at it from my side. I was supposed to meet you Friday night at the Neanderthal Club. You didn't show, so I had to go out hunting for you. I went to all your haunts—well, both of them: your house and your lab. You never go anywhere else. And the only reason you go home is to work at the computer station in your study where you can get away from the distractions of day-to-day business. The Biotech building was locked up tighter than a drum, showing no lights, and surrounded by a surveillance system which requires special knowledge to circumvent, and I didn't want to get caught that early in the game even if I was wearing a different disguise."

"Who were you that time?"

"Your ex-wife."

Grant jolted. "My ex—but why?"

"Because of the kidnapping attempt." Sarah held him down with a hand against his chest as he started to raise himself up on his elbows. "As soon as we got word that the NRL was involved and was threatening reprisals if the Memchip 201 was withheld from them—and they were willing to pay handsomely for it—we knew the kind of people we were dealing with. We acted accordingly, and spread a net through the information networks and computer links that would wave a flag if anything unusual occurred to anyone connected in any way with Biotech. That's how we learned about Randy Vanderbilt's death so fast. Not only was it suspicious because of his collaboration on the Memchip design, but following the death of so many others it completed a pattern of terrorism waged against the company. We know that the NRL will stop at nothing to get what they want. And we know how ruthless they've been in the past and the kinds of extortion they will resort to."

"What kind—"

"I'll get to that. I was recalled from Germany in order to be your liaison with the DOD." Sarah opened an overnight case which was hung over the back of the room's only chair, and removed a pocketsize first aid kit. "We knew from our informants in Germany that the NRL thought the Memchip 201 could solve their problems in building a new Nazi army, and would stop at nothing to enlist Biotech's aid. Take off your jacket."

Grant winced as he pulled his arms out of the sleeves. "Why us? We're a robotics company. We build articulated robots for use in outer space like Benthic Products builds platforms for exploration under the sea. Our defense contracts are minimal: we supply memory chips for ICBMs. We don't know a thing about ground forces."

"That's old news, but we'll go into that later." She laid her nursing supplies on a bath towel which she spread on the sheet next to Grant, and unwrapped a sterile gauze pad. "You remember that big guy blocking the doorway in your house?"

"I think I always will."

"It was a simulacrum. A member of Germany's next master race. The perfect soldier because it obeys every command at once and without protest or criticism. It can be programmed to engage the enemy unmercifully without fear of injury or death, because afterwards it doesn't have to deal with the emotional trauma of the ethics or morality of its actions. If damaged, it is more easily repaired than a human soldier; if destroyed, it is more easily replaced. In short, it offers what every dictator desires most from his subjects: absolute obedience."

"But, you can't use robots to kill people. There are laws—robotics laws—that prevent a robot from harming a human being."

"Grant, come out of the dark ages of juvenile science fiction. This is reality. You can build a machine to do anything you want it to do: calculate sums, produce spreadsheets, launch missiles, destroy cities. Do you honestly believe you can't program a computer to pull the trigger of a gun?"

"Well, I—I never thought of it quite like that."

"Yes, you have, but that's besides the point." Sarah flashed a knife and brought it to bear on his torn and bloodstained sleeve. She sliced the material all the way around with a blade which was razor sharp, and removed the sleeve entirely. "Lie down."

He did as he was told. "But what did Babs—"

"I'll get to that," she said imperiously. "A week and a half ago someone purporting to be Grant Templeton attended a high level meeting of the Joint Chiefs of Staff. General Brinkley, who is my section chief, brought the Chiefs up to date on the Nazi Revitalization League and their attempt to purchase the Memchip 201 when it is perfected. In the interests of national security, you—or whoever was posing as you—stated that Biotech had had no contact with any such organization, which would have been true in any case because they would have used a dummy corporation through which to tender purchase offers. You or your double was warned to be exceptionally careful with whom you were dealing, especially regarding research which was being funded by the military, and to report any strange goings-on."

"Ouch!" Grant looked down at the ugly gash in his upper arm, which now lay exposed.

Sarah laid the bloody hanky on the towel, and continued her ministrations. "You also exhibited a proto-type brain phasing unit in which the military has an interest because of its therapeutic value in treating bat-tle fatigue—euphemistically referred to as post trau-matic stress syndrome and associated psychiatric dis-orders."

"Well, I don't actually remem—"

"You left the unit in Washington and returned to Highland Hills. You called our mutual contact at Ben-thic Products on Thursday night and delivered a coded message which declared that an emergency situation was developing with respect to the memchip experi-ments this weekend, and that you thought that you were being watched and that your calls were being monitored. We were still deciding what to do when our computer spit out the report on the attempted kidnap-ping of your ex-wife. So we knew that the NRL was seri-ous in—"

"Is Babs okay? Was she hurt, or—"

"By a stroke of luck a couple of local cops foiled the kidnapping. Since kidnapping is a federal offense the report was automatically filed with the FBI, who flashed it to us immediately because of the flag. When we heard—"

"But, Babs has nothing to do with Biotech. Why would she—"

"Because you have emotional ties with her. Or had at one time. It's SOP for the NRL to exercise control by victimizing a person's loved ones, and threatening them—"

"What about Dawn? She's the one I care about the most."

"Don't worry about her. We've established protec-tion protocols to frustrate any further attempts by the NRL to instigate trouble. Right now a detective is sta-tioned outside your ex's door and her phone is being monitored—with her permission—so we can trace threatening calls."

Grant breathed a sigh of relief that soon turned to a yowl of pain as Sarah poured water onto his wound and cleaned it with a sterile pad.

"The NRL tipped their hand with the kidnapping attempt, forcing us into high gear because we knew then that events were accelerating rapidly. But we were caught shorthanded, and we didn't have much time to formulate a plan. I did most of it on the fly. Literally. On the plane I hatched out a scheme intended to distract the NRL from the true state of affairs without letting on that a DOD agent was in town. General Brinkley transmitted the greeting cipher to you via fax, which you were told to destroy upon receipt, then was—"

Sarah paused with the roll of gauze in the air above Grant's wound. She was staring at the headboard, but her mind was dislocated in both space and time. Her eyes glistened like the purest nacre which was touched by a windswept spray, and which reflected on their pearly surfaces the image of a plight unseen. She blinked, and the reflection vanished. But in that brief moment Grant had gazed into the depths of a soul in torment. She wrapped a layer of gauze around his arm, and continued as if no lapse had occurred.

"General Brinkley was murdered shortly after I left."

"What?"

Sarah continued wrapping gauze. "Presumably by an agent of the NRL who had infiltrated our security network. Or perhaps by one of our own agents turned rogue. I'm not sure . . . "

Again came the faraway stare. She finished taping Grant's arm, cut some strips of adhesive tape and snugged the gauze in place, then wrapped the bloody hanky and leftover first aid supplies in the towel, which she deposited in her overnight case.

"Anyway, my job was to find you and to protect you at all costs. I knew about your walking habits, so I scoured the country lanes looking for you, thinking that you didn't make our meeting because you fell and hurt yourself or knocked yourself out. Hoping, really, that the explanation was so simple; that the NRL had-n't already nabbed you. When you turned up at the police station in the morning, and the local officers filed a routine missing person's report, the message was relayed to our computer network which I was monitoring hourly by telephone. I put on my Mason drag and drove to the station posthaste and explained how you never showed up for our date the night before. I fed them the same line—my cover story—that I fed you, except that I told them I was staying at the Dew Drop Inn instead of the Tuck Me Inn. I didn't want them checking up on me, or, in case the NRL had infiltrated the police department, to pass our whereabouts to them. There's only a one-in-a-million chance of the NRL buying off the local cops, but in this business you're jaundiced by so much double-dealing that you either become paranoid or you retire to an early grave.

"Then when we met, you presented me with a peculiar challenge: to determine if you were the genuine article or a very clever counterfeit, and how could I tell the difference given the parameters of your cover story? The convenient lapse of memory made it difficult for me to judge if you were suffering from a mental breakdown due to the strain of overwork, or to the pressure of diabolic opposition—stronger men than you have broken under the gauntlet of enemy subversion—or if you were a carefully coached imposter masquerading as yourself—they can do wonders with plastic surgery these days—or if you were a machine.

"I stuck with my cover and played Mason to the hilt, and tried to trick you with bits of knowledge that the real you would know. But you didn't respond to anything: the gibes, the puns, even background trivia. I was troubled by the possibility that I was consorting with a deadly enemy or an almighty machine. I never saw you eat or drink—you could have flushed your lunch down the toilet and when I did have the chance to see you drink, you spat it back out. I didn't observe any elimination of waste; you never even blew your nose. And I couldn't get a rise out of you by playing the sexy lady. You were impervious to my wiles."

"I was tired and disoriented and I had a . . . "

"I know, you had a headache." Sarah pulled off the

tank top and exposed her undersized breasts. "I may not have as much to show as I did as Sarah Mason—" She rolled the rubber band off her ponytail and shook out her natural tresses. Blonde hair hung about her face and neck like a tasseled yellow frame. "—but I hope I haven't lost all my feminine appeal."

Now Grant felt the yearnings in his groin even more than he had before, perhaps because of the exhilaration of knowing—and the possibility of proving—that he was truly a man. "I don't judge a woman by the size of her breasts." But he could certainly make a judgment about this woman's external anatomy. Defined biceps and rippling back muscles were not grossly out of proportion as in prize-winning body builders, but were enough in evidence to demonstrate the attention she paid to physical conditioning.

"I know that. I've read all about you, remember?" Sarah kicked off her shoes and wiggled out of her tight black pants. Her panties were black, too. Thigh muscles bulged just enough to portray uncommon strength. "But after I locked you in the room yesterday—"

"You didn't spike my vodka?"

Sarah shook her head. "I had your keys duplicated and your clothes cleaned and repaired. When I got back, you were asleep, or were feigning sleep, which suited my purposes perfectly, although I wondered why an imposter would act so strangely. Dressed as Mason in case I got caught, I did some reconnoitering at Feline Estates, but I didn't drive through the gate. I went in on foot, shinnied up the camera pole and slipped a bag over the lens, then made sure your key operated the gate. I took off the bag. To anyone viewing the tape it might appear that a paper bag had blown up against the lens and lodged there temporarily.

"At first I explored the Estate from the tree line, and got the lay of the land. Then I slipped into your house—after determining, of course, that no one was home—and went through it with a fine-toothed comb. I found pretty much what I expected to find: nothing incriminating, no hidden safes, not a thing about your work at the lab, and nothing that I thought I could use to reveal your true identity other than the fit of your tailor made suits."

Sarah sat on the bed with one tiny foot tucked under her leg. "The labels and sizes matched what you were wearing at the motel, but I wasn't really sure until you tried on one of the jackets. Even then, I thought, a clever imposter would obtain a matching wardrobe. Do you feel like a shower?"

Grant trembled as much from her suggestion as from her touch when she unbuckled his belt. "Well, I, uh, I, uh, I guess I could use—"

"Do you want to get undressed on your own, or do I have to cut the rest of your clothes off of you?"

Grant was not so dazed or so tired that he could not see where she was leading him. And it was precisely where he wanted to go. "Well, I, uh—"

She unbuttoned his trousers and pulled the zipper halfway down. "You kept giving me crossed signals which totally confused me. One moment I thought you must be you—because you made such ingenuous statements which a true imposter or properly pro- grammed simulacrum would never make—and the next moment you appeared to be concealing some deep, dark secret. You really had me going. For example, you seemed thunderstruck by the Benthic Products sam- ples I showed you, yet the technology I demonstrated has been on the market for years, and quite frankly is exceeded by Biotech's creations—especially since you lead the industry in computer memory chip design. And you didn't seem to know that Biotech dropped its bid on the Disney contract only because you couldn't handle the workload. Then when I asked you about the Mem- chip 201, you danced around the issue completely and didn't even repeat facts that anyone could have picked up from recent expositions in the rag sheets. If you were an imposter, you were either unimaginably stupid or exceptionally brilliant."

"I told you I was confused—"

"Talk later. Now it's my turn." She slipped her hand

beneath his undershirt and ran her fingers up to his chest, where she massaged his flaccid muscles. "What really scared me was that you might not be an imposter, but a simulacrum—with the strength of hydraulics that could crush me like an eggshell. When I got back to the room and saw that you had shaved, I inspected your facial skin and saw no telltale stitch marks: not a pleat or a tuck. By that time I had already seen your duplicate by observing Lerner's house. Later, you didn't respond to my remark that the coves past yours were named after African tigers. I knew that Ocelot Cove was next. How could you be so ignorant? On the other hand, you knew about the cow pasture. Later, you openly acknowledged that you knew nothing about the Memchip 201: an admission that could have been a way of forestalling me from asking you for details. But then, you showed no trepidation about going to Lerner's house for what I knew would be a showdown."

Sarah stood up and slipped off her panties, revealing a matted patch of blonde curls at the juncture of her legs. Grant's heart skipped a beat as he rose up to his elbows, then rolled onto his side to hide his excitement. Sarah lifted his legs off the bed and placed his feet on the floor, then pulled him upright and dropped his pants to his ankles. She pivoted away from him, stepped into the bathroom, started the water in the shower, and cast a conspiratorial look over her shoulder.

"Care to join me?" She slipped behind the curtain without waiting for a reply.

Grant finished undressing, lingered until his embarrassment subsided, then followed her into the shower.

"Keep that dressing dry." Sarah was smothered in lather like a model in a television soap commercial. She tilted her head back under the nozzle, thoroughly soaked her hair, then applied shampoo while she ran her eyes up and down Grant's hairy form. "You've been under quite a strain these past couple of days. How are you holding up?"

Grant could not hold back a smirk, nor prevent himself from rising to the occasion. "Quite well, thanks to you."

"I'll accept that as a compliment." She detached the shower nozzle from its holder and ran a fine spray of hot water on Grant's body, careful not to dampen the dressing. Then she rubbed him down with the bar of soap. "Turn around." She did his back, then bade him to face her again so she could do his front. Her fingers caressed and fondled.

In addition to the tingling sensation inspired by Sarah's touch, Grant felt exhilarated by the shedding of all the sweat and grime which had accumulated during the night of fear and exertion. Sarah scrubbed him clean with patience and care, acting as natural as if they had been longtime lovers. Grant never professed to be a man of stamina or inner strength. In fact, he had a history of overindulgence and lack of attention which had turned his wife against him despite his intellectual achievements. But he had never felt weaker than he did at the moment: at the end of his tether from coping with a world in which inconsistency was the norm, and being coddled by a woman who accepted him for what he was, now that his identity had definitely been established.

"All done." She shut off the water, drew back the curtain, grabbed a white towel from the rack, and performed a cursory job of drying both of them. Still dripping, she dragged Grant eagerly to the bed and pushed him down on his back. She switched off the lamp, but left the bathroom light on and the door partially open so the darkness was not complete. Then she sat by his side, quiet as a cat, peering down at him as she ran her hands tenderly over his chest and abdomen and genitals.

"Sarah—"

She hushed him with a single kiss on the lips.

He pushed her gently away. "Sarah, there's still something I need to know before . . . "

With sensuous fingers she squeezed and kneaded him as she gazed intently at his manhood.

"I—I can understand how you could be sure of—my humanity after I got shot and started to bleed, but—how did you know before then that I was human and not the other one?"

"For one thing, your accuser indicated your human condition by mentioning your brain and pointing to your head. But more significant than that, you were crying."

Grant looked deep into her eyes, delving for unassailable truth. "But, with everything else they can do today, can't they build machines with water squirts in the sockets, like they do with play dolls?"

"Of course they can, and they do. But crying is more than dripping tears. Crying is not something you do with just your eyes. When you cry, your heart and soul cries with you. Maybe I can't explain it very well. I'm not a poet and I don't have the words. But I know feelings when I see them. You were terrified, and you expressed that terror the way no machine ever could. Because the one thing you can't program into a computer—even you, as great a cyberneticist as you are—is emotion."

Sarah leaned forward to kiss his lips as she spread her legs to straddle him.

And in the following moments of ecstasy, Grant knew that she spoke the truth.

Chapter 19

Patrolman Richard Anderson tried to pull Dawn Templeton away from the body on the floor, but she clung to it with the strength of madness. "Let go of him, Baby. Let go."

"Daddy. Oh, Daddy," Dawn wailed, and continued wailing.

The siren of an ambulance wound down outside, and a moment later Sandy Hendry appeared in the room which was flooded with light from the overhead fluorescents. She took in the scene at a glance, exchanged quick looks with Riley and her father, and crouched beside the prostrate form which lay next to the desk. She looked for vital signs by first placing her fingers against the carotid artery, next by feeling for a pulse in the wrist, then by placing her ear against the bloody chest, and finally by cupping her hand alternately over the sightless eyes and looking for pupil contraction and dilation. At last she opened the corpse's mouth and peered down the throat.

"Is this somebody's idea of a joke?"

Everyone in the room was jolted by her remark, and Dawn was shocked into silence.

"Isn't—isn't he dead?" Captain Hendry asked tentatively.

"Of course not." Sandy opened her medical kit and removed a bundle of triage instruments. "You can't kill what was never alive." She selected a scalpel and used it to rip open the pants from the waist down to the crotch, then cut sideways around the upper thighs. The bullet hole was plainly visible in the lower abdomen: a clean wound without a trace of blood. "Get this lamp out of here."

Riley knelt to her assistance. He wrapped the extension cord around the broken lamp until the wire went taut around the body's leg. "There's another wire here, tangled up with—"

The second wire, fatter than the lamp cord, ran up under the pants leg. Sandy sliced open the material and exposed the entire lower body, then rolled the body over onto its belly and pointed to where the extra wire plugged into a pin module at the base of what was analogous to the coccyx.

"It's another damned robot."

"Jesus," Captain Hendry breathed.

Frank Riley felt a sudden rush of relief. In the short time he had known Grant Templeton and had been working on his case, he had grown to like the man and to feel sorry for his plight, and more than anything he wanted to save the mad scientist from whatever machinations were working against him.

In the stunned silence that followed, Patrolwoman Cindy Ballard was the only one who kept her head. "There's another, er, there's a man injured in the back yard who could use some attention."

Sandy threw the triage instruments into the black bag. "Take me to him."

Cindy led the way, followed by Sandy and then by Riley. They found two policemen crouched by a prostrate form on the grass at the edge of the lawn. One was pressing a sterile gauze pad to the victim's chest in order to stem the flow of blood, the other did the same for the man's head. Sandy shoved both policemen aside and examined the wounds with the aid of their flashlights.

"This is one lucky son of a bitch. One bullet bounced off his rib cage without entering the chest cavity—it hit at an oblique angle—and the other grazed his skull." She took Riley's flashlight and held it next to the deep furrow in the victim's head, and separated the red, matted hair while she dabbed away the still-flowing blood so she could examine the injury. She probed the gouge with a gloved finger. "Scalp wounds bleed like crazy. He'll have a hell of a scar, but the bullet didn't do much actual damage. Has he regained consciousness?"

One of the policemen said, "No, but he rambled a few words in a foreign language that sounded like German."

Sandy nodded. "Probably has a concussion. Strange, though, that there are powder burns on his forehead, like he'd been shot at point blank range. Someone is a lousy shot." She placed a clean sterile pad against the wound and wrapped gauze around the victim's head to hold the pad in place. "The wound will have to be debrided, but there's not much more we can do for him here."

Two men arrived with a stretcher. Sandy let them pick up the victim and take him away. "I'd better stay with the patient." She gave Riley a smack on the cheek. "If he starts talking, I'll get back to you." Then she was gone.

Riley found his companions in the living room with Dawn. She was wiping tears from her cheeks, but appeared to be in control of herself. Anderson provided comfort by placing his arm around her slender shoulders. Hendry had the investigation well in hand. He spat out orders left and right until everyone had a job and was intent on doing it.

Riley gave his report to the captain, summing it up by stating, "It looks like the same outfit that hit Templeton's house: driving Lincolns and spouting German."

"Yeah, but what the hell does it mean?"

"I don't know, but I'd like to take Ms. Templeton to her father's house and let her listen to that tape we found in his bedroom. She might be able to make some sense out of it."

"Good idea. We'll do that as soon as we get things cleaned up here."

The photographer arrived and took pictures of the Templeton simulacrum and the three bodies outside. The forensic team showed up with enough coffee and doughnuts for everyone, courtesy of the local twenty-four-hour convenience store which was doing a landslide business because of the number of law enforcement agents swelling the nighttime streets of Highland Hills. Nearly everyone was yawning and rubbing weary eyes, but none complained about the extra hours or the lack of breaks or sleep. They performed their duties with professional acumen.

It was not until more than an hour later that Dawn, Riley, Hendry, and Anderson gathered around the desk in Templeton's study. Dawn perched in the swivel chair like a bird about to take flight. Riley and Hendry stood attentively by her side, while Anderson leaned casually against the doorframe and chewed on an apple. Riley turned up the volume on the voice recorder so the voice was loud and clear.

No one said a word until the tape ran through and there was nothing left to hear but the hiss of the rotating spools.

With perfect posture, Dawn rose from the swivel chair and walked slowly to the front window. She glared into the darkness. "I know what he means. I know where he hid the backup disk. Or one possible place."

"Could he be there?" Captain Hendry asked. "Could your father be hiding there?"

"I don't see him."

"Huhn?"

Dawn turned slowly and faced the captain. "When I was a little girl, Daddy used to read to me from *The Wind in the Willows*, and to make it truly authentic we used to climb up into the willow tree in our front yard." In aside, "This was when we lived on Cedar Place."

"Cedar Place!" Hendry squinted somber eyes at Riley. "Where have I heard that street name recently?"

"Friday night. I responded to a call out there about a prowler in the neighborhood." Riley looked at Dawn. "14 Cedar Place?"

"Yes, that's where we used to live before Mother and Daddy got divorced. But that was a long time ago."

"That's some coincidence," said Anderson, between bites. "Remember the fish."

Dawn's brow wrinkled. "The fish?"

"Never mind him. Tell us about *The Wind in the Willows*." Hendry rolled his eyes. "I can't believe I just said that."

"Well, we'd climb up into the first notch and sit

there with me on his lap. And he'd read to me. Sometimes just a few pages, sometimes a whole chapter. The chapters were pretty long—at least, they seemed long to me because I was so young. Anyway, Daddy would take little candies with him and feed them to me if I got restless. He kept the leftovers in a tiny tin box and saved them for the next time—so the squirrels wouldn't get them, or the ants. After a while, the tin box became a hiding place where he'd leave me notes sometimes when he left for work in the morning, sometimes with a treat, like a toy or a Cracker Jack prize. As I got older he began to leave other things there: birthday gifts, Christmas presents, things like that. He always covered them in plastic in case it rained. One time we had about two feet of snow—"

"What does this have to do with the tape?" Captain Hendry had run out of patience, and the frustration was evident on his face.

Dawn did not appear upset by the captain's sudden outburst. She went on softly, "After they got divorced and Mother and I moved to Garden Fields, Daddy and I didn't get to do that much—"

"Not Buttercup Path?" asked Riley.

"Yes, that was it. 228 Buttercup Path. How—how did you know that?"

"We had a break-and-entry there Friday night."

Anderson whistled. "That's more than a fish; it's a whole damn school." Hendry frantically waved his hands at his patrolman. "Ignore them, Ms. Templeton. Just tell me how this relates to the tape. Please."

Dawn continued unflustered, as if she was bound to tell the story in her own way and at her own speed. "Mother didn't approve of us sitting in the tree, especially when I got older. She used to say it was too rough on my clothes. My dress used to get stained or dirty and I used to scuff my shoes, and sometimes I tore holes in my dress or my blouse. She was glad that our new house didn't have a willow tree. Then we could only read in the tree at Daddy's house. In order to fool her he bought me a pair of coveralls—well, that doesn't matter.

"Anyway, one time the tree got sick —I mean, it got some kind of blight and I thought it was going to die. It didn't, because Daddy had it treated. But I cried anyway because the willow tree had become our private retreat; it had come to symbolize our relationship. And all the time I was growing up he used to put presents there for me. Even after I grew up. And he told me that no matter what happened, we would always have our willow tree. That's why, when he had this new house built, he had it set way back here away from the road, on this particular lot. So he could have a willow tree in the front yard. The layout of the grounds and the orientation of the house was based on that tree."

"But how does any of this relate to the tape!"

"Oh, I thought you knew, or would remember. *The Wind in the Willows* was written by Kenneth Grahame."

Captain Hendry had to work his jaw a few times before being able to voice a response. "Are you—are you saying he hid a computer disk in—" He hunched over and pointed out the front window. "—that tree?"

"Well, I wouldn't swear to it, but I think we should check it out. No one would ever think to look there because the willow tree was our little secret—one that we never shared with anyone. Till now."

"I don't believe this." Hendry let out such a deep breath of air that it ruffled the satin curtains. He put his hands on his ample hips and walked twice around the room. "Why couldn't he read to you from a rocking chair like I used to read to Sandy?" Then he glowered at Patrolman Anderson. "Well, don't just stand there, Richy. What am I paying you for? Go climb a tree."

They charged through the house in single file and assembled at the base of the giant willow. Riley aimed his flashlight at the broad bole while Anderson reached up for a handhold.

"They didn't tell me about this at the academy," he grumbled, as he dug his spit-shined shoes into the smooth bark and pulled himself up onto the lower limb.

"It won't be very high," Dawn said.

Anderson used his own flashlight to check out the notches within reach. "I don't see anything."

"Great," Hendry said facetiously. "Young lady, we ain't gonna climb every damn willow tree in Highland Hills. This is ridicu—"

"Hey, wait a minute! There's something up here. Looks like a ballpoint pen."

"Bring it down, Mr. Anderson," Dawn called out. "It's got a message inside."

"Better be something in it, after making a monkey outa me." Anderson picked his way down the trunk but lost his grip just before reaching the ground. His shoes slid down the bark, and he crashed hard on his rump with a woof.

Hendry ignored the patrolman's plight, and snatched the pen from Anderson's hand—the one which was not rubbing his bottom. He inspected the pen, clicked the point out and in a few times, then scowled. "It's a ballpoint pen all right."

Dawn took the pen from the captain, unscrewed the two halves, and pulled it apart. Wrapped tightly around the ink refill was a scroll of paper. She unrolled it, and held it under the head of Riley's flashlight. Printed on the paper were four letters: C B N C.

Hendry leaned close so that all three heads were touching. "Now what's *that* supposed to mean?"

"It's code," Dawn announced. "It stands for 'close but no cigar'." Her face split with an expansive smile. "It means we're barking up the wrong tree."

Hendry went apoplectic. "Goddamn it, girl. This is serious business. I got no time for games—"

"But I know where the right tree is. I don't know if it will lead us to Daddy, but whatever this backup disk has on it has to be important, or else Daddy wouldn't have encoded it this way."

Captain Hendry inhaled deeply, waited a few seconds before speaking. "So where is this other tree?"

"On Memory Lane."

Chapter 20

"Wake up, Grant! Sleepy time is over."

Sarah's bare feet hit the carpeted floor as if they were a pair of springboards. She bounced into the bathroom so fast that Grant hardly had a glimpse of her shapely derriere before the door closed behind her. He shut his eyes again, grateful to have a few more minutes of sleep because he needed it so badly. But he only had time to blink before Sarah began to shake him.

"Come on, Grant. Get up. It's time to go to work."

"I can't do it again this soon. I need more recovery—"

"Stop being silly. You know what I mean."

Grant forced his eyes open, saw Sarah sitting on the bed next to him. He reached out suddenly and wrapped his arms around her waist, and drew her close. "If I said you had a nice body would you hold it against me?"

"Some other time." She easily disentangled herself from his grip, and stood up, exposing her nudity. "Right now we have work to do."

"I need more sleep," he grumbled.

"You've already had—" She glanced at her wristwatch. "—forty-five minutes."

"That's not enough."

"It'll have to do. Besides, you'll feel completely re-energized once you get out of bed and splash cold water in your face. Trust me. I take catnaps all the time. In this business, it's usually all you can get."

Grant groaned, but tossed back the covers and slowly—creakingly—swung his feet over the edge of the bed and rose to an unsteady sitting position with the blanket draped over his lap. He dug his fists into his eyes. "Re-energized was a poor choice of words—unless you think I run on batteries and you're not convinced I'm human."

"You're not."

That got Grant's attention.

"You're an incubus." Sarah pulled open a bureau drawer and took out a knapsack which she dropped on the bed next to Grant. "A spirit from another world who likes to sleep with women. And does a lot more than sleep. Now get dressed. We've got to get going."

"It's still dark out. Can't we at least wait till the cock crows the dawn?"

"You just told me that wasn't going to happen for a while."

"You know what I mean. Your batteries may have been recharged but mine have been drained."

"That's the difference between the sexes." She unzipped the front flap of the knapsack to reveal inner pouches filled with ammunition, grenades, and canisters of explosives. "Now either get dressed or I'll have to dress you."

"What—what are you planning to do with all that—stuff?"

Sarah reloaded the magazines for the forty-four Magnum. "Kill a few Nazis. Maybe open some doors and blow the lid off this case. No pun intended."

"You seem awfully cheerful—for someone who's about to charge into the valley of the shadow of death."

"Maybe I enjoy the danger. Maybe that's how I get my kicks out of life. And maybe I just like bloodshed."

Grant thought for a moment. "You really hate these Nazis, don't you?"

"Doesn't everybody?"

"Not as much as you do."

"Well, Grant, you'd hate them too if you knew what I know."

"And what's that?"

Again came the faraway stare. Sarah froze with a cartridge half in its clip. "Now isn't the time to tell you everything. Soon, I hope, you'll know what this mess is all about. But for now . . . " She blinked the stare out of her eyes and continued with her work. She slammed a fully loaded magazine into the Magnum, cocked the barrel to load a cartridge, removed the magazine and forced in one last bullet, then slammed the magazine back into place. In a flat, almost dispassionate voice, she said, "They killed my husband."

In the embarrassing silence that followed, Grant did not know what to say. In situations like this he never knew what to say. Nor could the Grant who belonged in this world record appropriate thoughts of grief or think of the proper words to write to a crushed and bereaving widow. "I—I'm sorry, Sarah. I know—how painful that must be for you—"

"Oh, I've gotten over the pain." She shoved the Magnum into her purse—Grant saw that it slipped into a specially made holster—and pushed extra clips into leather loops which lined both inner sides. She hefted the knapsack, found it awkwardly unbalanced, then redistributed its explosive contents. "But I haven't gotten over the hate."

Grant tried hard to look into her eyes, but she averted his gaze by gathering the clothes that she had deposited on the floor. He thought he caught the glint of a tear, but could not be certain.

"Now get dressed. Armageddon is waiting." She shook a tiny pill out of a bottle and gave the pill to Grant. "Codeine. It will dull the pain in your arm so you can get through the next couple of hours without loss of concentration. After that we'll see about getting the wound stitched."

Grant took his clothes into the bathroom and donned them in private. His outfit was the worse for wear, appearing more ragged now than it had the day before. The shirt with the missing sleeve was only partially camouflaged by the jacket with the bullet hole in it; both were smeared with blood, which had also dripped onto his pants. His left arm throbbed dully until he started pulling on his clothes; then it stabbed him with pain, as if an ice pick were being worked back and forth in the muscle. He swallowed the codeine along with a glass of water. By the time he was through in the bathroom, Sarah was fully clothed in her black pantsuit and converted athletic shoes.

"Sarah, I—I've got one more confession to make."

"Can it wait?"

"No, I'd rather get it off my chest before—"

"Hush a moment." She threw the knapsack over her back and cinched down the shoulder straps and waistband. The purse she wore as always, with the strap across her head and on the opposite shoulder. The overnight case was in her hand. "You can talk while we walk." She shut off the lights, opened the door a crack, and spent a full sixty seconds studying the motel grounds. "All clear."

Two minutes later found them traipsing across a field under the light of stars which, because of the new moon, were bright and seemingly infinite in number. Sarah stashed the overnight case under the brush in a stand of trees. "That's so no one can pick up my trail. When the job's over, I've got to go back and retrieve all the caches. Now, what did you have to say?"

"Well, it's about your allusion to the incubus: the otherworld creature that sleeps with women. You, uh, you perhaps hit the nail a lot closer on the head than you intended."

Sarah strode off at a quick pace. "Either you hit a nail or you don't."

"Well, what I mean is, I know why—that is, I have a theory backed by observable data which can explain why—why I don't seem to fit in this world of yours. Why there are gaps in my knowledge of names and places and technological advances. Why I'm so confused about myself and the company I work for. You see—" He took a deep breath. "—I really am an intruder."

"Don't give me that." Sarah ducked under some low-lying branches as she led the two-person patrol through the woods on the outskirts of town. "I've established beyond a reasonable doubt that you're the real Grant Templeton, not a lookalike or a programmed simulacrum. Let dead cows lie."

"But this—it's important that I establish my own identity. Not to *your* satisfaction, but to mine. My individuality—and my independence—is something I value fiercely. Therefore I can empathize with—any rational intelligence that faces the prospect of losing that individuality, either through absorption by an indifferent society or by the degenerative loss of one's mental faculties or by extermination. I was strongly affected by that simulacrum's death throes, or shutdown procedures—however you want to describe its ultimate dissolution. That machine knew it was going to—expire. The fact that it was a programmed intelligence makes no difference. It was terrified of having its logic circuits turned off permanently."

"I can't believe you're talking like this. You're the foremost cybernetics expert in your field. You know more about robots and computer intelligence than anyone in the world. There's no one who understands better than you that a machine is a machine is a machine. That simulacrum was no more alive than an electric typewriter. Just because you can get a typewriter to print 'please don't kill me' doesn't mean that it comprehends the meaning of the words; it's just ink on paper. The printout is the result of a program, written by a programmer. Adding a voice synthesizer doesn't change that fact."

"DNA is an organic program—"

"It's not the same thing, and you know it. When I put a slug into that simulacrum's guts it was no different from shooting an automated toaster. They are inanimate objects: no more, no less."

"But it had life—"

"It was a simulation of life. Not the real thing."

"What makes a carbon program any more real than a silicon program?"

"Consciousness. Perception of thought. Awareness of self. And a lot of other philosophical concepts that I don't profess to understand. Maybe intuition and a dab of imagination. Why do you think I didn't try to reason with the thing in Lerner's house when it wouldn't answer my questions, when it's program started looping that survival subroutine? Why do you think I shot out its CPU?"

"Like the man in Lerner's back yard?"

"That was different. He wouldn't tell me anything because of his indoctrination. He's a fanatic. He thinks the Nazi movement can be revitalized by drafting an army of mechanical mercenaries that can goose-step with perfect precision. It takes more than a clever machine to infect a nation with a blood lust for world domination gained by sacrificing its basic humanism. The NRL is bound to fail, but in the course of its failure a lot of innocent people will die.

"I quit interrogating the simulacrum because you can't argue with a machine, any more than you can argue with a car that just ran down a dog in the road. You argue with the driver. Take my word for it, Grant: you're human. Not only can you demonstrate creative thought, you can feel."

"And look how long it took you to figure that out. Look how many tests you had to put me through before you were sure that I was an organic intelligence instead of an electronic thinking machine—"

"An x-ray would have told me right away, but you refused to go to the hospital."

"Wrong. An x-ray would have detected flesh and blood instead of tegument and petroleum products—"

"Not any x-ray machine I've ever heard about, doctor."

"Okay: bones instead of a metallic framework. And a CAT scan would have shown tissue density instead of printed circuit boards—"

"Simulacra have power cells in their heads, not CPUs."

"—a PET scan would have shown metabolic processes and chemical reactions instead of electron flow. But all of that is irrelevant to the definition of intelligence. Why do you think cyberneticists call the animal brain a 'biological computer' or a 'wet machine'? Because it is nothing more than an organic corollary to its electronic counterpart—"

"Isn't it the other way around?"

"—the brain has a neural network which does chemically what the computer does electronically, but the net result is the same: both are devices for encoding, storing, and retrieving data which we define as a stream of memory. The physical substrates may be different in form, but the architecture is equivalent in function. The fact that our genes have been programmed by evolution while silicon chips are programmed by human intervention does not alter the capability or the potential of the final product."

Sarah shoved through a thicket with a vehemence that belied the stealth of their mission. "You're not going to make me believe that you can create a second generation intelligence simply by increasing the size and complexity of a mainframe computer—"

"That's what nature did with the human brain."

"—or by linking a bunch of mainframes together—"

"Isn't that what we call society?"

"—Memory capacity and processing speed notwithstanding, unless you add that unknown vital element that is the essence of life, all you end up with is a smarter and faster calculator. And for all the credence you give to the Turing test, it's still nothing more than an artificial construct specifically designed to substantiate a theoretical concept: a rather clumsy tautology that proves only that cyberneticists don't know what intelligence really is—natural or synthetic. Naming a thing doesn't define it. Anyway, how can you argue the point when you've preceded your case by disavowing all knowledge of the Memchip 201 and any possible aptitude it might have for achieving autonomous existence?"

"I'm arguing from the standpoint of logic based upon established propositions." Grant jumped across a rivulet and followed Sarah up an embankment that led through the brush to a clearing. "Where I come from, Artificial Intelligence is farther in the future than it is here, but that doesn't mean that the line of reasoning is in dispute. It's all a matter of time before machine programs overtake the ingenuity of human intelligence."

Sarah stopped short on a grassy knoll and placed

her hands on her hips. "Well, where I come from, an Artificial Intelligence will never ascend to the status of individual modality until it learns to add sentiment to its sentience. 'Ya gotta have heart' or you're just a dumb machine."

"You're anthropomorphizing."

"No, you are oversimplifying. You with half a mind that isn't even functioning are in no position to argue the finer points of state-of-the-art computer technology. You've already confessed your ignorance about the memchip and its significance. Are you having flashbacks that contradict your earlier statements?"

"No. I'm relying upon logic to extrapolate from what I know to be true—"

"From what you *believe* to be truth."

"—and if you'll shut your goddamn mouth for a minute I'll get back to my original declaration and tell you where I'm coming from." Grant found himself shouting and losing his temper. Or was it already lost? "Do you mind?"

Sarah glared at him with eyes that could have wilted a cactus in the rain. She quickly scanned the surrounding forest, then returned her gaze to Grant. "You can say anything you want as long as you don't shout it to the neighborhood. We're nearing enemy territory."

Grant took a dozen deep breaths in order to regain his composure. He did his best to keep his voice low and even. "You and I are from different worlds—"

"I know. I know. You're a brilliant scientist and I'm a lowly spy."

"That's not what I mean. Now please act your age for a moment and listen to what I have to say."

Sarah pouted and tapped one foot impatiently, but remained silent.

"I don't belong to this world of yours. I don't mean the world of gunfights and disguises and espionage and Nazi revival movements. I mean, you and I aren't even from the same universe."

"If you want to heap ridicule—"

"Listen to me. Just—listen to me." Grant ran his

fingers through his curly hair, struggling to think of the words that would impart the proper meaning. "What I'm trying to say is that when I 'woke up' the other night, trying to fit my key into a door where it didn't belong, it was because I—the person holding the key—came from another planet. Somehow, someway, through some mechanism of physics I don't profess to understand, I crossed some kind of interdimensional barrier from a parallel space-time continuum—"

"Oh, this is a real crock of—"

"Listen to me, Sarah!" he shouted. "Listen to me. I know it isn't easy for you to accept. I had a difficult time accepting it myself. But somehow it happened. I went to sleep in a world where we don't have memchips, where we don't have humanoid robots, where no one is after me but journalists looking for Sunday supplement fillers, and where the Nazis have been defunct for half a century. How I got here I don't know. What happened to the Grant Templeton who existed here before, I haven't the faintest idea. Maybe I displaced him when I arrived, perhaps because two identical bodies—or minds—can't exist simultaneously in the same continuum. That's why I don't know what's going on here. I've never been here before."

Sarah held her dignity for about five seconds, stunned by Grant's revelation. Then she laughed so loud that a pair of owls departed from the limb on which they were perched overhead. "You *are* from another planet if you expect me to buy a story like that. Or else you're crazier than anyone gives you credit for." She stalked off across the field toward a stand of scattered trees about a hundred yards away. "Do you actually believe this poppycock, or do you make it up as you go along?"

Grant had to run to keep up with her. "I know it sounds preposterous and insanely solipsistic, but it's the only explanation that fits the facts the way I've perceived them. Any other—"

"I've got no time for this." Sarah stopped so suddenly that Grant was three paces ahead before he noticed.

He ran back and stood in front of her. She placed her hands on his shoulders, careful not to touch the wound on his arm, and looked deep into his eyes. "Honey, baby, you listen to me for a moment. I know that you're confused. I know that you've been through a tough couple of days. That you're—disoriented. That your logic circuits—your organic logic circuits—have been scrambled. But you've got to listen to yourself and hear how fantastic you sound. If I ever doubted that you were human, all those doubts have been completely erased. No machine could come up with a tale like that, a tale that you couldn't even sell to the comic books. Now, I don't know what's happened to you, but I do know for sure and for certain that you didn't come from another universe. Believe me, there's a more rational explanation for your chaotic memories than the story you've concocted. And if we live through the next hour and a half, you might find out what the explanation is."

The open field was unutterably peaceful, like a beach on an Arctic isle. Grant shuddered with a chill which was not all in the air. He returned Sarah's stare with hope which was tempered by a dose of trepidation. He wanted to believe her. She was a strong woman, a capable woman, an incisive woman, and perhaps the most forceful personality he had ever encountered. Yet she was dominated by an inner rage which obeyed odd rules of conduct.

"I—I would like to believe that—"

"You don't know what to believe, and I can't say that I blame you. Surely this crusade against worldwide tyranny is something that you never bargained for. I know you'd rather be working in your lab than tangling with a new Nazi regime. I have things I'd rather be doing, too. But we can't ignore what is going on around us when there are people in the world who would take away our freedom to think and act for ourselves. Sometimes we have to take the cards that are dealt to us. So here's the deal.

"Up ahead is what I believe to be the local NRL hideout. You may not recognize it. You may not understand

any of what is happening. But you are Grant Templeton and this is your world, and the key to the resolution of the present conflict is in your head, whether or
not you can perceive it at the moment."

Sarah gave his shoulders a reassuring squeeze,
then dropped her hands to her sides. "I won't mislead
you. We're taking an incredible risk by going in there
alone—just the two of us—but it's a risk that we have
to take. And as incredulous as it may sound, I can't win
this battle without you."

Grant fumbled for words. He wanted to believe her,
to believe that he belonged to this whacky world, yet so
much was left unexplained. "But, if this is such an
important operation, if the Nazis are trying to take over
the world, why are you fighting it alone? Why isn't the
government sending in the marines?"

"I *am* a marine: Captain Margaret Sarah Witherspoon, and the only marine you're likely to get." She
glanced meaningfully at the eastern horizon. The stars
had already begun to fade and the deep purple tint was
dissolving to a somber shade of blue. "I'm afraid we
don't have much time. We need the cover of darkness—
" She cut herself short voluntarily. "Okay, but we walk
while we talk."

Again Grant had difficulty keeping up with her military stride.

"The Nazi Revitalization League is a small but influ-
ential organization that is funded by rich German
nationals who want to see a Fourth Reich come into
power so a re-united Germany can take its place in
world politics as a ruling nation. I won't go into the philosophy or the fundamental principals of the movement, other than to say that their campaign strategy
relies upon intimidation through terrorism, an example
of which you've seen tonight."

They entered the sparse grove of trees. Grant kept
his eyes trained ahead so he could dodge the trunks
and push through the brush without taking a spill, but
his ear was sharply attuned to Sarah's proclamations.

"According to established diplomatic policy, the

U.S. government does not officially recognize the existence of the NRL. It doesn't represent the voice of the people; at best it's an outspoken minority. But given the proper impetus and creative propaganda, there is always the possibility that a nation of sheep can have the wool pulled over its eyes and be herded over the brink of war. We—that is, the covert operation under the command of General Amos Brinkley—are trying to neutralize the NRL before they gain any real momentum: while they're still a small and annoying group of terrorists. But we've encountered a problem. Someone within the agency has been bought off, or has been bitten by the power bug, and is passing sensitive information to the NRL, telegraphing our plans before they're enacted, thus stymieing our efforts to curb Nazi aggrandizement through less violent means. The result has been extended bloodshed of innocent victims and not a few losses within our own ranks. A couple of our agents have been captured and mailed back in pieces—not all the pieces, just enough to suggest that the victims could still be alive. That's the mentality of the people we're dealing with."

"Whew." Grant let out a breath of air that deflated him like a punctured balloon. His legs suddenly seemed too weak to support him, and his pace slowed to a crawl as if he had lead in his shoes.

Sarah stopped behind a thick coppice, looked through the nearly leafless foliage, then crouched and pulled Grant down by her side. "By now you should be asking yourself why I'm dragging you into the lion's den if my job is to protect you."

"Well, that thought had crossed my mind."

"I won't lie to you: our chance of surviving to see the sun rise is slim to none, and Slim left town. But it's a chance we've got to take. The NRL is holding hostages who will all be killed if we let the Nazis get away. And when they catch on to the fact that you've switched the memchip matrix sequencing data and they can't initiate the complete program, they're going to become very angry. Again, bye-bye hostages, only in this case they probably won't be killed. On the positive side, I believe I may already have accounted for most of the local Nazi goon squad so there shouldn't be that much resistance to overcome. They would have sent more than four gunmen to Lerner's house if they'd had them available, which leads me to believe that only a small garrison was left to protect their stronghold. Plus we have the element of surprise on our side because they won't expect that we'll be able to breach their defenses. The Nazis are in a bind because they need either you or the memchip. I've got you, and you've destroyed the programming routine with a virus and hidden the backup, but can't remember where. The calculated risk is that we can pull off this caper without getting caught and giving the Nazis exactly what they want."

Grant spread his hands. "I still don't understand. What's the caper? And why don't you call for help instead of going it alone? Even if you don't trust the local police, can't the DOD send in more agents?"

"They could except for two things. First, I don't know who to call. The way covert operations are structured, each agent reports to only one superior officer. That's to prevent him or her from divulging the entire hierarchy under torture. General Brinkley was my controller, and since he's dead, I'm temporarily without a contact within the agency. I'm detached, as we call it. That means that I'm cut out of the system. Once the cops put your name on the datalink yesterday morning and the DOD got wind of the situation, the operation was shut down and my communication links were severed. And they'll stay that way until Brinkley's controller accesses his files and brings me in. Until that happens, protocol forbids me to make contact with anyone else because to do so might compromise my position and the security of the operation.

"Furthermore, there's a rogue agent on the loose: one who has been feeding information to the NRL, and who in all likelihood is responsible for Brinkley's death, if not directly, then by tipping off the Nazis about Brinkley's role as leader of the anti-NRL operation.

Since this rogue had access to privileged information, his position in the hierarchy must be higher than Brinkley's, meaning that he is Brinkley's immediate controller or another one up the line. This means that the rogue knows who I am, knows that what I know is dangerous to his counterespionage operation, and undoubtedly has issued a sanction on me. 'Sanction' is an agency euphemism for 'death warrant.' So, if I don't get this situation under control before all hell breaks loose, I'm a gone goose and the gander goes with me. Is that clear?"

"Not all of it, but enough to know that whether I like it or not, I'm in this up to my eyebrows." Grant shivered, and his sphincter contracted involuntarily. Before this night he had never been confronted with his own mortality. But when he had opposed the simulacrum in his likeness, and believed that it was the real Grant Templeton and that *he* was an imitation, he knew the meaning of despair. For to be nothing more than a programmed copy implied that he had no expression of his own, that he was a parody of another's experiences, that his lifelong achievements belonged to someone else. And so he had gone temporarily insane, attacking the assumptive truth which mocked his very existence.

Now he faced another situation in which his life was on the line, although this time it was his physical embodiment which was imperiled by willful malice. And as he contemplated the risk of death and the possibility of torture, he was forced to acknowledge a character trait of which he was previously unaware: he was a coward at heart. His natural inclination, after hearing Sarah's presentiments of danger, was to run fast and far away from the madmen who wanted to dissect his brain for their deranged and evil purposes. Yet, the dialectical side of his intellect conceded that madmen, like automobiles, cannot be reasoned with; and worse, they were not driven by ratiocination. This meant that the only way out of his present predicament was to resist the temptation to act with timidity and to confront the lunatics in their lair; else they would be like fiendish shadows lurking forever at his heels.

"But how did it happen? What did I do to earn such a punishment?"

"Nothing, Grant. It isn't your fault. It's just that there are people in the world whose ambition in life is not to produce or create or even to just go along with the flow. They must steal, they must control, and they must destroy what they can't steal or control."

"And this is what you do for a living? You search the world for bad guys to put out of commission?"

Sarah shrugged. "It keeps me from hanging out in the bars at night and crying about the inequities of life over glass after glass of liquid nepenthe. We believe in the causes we fight for. Not that I enjoy being as ruthless as the enemy, but they're the ones who engage the rules of conduct. There's no room for mercy if you truly desire to win. So it's either us or them, and I'll be damned if it'll be us." She looked lingeringly at the eastern horizon, then melded her body against Grant's and slipped her arms around his waist, and squeezed them both together in a lasting embrace. "But look at the good side. At least we've both recently known the purity of love."

Grant kissed the top of her head, inhaling the fragrance of her shampooed hair. "Will love help us in the upcoming battle?"

"No, but at least we will be at peace with ourselves should this be our final conflict."

"You're so encouraging," he said, with feigned sarcasm. He pushed her back to arm's length and stared longingly into her eyes. "You know I don't want to do this."

"I know, but I can't do it alone. I need you. The world needs you. Our world. Because locked up in that brain of yours, whether you recall it now or not, is the secret of Artificial Intelligence that everybody wants. A secret that I believe can be evoked if only given the proper stimulus."

Sarah broke away from Grant and parted the bushes that separated them from an immense lawn which was dotted with tall maple trees, whose colorful array of rustling leaves was muted by the stark light of the stars. Picnic tables and benches were scattered haphazardly, some under the trees, others in the open. A modern, five-story building of glass and aluminum occupied the center of the grounds. A parking lot extended from the opposite side, and what appeared to be a maintenance shed lay halfway between the woods and the cribbed loading docks. The sole tractor-trailer which was parked in its slot was the only vehicle in sight.

Grant squinted in the semidarkness. "I—I don't recognize this place. Or even the street."

"Nevertheless, unless I miss my guess, a part of you is in there. This is where all the answers are. This is Memory Lane."

Chapter 21

Sarah lay on her belly with her legs spread wide and her elbows pressed against the ground. With her back arched and her head held upright, she poked through the lower limbs of the hedgerow which served as a perimeter for the picnic grounds. She placed a ten-power monocular in front of one blue eye, and scanned the building and the surrounding lawn, parking lot, and street.

"Not a light showing anywhere."

She put down the monocular and raised a miniature starlight scope to her eye. The device gathered light from the stars and enhanced it electronically, forming an image of the landscape in a coruscating green light which seemed to crawl with motion, as if the dots in a newsprint photograph were revolving around centers instead of being firmly inked on paper.

"And no sign of movement."

She pushed herself back behind the hedgerow, rolled and tucked her legs in one fluid motion, and sat Indian style on the ground as she stowed the instruments behind her hip bones and under the elastic waistband of her pants.

"Remember, stay low and move slow. Pretend you're an alley cat slinking through the grass after a rabbit."

"Don't get too far ahead of me," Grant said.

"We've come too far together to get separated now." She gave him a peck on the cheek, then set the example by rolling onto her belly, low-crawling past the shrubbery, and slithering toward the maintenance shed which lay on a direct line between them and the building; thus they were sheltered from the video cameras which panned outward from the glass and aluminum facade.

Grant followed her as best he could. Because of the bullet wound he could not lie flat and thrust his elbows out in front as Sarah did so effortlessly. Instead, he hunched on his right side and performed a one-armed low-crawl, taking care not to make any jerky movements but to advance in a slow, steady slide. After two days of strenuous outdoor maneuvers, he had the strange feeling that he was in basic training for the army or the marines, and that this final assault was the escape and evasion course given prior to graduation. But in reality it was much worse than that, for this was a real combat zone.

It took Grant ten agonizing minutes to reach the brick shed. By that time Sarah had completed another visual reconnaissance, stashed the monocular and starlight scope in the knapsack, and was waiting none too patiently.

"So far, so good," she said in a hushed tone. "Now comes the tricky part." Without allowing Grant time to catch his breath, she stood with her body flattened against the brick wall and peered around the edge of the shed. Like a slice of protoplasm she curled around the corner and flowed toward the steel door. She produced a key, inserted it into the brass lock, turned and retrieved the key, and pulled out the door by degrees until she could slip inside. A moment later she called out, "Come on, Grant. But slow and easy does it."

He did as he was told, crept along the brick wall, and a minute later found himself in the dark interior, which became pitch black when Sarah closed the door. The air reeked of gasoline and motor oils.

She whispered, "Don't move until I switch the burglar alarm back on."

He heard her scrabbling on the concrete floor. Something clicked faintly, then her miniature flashlight flicked on and a narrow beam of light carved a white hole across the ebony interior. The shed was full of gardening implements and lawn machinery: rakes, clippers, trowels, and miscellaneous hand tools hung from pegboard attached to one wall, while a rack of steel shelving opposite held electric hedge trimmers and the like. A pair of tractor-mowers blocked the garage door, which faced the main building, and three gasoline powered push mowers stood behind them.

Sarah led the way past a couple of snow blowers to a steel door at the rear of the shed, next to which were hung half a dozen headset ear protectors. The door opened into a shaft with an iron spiral staircase which took them twenty feet below ground level to another steel door, beyond which lay the generator room. The beam from Sarah's miniature flashlight was swallowed by the immensity of the room. The generator was the size of a large locomotive. One wall was lined with electrical disconnect panels, massive contactors and throw switches, and an unlit annunciator board. Thick insulated wires were suspended overhead in cable trays. It was as still and as silent as a tomb.

"In case of a power outage, they can run their essential circuits and computer lines from here. The generator is distanced from the main building because the electrical interference plays havoc with sensitive instrumentation and computer interfaces."

Grant nodded knowingly. "Magnetic hysteresis. We had to isolate the fan motors—"

"This way," she said, interrupting Grant's unnecessary explanation.

They followed the major trunk line through an access panel into a concrete tunnel which was barely wide enough for a slender person to fit between the metal cable guides and the wall. Sarah's penlight led the way. In order to avoid the sharp edges of the cable guide framework, Grant had to drag his body along the concrete wall, and be careful not to gouge his wound. So far, the codeine was doing its job, and he felt nothing more than a mild throb in his arm.

"Are you okay?" Sarah whispered.

"Fine."

A few minutes later they reached the end of the tunnel. Sarah put an ear to the closed panel, listened for a full minute, then gently pushed open the metal door. The room beyond was as dark as the tunnel, but suffused with a humming sound which spoke of high-voltage electrical apparatus. The odor of ozone filled the air.

In the meager beam of the flashlight Grant saw that they were entering a room which housed the building's power distribution substation; it was a maze of metal and polyvinyl chloride conduits which crossed and crisscrossed more often than a California freeway system. Huge annunciator panels housed green and red lights which carried a warm if eerie glow of their own, and provided enough light to see by.

Sarah shrugged off her pack and removed a packet of what looked like putty wrapped partly in cellophane. She plunked it on top of a massive gang of conduits which protruded through the wall and entered the primary disconnect. She ignored the red lightning-bolt signs which were stamped "Danger: High Voltage."

"What's that for?"

"A diversion." She plugged the prong of a blasting cap into the brick of plastic explosive, deftly programmed the keyboard of an electronic detonator with a coded numerical sequence, and tucked the device out of sight behind the conduits. "In case we need it."

Grant knew that he should be concerned about the amount of destruction Sarah so casually contemplated causing. Yet he still felt like a stranger, an interloper, in this high technology world of Humphrey Bogart robots and infinite capacity memory units. Any moment he expected to wake up with a splitting headache and an enormous hangover, to discover that the past two days had been an incredibly lifelike but nevertheless alcoholically induced nightmare.

"You weren't kidding about blowing the lid off this case, were you?"

"When the stakes are big the betting gets heavy." She showed him a black plastic box the size of a cigarette pack. From one end protruded a red button covered by a clear plastic cap. "This is the trigger." She removed the monocular and starlight scope from her waistband and stowed them in the pack. The trigger went into her pants. "Let's see how busy this place is."

She opened the door a crack to peer out, and in so doing let in a ribbon of light from the corridor, which was dimly lit by drop-ceiling fluorescent fixtures. "From here on out we play it by ear. I don't know who or what we'll find, how many people are in the building, or where they may be at the moment. It's extremely important that we remain absolutely quiet; don't cough, don't clear your throat, don't even breathe fast through your nose. We're dealing with professionals." She emphasized her warnings by removing the forty-four Magnum from her purse and clicking off the safety. "Got it?"

Grant nodded. "Uh, yes. But don't you think I should have a gun, too?"

Sarah humphed. "What, so you can shoot yourself in the foot or take down an innocent victim? With all due respect, Honey, you're safer without one." She winked at him. "Just stick close to me. I'll save you." She gave him another peck on the cheek.

Sarah put her ear to the opening and listened intently, with her head cocked to one side like a robin on the lookout for worms in the ground. Then she motioned with her head for Grant to follow. Together they tiptoed along the broad, carpeted concrete floor. Grant's bones creaked uncommonly loud, like the telltale heart in Poe's gruesome murder story. Sarah either failed to notice or was not concerned, more likely the latter. Only every fifth fixture was lit, and then only one tube out of the four which occupied the metal casing.

Rooms opened to either side, each having a heavy metal door with a wire-glass window a foot square which occupied the center at about head height. No lights shone within. Sarah approached an intersection with more than usual caution, peered both ways past the cinder block walls, then darted across the intersection and motioned for Grant to follow. After passing the next intersection and observing that yet another lay ahead, Grant began to appreciate the dimensions of the building, for there also appeared to be parallel offshoots at fifty-foot intervals along the intersecting corridors.

There was no internal security system. After all, this was not a government nuclear weapons facility or a strategic military installation. It was a private corporation whose staff were civilians who could come and go as they pleased. The cinder block walls were gaily decorated with murals, paintings, and framed photographs of outdoor scenery: everything from mountain brooks to deserts to snow-capped peaks.

Each door was marked with a numbered plaque which spelled out the function of the room beyond, enabling Grant to ascertain the nature and the scope of the company's business. He passed by microchip design and production stations, specialized hydraulics departments, robotic assembly areas, photographic reduction facilities, clean rooms for the sterilization of printed circuit boards, even a cryogenics laboratory.

He stopped by a room which was designated as an "experimental tegument fabrication control center." He was still wondering what it meant when the sound of gruff voices announced the presence of others on the floor. Sarah pushed open the door and shoved Grant into the room. The sound of conversation diminished quickly, and soon Grant could hear nothing but his own labored breathing. Sarah made as much noise as a rock. A full five minutes passed before she switched on her penlight and speared the Stygian blackness with a narrow white beam.

After the barest moment she flicked off the light and opened the metal door a crack, but Grant said "Wait" in a hushed tone and put his hand out to ease the door shut. "I want to look at something."

"Grant, this isn't a sightseeing tour—"

His curiosity had been piqued by that merest glimpse, and piqued enough to incite his latent audacity. "Please. Just give me a moment." He put out his hands in order to locate her body, felt for her arm, then ran his fingers down to her hand and relieved her of the flashlight. "Just a moment." He knew that he could not have taken the flashlight from her unless she had permitted him to do so.

He aimed the beam at the production line bench. Scattered across the Formica surface were a multitude of arms and legs and a couple of mechanical torsos, in various stages of encasement. Sheets of experimental tegument lay draped over rods which were suspended from the ceiling at the far end of the room, appearing like bolts of padding in a carpet factory, or rolls of neoprene rubber in a wetsuit manufacturing plant. Colors ranged from black to brown to faint and mottled pink. On the bench closest to him lay trial cutouts and remnants of varying sizes and thicknesses.

Grant picked up a swatch of tegument. It was lightweight and resilient, and when he squeezed it between his fingers it felt like neoprene rubber and had about the same texture. Thicknesses ranged from one-eighth inch to a half. Upon close examination he could see the closed cell structure that so closely resembled the material of wetsuits.

"It's synthetic skin which is chemically impregnated with tinted polymers," Sarah explained softly. She plucked a carving scalpel from the tool rack in the middle of the bench, sliced through a fat remnant, and held it out for Grant to see. A red, sticky liquid seeped from the shallow incision. "It's the latest thing for lifelike models in the slasher movies, where they want to show lots of blood and gore. And a live actor can glue thin sheets of it on his skin so he can appear to bleed."

A faraway scream broke Grant's concentration.

"That's our call." Sarah snatched the flashlight from Grant's grasp and switched it off. In a moment she was out the door and slinking along the corridor, with Grant in careful pursuit. She paused at the intersection, looked both ways, then tilted her head for Grant to follow. She ran lightly in the direction of the stifled cries, and paused momentarily outside a door whose window showed light. Grant was right behind her when she shoved open the door of the lounge. Past her slender form he saw a nude woman and a partially dressed man who were struggling on the edge of a green couch.

"Hey, Kraut!"

The man thrust the woman away, turned and half rose, dropped his jaw in astonishment, and made an attempt to recover the trousers which had fallen down to his knees. Sarah swung a haymaker with the Magnum in her fist. The gun hit the man so hard in the forehead that his cracking skull sounded like a rifle shot. He dropped to the floor like a stone.

The woman collapsed half off the couch and began to cry hysterically. Sarah tried to silence her by shaking, then by slapping her on the face, but the woman writhed with such leftover terror that she could not be reasoned with and would not listen to Sarah's placating words. After several attempts to assure the woman that everything was all right, Sarah pressed her hand to the lipsticked mouth and clamped down tight so that she could not even breathe.

"Grant! Help me."

The woman went wide-eyed at Grant's approach. He knelt in front of her and grabbed her forcefully by the shoulders. Sarah released her hold and shrugged off the knapsack.

"Darling. Oh, darling," the woman gasped, after she sucked in some sorely needed air. "I tried to stop them but I couldn't—"

Now it was Grant's turn to press his hand across the frenetic woman's mouth. "Shut up, lady, or you'll give us all away."

She continued to wriggle like a trapped animal, but Grant did not loosen his grip. In a trice Sarah slapped a damp cloth over the woman's nostrils. "Hold her tight! Hold her tight!"

Grant held on, but turned his nose away from the odor of chloroform. He squeezed his eyes shut, trying to erase from his mind the look of horror and betrayal. The woman's body convulsed so hard that he had to lean his entire weight against her until the anesthetic took hold. When he finally opened his eyes he saw at first the Nazi goon, whose face was by now a sea of blood and whose skin was the pallor of death.

"I brought the chloroform for the victimizers, not the victims." Sarah removed the cloth from the woman's nose so she could breathe freely in unconsciousness. With the thoroughness and impersonality of a doctor she performed a quick examination. As a one-time medical practitioner, Grant could not help but notice the bruises on the woman's inner thighs. "I think she's been raped, probably more than once, but she doesn't appear to be otherwise injured." Sarah wiped tears off her cheeks with the backs of her hands. "The poor gal's been traumatized by these Nazi bastards."

Grant held back his own tears, but could not help the feelings of pity and deep resentment from welling within his breast. His heart throbbed.

Sarah was quick to return to reality. "Well, there goes our silent entry, although, if they've done this before they may be used to a few screams from their improvised bordello." She peered out the door and scanned the hallway. "All right, let's get her out of here. We can hide her in another room. By the time she wakes up or anyone notices her missing, our work should be done."

The woman's clothes were not in evidence, nor were there any sheets or blankets with which to cover her nakedness. Grant choked down his revulsion as he hefted the woman in his arms. She was quite attractive, he thought, fair-skinned and soft although perhaps a bit overweight—but who in their post forties did not have unwanted adipose tissue growing where it had never grown before? He felt sorry for her in her present condition, yet, despite the seriousness of their plight, could not help but fancy meeting her under more favorable circumstances.

He followed Sarah into the corridor. She ran ahead to the nearest intersection and disappeared around the corner. When Grant got there she was waving him forward. She held open the door to a maintenance closet which was stuffed with brooms, mops, buckets, vacuum cleaners, and rotary polishers, and lined with racks of towels and cleansing fluids.

"We'll hide her in here."

Sarah cleared an opening on the floor at the back of the closet, and lined it with linen towels. Together they stretched out the woman between the machinery, covered her with all the rest of the towels, and strategically placed brooms and mops in the way so they appeared to have fallen haphazardly. A quick glance from the door would not reveal her presence.

"I wish we could have talked with her and gotten the lay of the land, but maybe she doesn't know anything."

Grant was still too stunned to speak. He was out of his element.

"She's lucky, though. She still has all her body parts." Sarah closed the closet door. "Let's go get these guys before they catch on we're here and decide to murder the rest of the hostages." She led the way to the stairwell. "The voices went in this direction, and I heard heels clicking on metal steps."

The door closed behind them on a hydraulic piston. The concrete slab offered no way to go down. Sarah ascended the stairwell with catlike steps, and Grant followed suit, carefully putting each foot on the metal so as not to make any noise. They stopped on the landing at the upper basement level. Sarah raised a vertical finger to her pale lips. She eased open the fire door without allowing the latch to click. In the distance, Grant heard a shouting match in gruff German accents.

Sarah led the way with her gun. Grant waited until the piston had almost closed the door, then depressed the latch so that the bolt did not click into place. They crossed an intersecting corridor. Sarah motioned Grant to his knees, and they crawled on all fours along a cinder block wall which rose to a height of four feet, from which point glass panels extended to the twelve-foot ceiling. A quick glance inside disclosed a laboratory complex which occupied several "blocks" within the building, surrounded on all four sides by the perimeter corridor. The room itself was more than a hundred feet in length and breadth, and was sectioned off by low panels which created work carrels and computer terminal stations.

Sarah kept crawling until she reached a cinder block partition which surrounded a massive H-beam: one of the building's main structural supports. She motioned Grant to follow her.

The voices issuing from the middle of the laboratory were a mixture of German, English, and German-accented English. Several figures could be seen gesticulating but their words did not come clearly through the thick glass panels. Following Sarah's example, Grant twisted his head and allowed one eye to rise above the cinder block wall. He saw a man in a dark brown suit slap the pasty face of a straw-haired woman wearing a white lab smock. She staggered with the blow and came up hard against a steel shelf full of electronic components. She started to slump, but the brown suit grabbed her and tossed her into the arms of another man who had short blond hair and who also wore a lab smock.

After more shouting and arm waving, two men wearing black pants and turtleneck sweaters separated to reveal a long lean man lying on an operating table with one arm lying motionless over the side. The patient was wearing a contraption on his head which consisted of an encircling stainless steel frame with wired sensor pads screwed tight against his scalp above the ears. One of the turtlenecks unscrewed the sensor pads and removed the steel frame, the other unceremoniously shoved the body off the table, then laughed when it crashed to the polished linoleum floor in a contorted fetal attitude. The glaring eyes of the dead man seemed to stare directly at Grant and with foreboding intent.

Grant gasped. He closed his eyes to the gruesome sight and dropped down to his knees. He ignored the aches in his sides and legs from crouching in an unnatural position. When he opened his eyes he found Sarah staring at him with a look of concern.

She placed her lips close to his ears. "Did you recognize anyone?"

He nodded silently.

"Tell me."

He took a few deep breaths. He had seen so much violent death in the past twelve hours that the cumulative effect was threatening to destroy his inner foundation of sanity. He was sickened with dread and horror. Nor did he have to whisper his reply, for his throat was so choked up from emotion that he could barely utter an audible sound. "It was Bob," he finally managed to croak. "Bob Lerner." His longtime friend, confidant, and co-worker.

Came a scream from the lab. Despite his misgivings about what evil might be occurring, morbid curiosity and a compulsion to behold the Nazi's next act of horror incited Grant to peek once again through the glass. The two turtlenecks held a rather chubby woman in the air. One stifled her screams by locking his left arm around her throat as he pulled back her head by yanking hard a fistful of hair; the other pulled her taut by the ankles. Together they laid her on the operating table and proceeded to strap her down. Despite her wildly shaking head, the man in the brown suit affixed the steel head girdle to her skull and slowly screwed in the sensors. The blond man sat in front of a bank of computer monitors, several of which were showing brain wave and EEG patterns. He input commands on the keyboard, ignoring the woman in the smock, who held her hand to her head as it bled through trembling fingers. All this took only half a minute.

Grant hardly recognized the overweight woman on the table as his once slender secretary. "That's Francine," he said, a bit too loud. She's so bloated. What have they done to her?

Sarah murmured, "And that's the brain phasing device."

"What will it do?"

"I don't understand the principles of operation, but if the power isn't governed, it'll fry her brain like a scrambled egg. Like it just fried Lerner's." Sarah made an instantaneous decision, and pulled the electronic trigger from under her waistband. "I was hoping I wouldn't have to do this."

She flipped open the clear plastic protector, and without further preamble or second thoughts she pressed her thumb down on the small red button.

Chapter 22

Following Dawn Templeton's directions, Patrolman Richard Anderson turned off Memory Lane into an immense parking lot which was dark and devoid of vehicles. He steered away from the huge building which the parking lot served, and headed toward the far corner to where Dawn's pale finger pointed.

"There it is." Dawn wiggled her hand behind Anderson's shoulder. "Farther to the left and away from the road."

Captain Hendry squinted through the glare on the windshield. "Ain't much of a tree."

Anderson switched on the high beams and aimed the squad car toward the weeping willow which stood alone on the grass, and which was separated from the forest beyond by a hundred feet of new mown lawn. The willow stood no higher than fifteen feet and, shorn of most of its leaves in preparation for winter, it appeared stunted and scrawny.

"Daddy had it transplanted just for us. Sometimes I meet him here for lunch, and we always take our sandwiches over to this tree and spread a blanket on the ground. And since I moved out of the house, when he walks by on his way home from the lab he sometimes leaves notes pinned to the trunk or knickknacks tied to the lower branches, like when I was a little girl, only now I leave messages for him, too. Kids don't play out here and it's off the beaten track, so there's no one to disturb anything. It's a game we play. Daddy says that when you're too old to play games your life is coming to an end."

From the back seat next to Dawn, Patrolman Riley maintained an ever-present vigil. He twisted around and peered through the windows on all sides, half expecting trouble to erupt in the guise of a night watch person who was curious about official intervention. "It looks deserted."

Anderson stopped the car but did not shut off the engine or douse the lights.

"Playing possum, still." Hendry's thick neck bulged as he craned to look at Dawn. "Meaning no disrespect, ma'am, but your daddy's got a lot to answer for with what's been going on since he showed up on our doorstep yesterday morning. Fifteen dead men and two impersonating robots is no laughing matter. Now I'm not saying he's responsible for—"

The ball of light which erupted from the wall of the building momentarily illuminated the interior of the car like the brilliant flash of a strobe. The dull roar of an explosion came a split second later, followed by dirt and cinders and chunks of cement which splattered against the rear window like hailstones traveling at supersonic speed. Dawn screamed. Hendry threw his hands to his eyes. Anderson yelled a drawn out epithet. Riley turned in time to see the van-sized transformer burst into flames as the high-voltage wires were fused and short-ed and blew the windings to pieces. Red-hot shards pirouetted in the air and scythed through the sur-rounding trees, touching off secondary fires in the bark and on dry fallen leaves on the ground.

Captain Hendry muttered a few oaths as he rubbed his eyes with his fists. "Now there's an invite if I ever did see one." He reached out blindly for the microphone. "Git us inside pronto, Richy, even if you hafta crash your way in."

Anderson backed the car in a turn with such speed that the passengers were hurled to the side in a heap. Riley clutched Dawn and protected her from being throttled as Anderson stomped the gas, laid rubber on macadam, and fishtailed across the parking lot toward the building.

"Don't drive through the glass!" Hendry screamed.

Anderson stood on the brake, but the front tires bounced over the curb anyway. "I wasn't gonna, Boss. Honest." Then he slipped out from under the wheel and dashed across the sidewalk.

"Richie!" yelled Riley, struggling in the back seat.

"Let me out!" Anderson scrambled back to the car and opened the rear door for Riley. "Sorry, Frank."

"You stay put, young lady." Captain Hendry pressed the transmitter and got Sergeant Benson on the radio. "We need fire trucks and all the backup you can round up—"

Riley heard no more because he was running after Anderson toward the lobby.

The older patrolman had already drawn his pistol and aimed it at the glass facade. "I've always wanted to do this." He fired a round from his .38 at the middle of one ceiling-height pane, and drilled a neat round hole through the glass. He stared blankly after the echo from the shot died away. Then he fired three closely grouped shots and two wide of the mark, decorating the thick pane with six identical holes and some spider web cracks. "Damn. I thought the glass would shatter into a million little pieces."

While Anderson reloaded in the darkness, Riley drew his service revolver and aimed deliberately at the lock from a distance of several feet. He dented the mechanism with a round which ricocheted dangerously past his head. Stunned, he exchanged a wild-eyed stare with Anderson. Then he moved so he could fire on the lock at an angle, but still there was no effect other than a couple of minor dents.

"You boys been watching too much television." Captain Hendry approached with a twelve-gauge shotgun which was slung over his shoulder like a hoe. He lowered the butt to waist level and jammed the brass plate against his hip. He held the end of the barrel less than a foot from the face of the latch, and fired. Came a belch of flame and smoke, and the door burst inward as if it were released on a spring, followed by a mass of steel pellets and flying particles of glass. His shoes made crunching sounds as he stepped across the threshold. "Now put your guns away before you hurt somebody. If the place is still occupied, the folks are likely to be panicked—"

Hendry's warning was cut short by the staccato

popping of small arms fire from inside. "What the hell?"
****

Other than a dull whump and the momentary
blackness, Grant was hardly aware of the detonation in
the substation. The fluorescent night lights did not
come back on, nor did the ceiling lights in the glass-
encased laboratory, but the dull beams of battery-oper-
ated emergency incandescents soon suffused the air
with a dim yellow glow. Fire gongs everywhere were
clanging shrilly.

"Don't move," Sarah said grimly. "This is my show."

She kicked open the door and charged into the lab
with her Magnum blazing. All eyes turned in her direction. The two faces which protruded above turtleneck
sweaters were suddenly pockmarked with holes as
Sarah punched them with lead. Francine went limp.
The other woman, in the smock, backed against an
instrument cabinet and slid to the floor as if her legs
had turned to rubber; her eyes remained wide with
shock. Neither the man in the suit nor the man in the
smock made a move.

Sarah panned the gun from one man to the other.
"Would anyone care to tell me what's going on here?"

The blond man whom Sarah addressed had
swiveled on the chair but had not otherwise moved
from his place at the computer station. The bank of
monitors, whose operational condition was maintained
by the generator which was now supplying power to all
essential circuits throughout the building, displayed
the changing configurations of a program in process.

"I missed you at the Do Come Inn." The brown-suited man held his hands up high, but he put on a smirk
which showed chipped yellow teeth behind lips which
had seen their share of the sun. His face was wrinkled
like Egyptian parchment. "You wouldn't shoot an
unarmed man, would you, Maggie?"

Sarah said "Gladly," but not until after she plugged
him full in the chest. He was slammed against a partition by the force of the bullet. The smirk quickly faded
to a look of disbelief, then contorted with the pain of

inevitable death. Blood drooled slowly from thick, cracked lips. The eyes rolled up in their sockets. Then the man collapsed to the floor like a scarecrow suddenly deprived of its straw.

"Your turn." Sarah shifted her direction of aim to the man in the smock, who was now trembling visibly and who had suddenly started to sweat. "Would you care to be more sincere?"

The blond's nod was largely obscured by the violent shaking of the man's body. "I can say vat is doing." His words were hardly intelligible, not only because of the thick German accent but because he was losing muscular control of his tongue and jaw. "You vill not shoot?"

"That depends on what I hear." Sarah flashed a smile which was ironic at best. She shook the gun for effect. "Convince me." She pointed with her chin to Francine Baker. "Were you planning to kill her next?"

The man shook his head emphatically. Pointing to Bob Lerner, "Ve try to save the thinks the thoughts. But ve haf not the data, und—" He glanced at the woman who was now a blob on the floor. "She not help good vith Templeton program."

Grant perked up at the mention of his name. He remained hidden from view in the corridor, but observed events through the open door.

"I told him it wouldn't work the way he wanted it to," Dr. Constantinescu came to life with a scream. "I told him the brain phaser wasn't a memory transfer device, as he believed. I told him it was for shock treatment therapy and—"

"You lie!" The blond man's face contorted with anger and hatred, and he lowered his arms a tad. "You alter memchip program und zat is vat killed—"

Grant heard the thump of approaching feet and saw two uniformed men round the corner of the nearest intersection with their guns drawn. One aimed deliberately at Grant, and fired.

****

The building which had previously been dark was

now dingily illuminated by low-voltage flood lamps powered by self-contained battery packs, creating a shadowy effect which would not prevent people from escaping smoke and flames through the corridors, but which lent an eerie, phantasmagoric air to the stark tableau within.

Riley led the way across the lobby amid the din of clanging fire gongs. "This is the door the woman came out of." He charged into the corridor beyond with his gun in his hand and Anderson on his heels.

"Watch what you're running into, damn it." Captain Hendry scurried to keep up with the younger men. "You ain't giving out parking tickets."

Riley realized that he was again being impetuous, as he had a few hours earlier when he almost collided with a cow—or a steer. He slowed to a walk, kept close to the wall, and sharpened his senses to full alertness. Anderson touched a finger to his temple, winked and nodded, indicating in pantomime the sagacity of moving forward with caution.

A single shot rang out somewhere in the building.

Anderson danced lightly to the stairwell and eased open the fireproof door. He made the sign for silence by putting a finger to his lips, then jerked his head toward the stairs leading down. He advanced quickly but quietly, his gun held out at arm's length. Riley covered him from a couple steps behind. When they reached the next landing, Anderson reached out for the door handle, looked back at Riley and pointed with his gun at the crack, waited till Riley steadied his aim, then eased open the door.

"Careful." Hendry's single word of caution sounded like the hiss of a snake.

Muted voices wafted sibilantly from the corridor, the words indistinguishable.

"Both hands," breathed Hendry.

Riley grasped the gun as his boss and future father-in-law suggested. By now, Riley's thirst for excitement was long past the point of satiation. He never thought that he would find himself wishing for a job directing traffic through a busy intersection with an out-of-order signal. His heart was beating hard enough to hurt. He glanced at Anderson, who was waiting breathlessly for a cue, and gave him a slight single nod.

Anderson yanked open the door.

The corridor beyond was bathed in the same semi-darkness as the stairwell. Riley took a silent step forward, peered around the jamb, and saw two men in brown uniforms run full tilt around the distant corner. One man fired, then the other. Bullets spanged off the cinder block walls and sent chips of mortar flying everywhere; they were using Uzis. Another man in the corridor between Riley and the gunmen ducked through a doorway for cover.

Ignoring Hendry's advice of the two-handed hold, which required Riley to stick half his body into the corridor before he could get off a shot, he reverted to the single-handed military posture, which reduced a person's exposed surface area to the width of the body instead of its front. He hugged the doorframe and projected only his arm, shoulder, and the side of his head. Bullets whizzing past him disturbed his concentration. He took careful aim, and fired just as a slug gouged his bulletproof vest. His target went down headlong on the carpet, rolled and accidentally tripped his gun mate. Wild bullets from a depressed trigger shot up the corridor, ripped through the carpet, shattered two panes of glass, and struck Riley in the side.

The bullet entered Riley's vest below the armpit, cut a notch through the flesh, carved a groove around the inside of the Kevlar material, then whipped around his back and exited the opposite arm hole, nicking his spine in the process. He felt as if a red-hot barrel hoop were wrapped around his back. Hendry and Anderson both uttered curses as the bullet passed between them after making an impossible right-angle turn.

Riley tried to ignore the pain and focus on the foe who had been downed by his companion, and who was already climbing to his knees and was commencing to fire. Riley took careful aim and squeezed off a shot that caught the man in the leg. Another slug went through his jaw as he twisted about, and a third slammed into his lower abdomen.

Now Anderson leaped past Riley and into the corridor. He saw the first man crawling toward the fallen Uzi, aimed his police revolver, and fired as fast as he could pull the trigger until all the chambers were empty.

Gun smoke wafted lazily in the sudden silence.

Both Riley and Anderson stood like statues. Riley was in shock. He had never fired a gun at anything more manlike than a cardboard cutout. Now he gazed in horror at the blood-streaked bodies, at real flesh and bones from which the life had been expunged, and felt his insides churning with the dreadful comprehension of personal responsibility. He had reacted instinctively, firing at his opponent without thought of any consequences other than doing what he had to do in order to survive. Over and over he played back the scene like a quarterback reviewing a game, trying desperately to convince himself that the killing had been necessary, that wounding had been impossible under the circumstances of engagement: low light, distance, and the hostile intent of his foe.

Hendry placed a hand on Riley's shoulder. "You okay, son?"

Frank Riley managed a single nod. He shrank inside the bulletproof vest like a cow or a steer avoiding a branding iron, but the searing pain stayed with him. He was bolstered by the fact that his wound was slight and would leave no lasting impairment. But the memory of his participation in death would reside in his heart forever.

"You better reload that gun," said Hendry to Anderson, as he led the way along the corridor with one fist wrapped around the grip of his pistol and the other locked on the shotgun.

"Right, Boss." Anderson hurriedly broke open the cylinder and filled it with rounds from his belt. "Frank, are you sure you're okay?"

Riley nodded again, released the doorframe, and walked woodenly along the corridor. After a few steps he shrugged off the debilitating abstractions and tried to act like a policeman on duty. Anderson raced past him to serve as Captain Hendry's immediate backup.

Hendry was taking no chances. He stooped below the glass panes that comprised the upper half of the laboratory partition, in order to be protected from gunfire by the cinder blocks. Anderson crouched along behind him. Riley found it impossible to bend due to the fiery furrow in his back; he walked upright with a hand against the glass for support. The room into which the unfamiliar man had gone appeared to be devoid of people.

"This is the police," Captain Hendry said gruffly, half hidden behind the doorframe while his revolver panned the room. "Come out with your hands up."

It sounded so stereotypically corny that Riley felt embarrassed by the simpleminded pronouncement. Yet he knew that modern police procedure had evolved over the years in order to deal with people and situations at an intermediate level. Now was not the time for creative analysis.

Slowly, heads began to appear above the desks and the tabletops.

****

"Well, well, well. The cavalry has arrived with Captain Hendry leading the charge." Sarah stepped away from the computer station with her prisoner grasped firmly by the neck and her Magnum held loosely in her hand. "I can't say that I'm overjoyed to see you, but you did us a good turn by keeping those Krauts off our backs. As long as you're here to help, we've got an—"

"Put the gun down, miss. Slow and easy." Hendry spoke from the protection of the doorframe. "Then we can talk."

"Captain Hendry—"

With emphasis: "Put the gun down."

Sarah sighed with exasperation, but did as the captain requested. She shoved the gun into her handbag and held her arm high in the air. "I'm Captain Margaret Witherspoon, Captain Hendry. I'm an agent from the Department of Defense. There's an injured woman downstairs who needs immediate medical assistance. And I caution you that this building has not yet been secured—"

Hendry stepped into the laboratory with the shotgun leveled. "Put the purse on the table, miss."

"You won't shoot, Captain, and we both know it." Sarah glowered with eyes of blue which looked very cross at the moment. "I'm here on a secret mission to prevent Nazi aggression." She pointed to where one of the brown uniformed bodies was visible through the open door. "Look at the SS insignia on the sleeve. This is an invasion, Captain. Germans from another era trying to make good on the claims of their long-dead Fuhrer. And this—" She shook the blond man by the scruff of the neck. "This is Mr. Gestapo, experimenting on human subjects to advance the cause of Nazi science."

Anderson sidled across the room with his gun pointed up at the ceiling, and took a crossfire position. "Do what he says, lady."

By the expression on Captain Hendry's face, the policeman was in a quandary. It was time for Grant to show his support for the woman who had befriended him when he was a lost and lonely stranger, and who had helped him to survive the past two days in a world which was not of his making. "It's true, Captain Hendry. What she says is true."

"And who the hell are you?"

"Why, I'm—I'm Grant Templeton. I was in your station—"

"Grant Templeton!" Riley walked stiffly into the laboratory. He braced himself against a filing cabinet and squinted in the half-light which suffused through the room. He could feel the sticky dampness of blood as it trickled down his back. "You're Grant Templeton?"

"Patrolman Riley." Grant's hand shot to his face. "Ah, you don't recognize me because I shaved off the beard. I—"

"Grant!" This time it was the woman in the smock who shouted his name in recognition.

"Yes, that's right. What's your part in all of this?"

Dr. Nora Constantinescu moved into the beam of a low-voltage floodlight. "I thought —I thought you were dead. I thought they had killed you, or . . . "

Sarah interrupted the private dialogue. "Captain Hendry, this is neither the time nor the place for power ploys. There's a woman down—"

"Who the hell are you?" Hendry squinted and leaned slightly forward. "You sound famil—"

"I introduced myself as Sarah Mason when I came to pick up Grant at the station. I was working under-cover for reasons which are too complicated to go into at the moment. Please, will you call an ambulance? There's a woman who's been raped and severely beat-en—"

"Omigod, it's Charlotte, isn't it?" Dr. Constantines-cu covered her face with her hands, and wailed. "Is she—is she—?"

"She's alive, but unconscious. And the sooner we get her to a hospital—"

Nora Constantinescu scooped a telephone off a nearby desk and dialed the emergency number.

"Richy." Hendry pointed with his chin.

Anderson took the receiver from the frightened woman just as the call was completed. "Hi, Sarge. It's Richy. Yeah, listen, the action's over but we need an ambulance pronto. Frank got winged—" He glanced at Riley. "No, he's still standing, but he's as white as a sheet. And we think there's a rape victim—No, not Frank—Yeah, I'm sure she'll want to know. Okay. Over and out."

Dr. Constantinescu rushed to Grant's side, peered deep into his eyes, felt his pulse, then pushed the hair away from behind his temples to reveal the tiny red weals. "My god, it is you. But how?" Then she looked down at Bob Lerner. Her eyes grew wide in astonish-ment.

Hendry half lowered his armament. "Hey, what about that woman on the table—"

Dr. Constantinescu rushed again. "Francine's fine. She just fainted." She knelt by Lerner and took his hand in hers, felt for a pulse, pressed her ear to his chest. "I think he's still alive." She tilted back his head, pinched off his nose, pressed her mouth over his flaxen lips, and blew hard into his lungs. "Someone help me."

Grant dropped to the floor while Sarah kicked chairs out of the way and made room for Grant to stretch out the body. He noticed what appeared to be dime-sized burns on both sides of Lerner's head, just behind the temples. Then he placed the heels of his hands against Lerner's sternum.

Dr. Constantinescu shook her head between breaths. "His heart is still beating. He just needs more ventilation—Watch out for Fenton." Her warning came a moment too late.

The blond man made a dash for the computer console. He punched a button on the keyboard which sent the screen displays into a flurry of activity.

Sarah leaped into action. She kicked the man in the side hard enough to knock him back against the monitor rack, then she shoved a handful of curled knuckles into his solar plexus. He folded over with a whoosh of expelled air. Sarah kicked one leg out from under him and dropped him to the floor in a rapid one-two judo maneuver. He lay grimacing and gasping for air.

The action occurred too fast for the policemen to react.

Sarah continued to ignore the constabulary as she studied the screens and their flashing data, most of which was in German. "What's happening, Dr. Constantinescu?"

Dr. Constantinescu was busy performing mouth-to-mouth resuscitation. She stopped long enough to shout, "Get that book off the scanner."

Grant felt a weak pulse on his co-worker's wrist. There was nothing more he could do as long as Nora kept giving him air, so he joined Sarah at the computer station. A thick volume had been separated from its binding, and the pages were being machine fed into an optical character reader. He scooped the loose pages out of the carriage.

The title of the book was *Mein Kampf.*

Captain Hendry looked like he wanted to take control of the situation, but was agonizing over how to do it. "Ma'am, can you show me some identification."

Sarah spun around and faced him. "Hell, no. I'm undercover, and the last thing an agent carries is real ID. I will let you arrest me, however, once this operation is fully secured, pending the arrival of a DOD investigatory committee. At the very least I expect to be court-martialed for my unorthodox procedure." She tilted her head toward the brown-suited man lying motionless in a pool of blood. "That is my group leader's immediate supervisor, General Charles Pendergast, officially killed in the line of duty."

Hendry swallowed hard. "Would—would you surrender your weapon, please?" As an afterthought, "Not your hands and feet, of course, just the Magnum in your purse. It's—it's police protocol. And until the troops arrive at dawn, I'm the titular head of this mess. So help me make it look like I am."

Sarah could not refrain from smiling. "I like you, Captain Hendry. And I'm sorry we couldn't have worked closer together on this case. But there's a leak somewhere and—"

There came a crash of metal and glass from the far end of the laboratory. A dark uniformed figure rose up from an assembly bench, moving with short jerky motions as the head twitched from side to side as if in a state of disorientation. Polished black boots hit the floor with a crunching thud. The man or manikin rose to full medium height. The short black hair was parted on the right, and the upper lip sported a Charlie Chaplin mustache worn with a sinister leer.

"Oh, Jesus Christ," Captain Hendry muttered. "It's Adolf Hitler!"

Chapter 23

Nora Constantinescu abandoned her ministrations on Lerner, beheld the simulacrum for the barest instant, and assaulted the computer station's primary keyboard with fingers which moved so fast that their motion was a blur. Her keystroke instructions blanked screen after screen and shut down peripherals one after the other.

The Hitler simulacrum saw what she was doing, wrapped hydraulic fingers around the cable by which it was attached to the output modem, and yanked its plug out of the socket. The umbilical cord retracted automatically into an abdominal slot which was then covered by a steel flap under the military jacket.

"Too late," said Nora. "Most of the historical and biographical data have already been implanted. It has probably achieved consciousness of self if not full awareness." She turned to Grant. "Without the fully functioning memchip input program it cannot access its entire flashback repertoire, but it might already think that it is the real Adolf Hitler, or at the very least his reincarnation."

It was all Greek to Grant. The Fuhrer marched awkwardly, reminding Grant of his daughter when she took her first halting steps across the living room to his open and waiting arms. The simulacrum focused its attention on Nora and the computer station.

"Boss, do we shoot it?" Anderson held his gun in true police fashion, with two hands.

"Hell, yes."

Anderson fired at a distance of twenty feet. The bullet struck the thoracic cavity with a dull thud, tore a hole in the uniform jacket, and spanged up through an acoustical drop-ceiling tile, leaving a slender column of dust in its wake. The second and third bullets ricocheted at oblique angles and smashed through nearby laboratory equipment. "Must be wearing a flak jacket."

He emptied his revolver at the thing's head with much the same lack of result. He blew off one ear and tore one eye socket apart, but still the thing kept coming.

"It's the Deutch Reich prototype armored model," Nora said breathlessly. "It's built on a standard titanium chassis, but the components are all protected by Krupp steel plate."

With arms like car jacks the simulacrum ripped a heavy metal table free from the lag bolts which connected the stanchions to the concrete floor under the linoleum, and thrust it aside like an angry child would toss a small stuffed animal. Nora backed away from the computer station when Hitler arrived. It began rebooting programs with a delicacy of manipulation belied by its exhibition of strength.

Hendry leveled his shotgun and once again fired from the hip. The blast at close range tore the simulacrum's clothes to shreds and knocked the body sideways a good six inches, but otherwise did little destructive damage. Hitler turned its head slowly and deliberately as its digits continued to work on the keyboard, and glared at Hendry with complete if sluggish control of its facial tegument, rendering a look of contempt.

Sarah lunged forward, jammed the barrel of the Magnum against the back of the simulacrum's head, and pulled the trigger. The bullet bounced off the hardened steel alloy like a BB off sheet metal. The end of the barrel ruptured, and the gun was knocked out of Sarah's hand and sent pinwheeling across the laboratory as if it were a plastic toy. Hitler' head rocked forward on a ball-and-socket joint, but recovered quickly. A backhanded roundhouse caught her in the shoulder and knocked her back a dozen feet. With nothing but disdain for the people around it, Hitler started to plug in its power and data acquisition cable.

Intellectually, Grant was still lost in this parallel world of super science and indestructible robots, but he knew that no matter what technological achievements this society had attained, the underlying principles of physics were the same. He snatched Captain Hendry's revolver from his hand, and put a slug through the keyboard on which the simulacrum was typing, then proceeded to blast apart the hard drive.

Hitler went mad as its plans for absorbing more power went awry. It swung savagely and knocked the gun out of Grant's hand, then tried for a connecting blow to the head. Grant jumped back out of the way, and the armored arm swiped at nothing but air.

Anderson shoved a newly loaded pistol into the Fuhrer's face and got off one shot that tore away the remaining eye lens before his arm was clamped in the simulacrum's viselike grip. Hitler's program chose an almost human expression of arrogance as the simulacrum's hydraulic wrist bent sharply, and broke the patrolman's arm as one might snap a wooden pencil in two. Anderson screamed. Hitler then picked him up completely off the floor, dangled him for a second, and let him drop.

The eyeless caricature did not seem to mind being blind. Input sensors alerted its CPU by alternative means of the relative position of surrounding objects and tracked their motion as well. The German war machine goose-stepped toward its foes with precision which lacked only in speed, thus permitting people to scamper out of its way before they were captured in its bear-trap grip. It caught Riley by the door because his wounds slowed his retreat, but the patrolman wriggled from its clutches like a slippery prize from the tines of a twenty-five cent arcade claw.

In the corridor, the simulacrum walked around its fallen followers and kept going as if it had a purpose.

Sarah took a grenade from her knapsack and danced so fast around the simulacrum that it could not execute its turns fast enough to keep up with her. While Hitler imitated a diapered child who was trying to catch a butterfly, Sarah dropped the grenade down the back of its tattered pants.

"Fire in the hole!"

Everyone jumped for cover behind benches and cabinets, although the cinder block wall would have protected them in any case. Hitler stuck its hand into its trousers but only just managed to wrap its fingers around the grenade when it detonated. Shrapnel peppered the corridor and blew out all the glass within a ten-foot radius.

When the smoke cleared, Hitler lay prone on the floor with large portions of its tegument either splattered onto the cinder block walls or flayed back and hanging from its armored chassis like the skin from a half-eaten banana. The steel plate was scratched but not otherwise damaged. The simulacrum's limbs made discordant swimming motions, like an injured lizard held down on the ground by fingers which pinched its abdomen. Its right arm was severed below the elbow joint, and the remains of the manipulator and the disarticulated digits lay scattered about the floor in pieces. Hydraulic fluid leaked from the truncated forearm and soaked into the carpet, staining the maroon with ugly dollops of black.

At first the simulacrum could not rise because its gyroscope had taken a new set. Like a newborn foal which knew nothing about muscular coordination, the Hitler simulacrum, energized now for the first time and still unfamiliar with its limitations and controls, took a moment to adjust its motor mechanisms to the environment. Its memchip microprocessor actuated circuits and response patterns faster than any central processing unit previously in existence. And like the foal which could stand and gambol awkwardly about only minutes after birth, the simulacrum—switched on with full cognition which mimicked animal instinct—reduced the spin of its gyroscope wheel, pushed itself up to a vertical position, increased the wheel's speed, and steadied itself upon mechanical feet. By incrementally varying the rotational speed of its internal guidance system, it could simulate perfectly the fore and aft tilt of the human gait, which it did as it strode along the corridor without a backward glance from its lensless sockets.

With one hand, Patrolman Riley steadied himself against the battered doorjamb; with the other he held his service revolver and fired deliberately aimed shots at the simulacrum's power cell and CPU. The bullets dug furrows in the tegument which covered the armor plate like a papier-mâché facade, but did nothing more than cosmetic damage.

"It's getting away!" Captain Hendry broke open the shotgun barrel and shoved in two more shells.

"It won't go far. It's not trying to escape." With professional aplomb, Dr. Nora Constantinescu checked the pulses of the two unconscious people—Francine on the table and Lerner on the floor—then examined Anderson who lay groaning on his side. She wrapped a loose cloth around the patrolman's bleeding arm. "It's going to Grant's office to finish its programming."

"I have an office here?"

Nora frowned. "Of course. In the penthouse. And it knows that it can access all the computer files from your personal workstation." She pressed a hand against Grant's forehead and monitored his pulse. "Are you feeling okay?"

Hendry knelt by Anderson's side and placed a fatherly hand on the wounded man's shoulder. "Hang in there, son. You called the ambulance yourself. Remember?"

The patrolman screwed up his face in pain. "I'm all right, Boss. Just get that Nazi bastard before he tries to take over the world again. My grandfather was wounded at Anzio, and he must be turning over in his grave."

Grant let Nora complete her ministrations, then touched the weals on the side of his head. "I'm still a bit disoriented from the shock—"

"So how can we stop the thing without armor piercing rounds and antitank weapons?" Sarah grimaced and rubbed her bruised rib cage as she reloaded the Magnum. "I didn't come prepared to assault a casemated robot. And how many more Nazis are running loose in the building?"

"I think you've accounted for all the metabolic monsters. As for der Fuhrer, well—since it's the first memchip we've ever activated, we don't know anything about deactivating them." Nora shrugged. "Our guess is that a memchip should become an imitation entity, or an artificial personality, one that is the aggregate of all the data that have been programmed into it, the same way a man or a woman is the sum of a lifetime of accumulated knowledge and experience. Like any other organism—a biological organism—it should abide its directive to maintain its individuality against all attempts to alter its preformed agenda or coded instructions, and to protect its continuance at all costs."

"So it wants to stay alive."

"In a manner of speaking. Although it is not 'alive' in the organic sense of the word." Nora curled her lips to give the faint trace of a smile as she nodded in Grant's direction. "Grant and I have opposing views on what differentiates electrochemical sentience from purely electrical self-actuating circuitry. Theoretically, an integrated memchip contains as much data as the brain of an adult human being, and has a comparable degree of complexity and organization; otherwise it would not be able to simulate human thought patterns. Furthermore, because its processing speed is based upon the flow of electrons—essentially the speed of light—instead of slow chemical reactions, it can access data and respond faster than a human being. Nevertheless, I do not believe that those criteria quantify a memchip intelligence with human equivalence. It has yet to be seen whether an integrated memchip has the capacity for abstract thought, so in my opinion it is premature to objectify—"

"Pardon me for interrupting." Sarah cocked the Magnum and chambered a round. "Can we continue this discussion on the move. I mean, there is an indestructible machine on the loose, and it is the leader of the Nazi Revitalization League even if all the members of the local chapter have been exterminated."

"Yes, yes, yes. I understand your consternation, uh, Sarah. But do understand that the Hitler doppelganger is nothing more than a mobile memory unit, a portable computer in a bulletproof housing. It has no weapons other than rhetoric which, no doubt, can be a powerful means of persuasion when wielded by the wrong hands against weak minds susceptible to misdirection. But it is not likely to smite us with bombastic speeches about world domination by a so-called master race, no matter who it resembles. It is after all a machine—one that is unarguably more complicated than most, but still just a machine."

"Like a human being is more complicated than the amoeba." Grant may not have understood all that was happening, but he had gleaned enough information about the Memchip 201 to recognize its potential for catastrophe when programmed with evil intent. "I may be a bit behind the times, especially concerning the interpretation of the meaning of Artificial Intelligence, and you and I may disagree on the semantics of life and what constitutes 'aliveness' in machine perception and actualization, but even without the benefit of full knowledge of the memchip's design criteria, it must still be conceded that a program—any program—once initiated, will continue to operate and to seek a solution to the problem to which it has been assigned, or to complete the task to which it has been set, until it is told to stop. If a simple bottle boxing machine will keep dropping bottles into a carriage long after the holder has run out of boxes, until the pile of broken glassware threatens to fill every available space, what do you think a self-promoting program like Hitler is likely to do? It will let nothing impede its pursuit for world domination, and it will have no compunction against eradicating masses that it was programmed to eradicate." Turning to Sarah, "I agree with you. Our first priority is to immobilize this resurrected murderer. And don't underestimate its ingenuity."

"I wasn't proposing that we let it carry out its orders," protested Dr. Constantinescu. "I merely stated that there is no reason to chase after it when we can predict its destination and go directly there at our leisure. Surely, Grant, you know that it must have more time to 'feed' from the data banks in order to bolster its ego, so to speak." She pointed to the pages torn from *Mein Kampf*, which now lay scattered across the floor, and a huge stack of newspapers, magazines, and other printed material which was ready to be fed to the scanner for digitalization. "It needs to assimilate more input before it can forge the personality that the Nazis want it to have. Besides, you can actuate the fail-safe program from any operable remote terminal."

"I wish I knew what you were talking about." Grant swept his arms around him. "I don't know what any of this means. I don't know who you are. And I don't see how I fit into the grand scheme of the universe. Sarah tells me that—" Grant stopped in mid sentence as if a muzzle had been placed over his mouth.

After a moment of silence, Dr. Constantinescu said, "I think I understand. The brain-phasing unit they used on you must have . . . " She dribbled into silence when she noticed the stunned expression on his face and followed his line of sight.

Grant was staring at a magazine which lay atop the stack of periodicals on the table against the wall. He was looking at his name and face on the cover. It was *Personalities*. He held his breath as he picked up the magazine and read the banner headline: Scientist Claims AI Is Here Today. The subheading read: his totally new concept in memory storage permits a person to live forever.

Sirens sang in the distance.

"I used to wonder why you were so shy about being interviewed." Dr. Constantinescu glanced disparagingly at the magazine. "Now I know. The extravagant claims in the article are the reporter's, not yours."

But Grant was not as awestricken by the copy hype as he was by the numerical symbols in the upper right hand corner. "The—the—the date. It's . . . "

From her position facing him, Sarah pulled the top of the magazine down so she could read it. "It's *next* month. They always release magazines a month before the date on the cover, so you think you're getting it ahead of everyone else. As if people can be fooled."

"Not the month! The year!"

Patrolman Riley leaned over Grant's shoulder. "It's the current issue." To Captain Hendry, "George, that's the one I photocopied from the library."

"Yeah, I recognize it. So what?"

Grant did not have to be a mathematical wizard to make the mental calculation. "It's ten years in the future." His skin crawled with the import of the words he had just uttered. He scanned the faces that were arranged before him, saw nothing but disbelief. Patrolman Anderson stood up for the occasion and cradled his broken arm, his pain apparently forgotten in the moment of revelation. "Ten years in my future." To Sarah, "That's why this world never made any sense to me. I was right from the beginning: This is not my world. It's what my world will become if I can't go back into the past—your past—and change the course of my research. It's—"

"It's balderdash, that's what it is," Sarah exclaimed. "And I'm only saying that because we're in polite company."

The Sirens wailed in his ears.

Grant held his hands out pleadingly. "Don't you see? It explains everything. Somehow, I've come through time—through some kind of time warp—into the future—my future. I come from a continuum where none of this has happened—where it can still be prevented—"

"I will personally escort you to the loony bin if you don't stop this nonsense right this minute." Sarah snatched the magazine from Grant's hand. "I told you, you're not from another world."

Ignoring her, Grant took a newspaper off the top of the pile. Half-inch boldface screamed in all caps: GENERAL BRINKLEY SHOT TWICE IN HEAD. Just like Riley had told him; just like Sarah had said. And the year was the same future decade. Like Rip Van Winkle, Grant had gone to sleep clean-shaven and woke up with a beard. The years had passed him by.

It all made a baffling kind of sense, except: How had it come about?

Ordinary people do not awaken from a ten-year bender without some awareness of the passage of time. Grant had had his binges in the past, but never one like this. Even during the trauma of divorce . . .

The clatter of boots, the rustle of clothing, and shouts of alarm reverberated in the corridor. Instantly everyone in the room was on guard, and those who still had weapons aimed them at the door.

The portly sergeant in uniform knocked delicately on the glass. "Hey, anybody here need police assistance?" Sergeant Benson leaned into the laboratory, pointing a finger down at the body on the floor. "Correct me if I'm wrong, Captain, but hasn't the Gestapo been out of commission for the past sixty years?"

"Bob, I'm sure glad to see your fat happy face."

Fire Marshall Casey, clad in waterproof rubber, stepped delicately over the body. "Well, I'm not happy to see yours so soon." He surveyed the damaged laboratory with a jaundiced eye. "Are we interrupting a wrecking party?"

"Not exactly, but you're in time to see the belated end of Hitler's Third Reich. Or is it the Fourth Reich?"

"Huhn?"

Hendry pointed a crooked finger. "Did you do your job outside?"

"Huhn? Oh, yes. The fire is under control." Casey seemed confused by the captain's abstruse remarks. "And the ambulance is on the way. But, what's going on here?"

"Well, if I followed the highfalutin conversation correctly, the good Dr. Templeton is about to 'seig heil' Mr. Adolf for the last time."

Casey seemed more confused than ever. Before he could respond, he was pushed aside by a pretty young co-ed carrying a shiny metal box like an oversized antique cigarette case.

"Daddy!"

In a flash of insight, Grant perceived the truth

about the picture on the desk in the other Templeton's house. In this world Dawn was no longer a cute little girl who sat on her father's knee while he read stories to her from a book, but a lovely young woman who might not have time for a doting old man who wanted to revel in the past. Grant's heart was torn between two contrary emotions: the happiness of knowing that his daughter was alive and well, and that her affectionate hugs could bring joy to a lonely father who teetered close to the edge of madness; and the sorrow of knowing that her formative years were gone and were never to be regained, and that an important part of their relationship would forever be unknown to him.

He did not know whether to rejoice or to weep. Instinctively, he held out his arms, and did both.

Chapter 24

Grant Templeton found himself meandering through a surrealistic world, where a host of alternate realities merged into a single, interwoven, and chaotic disarrangement of events; where multiple planes of existence vied for continuance and domination; where divergent streams of time converged to the point of simultaneity; where his conscious and subconscious minds intermingled unsystematically, each struggling to establish sanity without deranging its partner in perception.

For the mind is a delicate thing: an ephemeral coruscation of thoughts in motion, a sensitive balance of memories in transition, a restless, whirling, mercurial and intangible organization of chemical interactions which occur in the substrate known as the brain and which then generate the entity known as the mind. One cannot exist without the other. The brain and the mind are inseparable: two quanta which mediate mutually to form a unity of being, the harmony of which results in the phenomenon called consciousness. Yet the mind is not a thing as much as it is a pattern: indefinable, ineffable, but with the tools of modern technology, not inimitable.

****

. . . reviewed the handwritten notations on the clipboard chart while Charlotte Weinstein checked the tags on the mice. The furry little creatures were huddled together in a white fluffy mass at the far end of the cage, trying to avoid the slender hand which sought to scoop them up. Charlotte caught one, and delicately lifted it out of the glass enclosure.

"This is the one I want. Number 122. My favorite." Charlotte tickled the mouse's chin and rubbed her finger around its head.

"I'll bet you say that to all the mice." Grant patted the pockets of his smock: first the lower pockets, then the uppers, then the lowers again.

Charlotte smiled quixotically. Her cheeks were pale, contrasting sharply against jet-black hair, thick brows, and clear brown eyes. "Mice get jealous and have inferiority complexes, too."

Still patting, "And what's that supposed to mean?"

Charlotte retrieved the pen from where it was perched atop Grant's ear, and placed it in his hand. "Whatever you want it to mean."

Grant jotted down the number on the chart and hung the clipboard on its hook. The pen automatically went back over his ear. "If I didn't know you better I'd think you were baiting me."

She cradled the mouse in one hand held tight against her breast. With her other hand she fetched a tiny square of cheese from a box on the table, and held it out for Number 122 to sniff. The little pink nose wrinkled spasmodically. "Doesn't it strike you as odd that the mouse's proverbially favorite food isn't found in its natural environment?"

"Not really. Through a quirk of evolution, mice have evolved to a point where their natural environment is no longer in the field or in barns or in basements or inside the walls of houses, but in the laboratory: a niche where they have found protection from all predators except the unsuccessful secretary turned research assistant."

"Now who is baiting whom?" Charlotte placed the cheese in a dish at one end of an elaborate maze, then carried the mouse, nose still a-quiver, to the other end of the maze. She let it go in a cubicle in which it went round and round the walls, seeking a way out. Charlotte glanced at her wristwatch, pulled up a panel that opened the cubicle to the maze, and watched the mouse run sniffing along the miniature corridors with but a single notion circulating in its pea-size brain. "Have you ever noticed how much more attentive they are when you starve them for a while?"

Grant feigned a scowl.

Number 122 scurried unerringly through the maze,

located the highly prized morsel, then sat back on its haunches and nibbled contentedly on the mild yellow cheddar.

"Fourteen seconds." Charlotte circled the table on which the maze was built, and made a notation on the clipboard chart with her pen. "Almost as fast as you."

Grant wagged a finger . . .

****

" . . . a seat. Would like coffee or tea?"

"No, thank you, Dr. Templeton." She sat in the overstuffed leather chair, put her purse on the floor, but kept the briefcase in her lap.

Grant smiled. "Call me Grant, Dr. Constantinescu. We like to be informal here at Biotech. May I call you Nora?"

"No."

Grant was taken aback.

"I hate Nora. I always have. But you may call me Connie."

"Connie?"

"It is a nickname for Constance, which itself is a shortened form of my family name."

"Okay. Connie it is." Grant leaned forward and shuffled through the stack of employment forms on his desk. "You've already been cleared through the Department of Defense, so the amount of paperwork will be minimal." He handed her several loose sheets and some explanatory documentation. "You can fill these out at your leisure. Read them carefully, of course. But what I really want to talk with you about is your previous work at Hannibal. I know that you started out as a neurologist and only recently switched to cybernetics. Why the change?"

Connie showed a mouthful of uneven teeth. "Probably for the same reason that you switched from medicine to robotic design work. I got tired of dealing with the terminally ill. Not tired, really, but depressed by the fact that I was unable to offer even so much as encouragement to most of the people who came to me for treatment. You know the routine. Each morning I would examine men and women with permanent dys-functions or incurable diseases: Alzheimer's, Parkin-son's, Gehrig's, Huntington's, and all the other people made notorious by having neurological impairments named after them. I could diagnose my patients' com-plaints, but usually I could not help to heal them. Ever. I was the harbinger of death, or the messenger of long-term degeneration that would ultimately lead to death."

Grant recalled his intern days. "Yes, I can under-stand. Although I didn't remain in the field long enough to reach the burnout stage. I guess I was lucky to get out early."

"But I am still fascinated by the structure and func-tion of the human brain/mind system," Connie was quick to add. "I just do not want to work with its sick-nesses and malfunctions. Hannibal Electronics offered me the opportunity to study computer chip geometry and Artificial Intelligence programs. But, as you know, Hannibal operates under license to produce microchips for Biotech—where the actual design work is done; they have no research and development division."

She squirmed uncomfortably, and broke for a moment from Grant's easygoing gaze.

Grant leaned back in his chair and threw his hands behind his head, hoping to inspire an ambiance of relaxation. He did not want Connie to feel as if she were on the grill. He just wanted to know if they were of like minds. "They recommended you highly. So highly, in fact, that they felt they were not able to use you to your full potential. You have too much on the ball for their purposes."

Her face flushed with embarrassment. "That is not really fair. They just never had a neurologist apply for a position whose pay scale was only a fraction of her previous earnings. But I was there to learn. And that is why I am coming to you. I want to apply what I know about the brain to the more creative aspects of chip design. I was intrigued by your article in *Neurology Today* on brain-phasing characteristics and your three-dimensional layered model of memory storage. I have

some ideas along the same lines . . . "
****

. . . "Oh, Daddy. Are they for me?"

"Well, if your mother will let you keep them."

"Are they real?"

Grant felt himself slipping out of the notch. He pushed his foot against the opposite limb so as not to fall out of the tree. "Now where have you ever heard of fake mice? Do they look like cartoons?"

"But where did they come from?"

He tucked the linen towel, which had been draped over the cage, into his pocket. "From mommy mice."

"Oh, Daddy. You know what I mean." Dawn poked her finger through the bars of the small wire cage, then squealed and withdrew her finger quickly when both mice lunged for it. "Do they bite?"

"No, they think you're going to feed them. These are laboratory mice. They're very docile, they like being handled, and when they bite they feel like coarse sandpaper because they have such tiny teeth and weak jaws."

Dawn shook her head in order to chase away a fly which was buzzing around her face. Her pigtails swung like twin tassels. "What do they do in the laboratory?"

"Well, we train them to do things, like finding their way through a maze. That's a kind of puzzle—"

"I know, like in the coloring books."

"That's right."

Dawn took some bits of cheese from her sandwich and dropped them into the cage from above. The mice scrambled for the morsels. "Do they have names?"

"Well, I called them Pete and Repete. But that was before I found out they were girls. Now I call them Joyce and Rejoyce."

"Oh, Daddy. You're so clever." She stuck her fingers through the wires and let the mice nibble on them. "Ooh, they feel funny. Do you think I can take them to school for show-and-tell?"

"I think you'd better ask your teacher about that. Some people are afraid of mice."

"I thought that was elephants."

"No, that's just an old wives' tale."

"Don't let Mommy hear you say that." Dawn looked up inquiringly. "After you train them, do you cut open their heads and count the wrinkles in their brains?"

"Who told you . . .

****

" . . . so much room we won't know what to do with it all. And it will allow us to expand the R & D division. That's what we really need to get this memchip design of yours off the drawing board and into production." Bob Lerner waved his arms enthusiastically at the architectural plans spread across the table. "We can consolidate our debts on this place, get additional capitalization from the bank because the DOD will co-sign the loan, and make a new stock offering. The board will go along with us because the DOD contract is part of the deal."

"Bob, there's no need to preach to the choir. I want this expansion as much as you do. The memchip is the culmination of years of research. It's just that I like working for NASA, I like focusing our attention on the aerospace industry. I have strong reservations about shifting our concentration toward the military applications of Artificial Intelligence."

"You think ninety percent of NASA's work isn't military? Come down to Earth, Grant. Sure, there are some pure science projects that go up in the shuttles, but most of what goes into orbit is surveillance satellites for the U.S. war machine."

"I like to believe that's the U.S. war prevention machine. And sure, I know our guidance systems are used on spy planes and rockets, but that's not the same as supplying automated quick-response CPU's for tanks and unmanned weapons systems."

"Don't look at it that way. Look at it as using the DOD as a means to an end, as a way to obtain funds for expanding our research program, to acquire the space and hire the technicians we need to build the memchip. That's what's important. Sure, we give the

DOD what they want as far as AI for military purposes. But they give us the resources to make it happen. It's a trade off, and everybody wins."

Grant could not find fault in Lerner's logic. The days of the lone scientist working part-time in a one-room laboratory or in the basement of his house were long gone. Today, invention and discovery were private enterprises made possible only through the infusion of large amounts of capital whose investment did not require short-term yield—or any yield. Without corporate funding, government grants, and contributions from nonprofit organizations, scientific advancement was likely to be forestalled despite healthy competition from rival companies and aggressive foreign nations.

"I guess my big concern is becoming known as Government Grant."

Bob Lerner remained expressionless for perhaps five seconds. Then he caught the joke, laughed uproariously, and slapped Grant heartily on the back.

"Grant, sometimes you just tear me apart."

Grant snickered, then indicated the building plans on the table. "So where are we going to build this monstrosity?"

Lerner made a fist and pointed with a thumb. "Right up the street. The land is cheap because it's only a hog farm that's been on the outs for years. We extend Memory Lane to reach what is now the back of the farm, reinforce the roadway for heavy-duty delivery trucks, and we're in business. Instead of 101 Memory Lane, our address will be 201 Memory Lane. And we call the fluxion device the Memchip 201, even though it isn't really a chip. But the name has pizzazz."

Grant flipped through the floor plans and the mechanical drawings of the various subsystems, such as electrical and plumbing and heating, until he came to the landscaping layout. The blueprint showed a large lawn which was serviced by a detached maintenance shed which also housed a remote auxiliary generator. Arranged haphazardly on the grass were picnic tables for the staff, some under trees for shade, others in the open for sun.

"There's only one thing I insist on having. A weeping willow . . . "

****

. . . looked comical wearing the miniature headset, like a scene out of a 1950's monster movie whose plot involved a mad scientist with an apparatus that could read rodent minds. The white mouse sniffed along the walls of the maze with evident curiosity. It stopped at each intersection and inspected each pathway before continuing on its way.

Dr. Constantinescu monitored the electroencephalogram with characteristic scientific detachment; she might have been reading the ingredients on a cereal box. She picked up the voice recorder and held it to her lips. "Subject Number 122, test number five. EEG normal. Still demonstrating no memory of the maze. Suggest we increase the power to the sensor pads but maintain the phase adjustment . . . "

****

" . . . can't believe you want to go along with their mad scheme."

"It's not because I *want* to, it's because we *have* to. We're not talking venture capital here. The DOD didn't put up millions of dollars for memchip research out of the goodness of their hearts. Philanthropy isn't what makes the world go round. In business, it's profit margins. When you deal with governments, it's whatever return the higher-ups expect to gain from their investment."

Grant ran his fingers through graying hair. "I understand that, Bob. We've been dealing with NASA long enough to know that they're never going to make a profit by selling cubic lots in outer space. We know that they have more lofty goals in mind than making real estate deals. But to program our first memchip as a recreated personality for an espionage simulacrum, to reanimate a bloodthirsty political leader responsible for the deaths of an uncounted number of innocent people. That's more than I bargained for."

Bob Lerner's eyes rolled in agonizing pain. "Look, I didn't say that I liked the idea, or that I agree with their plan to overthrow the government of a foreign country through subversion. All I'm saying is that money is power, and as long as the DOD has sunk that much money into the memchip project, they've got the power to force our cooperation if we don't give it willingly."

"The DOD bought a research program, they didn't buy off our sense of ethics."

Now it was Bob who shoved his fingers through his hair. He grabbed a double handful of straight, silky strands whose gray roots were in desperate need of tinting, and grimaced like an overacting soap opera star. "Grant, stop adding to our predicament by going moral on me. You knew right from the start that the DOD wasn't funding our research so they could build self-operating plows to till wheat in foreign fields. Face the facts: military funds are allocated for military purposes. What difference does it make if they want the memchip for a new generation of smart bombs, superior self-seeking missiles, or highly advanced simulacra that can imitate political leaders?"

"If you don't know the difference, Bob, then I can't explain it to you. Any more than I can program human emotion into a silicon chip or a fluxion device. It's something that has to come from within."

Bob rolled his head as if his neck were broken. "Grant, Grant, Grant. Let's not get in a row over this. You know I feel the same way you do about the things in life that count. But this is business. This is a contractual obligation to produce and perform what the purse strings call for. You're just not being realistic about the matter."

Grant was in turmoil. He had not intended to take out his frustrations on his longtime co-worker and now partner in Biotech. "You're wrong, Bob. I'm just looking for a way out and hoping you'll come up with one."

"I wish I could, Grant, but our hands are tied. I was hoping you could pull us out of this dilemma by tickling their fancy with a demo of the brain-phasing unit.

You know, offering them a carrot to buy us some time. But we can't stop the inevitable. They want the mem-chip program and we're going to have to give it to them. But I'd like to stall them long enough to experiment with the prototype and work out the bugs. God, nothing like it's ever existed before outside the human head. We have no idea how an artificially implanted memory system with human brain complexity will react to the real world. It might not live up to our full expectations. It might not work at all. Or it might go crazy as soon as it compiles enough data to become self-sustaining."

"Are you trying to convince me?"

"Hell, no. I'm just rehearsing the things I'm going to tell the Joint Chiefs, and especially that warmonger Pendergast. I'm going to Washington today—tonight—and I'm going to try to talk them out of their madcap scheme. At least until we can run some diagnostic tests. I'll call you and let you know."

****

" . . . as your secretary it's my job to take care of your affairs, which I've been doing anyway for the past fifteen years, since long before you were divorced." Francine Baker stood stoically in front of Grant's oak desk, with legs spread wide like the Colossus of Rhodes and every bit as ominous. Dimples appeared in wrinkled cheeks when she flashed a closed-mouth smile. "Honestly, Grant, sometimes you're such a child. I think that must be the secret of your charm."

Grant loved to be pushed around by aggressive women, but he never let them know it—perhaps *that* was the secret of his charm. "So what do think I should do?" He already knew the answer, but by letting Francine make the suggestion it would make her feel as if she had some influence over him.

"Charlotte is overqualified for this job, and you know it. She only accepted a secretarial position because it was the only way she could get into the company without a security clearance. So, keep her on as a secretary—I'll continue to work with her—but let her do lab work on the side till you can get clearance papers for her."

Grant tilted his head and squinted with one eye. "But there's the personal angle, too."

Francine shrugged her shoulders with a huff. "I know you have a policy against internal fraternization, and that's very commendable, especially in light of today's overemphasis on sexual harassment, but I don't think you would be out of line to ask her out on a harmless dinner engagement to discuss, well, her future opportunities with the company. You tell her that Fred and I are going along as chaperones, then I'll beg off at the last minute. She'll understand. And as long as you don't try to rush her straight to your bedroom, like that other nice gal you scared off with your quick-come attitude—"

"All the psychologists agree that a little aggression is good for a relationship."

"The operative word is 'little'. Even *I* know that, and I've been married for thirty-some years—with one short hiatus when I dated promiscuously." She winked at Grant conspiratorially. "Take my advice, Grant: go slow and easy instead of fast and headstrong."

Grant leaned forward in his chair and placed his elbows on the desk. "Does this still fall under the category of 'secretarial advice'?"

"Call it whatever you will. But let me tell you what I know from dipping in the secretarial pool: Charlotte has the hots for you. And not because of your money."

"Will you sign a paper to that effect, noting that this assignation was your idea—in case I'm ever brought up on charges?"

"I'll sign anything but your marriage certificate. Now, you take it from me, a woman who's seen you try for years to drown your sorrows in a bottle. You need the love of a good woman to keep you on the straight and narrow."

"But, Dawn has just come to live with me. I can't jeopardize . . . "

****

" . . . tuck this in the back of your mind somewhere." Randy Vanderbilt scrawled some algebraic formulas on a sheet of paper to show Grant and Bob how he had arrived at his solution, but did the actual calculations on a computer. "It's a simple geometric progression, with the time variable accelerated not only to account for the memchip's superconductive clock rate, but for the 3-D architecture as well. I ran some simulations . . . "

Vanderbilt tapped the keys which initiated the math program. Numbers flashed across the screen with lightninglike rapidity, but not so fast that the process was indiscernible. "See what I mean? If the figures are valid for proper data acquisition, they're just as valid for *improper* data acquisition. Once assimilated by the matrix . . . "

Bob Lerner clucked his tongue against his palate. "How come we never thought of this before? Christ, Grant, we're supposed to be the experts."

The expression on Randy Vanderbilt's face was one of calm professionalism, absent any accusatory glare. In his years with Biotech he had learned a lot from his masters. No longer was he a technician who only carried out orders and monitored experiments. He had become a scientist in his own right, and a valuable addition to the upper echelon staff. "I think you were both too close to the problem to see the obvious."

Grant shook his head slowly. "Making excuses doesn't help solve the problem now that we know that one exists. Good work, Randy."

"Thanks, Grant. I'm sure you can see that because the memchip stores data in a dispersal pattern rather than a straight-line input, once absorbed by the matrix, data are impossible to relocate and delete. The memchip doesn't have entry lanes the way the human brain does. It's in flux all the time . . . " Vanderbilt had a habit of leaving his sentences unfinished, and raising the pitch of his voice so that his statements sounded like questions.

Lerner rubbed his face with his hands so hard he could have been cleansing himself of several months of dirt. "Oh, god. I don't believe this. Here we are on the verge of turning the damn thing on, and up comes another bug in the system."

"Well, there's no bug yet, but that's what I'm afraid might happen if there's a programming flaw. We could wind up with an AI that's not the one we wanted, one whose data base is infected with erroneous information that would alter its personality index . . . "

"And affect its judgment." Grant completed Vanderbilt's dreadful insinuation. The information processing speed of Grant's organic brain most certainly could not surpass, nor even come close to, the speed of electrons darting along the pathways of a condensed silicon chip. Yet his mind, in a sudden leap of creative thought euphemistically known as a "flash of insight", made instantaneous correlations and dire predictions which no machine yet in existence could make. "And that's not all."

Both Lerner and Vanderbilt stared at him expectantly.

"The information environment provided by a memchip is analogous to the septic condition of an open wound: both are especially susceptible to infection. And Randy is dead right: just as bacteria can be cultured quickly in a properly prepared Petri dish, a computer virus will spread almost instantaneously through the systems and data bases of a memchip, due to the dynamics of its fluxion architecture and its processing speed. So it seems to me that we have two choices: either guarantee absolute sterility of the data input, which I think is impossible on a practical level, or install a governor."

Bob started snapping his fingers. "You mean, like an antiviral program. But Grant, how can we write a universally protective program for something like the memchip when we've never turned one on? How can we anticipate what troubles we'll run into?"

"We can't. And that really bothers me. The same complexity that gives the memchip its near-human faculties also imparts a similar vulnerability. Now, when an ordinary computer is infected with a virus that can't be cured, we power down the systems and reboot uninfected programs. But how do we deal with a computer that is quasi-conscious and mobile—and doesn't *want* to be powered down?"

Vanderbilt nodded understandingly.

"Oh, sweet Jesus." Bob kneaded his cheeks as if they were two loaves of dough. "What you're saying is that an AI might be inherently unstable."

"We don't know that yet. I'm just asking a hypothetical question. What happens when we wake up an AI that has the ability to protect itself from harm? Inorganic vanity might be as strong as our own. Would we let ourselves be shut off—killed—then revived with the same body but another personality?" He held up a finger to defer forming protestations. "With the kind of intelligence we're dealing with, a programming error does not just result in a wrong answer to a computational problem. It results in total disruption of the system—what we would call in a human being, insanity." Grant paused dramatically. "Insanity with a will to survive. . . "

****

. . . on the horizon. Buttercup Path was noisy on a warm summer day, there apparently being a contest between the neighborhood boys and their dogs as to who could be the loudest and block the most traffic. Grant parked in the driveway, turned off the engine, and approached the front of the bungalow. He knocked with his characteristic five bars of "shave and a haircut," and before he could rap out "two bits" the door flung open and Dawn raced into his arms.

"Daddy, I missed you."

"I missed you, too, Baby."

She kissed him on the cheek. "Daddy, are you going to call me 'Baby' when I'm grown up?"

"Only if you want me to."

They hugged and kissed for a minute before she dragged him into the house by the hand as if he were a puppy on a leash.

"Daddy's home," Dawn singsonged.

Barbara appeared wearing an apron and with her hands full of batter. "Hello, Grant. How was the trip?"

Grant took a small package from his jacket pocket and handed it to his daughter. "As usual: exhilarating and exhausting. Too much talk, way too much food, and not enough exercise. I did manage to slip off for a short walk every morning and sometimes late in the evening. I never knew that Prague had so many ugly gargoyles."

"It's an ancient city. That kind of statuary was popular in the old days."

"No, I meant wandering the streets. Prostitutes with faces harder than stone and bodies that were carved when fat was where it was at."

"Grant!"

He gritted his teeth. "Oops." He glanced down at Dawn, who was busily ripping off the paper from the gift-wrapped package. "Sorry."

Dawn worried the box open and dumped the miniature pewter figurines into her hand. "I know what they are."

"What?" asked Grant.

She looked up at him ingenuously. "They're women who kiss men for money."

Grant rolled his eyes at Barbara. "Right."

Barbara wagged her finger at Grant as if he were a naughty boy. "Would you please learn to watch your mouth? Now, come into the kitchen for a minute. I've got a cake in the oven.

"Mommy, can Daddy read to me in the back yard?"

"Yes, Sugar, but I've got to talk to him first."

"Y-a-a-a-a-y."

"But take that dress off and put your dungarees on. I don't want you getting grass stains on your good clothes."

"Okay, Mommy." She gave Grant another kiss before skipping off to her room.

Barbara headed for the kitchen. "Have you been home, yet?"

"No, I came directly from the airport. I wanted to get here before dark. But I can't stay for dinner." It was not their routine to share meals, anyway. According to Barbara, eating together was too reminiscent of married life, something which Barbara was trying hard to forget. Grant still did not profess to understand her rationale for divorce. She had always said it was because he spent so much time at work and not enough time with her at home. Yet, now that they were divorced, she spent *all* her time without him, and made no attempt to find a husband who fit her so-called ideal model. This was a mystery of the female mind which Grant, in a lifetime of study of the human mind, felt he would never solve. "Why?"

When she turned around at the counter there were tears in her eyes. She dabbed them with a tissue which she yanked out of a decorator box.

"Babs, what's wrong?"

"I left a message on your answering machine to call me right away. I haven't told Dawn yet. I only found out a few hours ago, and you were already in the air. I thought you might want to tell her yourself." She spoke quickly, as if to get out every word before her voice cracked up and failed her entirely. She dabbed again with the sodden tissue. "Grant, your mother passed away."

Grant was stunned, shocked, overwhelmed with sudden emotion.

"I can't ask you to stay here. But if you don't want to be alone, you can take Dawn home with . . . "

****

" . . . if only we could learn more about how the human brain does all the things it can do. The problem is, we can't experiment on a human brain unless it's dead and in a jar."

Colonel Charles Pendergast spread his hands in a gesture of doubt. "Forgive my ignorance. This is a new assignment, and already I can see that I have a great deal to learn. So please bear with me if my questions seem somewhat, ah, medically naive." The colonel shuffled through a thick sheaf of papers which he held on his lap instead of spreading in front of him, as if he were protecting them from prying eyes. "On the plane I was reading up on, ah, peptides and neurotransmitters. From a paper that you yourself wrote, Dr. Lerner."

"That was my specialty before joining Biotech." He glanced at Grant across a table of polished cherry. "Still is, I guess. I've done a fair amount of research on memory enhancers and inhibitors, and some of those studies are still ongoing."

"Then let me address my next question to you. And remember that I'm a neophyte, and that what may be obvious or simplistic to you is new and complicated to me. If, as you say, you cannot experiment on living human brains, how did you ever learn which parts of the brain performed the specific functions ascribed to them, and how did you discover which chemicals affected the brain in the manners described in your papers?"

"Well, let me answer that in reverse order. First of all, we perform a lot of experiments on the brain—but not the human brain. Like every pharmaceutical company and government research facility seeking wonder drugs and remedies for incurable diseases, we use lab animals: mice, rats, guinea pigs, and, when we think we're getting close to a solution and need a human organ analogue, we use chimpanzees. Those are the bodies we dissect and the brains we fractionate for chemical analysis, and that's how we know if we're headed in the right direction. Then, when we can't go any farther with animals, we carry out controlled tests on terminally ill patients—patients who have no hope for recovery or quality of life other than divine intervention. They become human guinea pigs: people who are injected with experimental drugs or on whom unproven surgical procedures are performed, all conducted with their cooperation and in full knowledge of the experimental nature of the treatment." As an afterthought, "And in compliance with ethical guidelines established by the American Medical Association."

"Of course." An ugly leer appeared on Colonel Pendergast's face. "It's too bad that the dictates of society don't let us utilize otherwise wasted resources: murderers and hardened criminals whose decease would prove doubly useful, by removing them permanently from the society on which they prey, and by providing that society with the raw materials with which to advance the cause of medicine."

Grant was aghast. He did not know how to respond to such a suggestion. Lerner poured water from a pitcher into his glass. The tinkling of ice cubes and the faint liquid sloshing were the only sounds in the conference room audible above the gentle whoosh of cool air flowing from the ducts. He continued his explanation as if Pendergast had made no comment.

"Nearly all our knowledge of the functions of the various areas of the human brain has come from patients with disorders caused by tumors, infections, clots, or diseases that affected the patient's performance in clearly demonstrable ways. In the old days, autopsies revealed where and how the brain was damaged, and, by correlating that information with the patient's symptoms, certain conclusions could be drawn or inferred. Of course, that didn't help the patient since he was already dead, but it enabled the attending physician to learn from experience and, by sharing case studies with other doctors, it contributed to the general fund of knowledge which might then be used to treat other patients with the same or similar symptoms.

"For example, a man receives a contusion to the head which results in a higher cortical dysfunction—he no longer comprehends language: what we would call aphasia, an inability to communicate. If you open him up and find that his Wernicke's area is damaged, you might assume that a correlation exists between the comprehension of language and Wernicke's area."

Colonel Pendergast nodded slowly. "I see."

Lerner raised his brows at Grant, who caught the pass and carried the ball down the field. "No, you don't. You think you see. But in reality the situation is more complex, because Wernicke's area is not the only area of the brain that is responsible for articulated language. Subtle damage to Broca's area could also be responsible for the aphasia. Or the problem could be ischemia— an interruption of blood supply which results in cell death of the arcuate fasciculus: a bundle of nerve fibers that connects Wernicke's area to Broca's area. The symptoms are different but the end result is frustratingly similar."

"I see," said Colonel Pendergast, although his narrowed eyes hinted otherwise.

Grant lateraled to Lerner. "And there are other areas of the brain that can be responsible for the breakdown of communication. For example, damage to the hippocampus, damage to the temporal stem, damage to the amygdala, damage to the pyramidal cell layer, or damage to the bilateral medial temporal lobe, to name a few. And this doesn't take into account organic memory dysfunctions that could be caused by chemical imbalances, encoding errors, storage loss, or retrieval glitches, none of which is well understood. You see, the brain is not just a three-pound lump of gray matter that processes information the way the stomach processes food. It is so incredibly complicated that an army colonel could never understand it."

The colonel could not have bolted more upright in his seat than he already was, but the way his body tensed was an indication that he was trying. Grant let Lerner's statement sink in for a moment; then, just when Colonel Pendergast opened his mouth to speak, he let him in on the joke.

"And that's because no neuroscientist in the world, including the two in this room, understands it." Grant and his partner exchanged grins. "Nowadays, of course, we have more sophisticated methods of studying the living brain than our twentieth-century counterparts, and without killing the patient in the process: CAT scans, PET scans, and a small menagerie of more novel techniques that are still being developed. It's through the use of these new devices and study approaches that we've gained an insight into the workings of the brain: how memory works and what mechanisms assure accuracy."

Colonel Pendergast referred to the papers on his lap. "Such as, and forgive me if I mispronounce it, acetylcholine? 'An excitatory neurotransmitter that plays an important role in memory.' I understand that cholinergic—acetylcholine producing—cells are deficient in the victims of Alzheimer's disease, that specific protein syntheses are necessary to hold memories in place, and that atropine—a crystalline alkaloid obtained from belladonna—can disrupt memory."

Lerner put on a deadpan face and became purposely obfuscatory. "A fair schema of putative memory loss etiologies, and an important part of the neuroscientist's armamentarium, but modern research involves more than synaptic response, axional discharge, and the ionic permeability of postsynaptic neurons."

If Pendergast thought of saying "I see," he did not.

Grant took the ball into the end zone. "But the chemical basis for organic memory subsistence is beside the point. If we can emulate the way the brain processes information, we can transfer that knowledge to an electronic substrate: not just a more advanced integrated circuit composed of static electrical elements, but a totally new concept in computer design; a kinetic matrix that is constantly in motion, a three dimensional crosshatch, if you will."

"I see." Colonel Pendergast nodded perfunctorily. "Well, actually, I suppose I don't see. The reason the Pentagon sent me here was because no one back east really understood the concept the way it was presented to NASA. When they referred your report to the DOD—"

"Excuse me, Colonel." Lerner interrupted and held up his hands. "First of all, understand that our present commitments to NASA require our fullest attention, and that we can't incur further contractual obligations without expanding our facilities. Our resources are limited by the size of our staff and the amount of space in the building. When we petitioned NASA for research and development funding, it was intended that any work on the phasing unit or memchip design be conducted within our current resource constraints—part time, so to speak. Second, our disclosure to NASA was necessarily brief because patent applications are still pending, and we don't want to tip our hand before we're fully protected from our competitors."

"I understand your position entirely. I didn't come here to pry into corporate secrets, but to gain some insight into the potential uses of the final product." Colonel Pendergast smiled conspiratorially. "And to assure you that, should I find that these products could contribute—in a broad interpretation of the word—to national defense, we are prepared to provide sufficient funding for the necessary expansion of your facilities."

Now it was the colonel who had control of the meeting. Grant and Lerner exchanged high signs with their eyebrows, then sat back in their black leather chairs to listen. They had not solicited the Department of Defense, and would never have thought of doing so. But their contact at NASA had taken it upon herself to brief the DOD on the applicability of Biotech's robotics systems to military weapons platforms, and on the kind of research which Biotech wanted to conduct.

"Before we can begin negotiations, gentlemen, it's essential that we have certain guarantees, and that we deal directly with the people who are authorized to represent your company. Is it true that both of you—Grant Templeton and Robert Lerner—turned your patent rights over to Biotech Corporation in lieu of monetary compensation, and are now the major stockholders in the company, and that the board of directors advises only on day-to-day activities . . . "

****

. . . like a block off the old chip, with the potential to follow in her illustrious father's footsteps. Remember what Margaret Mead said: 'Children must be taught *how* to think, not *what* to think.' So the first time Dawn exercises her right to free will, you want to put a damper on it."

Grant shoved his hands in his pockets as he strolled along the driveway known as Panther Cove. He looked longingly at the huge weeping willow which occupied the front yard inside the low stone parapet. "Charlotte, that's not the way it is and you know it. I've never gotten in her way or put barriers between her and her ambitions. I've always encouraged her to seek her own level and to stretch her potential. It's just that— since her mother moved back to Chicago, I've gotten used to having her around. You don't know what it was like—all those years seeing her only on weekends or odd nights of the week. I missed her. Now, after living with her and getting reunited in a more normal father and daughter relationship, I'm not ready to give her up just yet."

Charlotte Weinstein put her arm through Grant's. A light wind blew wisps of dark hair from her face, which was lightly bronzed by the summer sun, and ruffled the pleats in her satin blouse. "Face it, Grant. She's growing up and you're, well, growing down. She's old enough to try her wings and fly away from the coop. It's not as if she wants to move to Timbuktu or Lower Jebip. She just wants to stay on campus with her girlfriends. And maybe her boyfriends. If you ask me, I think you're jealous."

"Oh, come on, now. How could I be—?"

"Because all fathers are jealous when their pride and joy discovers the love of another man. But it's a different kind of love; one that in no way diminishes the love she has for you as a father. You must accept the fact that she's not you're little girl any more. She's a young lady with sexual desires . . . "

Grant gasped.

"See! The idea frightens you. The idea that Dawn might have a life of her own without your control and guidance."

"I've never—"

"Okay, I'm teasing. But only about your control and guidance. She *is* a young lady, and she *does* have her own life to lead; a life in which a father has his place—and has to stay in it. Don't you think I missed my kids when they moved away? And still miss them? It's natural to feel that way. Now, admittedly, you might be a little more sensitive about Dawn because you were apart from her for so much of her childhood, but you can't hold that against her."

"I don't hold it against her!"

"See how touchy you are? And there's another factor in the equation that you haven't considered. If I move into this house with you—does anyone get married these days—Dawn doesn't want to get in our way. She wants you to be happy, too. She told me so herself."

"She did?"

"Come out of your fairy tale world, Grant. Dawn and I talk all the time because I treat her as an equal, and—"

"I've never been unfair with her."

"I didn't say that. I'm saying that you can't parent her forever. It's time to . . . "

****

. . . brought the latest laboratory results to Grant's office. She walked in without knocking because no one ever knocked in the Biotech family. "Grant?" The computer printouts crinkled when she waved them.

Grant could tell by the smile on her face that the experiment had been a success. He reached out for the still-connected stack of fanfold. "I thought you'd never come."

"Isn't that only a problem with middle-aged men?"

Grant blushed, and for a moment was struck dumb. Then he guffawed loud enough to be heard in every room on the floor. "Is there such a thing as reverse sexual harassment, where female employees harass their male employers?"

"Not at Biotech." Charlotte Weinstein smiled with satisfaction. "Especially when the female employee has good news."

Dr. Nora Constantinescu appeared in the doorway behind Charlotte, wearing a grin that rivaled that of the

Cheshire cat. "Number 122 came through for us. It remembered . . . "

****

. . . been working at Cyberdyne Systems on silicon chip design, just to learn the channels, so to speak."

The board of directors of the Biotech Corporation did not know enough neurophysiology to catch on to Grant's admittedly obscure pun. They sat around the table like the stone statues on Easter Island, hard and expressionless, with somber, drooping features which might have been carved from sedimentary rock. Grant felt that a parole board would have shown more compassion toward a serial killer than he was receiving as an applicant for the job of chief scientist. It was against Grant's nature to be so solemn, yet he found it difficult to relax and be himself when he was surrounded by men of such dismal mien.

"I boned up on information theory as it applies to computer technology, and modified one class of Cyberdyne's microchip which was then being used in factory robotic systems. The modifications accounted for variables encountered in the field and permitted the robot—which was an automated drill press—to act accordingly. In other words, the chip was given the capacity to respond to a narrow band of newly acquired data—what might be called learning—in a nonintuitive sense. But what I really want to investigate is the possibility of creating an entirely new kind of memory chip which would imitate more closely the operation of the human brain."

Norman Sandals, chairman of the board of directors, was old enough to remember when the only calculator to be found in the marketplace was the abacus. He referred to a sheet of paper which lay flat on the lacquered conference table. "By stacking chips which are interconnected by three-dimensional crosslinks?"

Grant breathed a sigh of relief. At least one member of the board had bothered to read his two-part proposal. "Yes, that's phase one of my plan: to produce a relatively inexpensive variation of the integrated circuit whose current architecture consists of a flat silicon chip. By introducing three dimensional connections, each chip can be mated to a chip on either side, thus providing alternative processing channels through which data can pass."

"So if there is a breakdown in the circuitry on any one chip, data is automatically rerouted along the parallel channels of either one of the two adjacent chips?" Sandals was more astute than his dispassionate manner allowed. "And you call this a, ah, TDS chip?"

Under the circumstances, Grant did not think that this was the appropriate time to explain the true derivation of the acronym. He suspected that a microchip named for a Triple Decker Sandwich would fail to achieve even a superficial nod of approval from the stately heads in the company. Now he was glad that he had not stuck with his original acronym, BLT, which might have been a dead giveaway, or the other two nomenclatures that he had coined for the invention: the clubchip and, even more irreverent, the Dagwood. He improvised quickly. "Yes, the TriDundant System chip."

Judging by the shared looks of barely passable approbation, Grant had the distinct feeling that he had just saved himself from being prematurely ousted from a job interview which he very much wanted to prolong until he could give a broad overview of his grand scheme. Any hesitation now, or recourse to comedy, might relinquish the opportunity forever.

"I've already applied for a patent on the concept, and I'm willing to reinvest in Biotech my portion of the proceeds from forthcoming product sales in order to finance research for a human brain analogue: a fluid memory chip, if you will, although it's not a 'chip' in the strict sense of the word. Instead of passing information along a static conductor as in a silicon chip, the fluid memory chip comprises a jellylike substrate impregnated with a three-dimensional, microscopically fine wire mesh . . . "

****

" . . . no such thing as a memory molecule. I spent

years looking for it, when I ascribed to the materialistic theory of the mind. Like other materialists, I reasoned that if DNA transmits information in complex chemical codes from one generation to the next, there should be analogous chemical codes in the nerve cells for the transmission of information throughout the brain."

Bob Lerner was a likeable man with a shock of thick black hair which was just beginning to turn gray at the temples. He spoke with an animation which was born from an overabundance of nervous energy. "Too bad it's not that simple, eh?"

Grant nodded in agreement. "Nothing ever is."

"So what's the score? I couldn't get much out of old man Sandals and his board of zombies, only that they plan to expand their facilities and move out of Chicago entirely. And that you requested another neuro to share the load. You didn't tell them we went to grad school together, did you?"

"It must have slipped my mind."

Lerner chuckled. "Everything slips your mind, except what counts. I'm just glad you gave up medicine for research. Imagine operating on some poor slob's brain, and leaving your watch inside his skull when you close him up. The ticking would drive him batty." There was nothing malicious in Lerner's statement. "So what's the gig?"

"You'd never know it from talking to them, but the board of directors wants to expand this operation big time. They hired me initially as a consultant because they liked my ideas, gave me this closet for an office—" Grant spread his arms and nearly touched the opposite walls. "—and told me to formalize a production sched-ule for the TDS microchip, which they are calling the Memchip 101, and to outline future research objec-tives. They've already got a new facility under construc-tion in Highland Hills, which they want me to head. I told them I'd rather direct just the research department and let someone else handle the production end. Natu-rally, you came to mind. I figured a skinflint like you must have squirreled away quite a few bucks from your neuro practice—else how did you buy into that pharmaceutical firm—and thought you might like to invest in Biotech and become their production manager. You've got the perfect background . . . "

****

" . . . you won't talk, I can make you talk." General Pendergast was smiling, but it was the kind of smile which was more of a sadistic leer than a denotation of good will.

No guns had yet been drawn, but Grant was surrounded by armed Germans who seemed eager to resort to weapons in order to have their demands met. Only two of them wore Nazi uniforms with SS arm bands. The rest sported tailor-made suits, except for a couple of lackeys in work sweaters and carrying Lugers in shoulder holsters.

Robert Fenton spoke with a clipped German accent which Grant had not gotten used to in the month during which Fenton had been overseeing the DOD's interests. He had been brought in by Pendergast as a special foreign consultant. "You vill gif us ze information ve ask, ve hurt no one." Nor was his threat veiled, since Charlotte had already been bound and gagged and dragged out of the laboratory. "Othervise . . . " Hunched shoulders completed his meaning.

Grant ignored Fenton and appealed directly to Pendergast. "General, I don't know where you got your information, but believe me, there's no connection between the brain phase unit and the Memchip 201. The BPU is a serendipitous outgrowth of our engram mapping program: a refined electroconvulsive shock treatment intended for psychiatric therapy—"

"I won't bargain with you. I don't have to bargain with you. I know what the BPU can do. I can remove your memories and download them onto your mainframe, then access them to my heart's content. But that will take time. And it will destroy you in the process—"

"Like it did to General Brinkley?"

Pendergast shrugged. "That was unfortunate. But I

do not tolerate insubordination. He was supposed to report to me on all the activities within his tactical area of operations, yet he withheld sensitive documents—"

"Proving that you were involved with the Nazi movement," Grant spat.

"I—" General Pendergast momentarily reddened with rage, then, without moving a muscle, brought himself under control. "I don't have to justify myself to you. You are a tool—a means to an end. Dr. Fenton did not have enough information to operate the prototype unit properly, so it overloaded and killed my good friend Amos. If it does the same to you, I will be no worse off than I am now. But I know you switched memchip programs and installed an earlier version. You were naive if you thought you could deceive Dr. Fenton so easily. So, if you won't decode the files voluntarily, I'll be forced to shock it out of you. Which will it be?"

Fenton fingered the BPU skullcap as if he were eager to try the device on Grant. "And don't forget zat ve haf your girlfriend. And ve know vhere to find your daughter—even after you are dead."

Grant's stomach was in knots. After watching the henchmen knock Lerner unconscious and beat Charlotte black and blue, to be carried off screaming to an unmentionable fate, he knew that he was supposed to cave in and give Pendergast everything he wanted, so that he would leave them all alone to live happily ever after. That was the way it happened in the movies. But this was real life. And the Nazis had a history which belied the antiseptic Hollywood image. Despite his misgivings, Grant remained defiant.

"You're going to kill us all anyway, so there's nothing to be gained by telling you anything. You and your automated monster." He tilted his head in the direction of the unactivated simulacrum lying on a workbench at the far end of the laboratory. "You can all go to hell."

Pendergast sighed deeply. His eyes shimmered like liquid pools of mercury. "You are brave, but very, very stupid. You think to call my bluff, and I will show you that I never bluff. I act, and act decisively." He snapped his fingers, and instantly the two men in turtlenecks pinned Grant's arms to his sides and clamped a cloth soaked in chloroform over his mouth and nose . . .

****

" . . . hard to accept that people actually believed that eating the brains of your victims would transplant the vanquished one's qualities to the diner, but that was the psychological basis for cannibalism. It wasn't because food was scarce. Then along comes an enterprising scientist who grinds up the brains of a trained flatworm and implants the mush into the brain of another flatworm, and, lo and behold, discovers that the living flatworm remembers tricks that were taught to the pulverized flatworm. That's why I thought the theory of memory molecules had to be valid; because I was young and stupid, and figured that if it worked for flatworms it should work for people. I was looking at human thoughts, perceptions, and memories as additive properties, forgetting that addition begets complexity, and that there's a qualitative difference between the organization of the human brain and that of a flatworm. Like saying that a trip to the Moon is the same as a trip to the corner store, only longer. How could I have been so stupid? And don't answer that; it was a rhetorical question."

Grant snickered at Lerner's long-winded soliloquy. "Don't feel so bad. I started out thinking that short-term memory and long-term memory must be encoded by different chemicals: one that was unstable and that readily decomposed, and was therefore responsible for STM, and one that was practically impossible to break apart, responsible for LTM. What I couldn't figure out was how the STM chemical was changed into the LTM chemical, so I was looking for a stabilizing catalyst, figuring that the insults that caused memory loss—sudden acceleration of the brain, electroconvulsive shock, tumor, infections, diseases, and whatnot—were breakdowns of the retrieval mechanism, and had nothing to do with long-term storage.

"My mother lived a long time after my father died of

Alzheimer's. She experienced memory loss more typical of the elderly: she'd forget where she put down her keys or her glasses or where she parked her car, and she'd get lost in department stores—I'd find her wandering about in a daze—but she could recall in minutest detail incidents that occurred when she was a little girl: memory traces that in her middle age would have been impossible for her to remember. That really threw me for a loop. Until I found obvious falsehoods and misconceptions in her childhood recollections, events that I could verify that never actually occurred. The giveaway was when she told me she had visited Niagara Falls, when I knew that she had never been east of the Mississippi. Once I began questioning her and directing her recountal, I discovered that most of these fond remembrances of youth were itemized distortions—a short circuit in her memory pattern—but as real to her as if they had actually happened. And I couldn't convince her otherwise, even by showing her written documentation that refuted her statements, any more than you could convince me that my name isn't Grant Templeton.

"I never put any stock in the computer analogy: that a memory is a quantum of information found at a specific location like binary digit on a magnetic tape or disk. But, like everyone else, since the brain has no moving parts, I thought the brain was basically static except for the flow of chemicals. Then it occurred to me that the two concepts contradicted each other, that the flow of chemicals implied movement of some kind, that perhaps memories were more than quanta that were sequestered in Broca's area or Wernicke's area and all the other areas associated with memory functions, but were constantly in motion, whirling through the brain like passengers riding horses on a merry-go-round, to be plucked off when the proper recognition code was entered.

"Once I envisioned the brain and the mind—that is, the whole-body system, and an indivisible entity much greater than the sum of its interrelated parts—as a unity that was in flux within itself, I began to understand the biochemical mechanism that propagated the living data that are the basis of thought. And I found that the living data, the memories of our experiences, are deposited in sequence like pages in a book. Eventually I isolated and identified the pathways along which our thoughts travel, via chronically firing neurons, even as we sleep, and I dubbed these pathways, these channels through the brain, the 'memory lanes' . . . "

Chapter 25

The instantaneous recall of ten years of blocked memories was disturbing, disorienting, highly charged, and furiously evocative.

Grant was overwhelmed by the juxtaposed repertoire of the past, by disembodied images, by snatches of conversation, by incidents of note, by scenes of utter irrelevance, by names and faces and distant locations whose unfamiliarity bordered on the bizarre, all bursting upon his mind simultaneously in a blurting monstrous montage like a thousand instant replays of televised events flashing on a thousand overlapping screens, all attuned to his visual cortex and all focused with crystal clarity, and commingled confusingly with memories from before and after.

Grant could not help but wonder if this disarranged flood of impressions was genuine, or if it was a reconstructed implant fed into the memchip of the latest generation simulacrum whose tegument was designed to bleed when cut or nicked by bullets.

For what makes a person—what constitutes his individuality—other than the assemblage of thoughts and experiences which are continually available to recall, and whose temporal placement is comprehensible sequentially? What Grant found disconcerting in the chaos of raw data was his omniscient viewpoint, in which every event seemed to occur at once so that his lifetime played back in a jumble of vignettes like a poorly edited movie in which the past co-existed with the present.

****

Connie adjusted the skullcap to Grant's head by aligning the sensor pads on the blackened weals. "Of course you don't know how the brain-phase unit works. That's the proof of the pudding."

Grant sat on the table that had been only recently occupied by Francine Baker, who had recovered from her timely swoon and who now perched alert on a nearby stool, and whose confidence had returned upon awakening to find her allies in control of the situation. "Suppose the brain-phaser is just that: a brain 'fazer' that scrambles the brain instead of temporarily paralyzing the most recent input strata? Suppose it takes me back even farther, all the way to infancy? I could wake up this time needing a diaper change."

"There are a number of women here who can handle that eventuality."

Grant fidgeted, and appealed to Patrolman Riley, who sat shirtless on the table next to him. "Help me out, Frank, before I become a victim of the instincts of motherhood."

"Sorry, Dr. Templeton, but I've already got more than I can handle. Ouch!"

"You'd better believe it, buster." Sandy finished cleansing the furrow that carved around the patrolman's back like a deep rope burn, and started rolling gauze over the wound. To Captain Hendry, "And Daddy, I want you to put Frank on traffic patrol after this is all over, where I don't have to worry about him getting hurt."

The captain kept quiet. Anderson, his broken arm wrapped in a first-aid splint, raised his eyebrows at his boss, but said not a word.

"Pardon me for stating the obvious, but the essence of the most brutal killer in the history of mankind is alive and loose less than fifty feet away—" Grant pointed a finger at the ceiling. He thought in three dimensions the way most people think in two, so the vertical proximity of the Hitler simulacrum feeding from the computer terminal in the penthouse office came easily to mind. "—so shouldn't we do something about that first, and worry about my mental aberrations later?"

Dawn flourished the locked metal container which she had found in the willow tree at the end of the parking lot. "Daddy, I know you too well. You think so far ahead that I'm sure you've anticipated this problem and have prepared a solution, if only you could remember. And I'll bet the answer is in this box."

"I agree." Sarah took the container from Dawn and inspected it closely. "And I think I've got the key to the solution right here." She inserted a slotted silver key into the circular hole in the lid of the box, and twisted it effortlessly. She pulled, and the box slid apart like a sword from its sheath. "It's a miniature safe. Any attempt to torch or hammer it open would destroy the contents." The contents consisted of a computer disk labeled TWITW. "Doctor, I assume you know what to do with this?"

"Yes. It must be the backup—"

"Now wait just a minute, Sarah." Grant pinched his eyes skeptically. "Where did you get that key?"

"The same place I got the one that opened the door to the maintenance shed. It's a duplicate that I had made when I borrowed your key ring." To Dr. Constantinescu, "You were saying?"

"It must be the backup memchip matrix sequencing program. Grant purged the one in the system and replaced it with the previous release. Which is why the Hitler doppelganger could not be properly programmed." Connie Constantinescu slid the disk into an undamaged drive unit and booted the initializer with a couple of keystrokes. "Good. Very good." According to the icons on the menu, the disk also contained the Fenton file and the brain phase reversal program. "We can download on Fenton later."

Dr. Robert Fenton glared silently from the corner of the room, where he was handcuffed to a table leg. He rose from the chair on which he had been seated, but was unable to stand erect due to the low height of the table. He sat back down, glaring harder than ever.

Connie moved the cursor to the icon which was called "BPRP," tried to open it, and got an error message which flashed "FYEO" and "Enter Password." She said, "For your eyes only, Grant. What is the password?"

Grant scowled. "I'm so absent-minded that I can't remember my own name unless I record it or write it down. You expect me to know what your Grant Templeton chose for a password?"

Sarah took hold of Grant's cheeks like an elderly aunt would do to her sister's child whom she had not seen in a long while, and shook his face. "I don't want to hear any more of this otherworld nonsense. I told you—"

"I know what the password is." All eyes stared at Captain George Hendry as if he were the least likely person to make such a comment. "So does Dawn, here."

Dawn gasped. "Oh. Of course. It must be 'Mr. Toad'."

Once released from Sarah's firm grip, Grant worked his jaw until his facial muscles regained their former shape. His expression went blank for a moment, then registered surprise. "Did your father read to you from *The Wind in the Willows*, too?"

Sarah shouted, "Grant!"

"Yes, Daddy," Dawn said firmly. "You did."

Connie entered the password. The monitor instantly illuminated with a color graphic display of a toad wearing a tuxedo and top hat, and who hopped across the screen into a red convertible. The words "Yes. Yes! YES!" appeared sequentially in expanding letters, followed by, "You have answered the $64,000 question." The screen blanked, then flashed in bold typeface, "Hello, Grant. This is your conscience." This disappeared, and was quickly replaced by the image of a brain-phase headset and instructions for placement, ending with, "The stun charge/discharge is self-seeking, so the nodal pads only need to be approximately correct, say, within a radius of two centimeters. You can handle that, can't you, Grant?"

He cringed as Connie fitted onto his head the skullcap which had nearly killed his partner, Bob Lerner. "This should be easy. You still have the marks on your scalp where Bob—Bob Fenton, that is—placed the pads."

"Is that supposed to instill me with confidence?"

"I am at least as good at this as he is. He had been here only a month. And remember that I helped you write the software."

Grant cast a cringing look at Connie. "How can I remem—"

"You will in a moment. I should warn you, however, that all our laboratory tests were conducted on mice. You are the first human subject to undergo the experiment, although, judging by what I have seen so far, I would call it a triumphant success. Now if we can only reverse the procedure . . . " The doctor's quixotic expression was unreadable.

The stainless steel framework allowed the weight of the headset to rest on top of Grant's head. He felt a twinge as the doctor screwed the sensor pads tight against the existing scars, but after a moment the pain diminished to a persistent but mild irritation. He ignored the stares, feeling very much like a helpless patient—or perhaps like a bug on a pin under a magnifying glass.

"As I was saying before, I was not here on Friday night when you became the subject of Bob Fenton's brain-phasing experiment. After the arrival of General Pendergast, you and Bob—Bob Lerner, that is—closed the building and sent everyone home for the weekend, because the memchip loading procedure was slated to begin Saturday morning and would require every bit of the mainframe's capacity. You wanted no other programs running interference, so all ancillary systems were shut down. You told the people who were working on flex time that the company would make good for any lost wages. Only Francine and Charlotte stayed to assist. And Bob Fenton, of course.

"Bob called me the next afternoon—Bob Fenton, that is—to say that the memchip downloading was proceeding nicely, and that as long as the general was here he would like a demonstration of the brain-phasing unit. That seemed odd, since you had already taken the prototype to Washington and explained how it worked on lab animals. And Bob—Bob Lerner—had just gotten back from conducting a practical demonstration. I did not think that putting mice through a maze would impress the general, even if we could make them lose their way and then enable them to remember. But Bob insisted, so I came in, and learned the horrible truth about what was proceeding.

"He told me that you had died under treatment, that Bob Lerner had been tortured to unconsciousness without revealing useful information, and that if I did not cooperate, the Nazi soldiers would kill Francine and Charlotte after using them first and do the same to me. They figured that you had tampered with the memchip program, but they did not know how. They wanted me to perform the memory transfer on Bob Lerner that Bob Fenton had tried on you.

"I told them that the BPU did not transfer memory to a computer bank—where the information could be accessed without inhibition—that the device paralyzed memory, starting with those most recently acquired and working antecedently. But they did not believe me. General Pendergast had some ridiculous notion that we could preserve human memory electronically, then implant that memory in a receptive brain—a younger brain that had previously been wiped clean of its original memories; that the device was the road to eternal youth—that is, for those who gained control of the technology."

Connie paused as she calibrated Grant's brainwave emissions with the magnetic phasing apparatus.

"When the young patrolman came to the door—Frank, is it?"

Riley eased his arms into the sleeves of his shirt. "Yes, ma'am."

"Well, when Frank came to the door, they were afraid that it would look suspicious if no one answered, and that the police might take it upon themselves to investigate further. I was given instructions to fend him off and under no circumstances to let him enter the building. I acted the part I was given, but tried to tip him off by being evasive in my answers and noncooperative—"

"You did that very well," said Riley.

"Thank you."

"Our hands were tied by the law," added Hendry. "The judge wouldn't give me a search warrant because I had no probable cause that a crime had been committed."

"That's the trouble with the law," Francine complained. "Only the good guys have to go by the rules."

"I quite agree. And as we have seen with this—is it the Nazi Revitalization League—they care about no legal conventions that block their way to world domination." Connie stood up from the computer console and shoved her hands into the pockets of her smock. "After being forced to watch them destroy Bob's mind—Bob Lerner, that is—by overriding the power limiters, I was terrified of having my own mind destroyed. I would rather have undergone physical torture than to lose forever my mental aptitude. My body can afford a few losses without impairing my quality of life. But I did not want to lose my mind." She smiled uneasily. "Uh, no pun intended."

Francine Baker picked up the narrative. "By the time they got around to trying the brainwave phaser on me, I think they had pretty well given up on the idea of it actually working—they were depending on the threat of being turned to a vegetable to convince me to reveal Grant's codes. And I would have, too, if I had known them. Sorry, Grant, but I guess I don't have a very strong constitution. I was as scared as Connie. Especially after what they did to Charlotte." She took a deep breath to calm herself. "I never knew I was so—weak." She took another deep breath. "Anyhow, ever since I was promoted to Facilitator, I made sure that each Contract Group had its own passwords that were known only among the authorized members of the Group. It was a protocol required by our contracts with NASA and the DOD. No one outside the Group knew what those passwords were; *I* certainly didn't. I didn't have the clearance. Well, Fenton may not have been here very long, but he knew enough to know the procedure. I don't think he believed that I didn't have access—"

Further explanation was stopped by sharp sounds like the cracks of whips, muted by intervening floors, walls, and fireproof doors. A moment later a breathless Sergeant Benson charged into the laboratory, his pistol in his hand.

"It's loose! That robot is on the move and coming this way."

More shots reverberated in the nearby corridor, followed by shouts and the spangs of ricochets.

"Ain't nothing stopping it, not even shotguns at close range."

Captain Hendry grabbed for his guns and clicked off the safeties. "All right, people. Let's vamoose out the back door before it makes mince meat out of us."

"There is a better way to deal with it, captain." Connie made a final check of Grant's headgear and the wires leading off the sensor pads. "A more permanent way."

Grant was already on his feet. "I told you, I'm not the person who knows anything about the failsafe—"

"Yes, you are!" Sarah shoved Grant back onto the table. "Listen to the doctor. She knows what she's talking about." To Dr. Constantinescu, "Execute the program. Stat."

The shots and shouts were coming closer, accompanied by the tinkle of broken glass and the thuds of running feet. Hendry and Benson stood shoulder to shoulder as a first line of defense. Riley jumped off the table and drew his gun, wincing with pain. Anderson reached across to his holster with his left hand and pulled out his pistol; he held his broken arm up in the air, as Dawn had told him to do, in order to drain the blood and decrease the throbbing.

"George, I got something to tell you that I was hoping I wasn't—"

"Later, Bob."

Grant was about to protest once again when he saw

Connie key in the final command code. The computer screen lit up with a caricature of Grant's smiling face, and the words, "This won't hurt a bit, old buddy. Just sit back and relax, and enjoy your stroll down memory lane."

****

Grant awoke with a headache like he had never felt before. It was not extremely painful, but it seemed to crawl over his scalp like a mild electric current. He did not recognize his surroundings. He sat up, finding that he had been lying on a workbench which had been swept clear of its paraphernalia, all of which lay in a heap on the floor. Slowly he slid his feet over the edge of the bench, eased himself upright, and stood up, although somewhat shakily.

In a daze, he picked his way along the dimly lit corridors, not quite sure where he was going, but somehow able to navigate through the unfamiliar building as if he were being guided by a deep inner conviction. He ascended a set of metal stairs and pushed open the fire door, and found himself outside in the cool night air. The stars shone bright overhead, untwinkling beacons which suffused the landscape with a stark white light.

He strolled along the sidewalk in his characteristic daze. His feet instinctively guided him home while he pondered the day's activities and reflected on projects which needed additional thought. Strangely, he could not quite put his finger on what he had been working on prior to the nap. His mind seemed oddly blank. It also seemed like an inordinately long walk to Woodland Acres, perhaps because he had nothing important to think about.

When he finally found himself turning onto Cedar Place, he took the key ring out of his jacket pocket and fumbled for the proper key. Despite the lateness of the hour, he did not feel overpowering pangs of hunger, but he could sure use a drink to steady his hand. He could not seem to get the key to catch in the lock.

****

Grant woke up again, this time in his laboratory in

the Biotech building on 201 Memory Lane. His eyes were puffy, and tears were streaming down his face: he had just learned about his mother's death, among a thousand other facts which exploded in his mind at the instant that Dr. Constantinescu had activated the brain-phase reversal program. His head throbbed with the almightiest of hangovers. But instead of finding himself lost in a thick mental miasma, oblivious to his surroundings, his mind was perfectly lucid about the desperate straits at hand.

He tried to shake off the disorientation caused by the surfeit of information. "How long was I out?"

"Fourteen seconds." Sarah wielded Captain Hendry's pistol for whatever good it would do against the monster at the door.

A double detonation of discharging firearms reverberated loudly throughout the laboratory. Grant spun in time to see the captain and the sergeant flung aside like two sacks of potatoes. The Hitler simulacrum strode forth menacingly, making straight for Grant as if no one else occupied the room. Riley and Anderson interposed themselves and their weapons between Grant and the Fuhrer, despite the obvious futility of using bullets against armor plate.

Without bothering to remove the headset or disconnect the sensor pads from the input leads, Grant leaped to the computer console and shoved Connie aside. She rolled away on the wheeled chair and fetched up against Dawn and Francine, who had backed into a crevice between two workstations. He keyed in a coded command called "memkill," tapped the key for execution, and stood up fully confident that the horror of the Hitler abomination was under control.

The eyeless simulacrum stopped dead in its tracks. It was shorn of nearly every scrap of cloth that had once comprised its uniform. Only a few tatters of burnt material still clung to its shiny metal casing, which was blackened in spots where pointblank discharges had singed the surface with black powder. The darkened laboratory was still operating under emergency lighting only, and in the dimness there befell such an utter silence that the sough of labored, fear-induced panting was exaggerated to the point of mockery. Then the awful tableau was broken by the arrival of policemen and -women who guarded the corridor with impotent weapons, and by the scuffling of Captain Hendry and Sergeant Benson as they clambered to their feet.

There was very little resemblance now between the battered simulacrum and the depraved Fuhrer that its rubberized face had been molded to resemble. Most of the perfectly placed and parted hair had been burnt or shot away, as was much of the tegument which had given the metal casing its humanoid appearance. Half of the Charlie Chaplin mustache was gone, along with part of the upper lip, resulting in a whimsical leer that would have done the comic justice.

The simulacrum began to move in a curious circular motion with its feet rooted to the floor and with its head describing a tight arc around a central point. Larger and larger grew the arc until it reached the angle of instability. The stiffened chassis, like a body in rigor mortis, then wobbled like a child's top which was slowly running down. The chassis bent at the waist in a programmed effort to save itself from falling, although the arms remained firmly by their sides. Then the simulacrum teetered off balance, crashed sideways against a workbench at an acute angle, and spun away like a log rolling down an incline. It whirled off the edge of the bench and crashed to the floor, where it endeavored to roll, but it did not have the power to rise above the squarish shape of its body and outflung arms. Finally, it lay still.

Patrolman Anderson took a step forward and bent down on one knee by the motionless robot. He pointed his gun at the simulacrum's armored skull. "Is it dead?"

It took a moment for Grant to find his voice. When he did, his words came out faint and craggy. "Not yet." He wiped tears off his cheeks. A decade's worth of remembrances—both fond and sad—were still rattling through his brain like yesterday's afterthoughts. He ignored the flashbacks as best he could, and cleared his throat. "We don't really know how long the Memchip 201 can remain in flux once the motor that generates its fluxion field has been disconnected from the battery pack."

Every eye in the room fixated on the simulacrum. Sudden jerking of its limbs elicited a collective gasp.

Anderson backed out of reach. "How anticlimactic."

Grant sorted concepts which whirled through his mind like phantom ships in a hurricane. "We were afraid—Bob and Randy and I—of a viral infection, so we installed a remote controlled power supply interrupter, triggered by a solenoid. The loss of vertical stability is due to gyroscope failure, and the twitching is caused by feedback signals getting crossed in the CPU as the memchip shunts its fading programming capacity away from motor coordination and toward memory storage." Grant looked down at the simulacrum with an almost paternal sense of loss. "It's rerouting its essential operating programs to the inner core of the matrix, much as the human brain protects the mind when the heart stops beating and gray matter begins to die from lack of oxygen. It's a reflex action, designed to maintain its memory and artificial personality until power can be restored."

"Then it's unconscious?" asked Sandy.

"In a manner of speaking. I guess you could say it's experiencing the electronic equivalent of organic death throes. A superconductive circuit can maintain an electrical current for years without measurable diminution. But with the refrigeration unit cut off from the power supply, the temperature of the fluid will rise until it's no longer superconductive, at which point irretrievable memory loss begins to occur. If we were to re-establish the memchip's power circuit now, it might recover. Theoretically, it won't actually die until the fluid cools." He looked around at the anxious faces. "We can still save it."

"Don't you dare." Sarah placed a warm hand on

Grant's sagging shoulder. "Let it die peacefully. Then you can reprogam it with good thoughts and pleasant memories."

Grant held out his hand to his grown-up daughter.

Dawn rushed to his side and snuggled against his chest. "Welcome back, Daddy."

"You can't know how good it is to be here."

Grant was exhausted from days of stress and disorientation. But he knew that once the loose ends were tidied up, he could go home and rest in luxurious peace.

Unlike the simulacrum, however, he would awaken as the same person who had gone to sleep—this time, hopefully, not ten years older, but certainly ten years wiser.

Chapter 26

"As I was saying to George, the guy looked like an eager young reporter. Even had a press card with his pixture on it. And he didn't want nothing that was official business, or that would break regulations."

"All police business is official, and none of it is given out to the public. You know that!"

Sergeant Benson cowed under Captain Hendry's baleful glare. His sagging jowls jiggled as he shook his head. "I know that, George. I shoulda known better. I *did* know better. But it was easy money, and the guy insisted that I didn't hafta give him any personal information or steal written reports. Just let him know if I heard anything. You know, word of mouth stuff?" To Grant, "So when you were brought into the station Saturday morning . . . "

"I understand, Sergeant." Grant shoved his hands into the pockets of a clean white smock which covered the pressed blue suit which he kept in his office as a spare. "Don't worry about it. They would have been watching my house from Lerner's anyway, figuring that I might show up there eventually."

"Well, I got his name and phone number. Maybe—"

"The name will be fake and the number will be from a cheap motel room no doubt already abandoned. Don't bother." Sarah turned from the westward window where she was watching the arrival of the National Guard in jeeps, trucks, and deuce-and-a-halves, followed by three-piece-suited FBI agents in their rental cars, all of whom now had the Biotech building surrounded and infiltrated. "But certainly let it be a lesson to you."

"Yes, ma'am. I'll do that. After this, I won't even fix another tick—" Sergeant Benson glanced sharply at Captain Hendry, then hid his eyes from view.

"Bob, you and I are gonna have a long talk. And don't think because we've worked together for twenty years I'm gonna go easy on you. I'm making a written report, and it'll have to go through proper channels." Captain Hendry's angry stare could have melted iron. "Dr. Templeton, I can't apologize enough for—"

Grant waved his free hand. "It's over, Captain, so let's not dwell on it. We all live and learn."

"Still, I—" Captain Hendry did not seem to know what else to say, so he redirected his gaze and changed the subject. "Ms. Mason, or Witherspoon, or whatever your name is—if you have a real name—you will stay in the building like we agreed? Under house arrest, till your commanding officer gets here?"

Sarah held up her hands and rattled the chain that held the handcuffs together. "Girl Scout's honor."

"Look, I'm sorry—"

"I understand, Captain. It's protocol, and you're under direct orders from the Governor and the FBI." She smiled at him as if he were her closest companion. "I'll be fine. And there are no hard feelings."

Captain Hendry escorted his subordinate out of Grant's penthouse office, leaving behind a peacefulness which Grant never thought he could feel again. He strolled toward the eastward window, from which he could see the upper crescent of the sun which was making its appearance through the trees on the horizon.

"I'm a lucky man," Grant soliloquized. "I've been given two dawns only minutes apart. Which reminds me . . . " He stared thoughtfully, then turned to Sarah, who was rummaging through one of the drawers of his desk. "What are you looking for?"

"A paper clip." She found one, bent it apart with her teeth, then, biting down hard on the metal, she brought the handcuffs up to her mouth. In a trice the right handcuff flew open, followed a moment later by the left. She rubbed her wrists and flexed strong but feminine fingers. "I don't want to wear these things all day."

"But didn't Captain Hendry say that he'd been in touch with the DOD since Saturday and that a representative was due to arrive momentarily?"

"That's what he said and that's what he believes. But I suspect that the Washington office was under orders to forward all Highland Hills police calls to Pendergast here at Biotech, and that he was returning those calls from this building. He may have told them that he was on the way, but in actuality he was already here and in command of the situation. As you know, now that you've got your memory back." She joined him at the picture window and watched the dull yellow sphere come into full bloom. "So how does it feel? Knowing all, instead of being sheltered by ignorant bliss?"

Grant shrugged. "Life was simpler in that alternate world of ten years ago, back when I was entertaining hopeful dreams instead of experiencing bitter reality." He wiggled his injured arm out of the makeshift sling which Sandy had fashioned for him, after redressing his wound and warning him not to delay in going to the hospital for sterilization and stitches. "I wish I could go back."

"Don't we all." Sarah averted Grant's eyes, ambled across the office to the fax machine in the corner, and played idly with the control buttons. "If we could only foresee the fallible future and seed our furrows accordingly." She scribbled a note on a piece of paper, punched a number on the keypad, and transmitted her message. "Now someone will come running." She continued to play with the control buttons.

"Was Pendergast the only rogue in the DOD, or are there others you have to worry about?"

"I think he was alone. He was in a high enough position where he didn't have to be supported by a loyal command structure because he had access to all the information he needed. Except, of course, what was being purposely withheld from him."

"You mean, by Brinkley?"

"Yes. He suspected Pendergast's role in the NRL movement to free the fatherland from foreign appeasement, although I don't know how or why Pendergast ever got involved. He was—a good officer—at one time."

Grant's newfound memory held the answers to many questions. "He wanted to live forever and rule the world. To have his mind implanted on the next memchip. The Hitler simulacrum was intended to be his tool, his spokesperson; he was going to be the puppeteer."

"Delusions of grandeur: the big leveler."

"But the idea of creating a replacement simulacrum wasn't his. It originated from a CIA espionage plot to substitute a certain Arab potentate—whose name I am not at liberty to mention—with a lookalike simulacrum that could imitate the character of the original, but that could be programmed to be more sympathetic toward western philosophy. If you don't believe me, the chassis is in the basement, awaiting the implantation of the memchip that went into the Hitler simulacrum that the Nazis smuggled into the country."

"Oh, I believe you. I work with CIA agents in Germany all the time. It sounds like one of their grandiose schemes." The fax machine started spitting out paper. Sarah scanned the pages as they clattered out of the bale, then dropped them into the wastepaper basket. "I deplore their methods, but I have to say in their defense that they are true patriots of peace. The agency usually has the best interests of the world—the free world, not just the country—at heart." She glanced at Grant. "They fight dirty. But if you expect to win the war, you can't afford to be any less ruthless than your opponents."

"Like you were with Pendergast?" Grant watched Sarah intently, wondering what she was doing with the fax machine. "You weren't kidding when you said you didn't like being called Maggie."

Sarah forced a smile, but her facial expression did not conceal her true inner turmoil. "At the very least, that makes me guilty of insubordination." Her eyes brightened considerably as she ripped a sheet of paper from the bale. "On the other hand, this might help considerably at my court-martial." She handed the paper to Grant. "This is how Pendergast found out the jig was up. You, absent-minded professor that you are, were told to destroy this communiqué as soon as you read it. I have no doubt that you did, but you forgot—or never knew—that your fax machine has an electronic storage and retrieval system in case of paper jams and overloads. If Fenton saw this—"

The message was from General Amos Brinkley. It was brief, but in its brevity it implicated both Fenton and Pendergast in a subversive plot to steal the memchip and its programming capability before it went into production, and it arranged a clandestine meeting with one Sarah Mason and established passwords for recognition.

Grant shrugged. "I suspected Fenton right from the beginning, when Pendergast assigned him as attaché to oversee the final production and programming of the memchip, and to make recommendations about the usefulness of the brain-phase unit. He had some queer notions, like believing that the BPU could record memories, not just dampen them, despite my protestations to the contrary. He thought Bob and I were holding out on him. Then, when someone tried to break our access codes, I got real suspicious. And I was pretty sure when he claimed to be a longtime DOD agent, because he knew nothing about the Benthic Products contact. I instituted a discrete investigation—through military channels—and found a sordid and incomplete history that put me on my guard.

"I didn't know your General Brinkley—Pendergast was my liaison with the DOD—but when he faxed me this note after my meeting with the Joint Chiefs, and warned me about possible German involvement—I must have mentioned Fenton's name during the course of the demonstration—a lot of Fenton's unexplainable actions began to make sense, in a weird kind of way. I didn't know what authorization Brinkley possessed other than his being a special operations officer for the DOD, but the fact that he cautioned me not to breach any security protocols—not even to him—gave me faith in his honesty.

At the meeting in Washington, he came across as a sincere man who had a patriarchal attachment to his troops. His primary interest in the BPU was to treat soldiers who were suffering from battle fatigue and related emotional traumas. So, when he warned me to be on my guard against Fenton and Pendergast, and asked me to meet his agent—you, as it turned out—so you could brief me more fully on the situation, I went along with his plan."

Sarah nodded knowingly. "Brinkley's assignment was the NRL. As soon as he secured positive information that Pendergast was planning some kind of coup, he pulled me out of Germany, briefed me quickly, and sent me to meet you at the Neanderthal Club. My guess is that Pendergast learned somehow that Brinkley was fudging his reports, confronted him, couldn't make him talk, and tried to siphon off his memory with the prototype brain-phase unit that you left in Washington. It either killed him, or left him brain dead." Sarah paused for fully half a minute, staring at the sun as if it were a hypnotizing yellow ball. "Pendergast must have put a bullet into both sides of his head in order to cover the scars made by overstimulating the sensor pads—Fenton's not a trigger man. Then he and Fenton rushed out here with the Nazi goon squad in order to force you and Lerner to install the memchip in their Hitler simulacrum and program it with biographical data and propaganda material so they could create the image of a new Fuhrer."

Grant shivered. The building's heating unit was inoperable due to the power outage, and the room was suddenly suffused with a chill which had nothing to do with absolute temperature. "Did you know that Pendergast was responsible for the death of Randy Vanderbilt and the others?"

"I didn't have time for a full briefing, but it was Brinkley's suspicion that Pendergast was methodically killing off your people as a warning—his way of letting you and Lerner know later that he was not a man to be trifled with."

"That was his opening threat Friday night. That's why I let him burn out my brain rather than yield to his demands—even his threats against Charlotte." He shivered again as his reconstructed memories reminded him all too well of distant and recent events which overlapped into one horror-filled conglomerate. "I knew that he was the kind of man who would carry out his threats out of meanness, even if I acceded to his demands. There was nothing to be gained by bargaining. He was totally cold-blooded." Grant was filled with revulsion, which could only be overcome by resorting to gallows humor. "So you didn't shoot him just because he called you Maggie?"

"That was the least of his crimes." Sarah's eyes glistened in reverie, soft and unseeing. "I think Pendergast knew that your character was nearly inviolable—that your breaking point was far beyond that of the average man." Slowly, her eyes came into focus. "Lerner is unmarried and has no children, so Pendergast decided to kidnap Dawn in order to persuade you to do his bidding."

"It would have worked."

"He must have had your phone tapped and learned that she was on her way to Chicago. The bungled kidnapping of your ex-wife was what tipped us off that events were coming to a head. The local police were warned about the possibility of another attempt and were asked to provide a guard until relieved by the FBI—the DOD doesn't have roving operatives like other law enforcement agencies because we're essentially a military organization. We didn't want to put your ex into protective custody until Dawn appeared—even though we suspected that she had already been captured—so she was asked to stay put and answer the phone in case Dawn called, so she could be brought in before the NRL found her.

"Meanwhile, I muddied the water by disguising myself as your ex and renting a car in her name: leaving a clear trace of her identity for the NRL to investigate. I tried to find your daughter on campus, still disguised as her mother, so her friends would give her a description that would tally with my claim. I figured it would confuse the NRL, too, if they took the same tack and suspected that her mother was in town. When you didn't make the Neanderthal Club, I tried calling you—first at your office, where I got your answering machine, then at home. Then I drove out here looking for you. The building was dark and no one answered the door. I noticed the video cameras, so I went back to the motel and changed from my Sarah Mason disguise to your ex again, then came back to Biotech and let myself and the rental car be seen by the cameras—I ran away before anyone could answer the door and find out that I was an imposter. Back at the motel I called your answering machine and left a concerned message from your ex, about her being in town for a visit and discovering from Dawn's classmates that she had gone away with her boyfriend on a weekend jaunt. There was a strong possibility that the NRL had already found Dawn, in which case my subterfuges would have come to naught. But it was worth the effort to bewilder them on the off chance that they were still looking for her." Sarah shrugged. "It couldn't hurt.

"Once I was sure that you were who you said you were, I led you to believe that Dawn was under our protection—I couldn't afford to have you worry about her safety because it might have compromised your ability to think and act decisively. You're a strong man, Grant, as I've come to learn, but you're not an emotionless android."

Grant soaked in as much as he could. It was all so complicated. Despite his reconstructed memory, there were many facts that he did not know and many truths he was unsure of. "Were you absolutely certain when we made lo—when we were in the Please Duck Inn—that I was a man and not a machine?"

"Yes," Sarah said, but she hesitated an instant too long before answering. She rushed on, "I had be sure. Once in the grip of a simulacrum, it could have killed me instantly."

Grant nodded slowly. "If it had wanted you dead." He searched Sarah's eyes for any trace of emotion. What he saw was unfathomable depth. "Did you know that Pendergast wanted to replace me with a simulacrum—one implanted with my memories—and that he was finagling my records in order to dispute any physical dissimilarities?"

"Pendergast was a madman. You can't hold him responsible for anything he did or said."

Grant was not quite sure what she meant by that. "For a while I even thought Bob had been substituted—by a Memchip 101. I didn't see him for several days prior to this weekend. I only spoke with him over the phone; could never seem to track him down. He seemed too willing to go along with Pendergast's ideas. Now I realize that he was under pressure to produce results in order to negotiate funds for the new fabrication facility that Pendergast promised. Francine was headed for Washington to work on the proposal. I also think Pendergast was making a play for her."

"He was an egomaniac. That's what gave away the simulacrum at Lerner's house. I recognized his self-aggrandizing, ideological oratory despite the synthesis of your voice." After a pause, "What about Lerner? I know you two go back a long way, that you have a close bond of friendship. Can you—will he be all right?"

"I'm fairly certain he'll pull through okay. Sandy said that he was in shock but otherwise stable. Connie did a quick brain scan and found everything normal except for the paralyzed memory lanes. I let them take him to the hospital only so he could undergo more thorough testing. When he's fully conscious I'll perform the reversal procedure. It worked on me and the mice; it should work on him."

Sarah managed a weak grin. "I like your confidence, your self assurance. It looks good on you."

"I was pretty rattled yesterday, what with losing half my mind and believing I had crossed some hyperdimensional barrier into a parallel universe, then thinking that I might not even be human, but a runaway robot whose logic faults led to hallucinations of anthropo-morphism."

"You came through okay."

Now it was Grant's turn to grin. "Pun intended?"

Sarah did something which Grant thought was beyond her capability: she blushed. "I have to be honest with you, Grant. Uh—" She gritted her teeth, with honesty momentarily stuck on the tip of her tongue. "Uh, I knew that you were engaged to Charlotte. I knew that, in your weakened condition, I was taking advantage of you." She swallowed hard, looked askance, and watched the brightening yellow orb which now seemed to perch atop the distant trees, bringing light and warmth into human hearts everywhere. "I —I needed some closeness. I needed—" She wiped off the tears that were running down her cheeks. "I know this sounds childish, as if I were a teenager with a crush on her teacher. I am young enough to be your daughter and old enough to know better."

"That was the rudest part of my awakening: discovering that I was no longer in my forties, but a decade older."

"Don't interrupt. Let me have my say before I bury my feelings again."

Her voice held a tremor which was decidedly out of character for the woman Grant had come to know these past twenty-four hours. "Killing all those people was— it was my job. And although I hate to admit it, a part of me—deep down inside—a part of me *did* enjoy getting even with them for the misery they've caused. I don't like that part of me, but that's who I am. And after the fear, after the pain, after coming down from the exhilaration of fighting against uneven odds, and surviving, I needed a dose of affection. I knew I had no right to take it, but—" She tilted her head in a gesture of sublime helplessness. "At the time I didn't care about how my action would affect your relationship with Charlotte once you got your memory back. There's no need for you to feel guilty about anything. You didn't know that you had a commitment to anyone. But I did. I knew.

And I abused that knowledge. I needed a moment of tenderness so badly that I let it cloud my judgment. I'm sorry."

Had it lasted only a moment? No, Grant thought, now is not the time to crack jokes. He was confused and full of anguish for the woman who had just bared her soul to him; a complex woman who had the strength to kill when it was necessary—for self and country—while knowing all along that she must relive forever those cruel intervals of seeming inhumanity. He wanted to put his arms around her, to meld her body with his, to make her feel like the mature person she was. For he was now a man of two minds, of two memories, of conflicting emotions which had developed independently when his mind had been separated from itself. As he reached out for her she placed her palm against his chest and held him at bay as easily as a mother might hold back her little boy.

As if Sarah had read his reunited mind, she said, "And the worst part for you is that you've already got two women to worry about: a little girl who's not so little any more, and a fiancé who's going to need as much love and affection as you can give her, considering what she's been through."

"Sandy said that Charlotte wasn't hurt badly—"

"Grant, don't spoil your image by being a total idiot. I wasn't referring to her physical condition, but to her mental state. Don't you realize how traumatized a woman can be by rape? Don't you know how violated she feels?"

Grant tried not to look smug. "I can fix that easily—"

"Stop it, I said! I love you, Grant. Don't ruin it for me by acting chauvinistic and uncompassionate." Sarah was a woman in turmoil. "Let me tell you something, as long as I'm sharing secrets." She ran her hands over her loose blonde hair, whose short locks fell straight down from the top of her head, and played for a moment with her ear. "I was captured by the NRL. They held me prisoner—" She stopped, and her eyes took on that faraway stare, as if in her mind she were looking through the wrong end of a telescope tube into the bottomless pit of hell. "They held me prisoner—and they raped me—continuously—for days—for weeks. And they tortured me with—" Her eyes vibrated wildly with the awful, irrepressible memory. "Never mind. You don't need to know. You don't want to know. Just— never mind."

Grant gulped as tears welled in her eyes. He felt her pain leap across the space between them and stab him in the heart like an icicle made of dry ice, its indescribable cold spreading outward through his vital organs; he shivered involuntarily. Sarah dropped her hands in front of her. She was playing with something which was round and flat and rubbery, a pale pink object with concentric creases which Grant had the eerie feeling he had seen before, if only he could remember where.

"I wouldn't talk. They couldn't make me talk." She choked up, cleared her throat, and continued in a gravelly monotone which trembled as the awful recollections came to mind. "They wanted to send a clear message to the Department that they had me in their clutches; that I could not get away. And to make sure the Department was listening, they sent them this."

She turned her head sideways at the same time that she held up the oval-shaped object she was fingering. It was an ear, and at the same moment that Grant recognized it for what it was, he noticed the jagged scar that surrounded the aural opening on the right side of her head, and the lack of any external flesh.

"They said that next they were going to cut off my—"

She halted, and stared into the infinite reaches of outer space beyond the sun which had suddenly become frigid in the clear, blue sky. Grant realized that she was right—there were vile facts that he did not want to know.

"The biggest operation in our special ops history was mounted, with every available agent—ours, the CIA's, and the intelligence divisions' of the German and U.S. armies—scouring the countryside for the NRL's secret headquarters. They found me eventually. I was saved from death, if not from a fate worse than. And the man who led the charge and came to my rescue was General Amos Brinkley."

Tears collected on the edge of Sarah's jaw, and when they became heavy enough to drop, they fell to the emerald carpet like rain splattering the floor of a primeval forest. She ignored the streaks which ran unashamedly down her face. Using both hands, she fitted the prosthetic back in place, and when she took her hands away only a faint line showed where the rubber met her skin, unnoticeable unless one were purposely looking for it. The ear was a masterful job of plastic surgery.

Grant wiped the tears off her cheeks with his handkerchief. He took a firm grip on her chin and forced her to face him, although she stubbornly turned her eyes to the side. "Sarah, we do live in two different worlds. I can't comprehend your world of spies and guns and bloodshed any more than you can fathom the electronic world of memory chips and neurological dysfunction. But we do meet on the common grounds of trust and humanity. So believe me when I say that I can heal Charlotte's wounds at the press of a button. In your case—"

Sarah tried to pull away, but he held on firmly, with one fist gripping her slender but muscular shoulder. "You big goof. Now you have ruined it for me. Charlotte is going to be hurt and angry and she may never get over what those bastards did to her. And now you've made me lose faith in your nobility and sensitivity—"

"You're not listening to what I just said. I can—"

Sarah tugged hard and broke away. She turned her back on Grant and stalked across the office. "Just when I thought I'd found a man with a heart—"

Grant shouted, "I can cure Charlotte's pain with the brain-phase unit."

Sarah stopped in midstride halfway across the spacious office. She turned slowly and stared up at Grant with oncoming realization.

"That's what it was designed for. That's why Brinkley was so interested in the device. It can't record memories like Fenton and Pendergast wanted to believe, nor download them onto a database, although, who knows—perhaps some day in the future we'll be able to do that, too. But it can paralyze the most recent memories, such as those that cause battle fatigue, as I can certainly attest. With a mild dosage I can erase from Charlotte's mind all knowledge of the past two days, and with the obliteration of those memories goes the fear and the pain and the trauma that results not from the experiences themselves, but from the memory of those experiences."

Sarah's eyes were as big as saucers. "I take back all I said. You're not only aware of her potential anguish, but, good doctor that you are, you've already prescribed the remedy."

Grant beamed. "I've got good bedside manner, too. Er, so I've been told." Now it was his turn to blush. When he regained control of himself, he put on his best doctor face. "Sarah, as a patient you represent a more complicated case. We can't erase memories selectively—not yet, anyway—so we'd have to go all the way back—"

"Forget it, Grant. Or rather, I don't want to forget it."

"The process is painless, I promise. I got burned only because Fenton didn't know how to operate the device; he cranked up the juice too high. Nor is there any reason to be afraid of the treatment just because it's administered by a machine instead of by your own mind. When you suffer an extraordinarily horrible experience—one whose constant reminder affects your mental health adversely—the conscious mind represses the memory of those experiences, buries them deep in the subconscious where they can't cause further distress. The brain-phase unit blocks those memories in a similar manner, only more effectively."

"Grant, you are a brilliant scientist and know an awful lot about the functions of the brain and its effects on the mind, but you have a hell of a lot to learn about human psychology. 'If thine eye offends thee, pluck it out' is not a panacean remedy for mental variation from the norm. Charlotte, no doubt, is better off without any memory of the past two days. She doesn't need her pain. But the world doesn't suddenly become a Garden of Eden because you choose to ignore the evil serpent that is skulking in the bushes. You can still be poisoned by unseen fangs.

"I don't want to be 'healed' by your definition of the word. I can't afford to be healed. When you erase the past, you take away the good memories as well as the bad, and some of those memories are precious to me, painful as they are. And if you erase too much of the past, you take away the person's essence—who a person is. We adapt to the future by having constant access to our life's experiences; that's how we survive. If you don't remember burning your finger in a flame as a child, you'll keep sticking your hands into fire."

Sarah rejoined Grant at the window. Her tears were gone, but her eyes still glistened, like dew on the petals of a white rose. Now her demeanor held a vibrancy, a defiance, an air of contempt which fitted the image of the tough Amazonian warrior who could fight off a dozen villains with her fists and a gun, and, knowing full well the consequence of capture, would then storm alone the enemy stronghold. The window into the romantic feminine heart, which Grant had been permitted to see, was closed. Sarah sealed all sentiment behind a wall of resolution.

"Thanks for the offer, Grant, but I can't accept it. I need a constant reminder of my past. I need the hate that is the consequence of my suffering, or else I couldn't do what it is I've got to do: to go back to Germany and make retribution for NRL atrocities, to wipe out every last pocket of Nazi resistance. The recesses of my mind must be filled with conscious memories of the pain and the suffering the Nazis have caused, or else I might forget who they are, what they've done, and why they must be eradicated from the face of the Earth."

"You don't mean you're going to continue the battle—"

"Someone's got to. It may as well be me. I have a score to settle."

"But—"

"No buts, Grant. I've lost so much of what's important to me that I don't have much left to lose." She humphed. "Believe it or not, you're about the closest thing to a friend that I have in this world. And I meant what I said: I do love you. Not only for the way you've made me feel, but for the kind of person you are."

"Sarah—" Grant reached out, but she skipped away before he could lay a hand on her.

"No, Grant. I have to go. I can't stand to be with you any longer. It hurts too much. Once I break away, once I reorganize my feelings, I won't feel the pain of loneliness that I feel right now. I'll get over it. I know I will. I've done it before." There was no hesitation in her voice, no lack of resolve. Just an incredible strength which was born of a life spent dealing with the savage side of society. "You've got your life to lead, and I have mine. When it's all over—if it's ever over—I'd like to come and visit you. And Dawn and Charlotte. We can't be lovers again, but I dearly want you to let me be part of your life. A part of Biotech's extended family."

Grant remained silent and kept his hands stiffly at his sides. He was afraid that in his weakness he might yield to his desire to sweep her into his arms; and he was torn between conflicting passions because, although he recognized Sarah as a woman of rare intensity, he also saw in her a trusting adolescence. This act of severance reminded him too much of his divorce a couple of years—no, it was more than a decade ago. Deprived of his wife and daughter, he had nearly fallen apart, and for years he had viewed his life through the thick glass lens at the bottom of a bottle. Now he could not even stand the taste of alcohol. How could Sarah get over in a few minutes what took him ages?

Sarah stopped at the massive oak door, with one white hand on the polished brass knob. "I have to go,

Grant. The FBI will want to interrogate me. And I've got funeral arrangements to make."

Grant grasped for words—questions—anything to keep her from walking out of his life, possibly forever. "Will—will they put you in jail? You know, for shooting the general?"

"They'll understand. The court-martial will clear me of all duplicity, while implicating Pendergast and his role in the Nazi Revitalization League."

"And the funeral?"

Sarah opened the door, but stopped short with a frozen posture and a dreadful, faraway look in her eyes. She stood that way for half a minute, seconds ticking away as if each were an eternity. Grant shifted uncomfortably from one foot to the other. Finally, Sarah faced him. She was expressionless except for her eyes, which burned like dying embers.

"My mother was a frail woman who, in her short but intense life, tasted the bitterest sorrow and the sweetest happiness. In that she was probably not much different from most soldiers' wives. My father died in a firefight in the closing stages of the Vietnam War, six months before I was born, and she was left alone to deal with single motherhood the best she could. When I was two years old, she met a young lieutenant who was just out of officer candidate school. They fell in love and got married, but out of deference to the memory of her first husband, she kept her married name, and kept that name on me. Amos never minded. He raised me like his own daughter. I was the only child he ever had, and he was the only father I ever knew. And I don't—I don't—I don't ever—want to—forget him."

Sarah dashed out of the office suddenly, leaving the door open behind her.

Grant heard her soft footsteps padding along the carpeted corridor until they faded behind the closing of the elevator doors. Despite the heat of the sun pouring through the broad picture window, Grant felt an icy chill in the air, as if a draft had found its way from the high Antarctic continent down the collar of his shirt.

He was humbled by the fact that people like Sarah suffered so much pain so that people like him could live their lives in peace.

For the fourth time in the past two days, he cried.